REGENCY
Beauty

Sarah Mallory

MILLS &
BOON

First Published in Great Britain 2017
By Mills & Boon, an imprint of HarperCollins*Publishers*
1 London Bridge Street, London, SE1 9GF

REGENCY BEAUTY © 2017 Harlequin Books S.A.

Beneath the Major's Scars © 2012 Sarah Mallory
Behind the Rake's Wicked Wager © 2013 Sarah Mallory

ISBN: 978-0-263-92376-6

52-0117

Our policy is to use papers that are natural, renewable and recyclable products and made from wood grown in sustainable forests. The logging and manufacturing processes conform to the legal environmental regulations of the country of origin.

Printed and bound by
CPI Group (UK) Ltd, Croydon, CR0 4YY

A REGENCY

Collection

Carole Mortimer — REGENCY *Scandals*

Bronwyn Scott — REGENCY *Gamble*

Julia Justiss — REGENCY *Betrayal*

Annie Burrows — REGENCY *Rumour*

Margaret McPhee — REGENCY *Desire*

Sarah Mallory — REGENCY *Beauty*

Michelle Styles — REGENCY *Bride*

Lucy Ashford — REGENCY *Seduction*

Ann Lethbridge — REGENCY *Proposal*

Diane Gaston — REGENCY *Reputation*

Christine Merrill — REGENCY *Temptation*

Gail Whitiker — REGENCY *Disguise*

Beneath the Major's Scars

For P and S, my own twin heroes

Sarah Mallory was born in the West Country and now lives on the beautiful Yorkshire moors. She has been writing for more than three decades—mainly historical romances set in the Georgian and Regency period. She has won several awards for her writing, most recently the Romantic Novelists' Association RoNA Rose Award in 2012 (for *The Dangerous Lord Darrington*) and 2013 (for *Beneath the Major's Scars*).

Prologue

Cornwall—1808

The room was very quiet. The screams and cries, the frantic exertions of the past twelve hours were over. The bloodied cloths and the tiny, lifeless body had been removed and the girl lay between clean sheets, only the glow of firelight illuminating the room. Through the window a single star twinkled in the night sky. She did not seek it out, she had no energy for such conscious effort, but it was in her line of vision and it was easier to fix her eyes on that single point of light than to move her head.

Her body felt like a dead weight, exhausted by the struggle she had endured. Part of her wondered why she was still alive, when it would be so much better for everyone if she had been allowed to die with her baby.

She heard the soft click of the opening door and closed her eyes, not wishing to hear the midwife's brisk advice or her aunt's heart-wrenching sympathy.

'Poor lamb.' Aunt Wilson's voice was hardly more than a sigh. 'Will she survive, do you think?'

'Ah, she'll live, she's a strong 'un.' From beneath her lashes the girl could see the midwife standing at the foot of the bed, wiping her hands on her bloody apron. 'Although it might be better if she didn't.'

'Ah, don't say that!' Aunt Wilson's voice cracked. 'She is still God's creature, even though she has sinned.'

The midwife sniffed.

'Then the Lord had better look out for her, poor dearie, for her life is proper blighted and that's for sure. No man will want her to wife now.'

'She must find some way to support herself. I cannot keep her indefinitely, and my poor brother and his wife have little enough: the parish of Cardinham is one of the poorest in Cornwall.'

There was a pause, then the midwife said, 'She ain't cut out to be a bal maiden.'

'To work in the mines? Never! She is too well bred for that.'

'Not too well bred to open her legs for a man—'

Aunt Wilson gasped in outrage.

'You have said quite enough, Mrs Nore. Your work is finished here, I will look after my niece from now on. Come downstairs and I will pay you for your trouble...'

The rustle of skirts, a soft click of the door and silence. She was alone again.

It was useless to wish she had died with her baby. She had not, and the future seemed very bleak, nothing but hard work and drudgery. That was her punishment for falling in love. She would face that, and she would survive, but she would never put her trust in any man again. She opened her eyes and looked at that tiny, twinkling orb.

'You shall be my witness,' she whispered, her lips painfully dry and her throat aching with the effort. 'No man shall ever do this to me again.'

Her eyes began to close and she knew now that whenever she saw that star in the evening sky, she would remember the child she had lost.

Chapter One

Exmoor—1811

'Nicky, Nicky! wait for me—oh!'

Zelah gave a little cry of frustration as her skirts caught on the thorny branches of an encroaching bush. She was obliged to give up her pursuit of her little nephew while she disentangled herself. How she wished now that she had put on her old dimity robe, but she had been expecting to amuse Nicky in the garden, not to be chasing him through the woods; only Nurse had come out to tell them that they must not make too much noise since the mistress was trying to get some sleep before Baby woke again and demanded to be fed.

As she carefully eased the primrose muslin off the ensnaring thorns, Zelah pondered on her sister's determination to feed the new baby herself. She could quite understand it, of course: Reginald's first wife had died in childbirth and a number of wet nurses had been employed for Nicky, but each one had proved more unreliable than the last so it was a wonder that the little boy had survived at all. The thought of her sister's stepson made Zelah smile. He had not only survived, but grown into a very lively eight-year-old, who was even now leading her in a merry dance.

She had allowed him to take her 'exploring' in the wildly neglected woodland on the northern boundary of West Barton and now realised her mistake. Not only was Nicky familiar with the overgrown tracks that led through the woods, he was unhampered by *skirts*. Free at last, she pulled the folds of muslin close as she set off in search of her nephew. She had only gone a few steps when she heard him cry out, such distress and alarm in his voice that she set off at a run in the direction of his call, all concerns for snagging her gown forgotten.

The light through the trees indicated that there was a clearing ahead. She pushed her way through the remaining low tree branches and found herself standing on the lip of a steep slope. The land dropped away to form a natural bowl and the ground between the trees was dotted with early spring flowers, but it was not the beauty of the scene that made Zelah catch her breath, it was the sight of Nicky's lifeless body stretched out at the very bottom of the dell, a red stain spreading over one leg of his nankeen pantaloons and a menacing figure bending over him.

Her first, wild thought was that it was some kind of animal attacking Nicky, but as her vision cleared she realised it was a man. A thick black beard covered his face and his shaggy hair reached to the shoulders of his dark coat. A long-handled axe lay on the ground beside him, its blade glinting wickedly in the spring sunlight.

Zelah did not hesitate. She scrambled down the bank.

'Leave him alone!' The man straightened. As he turned towards her she saw that beneath the shaggy mane of hair surrounding his face he had an ugly scar cutting through his left eyebrow and cheek. She picked up a stick. 'Get away from him, you beast!'

'Beast, is it?' he growled.

'Zelah—'

'Don't worry, Nicky, he won't hurt you again.' She kept her gaze fixed on the menacing figure. 'How dare you attack an innocent boy, you monster!'

'Beast, monster—' His teeth flashed white through the beard as he stepped over the boy and came towards her, his halting, ungainly stride adding to the menace.

Zelah raised the stick. With a savage laugh he reached out and twisted the bough effortlessly out of her grasp, then caught her wrists as she launched herself at him. She struggled against his iron grip and her assailant hissed as she kicked his shin. 'For heaven's sake, I am not your villain. The boy tripped and fell.' With a muttered oath he forced her hands down and behind her, so that she found herself pressed against his hard body. The rough wool of his jacket rubbed her cheek and her senses reeled as she breathed in the smell of him. It was not the sour odour of sweat and dirt she was expecting, but a mixture of wool and sandalwood and lemony spices combined with the earthy, masculine scent of the man himself. It was intoxicating.

He spoke again, his voice a deep rumble on her skin, for he was still holding her tight against his broad chest. 'He tripped and fell. Do you understand me?'

He is speaking as if to an imbecile! was Zelah's first thought, then the meaning of his words registered in her brain and she raised her head to meet his fierce eyes. She stopped struggling.

'That's better.' He released his iron grip but kept his hard eyes fixed upon her. 'Now, shall we take a look at the boy?'

Zelah stepped away, not sure if she trusted the man enough to turn her back on him, but a groan from Nicky decided it. Everything else was forgotten as she fell to her knees beside him.

'Oh, love, what have you done?'

She put her hand on his forehead, avoiding the angry red mark on his temple. His skin was very hot and his eyes had a glazed, wild look in them.

The man dropped down beside her.

'We've been clearing the land, so there are several ragged tree stumps. He must have caught his leg on one when he tumbled down the bank. It's a nasty cut, but I don't think the bone is broken.'

'How would you know?' demanded Zelah, carefully lifting away the torn material and gazing in horror at the bloody mess beneath.

'My time in the army has given me considerable experience of injuries.' He untied his neckcloth. 'I have sent my keeper to fetch help. I'll bind up his leg, then we will carry him back to the house on a hurdle.'

'Whose house?' she asked suspiciously. 'He should be taken to West Barton.'

'Pray allow me to know what is best to be done!'

'Please do not talk to me as if I were a child,' she retorted. 'I am quite capable of making a decision.'

He frowned, making the scar on his forehead even more ragged. He looked positively ferocious, but she refused to be intimidated and met his gaze squarely. He seemed to be struggling to contain his anger and after a moment he raised his hand to point towards a narrow path leading away through the trees. He said curtly, 'Rooks Tower is half a mile in that direction; West Barton is at least five miles by carriage, maybe two if you go back on the footpath, the way you came.'

Zelah bit her lip. It would be impossible to carry Nicky through the dense undergrowth of the forest without causing him a great deal of pain. The boy stirred and she took his hand.

'I d-don't like it, it hurts!'

The plaintive cry tore at her heart.

'Then it must be Rooks Tower,' she said. 'Let us hope your people get here soon.'

'They will be here as soon as they can.' He pulled the muslin cravat from his neck. 'In the meantime I must stop the bleeding.' His hard eyes flickered over her. 'It will mean moving his leg.'

She nodded and squeezed Nicky's hand.

'You must be very brave, love, while we bind you up. Can you do that?'

'I'll try, Aunty.'

'Your aunt, Nicky? She's more of an Amazon, I think!'

'Well, she is not really my aunt, sir,' explained Nicky gravely. 'She is my stepmama's sister.'

Zelah stared, momentarily diverted.

'You know each other?'

The man flicked a sardonic look towards her.

'Of course, do you think I allow strange brats to run wild in my woods? Introduce us, Nicky.'

'This is Major Coale.' The boy's voice wavered a little and his lip trembled as the major deftly wrapped the neckcloth around his leg. 'And this, sir, is my aunt, Zelah.'

'Celia?'

'Zee-lah,' she corrected him haughtily. 'Miss Pentewan to you.'

'Dear me, Nicholas, you should have warned me that your aunt is a veritable dragon.'

The scar cutting through his eyebrow gave him a permanent frown, but she heard the amusement in his voice. Nicky, clinging to Zelah's hand and trying hard not to cry, managed a little chuckle.

'There, all done.' The major sat back, putting his hand on Nicky's shoulder. 'You were very brave, my boy.'

'As brave as a soldier, sir?'

'Braver. I've known men go to pieces over the veriest scratch.'

Zelah stared at the untidy, shaggy-haired figure in front of her. His tone was that of a man used to command, but beneath that faded jacket and all that hair, could he really be a soldier? She realised he was watching her and quickly returned her attention to her nephew.

'What happened, love? How did you fall?'

'I t-tripped at the top of the bank. There's a lot of loose branches lying around.'

'Aye. I've left them. Firewood for the villagers,' explained the major. 'We have been clearing the undergrowth.'

'And about time too,' she responded. 'These woods have been seriously neglected.'

'My apologies, madam, if they are not to your liking.'

Was he laughing at her? His face—the little she could see that was not covered by hair—was impassive.

'My criticism is not aimed at you, Major. I believe Rooks Tower was only sold last winter.'

'Yes, and I have not had time yet to make all the improvements I would wish.'

'You are the *owner*?'

Zelah could not keep the astonishment out of her voice. Surely this ragged individual could not be rich enough to buy such a property?

'I am. Appearances can be deceptive, Miss Pentewan.'

She flushed, knowing she deserved the coldness of his response.

'I beg your pardon, that is, I—I am sure there is a vast amount to be done.'

'There is, and one of my first tasks is to improve the road to the house and make it suitable for carriages again. I have men working on it now, but until that is done everything has to come in and out by packhorse.'

'Major Coale's books had to be brought here by pack-pony,' put in Nicky. 'Dozens of boxes of them. She likes books,' he explained to the major, whose right eyebrow had risen in enquiry.

'We have an extensive library at home,' added Zelah.

'And where is that?'

'Cornwall.'

'I guessed that much from your name. *Where* in Cornwall?'

A smile tugged at her mouth, but she responded seriously.

'My father is rector at Cardinham, near Bodmin.'

Zelah looked up as a number of men arrived carrying a willow hurdle.

She scrambled to her feet and stepped back. The major handed his axe to one of the men before directing the delicate operation of lifting Nicky on to the hurdle. When they were ready to move off she fell into step beside the major, aware of his ungainly, limping stride as they followed the hurdle and its precious burden through the woods.

'I can see you have some experience of command, Major.'

'I was several years in the army.'

Zelah glanced at him. He had been careful to keep to the left of the path so only the right side of his face was visible to her. Whether he was protecting her sensibilities or his own she did not know.

'And now you plan to settle at Rooks Tower?'

'Yes.'

'It is a little isolated,' she remarked. 'Even more so than West Barton.'

'That is why I bought it. I have no wish for company.'

Zelah lapsed into silence. His curt tone made the meaning of his words quite clear. He might as well have said *I have no wish for conversation.* Very well, she had no desire to intrude upon his privacy. She would not speak again unless it was absolutely necessary.

Finally they emerged from the trees and Zelah had her first glimpse of Rooks Tower. There was a great sweep of lawn at the front of the house, enclosed by a weed-strewn drive. At the far side of the lawn stood a small orangery, but years of neglect had dulled the white lime-wash and many of its windows were broken. Zelah turned away from this forlorn object to study the main house. At its centre was an ancient stone building with an imposing arched entrance, but it had obviously been extended over the centuries and two brick-and-stone wings had been added. Everything was arranged over two floors save for a square stone tower on the south-eastern corner that soared above the main buildings.

'Monstrosity, isn't it?' drawled the major. 'The house was remodelled in Tudor times, when the owner added the tower that gives the house its name, so that his guests could watch the hunt. It has a viewing platform on the roof, but we never use it now.'

She looked again at the house. There had been many alterations over the years, but it retained its leaded lights and stone mullions. Rooks Tower fell short of the current fashion for order and symmetry, but its very awkwardness held a certain charm.

'The views from the tower must be magnificent.' She cast an anxious look at him. 'You will not change it?'

He gave a savage laugh.

'Of course not. It is as deformed as I!'

She heard the bitterness in his tone, but could not think of a suitable response. The path had widened and she moved forwards to walk beside Nicky, reaching out to take his hand. It was hot and clammy. Zelah hid her dismay beneath a reassuring smile.

'Nearly there, love. We shall soon make you more comfortable.'

The major strode on ahead, his lameness barely noticeable as he led the way into the great hall where an iron-haired woman in a black-stuff gown was waiting for them. She bobbed a curtsy.

'I have prepared the yellow room for the young master, sir, and popped a warm brick between the sheets.'

'Thank you, Mrs Graddon.' He did not break his stride as he answered her, crossing the hall and taking the stairs two at a time, only pausing to turn on the half-landing. 'This way, but be careful not to tilt the litter!'

Dominic waited only to see the boy laid on the bed that had been prepared for him before striding off to his own apartments to change out of his working clothes. It was a damnable nuisance, having strangers in the house, but the boy was hurt, what else could he do? He did not object to having Nicky in the house. He was fond of the boy and would do all he could to help him, but it would mean having doctors and servants running to and fro. He could leave everything to Graddon and his wife, of course, and the aunt would look after the boy until Buckland could send someone.

The thought of Miss Zelah Pentewan made him pause. A reluctant smile touched his lips and dragged at the scarred tissue of his cheek. She was not conventionally pretty, too small and thin, with mousy brown hair and brown eyes. She reminded him of a sparrow, nothing like the voluptuous beauties he had known. When he thought of her standing up to him, prepared to fight him to protect her nephew...by God she had spirit, for she barely came up to his shoulder!

He washed and dried his face, his fingers aware of the rough, pitted skin on his left cheek through the soft linen cloth. He remembered how she had glared at him, neither flinching nor averting her eyes once she had seen his scarred face. He gave her credit for that, but he would not subject her to the gruesome sight again. There was plenty for him to do that would keep him well away from the house for a few days.

'Well, I have cleaned and bandaged the leg. Now we must wait. I have given him a sleeping draught which should see him through to the morning and after that it will be up to you to keep him still while the leg heals. He will be as good as new in a few weeks.'

'Thank you, Doctor.'

Zelah stared down at the motionless little figure in the middle of the bed. Nicky had fainted away when the doctor began to work on his leg and now he looked so fragile and uncharacteristically still that tears started to her eyes.

'Now, now, Miss Pentewan, no need for this. The boy has a strong constitution—by heaven, no one knows that better than I, for I have been calling at West Barton since he was a sickly little scrap of a baby that no one expected to survive. I'm hoping that bruise on his head is nothing serious. I haven't bled him, but if he begins to show a fever then I will do so tomorrow. For now keep him calm and rested and I will call again in the morning.'

The doctor's gruff kindness made her swallow hard.

'Thank you, Dr Pannell. And if he wakes in pain…?'

'A little laudanum and water will do him no harm.'

There was a knock at the door and the housekeeper peeped in.

'Here's the little lad's papa come to see him, Doctor.' She flattened herself against the door as Reginald Buckland swept in, hat, gloves and riding whip clutched in one hand and an anxious look upon his jovial features.

'I came as soon as I heard. How is he?'

Zelah allowed the doctor to repeat his prognosis.

'Can he be moved?' asked Reginald, staring at his son. 'Can I take him home?'

'I would not advise it. The wound is quite deep and any jolting at this stage could start it bleeding again.'

'But he cannot stay here, in the house of a man I hardly know!'

Doctor Pannell's bushy eyebrows drew together.

'I understood the major was some sort of relative of yours, Mr Buckland.'

Reginald shrugged.

'Very distant. Oh, I admit it was through my letters to a cousin that he heard about Rooks Tower being vacant, but I had never met him until he moved here, and since then we have exchanged barely a dozen words. He has never once come to West Barton.'

A grim little smile hovered on the doctor's lips.

'No, Major Coale has not gone out of his way to make himself known to his neighbours.'

'I think Nicky must stay here, Reginald.' Zelah touched his arm. 'Major Coale has put his house and servants at our disposal.'

'Aye, he must, at least until the wound begins to heal,' averred Dr Pannell, picking up his hat. 'Now, I shall be away and will return tomorrow to see how my patient does.'

Reginald remained by the bed, staring down at his son and heir. He rubbed his chin. 'If only I knew what to do. If only his mama could be with him!'

'Impossible, when she is confined with little Reginald.'

'Or Nurse.'

'Yes, she would be ideal, but my sister and the new baby need her skill and attentions,' said Zelah. 'I have considered all these possibilities, Reginald, and I think there is only one solution. You must leave Nicky to my care.'

'But that's just it,' exclaimed Reginald. 'I cannot leave you here.'

'And *I* cannot leave Nicky.'

'Then I had best stay, too.'

Zelah laughed.

'Now why should you do that? You know nothing about nursing. And besides, what will poor Maria do if both you and I are away from home? I know how my sister suffers with her nerves when she is alone for too long.'

'Aye, she does.' Reginald took a turn about the room, torn by indecision.

Nicky stirred and muttered something in his sleep.

'Go home, Reginald. These fidgets will disturb Nicky.'

'But this is a bachelor household.'

'That is unfortunate, of course, but it cannot be helped.' She dipped a cloth in the bowl of lavender water and gently wiped the boy's brow. 'If it is any comfort, Reginald, Major Coale has informed me—via his housekeeper— that he will not come into this wing of the house while we are here. Indeed, once he had seen Nicky safely into bed he disappeared, giving his housekeeper orders to supply us with everything necessary. I shall sleep in the anteroom here, so that I may be on hand should Nicky wake in the night, and I will take my meals here. So you see there can be no danger of impropriety.'

Reginald did not look completely reassured.

'Would you like me to send over our maid?'

'Unnecessary, and it would give offence to Mrs Graddon.' Zelah smiled at him. 'We shall go on very comfortably, believe me, if you will arrange for some clothes to be sent over for us. And perhaps you will come again tomorrow and bring some games for Nicky. Then we shall do very well.'

'But it will not do! You are a gently bred young lady—'

'I am soon to be a governess and must learn to deal with situations such as this.' She squeezed his arm. 'Trust me, Reginald. Nicky must stay here and I shall remain to look after him until he can be moved to West Barton. Now go and reassure Maria that all is well here.'

He took his leave at last and Zelah found herself alone in the sickroom for the first time. Nicky was still sleeping soundly, which she knew was a good thing, but it left her with little to do, except rearrange the room to her satisfaction.

Zelah took dinner in the room, but the soup the housekeeper brought up for Nicky remained untouched, for he showed no signs of waking.

'Poor little lamb, sleep's the best thing for him,' said Mrs Graddon when she came to remove the dishes. 'Tomorrow I shall make some lemon jelly, to tempt his appetite. I know he's very fond of that.'

'Oh?' Zelah looked up. 'Is my nephew in the habit of calling here?'

'Aye, bless his heart. If he finds an injured animal or bird in the woods he often brings it here for the master to mend, and afore he goes he always comes down to the kitchens to find me.'

Zelah put her hands to her cheeks, mortified.

'Oh dear, he really should not be bothering Major Coale with such things, or you.'

'Lord love 'ee, mistress, the boy ain't doin' no 'arm,' exclaimed Mrs Graddon. 'In fact, I think 'e does the master good.' She paused, slanting a sidelong glance at Zelah. 'You've probably noticed that the major shuns company, but that's because o' this.' She rubbed her finger over her left temple. 'Right across his chest, it goes, though thankfully it never touched his vital organs. Took a cut to his thigh, too, but the sawbones stitched him up before he ever came home, so his leg's as good as new.'

'But when he walks…'

The housekeeper tutted, smoothing down her apron.

'He's had the very finest doctors look at 'im and they can find nothing wrong with his leg. They say 'tis all in his head. For the master don't always limp, as I've noticed, often and often.' She sighed. 'Before he went off to war and got that nasty scar he was a great one for society—him and his brother both. Twins they are and such handsome young men, they captured so many hearts I can't tell you!'

'You've known the family for a long time?'

'Aye, miss, I started as a housemaid at Markham, that's the family home, where the master's brother, the viscount, now lives. Then when the master decided to set up his own house here, Graddon and I was only too pleased to come with him. But he don't go into company, nor does he invite anyone here, and I can understand that. I've seen 'em—when people meets the master, they look everywhere but at his face and that do hurt him, you see.

But Master Nick, well, he treats the major no different from the rest.'

Zelah was silent. In her mind she was running over her meeting with Major Coale. Had she avoided looking at his terrible scarred face? She thought not, but when she had first seen him she believed he was attacking Nicky and she had been in no mood for polite evasions.

The housekeeper went off and Zelah settled down to keep watch upon her patient.

As the hours passed the house grew silent. She had a sudden yearning for company and was tempted to go down to the kitchen in the hope of meeting the house-keeper, or even a kitchen maid. She would do no such thing, of course, and was just wondering how she could occupy herself when there was a knock at the door. It was Mrs Graddon.

'The major asked me to bring you these, since you likes reading.' She held out a basket full of books. 'He says to apologise, but they's all he has at the moment, most of his books being still in the crates they arrived in, but he hopes you'll find something here to suit.'

'Thank you.' Zelah took the basket and retreated to her chair by the fire, picking up the books one by one from the basket. Richardson, Smollett, Defoe, even Mrs Rad-cliffe. She smiled. If she could not amuse herself with these, then she did not deserve to be pleased. She was comforted by the major's thoughtfulness. Feeling much less lonely, she settled down, surrounded by books.

It was after midnight when Nicky began to grow rest-less. Zelah was stretched out on the bed prepared for her when she heard him mutter. Immediately she was at his side, feeling his brow, trying to squeeze a little water through his parched lips. He batted aside her hand and turned his head away, muttering angrily. Zelah checked the bandages. They were still in place, but if he continued to toss and turn he might well open the wound and set it bleeding again.

She wished she had not refused Mrs Graddon's offer to have a truckle bed made up in the room for a maid, but rather than wring her hands in an agony of regret she picked up her bedroom candle and set off to find some help.

Zelah had not ventured from the yellow bedroom since she had followed Nicky there earlier in the day. She retraced her steps back to the great hall, too anxious about her nephew to feel menaced by the flickering shadows that danced around her. There was a thin strip of light showing beneath one of the doors off the hall and she did not hesitate. She crossed to the door and knocked softly before entering.

She was in Major Coale's study, and the man himself was sitting before the dying fire, reading by the light of a branched candelabra on the table beside him.

'I beg your pardon, I need to find Mrs Graddon. It's Nicky...'

He had put down his book and was out of the chair even as she spoke. He was not wearing his coat and the billowing shirt-sleeves made him look even bigger than she remembered.

'What is wrong with him?'

'He is feverish and I c-cannot hold him....'

'Let me see.' He added, observing her hesitation, 'I have some knowledge of these matters.'

Zelah nodded, impatient to return to Nicky. They hurried upstairs, the major's dragging leg causing his shoe to scuff at each step. It was no louder than a whisper,

but it echoed through the darkness. Nicky's fretful crying could be heard even as they entered the anteroom.
Zelah flew to his side.

'Hush now, Nicky. Keep still, love, or you will hurt
your leg again.'

'It hurts now! I want Mama!'

The major put a gentle hand on his forehead.

'She is looking after your little brother, sir. You have
your aunt and me to take care of you.' He inspected the
bottles ranged on the side table and quickly mixed a few
drops of laudanum into a glass of water.

The calm, male voice had its effect. Nicky blinked and
fixed his eyes on Zelah, who smiled at him.

'You are a guest in the major's house, Nicky.'

'Oh.' The little fingers curled around her hand. 'And
are you staying here too, Aunt Zelah?'

'She is,' said the major, 'for as long as you need her.
Now, sir, let me help you sit up a little and you must take
your medicine.'

'No, no, it hurts when I move.'

'We will lift you very carefully,' Zelah assured him.

'I don't want to…'

'Come, sir, it is only a little drink and it will take the
pain away.'

The major slipped an arm about the boy's shoulders
and held the glass to his lips. Nicky took a little sip and
shuddered.

'It is best taken in one go,' the major advised him.

The little boy's mouth twisted in distaste.

'Did you take this when you were wounded?'

'Gallons of it,' said the major cheerfully. 'Now, one,
two, three.' He ruthlessly tipped the mixture down the
boy's throat. Nicky swallowed, shuddered and his lip
trembled. 'There, it is done and you were very brave.

Miss Pentewan will turn your pillows and you will soon feel much more comfortable.'

'Will you stay, 'til I go to sleep again?'

'You have your aunt here.'

'Please.'

Zelah responded with a nod to the major's quick glance of enquiry.

'Very well.' He sat down at the side of the bed and took the little hand that reached out for him.

'Would you like me to tell you a story?' asked Zelah, but Nicky ignored her. He fixed his eyes upon the major.

'Will you tell me how you got your scar?'

Zelah stopped breathing. She glanced at the major. He did not look to be offended.

'I have told you that a dozen times. You cannot want to hear it again.'

'Yes, I do, if you please, sir. *All* of it.'

'Very well.'

He pulled his chair closer to the bed and Zelah drew back into the shadows.

'New Year's Day '09 and we were struggling through the mountains back towards Corunna, with the French hot on our heels. The weather was appalling. During the day the roads were rivers of mud and by night they were frozen solid. When we reached Cacabelos—'

'You missed something,' Nicky interrupted him. 'The man with the pigtail.'

'Ah, yes.' Major Coale's eyes softened in amusement. In the shadows Zelah smiled. She had read Nicky enough stories to know he expected the same tale, word for word, each time. The major continued. 'One Highlander woke to find he couldn't get up because his powdered pigtail was frozen to the ground. A couple of days later we reached the village of Cacabelos and the little stone bridge over the River Cua. Unfortunately discipline had become a problem during that long retreat to Corunna and General Edward Paget was obliged to make an example of those guilty of robbery. He was about to execute two of the men when he heard that the French were upon us. The general was extremely vexed at this, and after cursing roundly he turned to his men. "If I spare the lives of these men," he said, "do I have your word of honour as soldiers that you will reform?" The men shouted "Yes!" and the convicted men were cut down.'

'Huzza!' Nicky gave a sleepy cheer.

Major Coale continued, his voice soft and low.

'And just in time, for the enemy were already in sight. They were upon us in an instant, the French 15th Chasseurs and the 3rd Hussars, all thundering down to the bridge. All was confusion—our men could not withdraw because the way was blocked with fighting men and horses. Fortunately the chasseurs were in disarray and drew back to regroup, giving us time to get back across the bridge. We fixed bayonets and waited below the six guns of the horse artillery, which opened fire as the French charged again. The 52nd and the 95th delivered a furious crossfire on their flanks, killing two generals and I don't know how many men, but still they came on and fell upon us.'

He paused, his brow darkening. Nicky stirred and the major drew a breath before going on.

'I found myself caught between two chasseurs. I wounded one of them, but the other closed in. His sabre slashed down across my face and chest. I managed to unseat him and he crashed to the ground. He made another wild slash and caught my leg, but I had the satisfaction of knowing he was taken prisoner and his comrades were in full retreat before I lost consciousness.'

'Don't stop, sir. What happened then?' Nicky's eyes were beginning to close.

'I was patched up and put on to a baggage wagon. Luckily I had no serious internal injuries, for I fear it would have been fatal to be so shaken and jarred as we continued to Villafranca. I remember very little after that until we reached England. Someone had sent word to Markham, and my brother came to collect me from Falmouth and take me home. There I received the best treatment available, but alas, even money cannot buy me a new face.'

He lapsed into silence. Nicky was at last in a deep sleep, his little hand still clasped in the major's long lean fingers. Silence enveloped them. At length the major became aware of Zelah's presence and turned to look at her. She realised then her cheeks were wet with tears.

'I—I beg your pardon.' Quickly she turned away, pulling out her handkerchief. 'You have been most obliging, Major Coale, more than we had any right to expect.' She wiped her eyes, trying to speak normally. 'Nicky is sleeping now. We do not need to trouble you any longer.'

'And what will you do?'

'I shall sit with him...'

He shook his head.

'You cannot sit up all night. I will watch over him for a few hours while you get some sleep.'

Zelah wavered. She was bone-weary, but she was loath to put herself even deeper in this man's debt. He gave an exasperated sigh.

'Go and lie down,' he ordered her. 'You will not be fit to look after the boy in the morning if you do not get some sleep.'

He was right. Zelah retired to the little anteroom. She did not undress, merely removed her shoes and stretched out on the bed, pulling a single blanket over her. Her last waking thought was that it would be impossible to sleep with Major Coale sitting in the next room.

Zelah was awoken by a cock crowing. It was light, but the sun had not yet risen. She stared at the unfamiliar surroundings, then, as memory returned, she slipped off the bed and crept into the next room. Nicky was still sleeping soundly and the major was slumped forwards over the bed, his shaggy dark head on his arms.

The fire had died and the morning air was very chill. Noiselessly Zelah crossed the room and knelt down by the hearth.

'What are you doing?'

The major's deep voice made her jump.

'I am going to rescue the fire.'

'Oh, no, you are not. I will send up a servant to see to that.'

He towered over her, hand outstretched. She allowed him to help her up, trying to ignore the tingle that shot through her at his touch. It frightened her. His presence filled the room, it was disturbing, suffocating, and she stepped away, searching for something to break the uneasy silence.

'I—um—the story you told Nicky, about your wound. It was very…violent for a little boy. He seemed quite familiar with it.'

'Yes. He asked me about my face the very first time he saw me and has wanted me to recount the story regularly ever since.' He was watching the sleeping boy, the smile tugging at his lips just visible through the black beard. 'I was working in the woods and he came up, offered to help me finish off the game pie Mrs Graddon had packed into my bag to sustain me through the day.'

'You must have thought him very impertinent.'

'Not at all. His honesty was very refreshing. Most people look away, embarrassed by my disfigurement.'

'Oh, I beg your pardon. I hope you did not think that *I*—'

The smile turned into a grin.

'You, madam, seemed intent upon inflicting even more damage upon me.'

The amusement in his eyes drew a reluctant smile from Zelah.

'You did—do—look rather savage. Although I know now that you are very kind,' she added in a rush. She felt herself blushing. 'You have been sitting here all night and must be desperate for sleep. I can manage now, thank you, Major. You had best go…'

'I should, of course. I will send someone up to see to the fire and order Mrs Graddon to bring your breakfast to you.'

'Thank you.' He gave her a clipped little bow and turned to leave.

'Major! The chasseur—the one who injured you—was he really taken prisoner?'

He stopped and looked back.

'Yes, he was.' His eyes narrowed. 'I may *look* like a monster, Miss Pentewan, but I assure you I am not.'

Chapter Two

Nicky was drowsy and fretful when he eventually woke up, but Dr Pannell was able to reassure Zelah that he was recovering well.

'A little fever is to be expected, but he seems to be in fine form now. I think keeping him still is going to be your biggest problem.'

Zelah had thought so too and she was relieved when Reginald arrived with a selection of toys and games for his son.

'Goodness!' She laughed when she saw the large basket that Reginald placed on the bed. 'Major Coale will think we plan to stay for a month.'

Reginald grinned.

'I let Nurse choose what to send. I fear she was over-generous to make up for not being able to come herself.'

'And what did our host say, when you came in with such a large basket?'

'I have not seen him. His man informed me that he is busy with his keeper and likely to be out all day.' He glanced at Nicky, happily sorting through the basket, and led Zelah into the anteroom. 'I had the feeling he was ordered to say that and to make sure I knew that he had given instructions for a maid to sit up with the boy during the night. Setting my mind at rest that he would not be imposing himself upon you while you are here.'

'Major Coale is very obliging.'

'Dashed ragged fellow though, with all that hair, but I suppose that's to cover the scar on his face.' He paused. 'Maria asked me to drop a word in your ear, but for my part I don't think there's anything to worry about.'

'What did she wish you to say to me?'

He chewed his lip for a moment.

'She was concerned. Coale was well known as something of a, er, a rake before the war. His name was forever in the society pages. Well, stands to reason, doesn't it, younger son of a viscount, and old Lord Markham had some scandals to his name, I can tell you! Coale's brother's inherited the title now, of course, and from what I have read he's just as wild as the rest of 'em.' He added quickly, 'Only hearsay, of course. I've never had much to do with that side of the family—far too high and mighty for one thing. The Bucklands are a very distant branch. But that's neither here nor there. We were worried the major might try to ingratiate himself with you—after all, we are mighty obliged to him—and Maria thought you might have…stirrings.'

'Stirrings, Reginald?'

He flushed.

'Aye. Maria says that sometimes a woman's sympathy for an injured man can stir her—that she can find him far too…attractive.'

Zelah laughed.

'Then you may set Maria's mind at rest. The only *stirring* I have when I think of Major Coale is to comb his hair!'

* * *

Reginald stayed for an hour or more and after that Hannah, the chambermaid appointed to help Zelah look after Nicky, came up to introduce herself. By the time dinner was brought up it was clear that she was more than capable of nursing Nicky and keeping him amused, and Zelah realised a trifle ruefully that it was not Nicky's boredom but her own that might be a problem.

Zelah and Hannah had taken it in turns to sit up with Nicky through the night, but there was no recurrence of the fever and when Dr Pannell called the following morning he declared himself satisfied that the boy would be able to go home at the end of the week.

'I will call again on Friday, Miss Pentewan, and providing there has been no more bleeding we will make arrangements to return you both to West Barton. You will be the first to use the major's new carriageway.'

'Oh, is it finished?' asked Zelah. 'I have been watching them repair the drive, but I cannot see what is going on beyond the gates.'

'I spoke to the workmen on the way here and they told me the road will be passable by tomorrow. The road-building has been a godsend for Lesserton, providing work for so many of the men. The problems with grazing rights is making it difficult for some of them to feed their families.'

'Is this the dispute with the new owner of Lydcombe Park? My brother-in-law mentioned something about this before I came away.'

'Aye, Sir Oswald Evanshaw moved in on Lady Day and he is claiming land that the villagers believe belongs to them.' The doctor shook his head. 'Of course, he has a point: the house has changed hands several times in recent years, but no one has actually lived there, so the villagers have been in the habit of treating everything round about as their own. The boundaries between Lydcombe land and that belonging to the villagers have become confused. He's stopped them going into Prickett Wood, too, so they cannot collect the firewood as they were used to do and Sir Oswald's bailiff is prepared to use violence against anyone who tries to enter the wood. He's driven out all the deer, so that they are now competing with the villagers' stock for fodder.' He was silent for a moment, frowning over the predicament, then he shook off his melancholy thoughts and gave her a smile. 'Thankfully Major Coale is of a completely different stamp. He is happy for the local people to gather firewood from his forest. It is good fortune that Nicky chose to injure himself on the major's land rather that at Lydcombe.'

Zelah had agreed, but as the day wore on she began to wonder if she would have the opportunity to thank her host for his hospitality. With Hannah to share the nursing Zelah was growing heartily bored with being confined to the sickroom.

When the maid came up the following morning she asked her casually if the major was in the house.

'Oh, no, miss. He left early. Mr Graddon said not to expect him back much before dinner.'

She bobbed a curtsy and settled down to a game of spillikins with Nicky. Left to amuse herself, Zelah carried her work basket to the cushioned window seat and took out her embroidery. It was a beautiful spring day and she could hear the faint call of the cuckoo in the woods.

The sun climbed higher. Zelah put away her sewing and read to Nicky while Hannah quietly tidied the room around them. The book was one of Nicky's favourites, *Robinson Crusoe,* but as the afternoon wore on his eyelids began to droop, and soon he was sleeping peacefully.

'Best thing for'n. Little mite.' Hannah looked down fondly at the sleeping boy. 'Why don't you go and get yourself some rest, too, miss? I'll sit here and watch'n for 'ee.'

Zelah sighed, her eyes on the open window.

'What I would really like to do is to go outside.'

'Then why don't 'ee? No one'll bother you. You could walk in the gardens. I can always call you from the window, if the boy wakes up.'

Zelah hesitated, but only for a moment. The spring day was just too beautiful to miss. With a final word to Hannah to be sure to call her if she was needed, she slipped down the stairs and out of the house.

The lawns had been scythed, but weeds now inhabited the flowerbeds and the shrubs were straggling and overgrown. After planning how she would restock the borders and perhaps add a statue or two, she moved on and discovered the kitchen garden, where some attempt was being made to improve it.

The hedge separating the grounds from the track that led to the stables had been hacked down to waist height, beds had been dug and cold frames repaired. Heartened by these signs of industry, Zelah was about to retrace her steps when she heard the clip-clop of an approaching horse. Major Coale was riding towards the stables on a huge grey horse. She picked up her skirts and flew across to the hedge, calling out to him.

He stopped, looking around in surprise.

'Should you not be with the boy?'

She stared up at him.

'You have shaved off your beard.'

'Very observant. But you have not answered my question.'

'Hannah is sitting with him. It was such a beautiful day I had to come out of doors.'

She answered calmly, refusing to be offended by his curt tone and was rewarded when he asked in a much milder way how the boy went on.

'He is doing very well, thank you. Dr Pannell is coming in the morning to examine Nicky. All being well, I hope to take him back to West Barton tomorrow.' He inclined his head and made to move on. She put up her hand. 'Please, don't go yet! I wanted to thank you for all you have done for us.'

'That is not necessary.'

'I think it is.' She smiled. 'I believe if I had not caught you now I should not have seen you again before we left.'

He looked down at her, unsmiling. His grey eyes were as hard as granite.

'My staff have orders to look after you. You have no need to see me.'

'But I want to.' She glanced away, suddenly feeling a little shy. 'You have been very kind to us. I wanted to thank you.'

She could feel his eyes boring into her and kept her own fixed on the toe of his muddy boot.

'Very well,' he said at last. 'You have thanked me. That is an end to it.'

He touched his heels to the horse's flanks and moved on.

'I wish I had said nothing,' she muttered, embarrassment making her irritable. 'Did I expect him to thaw a little, merely because I expressed my gratitude? The man is nothing but a boor.'

Even as she spoke the words she came to a halt as another, more uncomfortable thought occurred. Perhaps Major Coale was lonely.

What was it Mrs Graddon had said? *He was a great one for society.* That did not sit well with his assertion that he had no wish for company. His curt manner, the long hair and the shaggy beard that had covered his face until today—perhaps it was all designed to keep the world at bay.

'Well, if that is so, it is no concern of mine,' she addressed the rosemary bush beside her. 'We all have our crosses to bear and some of us do not have the means to shut ourselves away and wallow in our misery!'

When Dr Pannell called the next day he gave Nicky a thorough examination, at the end of which Zelah asked him anxiously if he might go home now.

'I think not, my dear.'

'But his mama is so anxious for him,' said Zelah, disappointed. 'And you said he might be moved today...'

'I know, but that was when I thought the major's new road would be finished. Now they tell me it will not be open properly until tomorrow. Be patient, my dear. Major Coale has told me his people will be working into the night to make the road passable for you.'

With that she had to be satisfied. Nick appeared quite untroubled by the news that he was to remain at Rooks Tower. His complaisance was much greater than Zelah's. She hated to admit it, but she was finding the constant attendance on an eight-year-old boy and the company of an amiable but childish chambermaid a little dull.

After sharing a light luncheon with Nicky, Zelah left the boy reading with Hannah and went off in search of Mrs Graddon, to offer her help, only to find that the good lady had gone into Lesserton for supplies. Unwilling to return to the sickroom just yet, Zelah picked up her shawl and went out to explore more of the grounds.

Having seen enough of the formal gardens, she walked around to the front of the house and headed for the orangery. A chill wind was blowing down from the moors and she wrapped her shawl about her as she crossed the lawn. The orangery was built in the classical style. Huge sash windows were separated by graceful pillars that supported an elegant pediment. Between the two central columns were glazed double doors. The stone was in good order, if in need of a little repair, but the woodwork looked sadly worn and several panes of glass were broken.

Zelah was surprised to find the doors unlocked. They opened easily and she stepped inside, glad to be out of the wind. The interior was bare, save for a few dried leaves on the floor, but there were niches in the walls which were clearly designed to hold statues. A shadow fell across her and she swung around.

'Oh.'

Major Coale was standing in the doorway. She guessed he had just returned from riding, for his boots were spattered with mud and there was a liberal coating of dust on his brown coat. His broad-brimmed hat was jammed on his head and its shadow made it impossible to read his expression. She waved her hand ineffectually.

'I—um—I hope you do not mind...'

'Why should I?' He stepped inside, suddenly making the space seem much smaller. 'I saw the open doors and came across to see who was here. What do you think of it?'

'It is in need of a little repair,' she began carefully.

'I was thinking of tearing it down—'

'No!' She put her hand to her mouth. 'I beg your pardon,' she said stiffly. 'It is of course up to you what you do here.'

'It is indeed, but I am curious, Miss Pentewan. What would *you* do with it?'

'New windows and doors,' she said immediately. 'Then I would furnish it with chairs for the summer and in the winter I would use it as it was intended, to shelter orange trees.'

'But I have no orange trees.'

'You might buy some. I understand oranges are extremely good for one.'

He grunted.

'You are never at a loss for an answer, are you, ma'am?'

Yes, she thought, *I am at a loss now.*

She gave a little shrug and looked away.

'I should get back.'

'I will accompany you.'

She hurried out into the sunlight and set off for the house. Major Coale fell into step beside her.

'So you will be leaving us tomorrow. I met Dr Pannell on the road,' he explained, answering her unspoken question. 'You will be glad to return to West Barton.'

'Yes.' He drew in a harsh breath, as if she had touched a raw wound and she hurried to explain. 'It is not—you have been all kindness, and your staff have done everything required...'

'But?'

She drew her shawl a little tighter.

'I shall be glad to have a little adult company once more.'

There. She had said it. But as soon as the words were uttered she regretted them. 'Please do not think I am complaining—I am devoted to Nicky and could not have left him here alone.'

'But you have missed intelligent conversation?'

'Yes,' she responded, grateful that he understood. 'When I lived at home, in Cardinham, Papa and I would talk for hours.'

'Of what?'

'Oh, anything! Politics, music, books. At West Barton it is the same, although my sister is a little preoccupied at the moment with her baby. But when Reginald is at home we enjoy some lively debates.' She flushed a little. 'Forgive me, I am of course extremely grateful to you for all you have done—'

'I know, you told me as much yesterday. Yet it appears I am failing as a host.' They had reached the front door and he stopped. 'Perhaps you would join me for dinner this evening.' The request was so unexpected that she could only stare at him. 'No, of course that is not possible. Forget I—'

'Of course it is possible.' She spoke quickly, while an inner voice screamed its warnings at her. To dine alone with a man, was she mad? But in that instant when he had issued his invitation she had seen something in his eyes, a haunting desolation that burned her soul. It was gone in a moment, replaced by his habitual cold, shuttered look. But that brief connection had wrenched at the core of loss and loneliness buried deep within her, and Zelah found the combination was just too strong to withstand. 'I would be delighted to join you.'

His brows rose.

'There will be no chaperone.'

'Nicky will be in the house and your housekeeper.'

His hard eyes searched her face for a moment.

'Very well, Miss Pentewan. Until dinner!'

With that he touched his hat, turned on his heel and marched off towards the stables.

* * *

Zelah looked at the scant assortment of clothes laid out on the bed. Whoever had packed her bag had clearly assumed she would spend all her time in the sickroom. Neither her serviceable grey gown nor the dimity day dress was suitable for dining with the major. However, there was a green sash and matching stole that she could wear with her yellow muslin. Mrs Graddon had washed it for her and there were only a few drawn threads from her escapade in the woods. Once she had tied the sash around her waist and draped the stole over her arms she thought it would serve her well enough as an evening dress.

In the few hours since the major had invited her to dine, Zelah had pondered upon his reasons for doing so, and had come to the conclusion that it was twofold: he was being kind to her, but also he was lonely. If she thought for a moment that he was attracted to her she would have declined his invitation, but Zelah had no illusions about herself. Her mirror showed her a very nondescript figure, too thin for beauty and with soft brown hair that was neither fashionably dark nor attractively blond. And at two-and-twenty she was practically an old maid.

Sometimes she thought back to the happy girl she had been at eighteen, with a ready laugh and a sparkle in her eyes. Her figure had been better then, too, but at eighteen she had been in love and could see only happiness ahead. A year later everything had changed. She had lost her love, her happy future and her zest for life. Looking in her mirror now, she saw nothing to attract any man. And that could only be to her benefit, she reminded herself, if she was going to make her own way in the world.

* * *

Hannah had found her a length of yellow ribbon for her hair and five minutes before the appointed hour she presented herself to her nephew.

'Well, will I do?'

Nicky wrinkled his nose.

'I wish I could come with you, Aunty.'

'So, too, do I, love,' said Zelah earnestly. She had been growing increasingly anxious about meeting the major as the dinner hour approached.

'Ah, well, after I've given Master Nicky his supper we are going to finish our puzzle,' said Hannah, beaming happily. 'Now you go on and enjoy your dinner, miss, and don't 'ee worry about us, we shall have a fine time!'

Zelah made her way down to the great hall, where the evening sun created a golden glow. She had no idea where the drawing room might be and was just wondering what to do when Graddon appeared .

'This way, madam, if you please.'

He directed her to a door beside the major's study and opened it for her.

After the dazzling brightness of the hall, the room seemed very dark, but when her eyes grew accustomed she saw that she was alone and she relaxed a little, looking about her with interest. It was a long room with a lofty ceiling, ornately plastered. The crimson walls were covered with large paintings, mostly of men and women in grey wigs and the fashions of the last century, but there was one painting beside the fireplace of a young lady with her hair tumbling like dark, polished mahogany over her shoulders. She wore a high-waisted gown and the artist had cleverly painted the skirts as if they had just been caught by a soft breeze. Zelah stepped closer. There was a direct, fearless stare in the girl's dark eyes and a firm set to those sculpted lips. She looked strangely familiar.

'My sister, Serena.'

She jumped and turned to find the major standing behind her.

'Oh, I did not hear you—' She almost said she had not heard the scuffing of his dragging foot. Flustered, she turned back to the painting. 'She is very like you, I think.'

He gave a bark of laughter.

'Not in looks, I hope! Nor in temperament. She was not the least serene, which is why Jasper and I renamed her Sally! Very wild and headstrong. At least she was until she married. Now she is a model of respectability.'

'And is she happy?'

'Extremely.'

She took a last look at the painting, then turned to her host. Although she had seen him without his beard that afternoon, his clean-shaven appearance still surprised her. He had brushed his thick, dark hair and tied it back with a ribbon. The ragged scar was now visible, stretching from his left temple, down through his eyebrow and left cheekbone to his chin, dragging down the left side of his mouth.

The look in his eyes was guarded with just a touch of defiance. Zelah realised he expected her to look away, revolted by the sight of his scarred face. She was determined not to do that and, not knowing quite what to do, she smiled at him.

'You look very smart, sir.'

The wary look disappeared.

'Thank you, ma'am.' He gave a little bow. 'I believe this is still the standard wear for dinner.'

They both knew she was not referring to the black

evening coat and snowy waistcoat and knee breeches, but her smile grew.

'Your dress is very different from the first time I saw you.'

'I keep that old coat for when I am working in the woods. It is loose across the shoulders and allows me to swing the axe.' He paused. 'Graddon informs me that there has been a slight upset in the kitchen and dinner is not quite ready.' A faint smile lifted the good side of his mouth. 'Mrs Graddon is an estimable creature, but I understand my telling her I would be entertaining a guest caused the sauce to curdle.'

'Sauces are notoriously difficult,' she said carefully.

He held out his arm to her.

'Perhaps you would care to step out on to the terrace while we wait?'

Zelah nodded her assent and took his proffered arm. He walked her across the room to the door set between the long windows.

'You see the house has been sadly neglected,' he said as he led her out of doors. He bent to pluck a straggling weed from between the paving slabs and tossed it aside.

'The rose garden has survived quite well,' she observed. 'It needs only a little work to bring it into some sort of order.'

'Really? When I last looked the plants were quite out of control.'

'They need pruning, that is all. And even the shrubbery is not, I think, beyond saving. Cut the plants back hard and they will grow better than ever next year.'

'Pity the same thing does not apply to people.'

She had been happily imagining how the gardens might look, but his bitter words brought her back to reality. She might be able to forget her companion's disfigurement, but he could not. A sudden little breeze made her shiver.

'I beg your pardon. It is too early in the year to be out of doors.'

The major put his hand out to help her arrange her stole. Did it rest on her shoulder a moment longer than was necessary, or was that her imagination? He was standing very close, looming over her. A sense of his physical power enveloped her.

This is all nonsense, she told herself sternly, but the sensation persisted. *Run, Zelah, go now!*

'Perhaps, ma'am, we should go back inside.'

He put his hand beneath her arm and she almost jumped away, her nerves jangling. Immediately he released her, standing back so that she could precede him into the room. He had turned slightly, so that he presented only the uninjured side of his face to her and silently Zelah berated herself. Major Coale was acting as a gentleman, while she was displaying the sort of ill-mannered self-consciousness that she despised. That was no way to repay her host's kindness. She must try harder.

He escorted her to the dining room, where Zelah's stretched nerves tightened even more. A place was set at the head of the table and another on its right hand. It was far too intimate. She cleared her throat.

'Major, would—would you object if I made slight adjustment to the setting?'

She flushed under his questioning gaze, but he merely shrugged.

'As you wish.'

She squared her shoulders. The setting at the head of the table was soon moved to the left hand, so that they would be facing each other. She had to steel herself to turn back to the major.

The silence as he observed her work was unnerving, but Zelah comforted herself that the worst he could do was order her to go back to her room and eat alone. At last those piercing eyes moved to her face.

'Do you think you will be safer with five foot of mahogany between us?'

'It is more...seemly.'

'Seemly! If that is your worry, perhaps we should ask Mrs Graddon to join us.'

Zelah's anger flared.

'I agreed to dine with you, sir, but to sit so close—'

'Yes, yes, it would be *unseemly*! So be it. For God's sake let us sit down before the food arrives.'

He stalked to her chair and held it out. She sat down. He took his own seat in silence.

'I beg your pardon,' said Zelah. 'I did not mean to put you to all this trouble.'

It was a poor enough olive branch, but it worked. Major Coale gave her a rueful look.

'And I beg your pardon for losing my temper. My manners have lost their polish.'

The door opened and the footmen came in with the first dishes.

After such an unpromising start Zelah feared that conversation might be difficult, but she was wrong. The major proved an excellent host, exerting himself to entertain. He persuaded her to take a little from every dish on the table and kept her glass filled while regaling her with amusing anecdotes. She forgot her nerves and began to enjoy herself. They discussed music and art, the theatre and politics, neither noticing when the footmen came in to light the candles, and by the time they finished their meal Zelah was exchanging opinions with the major as if they were old friends. When the covers were removed the major asked her about Nicky and she found herself chatting away, telling him how they filled their days.

'Hannah is so good with him, too,' she ended. 'Thank you for sending her to help me.'

'It was Mrs Graddon who suggested it, knowing the girl comes from a large family.'

'Nicky adores her and would much rather play spillikins with her than attend to his lessons.'

His brows rose. 'Don't tell me you are making him work while he is laid up sick?'

She laughed.

'No, no, but I like him to read to me a little each day and to write a short note to his mama. He is reluctant to apply himself, but I find that with a little encouragement he is willing enough. And it is very good practice for me.'

'Practice?'

'Yes, for when I become a governess.'

She selected a sweetmeat as the butler came up to re-fill her glass. The major waved him away.

'Thank you, Graddon, that will be all. Leave the Madeira and I will serve Miss Pentewan.' He waited until they were alone before he spoke again.

'Forgive my impertinence, ma'am, but you do not look old enough to be a governess.'

She sat up very straight.

'I am two-and-twenty, Major Coale. Not that it is any of your business!' She bit her lip. 'I beg you pardon. I am a guest in your house—'

'Guest be damned,' he interrupted roughly. 'That is no reason you should endure my incivility. Being a guest here should not put you under any obligation.'

Zelah chuckled, her spurt of anger dying as quickly as it had come.

'Of course I am under an obligation to you, Major.

You have gone to great lengths to accommodate us. And how could I not forgive you for paying me such a handsome compliment?'

He gave a short laugh and filled their glasses.

'So why *are* you intent on becoming a governess? Can Buckland not support you?'

'Why should he do so, if I can earn my own living?'

'I should not allow *my* sister to become a governess.'

'But your father was a viscount. Reginald is only a brother by marriage, and besides, he has a family of his own to support.' She picked up the glass he had filled for her and tasted it carefully. She had never had Madeira before, but she found she enjoyed the warm, nutty flavour. 'I would not add to his burdens.'

He reached out, his hand hovering over the sweetmeats as he said lightly, 'Perhaps you should look for a husband.'

'No!'

The vehemence brought his head up immediately and she was subjected to a piercing gaze. She decided to be flippant.

'As I am penniless, and notoriously difficult to please, I think that might be far too difficult. I do like this wine— is it usual for gentlemen to drink it at the end of a meal? I know Reginald prefers brandy.'

To her relief he followed her lead and their conversation moved back to safer waters. She took another glass of Madeira and decided it must be her last. She was in danger of becoming light-headed. Darkness closed around them. The butler came in silently to light more candles in the room and draw the curtains against the night, but they made no move to leave the table, there was still so much to say.

The major turned to speak to Graddon and Zelah studied his profile. How handsome he must have been before his face was sliced open by a French sabre. It was a momentary thought, banished as soon as it occurred, but it filled her with sadness.

'You are very quiet, Miss Pentewan.'

His words brought her back to the present and she blushed, not knowing how to respond. In the end she decided upon the truth.

'I was thinking about your face.'

Immediately he seemed to withdraw from her.

'That is why I wanted you upon my right hand, to spare you that revulsion.'

She shook her head.

'It does not revolt me.'

'I should not have shaved off my beard!'

'Yes, you should, you look so much better, only—'

'Yes, madam? Only what?' The hard note in his voice warned her not to continue, but she ignored it.

'Your hair,' she said breathlessly. 'I am surprised your valet does not wish to cut it.'

'I have no valet. Graddon does all I need.'

'But I thought he was a butler...'

'He does what is necessary. He was with me in Spain and brought me back to England. He stayed with me, helped me to come to terms with my new life.'

'And Mrs Graddon?'

'She was housemaid at Markham and decided to marry Graddon and come with him when I moved here.' He raised his glass, his lip curling into something very like a sneer. 'You see, my misfortune is their gain.'

She frowned.

'Please do not belittle them. They are devoted to you.'

'I stand corrected,' he said stiffly. 'I beg your pardon and theirs.'

'I think you would look much better with your hair cut short. It is very much the fashion now, you know.'

He leaned closer, a belligerent, challenging look in his eye. It took all her courage not to turn away.

'I need it long,' he said savagely. 'Then I can bring it down, thus, and hide this monstrous deformation.' He pulled the ribbon from his hair and shook the dark curtain down over his face. 'Surely that is better? I would not want to alarm the ladies and children!'

He was glaring at her, eyes narrowed, his mouth a thin, taut line, one side pulled lower by the dragging scar.

'Nicky is not afraid of you,' she said softly. 'Nor do you frighten me.'

For a long, interminable time she held his eyes, hoping he would read not pity but sympathy and understanding in her gaze. He was a proud man and she was dismayed to think he was hiding from the world. To her relief, his angry look faded.

'So would you have me trust myself to a country barber?' he growled. 'I think not, Miss Pentewan. Perhaps next time I go to London—'

'I could cut it for you.' She sat back, shocked by her own temerity. 'I am quite adept at cutting hair, although I have no idea where the skill comes from. I was always used to trim my father's hair, and since I have been at West Barton I have cut Nicky's. I am sure no one could tell it was not professionally done.'

He was frowning at her now. She had gone too far. The wine had made her reckless and her wretched tongue had let her down. Major Coale jumped up and strode to tug at the bell pull. He was summoning a footman to escort her to her room.

'Graddon, fetch scissors and my comb, if you please.'

He caught her eye, a glint in his own. 'Very well, Miss Pentewan, let us put you to the test.'

'What? I—' She swallowed. 'Are you sure it is what you want?'

'Are you losing your nerve, madam?'

Zelah quite thought that she was. Two voices warred within her: one told her that to dine alone with a gentleman who was not related to her was improper enough, but to cut the man's hair would put her beyond the pale. The other whispered that it was her Christian duty to help him quit his self-imposed exile.

The glint in his eyes turned into a gleam. He was laughing at her and her courage rose.

'Not at all. Let us do it!'

'Major, are you quite sure you want me to do this?'

He was sitting on a chair by the table and Zelah was standing behind him, comb in hand. They had rearranged the candelabra to give the best light possible and the dark locks gleamed, thick and glossy around his head, spreading out like ebony across his shoulders. The enormity of what she was about to do made her hesitate.

The major waved his hand.

'Yes. I may change my mind when I am sober, but for now I want you to cut it.'

Zelah took a deep breath. It was too late to go back now, they had agreed. Besides, argued that wickedly seductive voice in her head, no one need ever know. She picked up the scissors and moved closer until her skirts were brushing his shoulder. It felt strange, uncomfortable, like standing over a sleeping tiger. Thrusting aside such fanciful thoughts, she took a secure grip of the scissors and began. His hair was like silk beneath her fingers. She lifted one dark lock and applied the scissors. They cut through it with a whisper. As she continued her confidence grew, as did the pile of black tresses on the floor.

His hair was naturally curly and she had seen enough pencil drawings of gentlemen with their hair *à la Brutus* since she had arrived at West Barton to recreate the style from memory—Reginald and Maria might live in a remote area of Exmoor, but they were both avid followers of the *ton*, receiving a constant stream of periodicals and letters from friends in London advising them of the latest fashions. She cut, combed and coaxed the major's hair into place. It needed no pomade or grease to make it curl around his collar and his ears. She brushed the tendrils forwards around his face, as she had seen in the fashion plates. Her fingers touched the scar and he flinched. Immediately she drew back.

'Did I hurt you?'

'No. Carry on.'

Carefully she finished her work, combing and snipping off a few straggling ends until she was satisfied with the result. It was not strictly necessary, but she could not resist running her fingers though his glossy, thick hair one final time.

'There.' She brushed the loose hair from his shoulders. 'It is finished.'

'Very well, Delilah, let us see what you have done to me.'

He picked up one of the candelabra and walked over to a mirror.

Zelah held her breath as he regarded his image. In the candlelight the ugly gash down his face was still visible, but it seemed diminished by the new hairstyle. The sleek black locks were brushed forwards to curl about his wide brow, accentuating the strong lines of his face.

'Well, Miss Pentewan, I congratulate you. Perhaps you

should not be looking for a post as a governess, after all. You should offer your services as a *coiffeuse*.'

Relief made her laugh out loud. She said daringly, 'You look very handsome, Major.'

He turned away from the mirror and made a noise between a growl and a cough.

'Aye, well, enough of that. It is time I sent you back to the sick room, madam. You will need to be up betimes.'

'Yes, of course.' She cast a conscience-stricken look at the clock. 'Poor Hannah has been alone with Nicky for hours.' She held out her hand to him. 'Goodnight, sir. I hope we shall see you in the morning before we leave?'

Again that clearing of the throat and he would not meet her eyes.

'Perhaps. Goodnight, Miss Pentewan.' He took her hand, his grip tightening for a second. 'And thank you.'

Chapter Three

The following morning Reginald drove over in his travelling chaise, which Maria had filled with feather bolsters and pillows to protect Nicky during the long journey home. Nicky looked around as his father carried him tenderly out of the house.

'Is Major Coale not here, Papa?'

'He sends his apologies, Master Nick,' said Graddon in a fatherly way. 'He went off early today to the long meadow to oversee the hedge-laying.'

'But I wanted to say goodbye to him!'

Nicky's disappointed wail touched a chord in Zelah: she too would have liked to see the major. However, she was heartened by Reginald's response.

'Your mama has already penned a note to Major Coale. She has not only given him permission to call at any time, but she has also invited him to dinner. And once we have you home, Nicholas, you may write to him yourself, thanking him for his care of you.'

'Yes, and I can ask him to call and see me,' agreed Nicky. He frowned, suddenly unsure. 'He will come, won't he? If I ask him 'specially.'

'I do not see how he can refuse.' Reginald grinned at

Zelah. 'But I might have to instruct the staff not to send him round to the kitchens—when I saw him last he looked so ragged one might easily mistake him for a beggar.'

'I think you might be surprised,' murmured Zelah, smiling to herself.

The five miles to West Barton were covered with ease and they were greeted with great joy by the household. Maria clasped her stepson and wept copiously, bewailing the fact that she had been unable to visit him, while Nurse promised him all sorts of treats to make up for his ordeal.

'I only hope being in That Man's house hasn't given you nightmares,' said Nurse, tucking Nicky into his bed. 'I believe he is truly hideous to look at.'

Anger welled up in Zelah, but she fought it down and said quietly, 'Nonsense. Major Coale has a scar on his face, nothing more.'

'Yes, and I don't care for *that*,' exclaimed Nicky. 'He's a great gun.'

'Of course he is, my pet. Now, you need to rest after your long journey.'

Obedient to her unspoken wishes the others left Nicky to Nurse's care and made their way back downstairs to the morning room.

'I don't like to think that he has been making a nuisance of himself.' Reginald frowned. 'When Coale told me he has been running free at Rooks Tower—'

'Major Coale and his people are very happy to see him,' said Zelah. 'With everyone here so busy with the new baby, Nicky has been left too much to his own devices.'

Her words were met with a short silence. Then Maria sighed.

'It is very true. Nurse has been giving all her attention

to me and little Reginald and we were only too happy to think that Nicky was amusing himself in the garden.' Her softly reproachful eyes moved to her husband. 'And you have been out of the house so much recently...'

'Trying to gather evidence for the villagers,' he replied defensively. 'I could hardly take the boy with me! I never thought—Nicky seemed quite happy.' He gave Zelah a rueful smile. 'No wonder he took to you so well, although looking after Nicky was not the reason you came to us. My poor sister, you have been with us for only a few weeks and we have turned you into a nursemaid.'

'I am pleased to help, you know that, but Nicky needs companions of his own age,' she said gently. 'Or at the very least a tutor...'

'But he is so young!' Maria clasped her hands together. 'I suppose I must stop thinking of him as a baby now.' She brightened. 'You are looking for a post as a governess, Zelah—perhaps you should start with Nicky. We could pay you—'

'Dear sister, that is a kind thought, but that is not what I meant. And I could not take a salary off you; I have no wish to be an added drain upon your resources.'

Reginald shook his head.

'No, it would not do at all. I believe Mr Netherby gives lessons to a few boys in the vicarage. I will make enquiries when I go into Lesserton this afternoon.'

Maria stretched out her hands to him. 'Oh, must you go, with Nicky just come home...?'

He squeezed her fingers.

'I'm afraid I must.'

'What is this business that takes you there so often, Reginald?' asked Zelah. 'Is it something to do with Lydcombe Park? I remember you saying the new owner was causing difficulties.'

'Aye. He is planning to open mines on his land.'

'But surely that is a good thing,' exclaimed Maria. 'It will provide work—'

'Not much. Evanshaw will be bringing in engineers and miners of his own. But the land he wants to mine is in dispute. The villagers believe it is theirs by ancient charter and have been using the land for years, grazing their animals on the hill as well as hunting in Prickett Wood. Sir Oswald claims it for his own and he has employed a bailiff, William Miller. A nasty piece of work who patrols the land with his henchmen.'

'And is there nothing they can do?'

'Those he has evicted are too poor to do anything themselves, but I have been organising the villagers. We have petitioned the Crown and put together a fund to pay for a lawyer to come to Lesserton and settle this once and for all.'

'But can you not talk to Sir Oswald?' said Zelah. 'Surely he does not want to be on bad terms with his neighbours.'

Reginald shrugged. 'I called upon him as soon as he took possession of the house on Lady Day, but he was not at all hospitable. I do not think he intends to live at Lydcombe. The house is merely a shell; everything of value in it has been sold. He told me he means to sell off the timber from his land and then sink his mine. He has no interest at all in the people.'

'Then of course you must fight this,' exclaimed Zelah. 'I quite understand now why you are so busy. And please do not worry about Nicky, at least for the moment. I am very happy to help you look after him.'

Zelah went upstairs to relieve Nurse, satisfied that Maria and Reginald would find a solution to Nicky's loneliness. Taking lessons at the vicarage would go a long

way towards filling his days and would also provide him
with the companionship of other boys. For the present,
her concern was to keep him entertained while the deep
gash on his leg healed.

The fine spring weather continued but Zelah was
too busy to go out, dividing her day between Nicky and
Maria, who was delighted to have her back and insisted
that Zelah should sit with her whenever she could. It was
therefore a full three days before she could find the time
to enjoy the sunshine. She tied a straw bonnet over her
brown curls, but declined her sister's offer of a parasol,
declaring that her complexion was past praying for.

Leaving the house by a side door, she set off across the
grass at a very unladylike pace. It was good to be out in
the fresh air again and she lifted her face up to the sun,
revelling in its warmth. She walked briskly, enjoying the
opportunity for a little quiet reflection.

She had been at West Barton for a month now and
had made no progress in finding a position. She could
make excuses, of course. Maria had told her how helpful
it was to have her there, looking after Nicky, but deep in
her heart Zelah knew she did not want to dwindle into
the role of favourite aunt, at everyone's beck and call and
willing to perform any little task in gratitude for being
allowed to live with the family.

'You are being very ungrateful,' she said aloud. 'A
position as governess would be far from comfortable.
Here you could more than earn your keep.' She climbed
over a stile and jumped lightly down. 'But as a governess I would be *paid*!'

She strode on. What she wanted, she realised, was independence. If she was fortunate enough to find a good
position, then it might be possible to save a little of her

salary each year until she had enough to retire. That, of course, would take many, many years, but what else had she to look forward to?

Perhaps you should look for a husband.

Major Coale's words came into her mind. She could almost hear his deep voice saying them.

A husband. That was the ambition of most young ladies, but it was not hers. Besides, no man would want her if he knew her past—and she could not consider marrying a man without telling him everything.

No, thought Zelah practically, she had only two choices: she could remain at West Barton, loved and valued at the present, but destined to become nothing more than a burdensome old maid, or she could make a bid for independence.

'I choose independence,' she said to a cow, regarding her balefully from the next field. 'I shall go back now and write out an advertisement for the newspaper.'

She crossed the field and scrambled over the stile on to the lane that led up to West Barton and as she did so she saw a rider approaching from the direction of Lesserton. Major Coale. In a panic she considered jumping back over the stile and hiding until he had gone by, but it was too late; he had already seen her.

'Good morning, Miss Pentewan.' He raised his hat to her. She felt a little rush of pride when she saw his short hair. His cheeks were still free of a beard, too. There was no sign that he planned to revert to his former shaggy appearance. 'I am on my way to enquire after young Master Buckland.'

'He is doing very well, Major, thank you. The doctor says he may leave his bed tomorrow.'

He professes to dislike society, she thought. *Perhaps*

*he will be satisfied with that report. He will touch his hat,
turn and ride away again.*

'I am glad to hear it.' He kicked his feet free from the
stirrups and jumped down. 'Are you walking back to the
house now? May I join you?'

'I...yes, of course.'

She waited until he was beside her and began to walk
on, very slowly, the grey mare clopping lazily along behind them. After a few yards the major stopped.

'Is this how you usually walk, Miss Pentewan? I am
surprised you ever get anywhere.'

'Yes—no, I...' She trailed off, her gaze dropping to
his booted feet. 'I thought, your leg...'

'I am not a cripple, madam.'

Mrs Graddon's words flashed into her mind and she
recalled when she had offered to cut his hair and he had
got up from the table to summon his servant. There had
been no dragging step, no sign of a limp then.

'Does the wound not pain you?' she asked him.

'Not at all, unlike this dawdling pace.'

She gave a little huff of irritation.

'I beg your pardon. I was trying to be considerate.'

His hard look informed her quite clearly that he did
not appreciate her efforts. She put up her chin.

'If the wound has healed and there is no pain, why,
then, does it affect your step?'

'Habit, I suppose. What does it matter? I do not go
into society.'

'But that might change.'

'I think not.'

She gave up the argument and walked on at her normal
pace. The major matched her stride for stride and Zelah
hid a smile. A little furrow of concentration creased his
brow, but he was no longer limping.

'Your journey back was not too tiring, Nicky did not suffer overmuch?'

'Not at all. The new road is very smooth.' She waved her hand at the lane. 'It puts our own track to shame.'

'My engineer used a new method of road-building: smaller stones, tightly packed. It seems very good, but we shall see how well it wears.' His glance shifted to her skirts and the band of damp around the hem. 'You have not been keeping to the roads, I think?'

She laughed. 'No, I have crossed a couple of very muddy fields. It was such a lovely day I could not bear to remain indoors a moment longer.'

'I suppose Nicky requires a great deal of attention. Your time cannot be your own.'

She was surprised by his concern.

'You are not to be thinking I begrudge him a moment of it, nor Maria, but sometimes one likes a little time alone—but I have had that now,' she said quickly, sensing his hesitation. She added shyly, 'This last stretch is the least interesting, and I am always glad of company for it.'

The house was in sight. She called to the gardener's boy to take the major's horse to the stables and led him in through the front door, sending a footman running to fetch Maria.

'Please come into the morning room, Major. My brother-in-law is out and will be sorry to have missed you, but my sister will be here directly.'

'Must I see her? I would rather you took me directly to see the boy.'

'You know I cannot do that. Besides, my sister will want to give you her thanks in person.'

He gave a little pout of distaste but the scar at the left side of his mouth distorted it into a full grimace. He muttered irritably that he wanted no thanks. Zelah felt a smile tugging her lips.

'You sound very much like a sulky schoolboy, Major.' She heard the door open and turned. 'Ah, Maria, here is Major Coale come to visit Nicky, if you will allow it.'

Maria hesitated at the door, then smiled and came forward.

'Major Coale, I am so delighted to meet you at last. I have heard so much about you from my son and I have been longing to thank you in person for taking such care of him.'

Watching him take her outstretched hand and bow over it gracefully, Zelah was aware of a little stab of jealousy that he had never saluted her in that way.

'My husband is in Lesserton at present, Major, and I am sure he will regret that he is not here to greet you. However, he is looking forward to seeing you next week at dinner—you received my note, I hope?'

'I did, ma'am, and I am delighted to accept.'

'Reginald is at a meeting,' said Zelah. 'There is a dispute over the boundary between the villagers' land and that belonging to Lydcombe Park. Have you heard about it?'

'Yes,' he said indifferently. 'I recall Netherby telling me something of it when he came to call.'

'Did he not tell you of the meeting?'

'He did, but it's no business of mine.'

His tone was final and Maria was quick to change the subject.

'Goodness, how the morning is flying! I am sure Nicky is anxious to see you, sir. Zelah, my love, perhaps you would escort Major Coale upstairs?'

'Oh—but I was about to retire to change my gown. It became sadly muddied during my walk....'

'Well, the major has already seen it and Nicky will not notice.' Maria laughed aside her objections. 'I must go and relieve Nurse—little Reginald will be waking up soon and demanding to be fed.' She turned to smile at the major. 'I shall say good-day to you now, sir, and look forward to seeing you here for dinner next week.'

Silently Zelah led the major away. The slight hesitation in his step had returned, but whether it was due to the exercise or the awkwardness of meeting his hostess she did not know and would not ask. Nicky's face lit up when the major walked in.

'I knew you would come!' Nicky greeted him enthusiastically.

'Did you doubt it, after you wrote me such a very polite letter?'

'It was Zelah's idea. She helped me write it.'

'But the sentiments were all Nicky's,' she said quickly.

The major turned towards her, amusement warming his hard eyes.

'Including the invitation to call? I am quite cast down.'

Zelah flushed scarlet, but she was saved from finding a response by her nephew, who had spotted a packet protruding from the major's coat pocket.

'Is that a present for me, Major?'

'It is, sir. It is the travel backgammon set from Rooks Tower. Hannah told me how much you enjoyed using it so I thought you might like to have it. She sends you her best wishes, by the bye.'

Nicky gave a little crow of delight and immediately challenged the major to a game.

'Oh now, Nicky, I am sure Major Coale is far too busy—'

'Major Coale has a little time to spare,' Dominic interrupted her. 'And my honour is at stake here—I cannot refuse a challenge!' He nodded at her. 'You may safely leave the boy with me for an hour, Miss Pentewan, if you wish to go and change your gown.'

'...and he stayed for a full two hours playing backgammon with Nicky. It was most good-natured of him. It left me free to look after baby and Zelah went off to write her letters.'

The family were at dinner and Maria was telling her husband about Major Coale's visit.

'Yes, I must say he struck me as very gentlemanly when I passed him on the road,' said Reginald. 'Quite a change from when I first made his acquaintance. *Then* he was looking very wild, but he is very much altered.' He cast an amused glance at Zelah. 'Having you in the house was a civilising influence, my dear.'

'Not that civilising,' she responded. 'I told him about your opposition to Sir Oswald's plans for Prickett Wood and he was not at all interested in supporting you.'

Maria was inclined to be sympathetic.

'One can hardly blame him, poor man. He is so hideously disfigured it must be a trial for him to go into society at all.'

Reginald paused, considering.

'Do you really think him so repulsive, my love? I can't say I really noticed his scar the last time I saw him.'

This response earned him a warm smile from his sister-in-law.

'Well, of course, it *was* the first time I had seen him,' said Maria. 'But his manners are so polished and he *is* the son of a viscount. Once he has been to dinner and I have seen him a little more, I am sure I shall grow accustomed.'

* * *

A week went by and Zelah waited hopefully each day
for a response to her advertisement for a position as governess. She had written it out in her best copperplate
and sent it to the newspaper offices in Barnstaple and
Taunton, but no replies were forthcoming.

'Oh, my dear, perhaps it is not meant to be,' said Maria,
when Zelah explained this to her. 'Can you not content
yourself with living here? You know we are very happy
to keep you with us.'

'Thank you, Maria, and I love being here as a guest,
but it was never my intention to become your pensioner.'

Maria cried out at that, protesting that she would always be a guest, never a burden, but Zelah had seen
Reginald poring over his accounts, she had heard him
discussing with Maria the possibility of selling off some
of their land to pay for Nicky to attend Mr Netherby's
school. Zelah did not mention it, merely saying cheerfully, 'I do not despair—tomorrow I shall write another
notice and send it off to the newspapers in Bristol and
Bath. I am sure someone there must require a governess.'

'I am sure they do, love, but for now let us forget this
plan of yours and look forward to this evening. Major
Coale is coming to dinner, had you forgotten?'

Zelah had not forgotten, but for some reason she did
not want to admit it and she was glad when her sister
continued.

'What will you wear, Zelah, the green robe you had
made up last summer?'

'I thought I might put on my grey gown.'

'What?' Maria sat up, scandalised. 'That gown has
done service for several years now and is very severe.
You should save it to wear when you are interviewed by

a prospective employer. No,' she said decisively, 'you will wear the green and I shall fetch out my Norwich shawl for you to drape over your arms, should the evening turn chilly.' Maria sighed loudly. 'There is certainly no reason for you to save your best silk any longer. If you are set upon finding work, then it is not at all suitable for a governess.'

Zelah hugged her.

'Pray do not be sad for me, dearest sister. I think it is quite exciting, and if I find the children are just too abominable, I shall give it all up and come running home to you!'

When the dinner hour approached, Zelah ran lightly down to the drawing room, her silk skirts whispering as she moved. She had to admit there was something very uplifting about putting on a pretty dress. Maria had even sent her own maid to put up Zelah's hair, restraining it by a matching green bandeau and leaving just a few loose curls tumbling artlessly to her shoulders. To complete the picture Zelah threaded a small jade cross on a green ribbon and tied it around her neck.

'There,' she told her reflection, 'a picture of simple elegance. What does one need with diamonds and emeralds?'

The approving looks of her sister and brother-in-law raised her spirits even more and when Major Coale arrived she turned towards the door, her eyes sparkling and a smile of genuine welcome parting her lips.

Dominic entered the room ready to bow and say all that duty required, but when his eyes alighted upon Zelah Pentewan he stopped, his brain refusing to function. In a matter of seconds he regained his composure, bowing to his host and greeting Mrs Buckland with the usual polite phrases, but all the time his brain was in turmoil.

He had not been looking forward to the evening. He remembered his first meeting with his hostess, recalled her hesitation and the way her eyes travelled everywhere save to his face. He hoped she would soon recover from the habit, but it did not surprise him. It was always thus with a new acquaintance.

Except Zelah, who had never shown any reluctance to look at him, save when he teased her or paid her compliments and made her blush. Gazing at her now, he wanted to shower her with compliments, for she looked quite charming. Her gown, which was the colour of new leaves, brought out the green flecks in those expressive eyes that now met his own and a delicate flush mantled her cheeks. She looked genuinely pleased to see him and for a moment his spirits soared.

It had been a long time since any young woman had smiled at him in quite such a welcoming way, save those he had paid on rare occasions to spend the evening with him in a vain attempt to relieve his loneliness. Dominic quickly damped down his pleasure. Her smiles were nothing more than natural friendliness. No woman could ever be attracted to him now.

So he retreated into the safety of his perfect society manners and quelled the impulse to hold her fingers an instant longer than was required, or even—as he really wanted—to kiss her hand.

Dinner should have been a relaxed affair. Maria and Reginald were at pains to put their guest at ease and the major responded with perfect civility. There was very little for Zelah to do other than eat her food and enjoy the sound of his deep, well-modulated voice, yet she could not be easy. Every nerve end ached, her skin was so sensitive she wondered if it was perhaps some kind of fever, but when she touched her own cheek the skin was not unnaturally warm. Zelah wondered at her reaction and finally concluded she had lived retired for too long and had forgotten how to behave amongst strangers.

At last Maria gave the signal to withdraw and the ladies left the men to their brandy.

'I think it is going exceedingly well,' said Maria, sinking into a chair and disposing her skirts elegantly around her. 'Major Coale is very well read and Reginald was right, now that we have been in his company for a while I hardly notice his poor face at all. But you have been very quiet, Zelah my love. I would have thought the major's knowledge of art and literature would have made him an interesting guest for you.'

'He is—that is, the conversation was flowing so well I didn't like to—I mean, I could find nothing to add.'

'That is most unlike you, little sister.' Maria patted her cheek. 'I do believe you are a little shy of the major, but there is no need. Indeed, you should know him better than any of us. You must try to be a little more sociable. I assure you, Zelah, you have nothing to fear. He is perfectly harmless.'

But Major Coale did not *feel* perfectly harmless. Zelah could not explain it. Part of her wanted to stay near him, to engage him in conversation and at the same time she wanted to run away. It was most confusing.

When the gentlemen came in she was prepared to make an effort to join in, but they were getting on so

well that the conversation flowed quite easily without any
contribution from herself and she remained beside her sister, a relieved and silent observer. Maria, however, was
determined that she should participate more and when
the tea tray was brought in she handed two cups to Zelah,
instructing her to carry one to their guest.

Bracing herself, Zelah moved across the room. Major
Coale accepted the cup with a word of thanks, adding, as
Reginald lounged away and they were left alone, 'Buck-
land tells me Nicky is to go to school.'

'Yes. Mr Netherby teaches a small group of boys for
a few hours each day and he has agreed to take him. It is
as much for the company as anything.'

'And when does he start?'

'As soon as he is walking again, which should not be
long now, he is making good progress.'

She sipped at her tea, trying to think of something to
say. She wanted to tell him how handsome he looked,
but that would be most improper, and unfortunately, everything else that came to mind was connected to their
having dined together, a fact that must remain secret.

'You are very quiet this evening, Miss Pentewan. Why
is that? I know you are not afraid of me.'

The glinting smile in his eyes drew an answering
gleam from her.

'Not when I was on your land, certainly. But here…'
she glanced around '…I fear I am less at ease with you
in these more formal surroundings.'

'That is singular—if anything you should feel safer
here, with your family.'

She smiled. 'You must think me very foolish.'

'Not at all. Have you found a suitable post yet, as a
governess?'

'No, and it is very lowering. Maria ascribes it to my lack of experience.'

'She may well be right.'

'But I am very well qualified! Papa himself took charge of my education. He taught me French and mathematics and the use of globes—and he allowed me free access to his extensive library.' She sighed. 'But of course, apart from my nephew I have little experience of children.' She turned her eyes upon him as a thought occurred to her. 'I wonder perhaps if you have a young relative in need of a governess?'

He threw back his head and laughed at that. Zelah smiled, surprised at the little curl of pleasure it gave her, to have amused him so.

'No, Miss Pentewan, I do not. I have only one sister, you saw her portrait. She is now married, but when she was younger she was such a minx that I have the greatest sympathy with every one of the poor ladies employed to instruct her.'

'Oh dear, was she so bad?'

'A perfect hoyden. She ran through at least a dozen governesses. Do not look so dismayed, ma'am, the Coales are renowned for being wild to a fault. Not all families will be as bad.'

'No-o.' Zelah was not convinced. She gave herself a little shake. 'I have not given up hope, Major. I have already sent off more advertisements. I am sure something will turn up.'

'Of course it will.' He put down his cup. 'It is growing late and I must get back.'

He rose and crossed the room to take his leave of his hostess. Zelah felt a deep sense of disappointment that he was going so soon, which was irrational, since she had avoided his company most of the evening.

Nicky was making good progress. By the end of the week he was hobbling around the garden, showing off his heavily bandaged leg to all the servants.

Zelah watched him from her bedroom window. He was in the garden, talking to the aged retainer employed to cut the lawn. She was too far away to hear what was being said, but she could imagine him recounting the tale of how he hurt his leg. The old man was leaning on his scythe and giving the boy his full attention, even though she was sure he would have heard the story several times over. She put her chin on her hands, smiling. Nicky had such a natural charm, no wonder everyone loved him. Reginald was taking him to join the vicar's little school next week and she hoped the other boys would take to him.

There was a knock at the door.

'If you please, miss, Major Coale is here to see you.'

'Is my sister not available?'

The maid bobbed another curtsy. 'He asked to speak to you, ma'am.'

'Oh.'

She turned to the mirror and picked up her brush, then put it down again. Without removing all the pins, brushing out her curls and pinning it all back up again, which would take far too long, there was not really much improvement she could make, save to tuck an escaping tendril behind her ear.

Zelah pulled the neckline of her gown a little straighter, smoothed out her skirts and, after a final look in the mirror, made her way downstairs to the morning room.

The major was standing by the window, his back to the room and his hands clasped behind him.

'Good morning, Major Coale.' He turned to face her, but with his back to the light Zelah could not read his expression. She said quickly, 'Nicky is in the garden, sir, if you wish to see—'

'No, it is you I came to see,' he interrupted her, his tone more clipped and curt than ever.

She sank on to a chair. He ignored her invitation to sit down and took a turn about the room. Zelah waited in silence, watching him. His right leg was dragging and he was frowning, the crease of his brow making the scar running down his face even more noticeable. Zelah clasped her hands tightly together and waited.

'Miss Pentewan.' His shadow enveloped her as he stopped before her chair. Then, with a slight shake of his head, he took another turn about the room, saying as he walked, 'You may think I should have spoken first to Buckland or perhaps to your sister, to sound them out on the matter, but you are of age, and knowing how you value your independence I decided to address you directly.'

Zelah dropped her gaze. There was a slight crease in her own brow now. Her heart was hammering so hard against her ribs she thought it might burst free at any moment. She hoped he would not expect her to speak, for her throat felt so tight she could hardly breathe. He approached, his steps thudding a soft, uneven tattoo on the carpet and soon she was staring at the highly polished toes of his topboots, yet still she could not look up.

He cleared his throat again. 'Miss Pentewan, I have a proposal for you.'

Chapter Four

Zelah closed her eyes, waiting for the world to stop spinning. After a few deep breaths she opened her eyes, but could not bring herself to look up into the major's face. Instead she fixed her gaze on the rather poor landscape painting on the wall.

'A p-proposal, sir?' Her voice was little more than a croak.

'Yes.'

She jumped up and went to the window, her hands on her burning cheeks. What was she to say? Could this really be happening? She kept her back to him as he began to speak again.

'You have honoured me with your confidence and informed me that you are seeking employment as a governess. I want to ask—that is, would you consider a rather… *different* form of employment?'

The heat and colour fled from her cheeks as swiftly as it had come. She wheeled around, this time firmly fixing her eyes upon his face. Her heart was still hammering but there was such a confusion of thoughts in her head that she felt sick. She swallowed, hard.

'Just what are you offering me, Major?'

He looked uncomfortable. She found herself praying. *Please do not let him say it. I cannot bear to think he would even ask...*

'Miss Pentewan, you will know I am alone at Rooks Tower.' Her heart sank even lower. She clenched her hands together, closed her eyes and prepared her answer even as he continued. 'I have been struggling for some weeks now but—madam, would you consider working as my archivist?'

'Sir, thank you, but I could not possibly—*what?*'

He shrugged. 'Archivist, librarian, I am not sure what title you would use, but I need someone to put my books in order. Rooks Tower has a large library and I intend to make use of it. I have had the room decorated, but have done nothing about unpacking the books I brought with me from Markham. I have collected a great number of volumes over the years and transported them all here, but they are in no particular order. It is the devil of a job and with the summer coming on I need to be supervising the work outside as much as possible. I just haven't the time...'

She blinked at him.

'You...you want me to, to *arrange your books*?'

'Yes. Oh, I know it is not the type of work you were looking for, but from our discussions I received the impression that you were intent upon becoming a governess because that is the only respectable occupation available to a young woman.'

'Respectable, yes, and...I know nothing about organising a library!'

A smile tugged at the corner of his mouth.

'You told me you knew nothing about children, but that has not stopped you advertising yourself as a governess. I need someone to sort out all those damn—dashed volumes.'

'But surely you should employ a scholar to do this, someone who understands the value of your collection—'

Again that grimace distorted his features.

'I am not interested in its value, only that the books are recorded in some sort of order and that they are on the shelves and to hand when I want them. They are, in the main, useful books that I have collected.' He took a turn about the room. 'Besides, I do not wish to have a stranger in my house. No, madam, I want the library organised and all the books catalogued during the next few months. I see no reason why you could not walk over there every day and continue to live with your brother and sister.'

'I—I am not sure…'

He waved an impatient hand.

'You need fear no impropriety. Mrs Graddon and the housemaids will be present and I spend most of my time out of doors. I am willing to pay you a total of fifty guineas for the work: twenty-five when you begin, and the rest once the library is complete. It should not take too long, two months, perhaps three at the most.'

'Then the remuneration you offer is far too generous.'

He shrugged. 'I want it to be done, and soon. The cost is not important.'

Zelah shook her head, trying to think clearly. In the space of a few minutes her spirits had experienced ecstatic heights, deep despair and a fury of indignation, and all for nothing. He was offering her nothing more or less than a job of work.

The major picked up his hat.

'Perhaps you would like to consider it. Talk it over with your sister.'

'No,' she answered him quickly. 'No, I have made my decision.'

If she discussed this with Maria or Reginald they might well try to dissuade her, but here was an opportunity to earn her keep, albeit for a short time, and remain with her family. She squared her shoulders, raised her head and met his gaze.

'I accept your offer, Major Coale.'

For a long, breath-stopping moment his eyes searched her face, then he smiled and she found herself responding, until he looked away from her.

'Thank you, that is excellent news,' he said crisply. 'I see no reason for delay. Report to Rooks Tower on Monday morning!'

'My dear sister, have you lost your wits?'

Zelah gazed up at her brother-in-law, a laugh hovering on her lips. 'Why should you think that? I have merely accepted a very lucrative engagement.'

She had kept the news of the major's proposal until they were sitting together in the drawing room after dinner. She had hoped that a good meal would put Reginald in a more mellow mood, but her announcement was still met with a mixture of indignation and amazement.

'You cannot accept,' declared Maria. 'It would be most improper.'

'But I *have* accepted and there will be nothing improper about the arrangement. Major Coale has already informed me that he spends his days out of doors.'

'For an unmarried lady to be alone in his house—'

'I shall not be alone, Reginald, I shall be surrounded by servants. Besides, who will know of it?'

'The whole of Lesserton by the end of the week,' replied Reginald drily.

'But it is a job of work. I shall continue to advertise for a position as a governess, but until then it will give me a measure of independence, and if the task takes only three months then I should be able to save a good proportion of my money against hard times.' Zelah looked at her sister, begging her to understand. 'I have been here long enough, Maria. I told you when I came I would not be your pensioner. Major Coale has promised to give me half my fee in advance. I intend to give some of it to you, to pay Nicky's school fees.'

'But there is no need of that, Reginald and I have already agreed—'

'To sell the seven-acre field, I know.' Zelah interrupted her. 'I would much rather you took my money.'

'Never,' cried Maria, pulling out her handkerchief. 'I would not dream of taking your wages—'

Reginald held up his hand.

'I think Zelah has a point,' he said slowly. 'To sell off the field would mean less return at harvest. If we keep it, we may well be able to repay your sister by the end of the year.'

Maria did not look convinced. She reached across and took Zelah's hands.

'Oh, my dear, for any young lady to take such a position, in the house of a man like Major Coale, would be to risk her reputation, but in your case—'

'In my case I have no reputation to risk.'

An uncomfortable silence followed Zelah's bald statement. She withdrew her hands from her sister's grasp and rose.

'I made up my mind when I left Cardinham that I would support myself. I have caused my family enough sorrow and will not compound my guilt by allowing you to keep me.'

'But you might marry—'

'You know I have set my mind against marriage.'

'Oh, sister, pray do not say that—'

Reginald put up his hand to silence his wife's protest.

'My dear, Zelah is right,' he said heavily. 'Any man who formed an attachment would have to be told of her... unfortunate past.'

Zelah winced.

'But if a man truly loved her—' cried Maria, looking beseechingly at her husband.

Zelah shook her head.

'Of all the requirements a man may have when looking for a wife three things are paramount: good birth, good fortune and a spotless character. I am afraid I have only the first of those requirements. So you see, it is much better that I should learn to make my own way in the world.' She smiled at them, knowing tears were not far away. 'If you will only allow me to continue living here while I work at Rooks Tower, then I shall consider myself truly blessed.'

'Of course you may.' Reginald came forwards to kiss her cheek. 'We could not countenance you living anywhere else.'

'Good day to you, Miss Pentewan. The master said you was coming. I am to show you to the library.'

Despite having told herself that she did not expect the major to be at Rooks Tower to greet her, Zelah was disappointed. She followed the housekeeper through the hall, heading away from the main staircase and towards a pair of ornate double doors. Zelah expected to pass through into a grand reception chamber, but she was surprised to find herself enveloped in shadows. When her eyes grew accustomed to the gloom she could see that it was indeed a large room with a magnificent marble fireplace and intricate linenfold panelling on the walls, but each of the long windows was shuttered to within a few inches of the top, allowing in only enough light to see one's way between the furniture.

'The master instructed that these shutters should remain closed,' explained the housekeeper. 'This is the yellow salon and everything here is just as it was when Major Coale bought it, but he never uses it. One soon gets used to walking through the gloom.' There was a tiny note of regret in the older woman's voice. She had reached the far end of the room and threw open the doors. 'This is where you will be working.'

The library was identical in size to the yellow salon, but here the morning light shone in through a series of long windows that filled one wall. The other three walls were lined with open bookcases in rich mahogany, their ranks broken only by the doors and the ornate chimney breast. A large desk and chair stood at one end of the room and a wing chair had been placed near the hearth, but the remaining floor space was taken up with a multitude of crates and boxes.

'Goodness,' murmured Zelah, her eyes widening. She felt a little tremor of excitement as she thought of all the books packed in the boxes. Who knew what treasures lay in store!

'It is indeed a sorry mess,' said Mrs Graddon, misinterpreting her reaction. 'I'm sure you'll soon begin to set it all in order. The master has left you new ledgers in the desk drawer and there's pens, paper and ink, too. Graddon will send someone to help you with the boxes.'

She went away and Zelah stood for a few moments, wondering just where to start.

She began by exploring the room, running her fingers

along the smooth polished wood of the empty shelves and then over the cold marble of the fireplace. She moved across the room. The long windows with their low sills looked out on to a wide terrace where little tufts of grass sprouted between the paving. Beyond the stone balustrade the grounds sloped down to the river before the land rose again, the park giving way to woodland that stretched away as far as the distant hills.

An idyllic setting, she thought, drinking in the peaceful tranquillity of the scene. Then setting her shoulders, she turned again to face the task ahead of her.

When the clock on the mantelpiece chimed four o'clock Zelah looked up, surprised. She had no idea where the day had gone. Books were piled haphazardly on the shelves and several opened crates littered the floor. The volumes had been packed in no particular order, novels and religious tracts jostling with books on wild flowers and a furniture directory. She would have to go through them all before she could begin to catalogue them. The room looked even more chaotic now than when she had started, but it could not be helped.

She tidied her desk and glanced around the room, mentally deciding just where she would begin tomorrow. Her eyes fell upon the small door in the far corner. The housekeeper had told her it led to the tower. Zelah stood for a moment, indecisive. Perhaps, while no one was about, she would take a quick peep at the tower.

The door opened on to a small lobby where a steep, wooden stairway wound its way upwards. There was an air of neglect about the plain painted walls and worn treads, but the banister was firm enough and Zelah began to climb the stairs. A door on the first landing opened on to a storage room which was filled with old furniture.

Zelah gave it only a cursory glance before moving on to the second floor. She found herself at last on a small landing. The wooden stairs gave way to a narrow stone spiral staircase at the side of which was a single door. Grasping the door handle, Zelah turned it, half-expecting it to be locked. It opened easily and she stepped into a room filled with sunlight. At first glance it seemed there were no walls, only windows from breast-height to ceiling, the leaded lights divided by thin stone mullions and giving an extensive view of the country in all directions.

The only solid wall was behind her, surrounding the door through which she had entered and housing a small fireplace. There were just three pieces of furniture in the room: a mahogany pedestal desk and chair and a much older court cupboard pushed under one window, its well-worn top level with the sill. Zelah knew that such pieces had been designed to display the owner's plate, a visible indication of wealth and status, but this cupboard was as empty as the desktop. There was nothing in the room to detract from the magnificent views. Zelah moved to the windows. From the first she could see right over the forest and vales towards Devon, from the next the road curled off towards Lesserton and the densely packed trees of Prickett Wood, while from a third she looked out across the park and woods of Rooks Tower to the uplands of Exmoor. She put her hands on the window ledge, drinking in the views.

'There are no books up here, Miss Pentewan.'

Zelah jumped. Major Coale was standing in the doorway, his hat and riding crop in one hand.

'Oh, I did not hear you come upstairs.' She noted idly that his broad shoulders almost brushed the door frame on each side and was glad when he moved into the room and his size did not appear so daunting. She waved towards the window. 'I was entranced by the view.'

'Obviously.'

'I hope you do not mind,' she hurried on, her eyes searching his face for some softening of his expression. 'I have done all I can in the library today and wanted to look at the tower and did not wish to disturb the servants...'

He placed his hat and crop on the cupboard.

'And is this what you expected?' he asked, drawing off his gloves.

Her smile was spontaneous, any nervousness forgotten.

'Not at all. I had not imagined the views would be so extensive. You can see all the way into the next county! It is such a lovely room. Imagine how wonderful to sit at this desk—why, in the summer you could work all day and never need to light a candle.' She looked up at him. 'Is this your desk, sir? Do you use this room?'

He shook his head.

'This room is as it was when I bought Rooks Tower and so far this year I have been too busy putting the estate in order to worry overmuch about the interior.'

'I would like to use it.' Zelah clasped her hands together, hoping her eagerness did not sound foolish. 'I could bring the books up here to catalogue them. That way, once the library is tidy, you would be able to use it for your guests—'

'There are no guests,' he said shortly.

'But one day—'

'It is not my intention to invite anyone here. Ever.'

She felt the last word was added for her benefit. It was uttered with such finality that it gave her pause, but not for long.

'Is... Would that be because of...?' She touched her

own cheek and saw him flinch. He turned slightly, presenting his undamaged side to her, his profile reminding her of how dangerously attractive he must once have been.

'I did not move to Rooks Tower to be sociable,' he said curtly. 'My years as a soldier have left me impatient of society. Its values and petty tyrannies disgust me.'

'But you have family and friends, sir. Surely you will not cut yourself off from them so completely?'

'Damn you, madam, we are not here to discuss how I choose to run my life!'

Zelah recoiled from his angry retort. She bit her lip against further argument, but was not daunted enough to forget her original idea.

'I beg your pardon, Major. Of course it is no business of mine. But I would like to make use of this room, if you will allow me.' She waited for a moment, then added coaxingly, 'I promise I will not let the view distract me from my work.'

His brow cleared.

'The view is even better from the roof, especially on a fine day like this.'

She waited expectantly. His hard eyes glinted and she knew he had read her mind.

'Would you like to see it?'

Zelah followed him out to the landing and on to the spiral stair. It was only just wide enough for one person and she was obliged to hold up her skirts as she climbed the steep steps. A series of tiny windows sent shafts of dazzling sunlight across her path, making it difficult to see the next step.

When they reached the top he threw open the door and the light flooded in.

'Do you not keep it locked?'

'No need. My servants never come up here.' He turned and reached down for her. 'Give me your hand. There is no handrail and these last few stairs are uneven.'

His fingers curled around her hand, warm and secure as he guided her up the final steps to the roof. She found herself on a flat roof, paved over with stone slabs and surrounded by a crenellated parapet.

'Oh,' she breathed. 'I feel I am on top of the world.'

She became aware that the major was still holding her hand and looked up at him warily. Immediately he released her. She gazed out across the hills, her hands clutched against her breastbone.

'Magnificent, isn't it?' He stood beside her, the rough wool of his jacket rubbing against her bare arm. 'Do not go too near the edge and do not lean against the battlements,' he warned her. 'The stonework is in poor condition.'

'But you will repair it, won't you, Major? I cannot bear to think that this view would be lost.' She swung round and peeped up at him, trying and failing to suppress a smile. 'Even though you are adamant you will not be having any guests here.'

The answering gleam in his eyes made her own smile grow and she gazed up at him quite unselfconsciously, thinking how much better he looked when he was not scowling at everyone and everything. In fact, she did not even notice his scarred face when he looked at her in just that way.

The playful breeze tugged a lock of hair free from her sensible topknot and whipped it across her face. She was going to sweep it away, but Dominic's hand came up first and his fingers caught the errant curl.

Zelah held her breath. Their eyes were still locked,

and instead of removing his hand after tucking the curl behind her ear, he allowed it to slip to her neck while he ran his thumb lightly along her jaw. Her heart began to pound against her ribs and she kept her hands clenched across her breast as if to prevent it breaking free. Her mouth dried. There was an almost forgotten ache curling inside her. Anxiety? Excitement?

With his hand on her neck he held her as surely as if she was in chains. She could not move. Indeed, she did not want to move, she wanted him to lower his head and kiss her. She wanted to feel his hands undressing her, exploring her body.

Oh dear heaven, where had such wanton ideas come from?

Something of her thoughts flickered in her eyes and immediately he released her. Zelah switched her gaze to the view, trying to recall what they were saying. Ah, yes. She had been teasing him. Well, that was clearly a very dangerous thing to do.

The major cleared his throat. 'If you have seen enough, perhaps we should go back downstairs.'

'Yes.' She was anxious to get away from his disturbing presence. 'Yes, of course.'

She went carefully down the steep spiral, one hand on the wall. Her legs were shaking and she was very conscious of Major Coale following her down. When they reached the landing she hurried on to the wooden stairs, halting only when she heard the major's voice behind her.

'I have to collect my hat and whip. Feel free to make use of the room if you wish, Miss Pentewan. I have no objection.'

'Thank you.' She forced the words out and glanced back at him. He was standing once again in the doorway, blocking the light and enveloping her in his shadow. Binding her to him by some force beyond her comprehension.

Zelah gave herself a mental shake. Fanciful nonsense. She must not give in to it. She nodded, trying to sound businesslike. 'If there is nothing else, sir, I shall go home now.'

'No, nothing.'

Dominic watched her hasten away. Her hand looked unsteady on the banister, but she descended the stairs without mishap and disappeared from sight.

He exhaled, his breath hissing through his clenched teeth. He had not meant to frighten her, but when they were up on the roof and she stood before him, her eyes shining with excitement, he had felt the desire slam through him. He should have known better. He could have moved away, turned his back on her, but the craving to touch her was so strong that he had given in to it. Even now he could feel her skin beneath his thumb, soft as a flower petal. And she had not moved away. Petrified, he thought sourly, for an instant later he had seen the horror in her face.

What if he had frightened her so much that she did not return tomorrow? Perhaps that would be for the best. She unsettled him, with her teasing and her challenging questions. He squared his shoulders. He was a soldier. He would not be beaten by this slip of a girl! They had an agreement and *he* would not be the one to break it. Let her come to Rooks Tower and organise his library. But perhaps it would be wise if he kept out of her way.

The walk back to West Barton did much to calm Zelah's disordered nerves. She had allowed herself to relax in Major Coale's company. After all, one did not tease a gentleman, unless he was a relative, or a very close friend. Certainly one did not tease an employer. She must be more careful. No one knew better than she the consequences of becoming too familiar with a gentleman!

Each evening at dinner Maria and Reginald asked Zelah about her day at Rooks Tower. They were naturally interested in her progress, but even more concerned about the behaviour of her employer. Each time Zelah was able to reply with complete sincerity that she had not seen Major Coale. For the first few days after the incident on the tower roof she was relieved that they did not meet, but gradually his elusiveness began to frustrate her. She had many questions to ask him and was obliged to leave notes, asking where he wanted certain books and how he would like them arranged. His answer, via the butler or Mrs Graddon, was always the same, 'The master says to do as you think best and he will discuss it with you later.'

It was nearly two weeks before she saw Major Coale again. By that time she had removed all the books from their crates and was working on making a record of every title, bringing small piles of books to the large mahogany desk to list in one of the ledgers provided.

It was a particularly sunny day and the room was uncomfortably warm, so Zelah had removed the fine muslin scarf from her shoulders and tossed it aside while she worked. She heard footsteps approaching and looked up, expecting to see Graddon or one of the footmen bringing refreshments, and she was taken by surprise when Major Coale strode in. He looked as if he had come direct from the stables; his hat was tucked under his arm and in one hand he carried his gloves and riding crop. His riding jacket hung open, displaying an embroidered waistcoat that fitted across his broad chest as snugly as the tight buckskins that covered his thighs. There was only the slightest drag on his right leg and his step was firm, brisk. He exuded energy.

Nonplussed, Zelah reached for her scarf and quickly knotted it across her shoulders as she rose and came around the desk to greet him.

His brows twitched together, the slight movement accentuating the ragged scar and deepening the unsmiling look into something resembling a scowl as they approached each other. Zelah tried not to feel intimidated.

'Have you come to see how I progress?' She summoned up a smile. 'The rooms looks much better without all the boxes, I think.' She waved her hand towards the bookshelves. 'Of course, they are not yet in any great order, but this way it is easier to see just what books we have.' She became more natural as she warmed to her theme. 'I need you to tell me how you want them arranged. Are you happy to have sermons and music ranked alongside books on ratcatching, shoeing horses and draining bogs?'

She observed a definite glint of humour in his eyes, albeit reluctant.

'I doubt if that is how you would place them. I think the last three should be grouped with estate management.'

'And your novels, Major? I thought to put them on these shelves, near your chair by the fire. They would be at hand then when you wish to sit in here and read.'

'That seems a good idea. You are not using the tower room?'

'No, not at present.'

The room held unsettling memories of the feelings he had roused in her. He tapped the riding crop against the palm of his hand as he glanced around the room, his expression unreadable.

'I came to tell you that you will soon have more books arriving. A few months back I purchased the contents of Lydcombe Park Library. The books have been in storage with my man of business since the sale. They are in a number of large crates, too big for the pack ponies, but now the road is finished they can be brought here by wagon, as soon as I can spare the men to fetch them.'

'Oh. Well then, it is a good thing I have not yet put everything in order.' She bent an enquiring gaze upon him. 'Are these *useful* books, sir, or might we find more classical texts in this consignment?'

'I have no idea. I have never seen them.'

'So we may well have more than one copy of some titles, sir.'

'If that is the case then I shall leave it to you to decide which one to keep.' His tone was cold, indifferent, and Zelah wondered if he was perhaps displeased with her way of working. She was framing the question in her mind when he reached out and flicked the edge of the muslin scarf. 'If you covered up your charms for my benefit then you were wasting your time, Miss Pentewan. I have no interest in hired staff.'

His words hit Zelah with the shock of cold water. She was rendered speechless, but thankfully she was not expected to respond. The major turned on his heel and marched out.

Zelah retreated to the desk and sank down on the chair, shaking. He had seen her put the scarf about her, was that the reason for his brusque manner? Had he taken her action as an insult? She shook her head. It had been a defensive gesture to cover her bare neck and shoulders, because she did not want him to think she was flaunting herself. He had taken it as a personal slight, as if she thought he had designs upon her virtue. She could have laughed, if she had not been so angry. Slowly, with trembling hands, she began to pack up. She would do no more today.

Chapter Five

Zelah set off across the grass, heading for the woodland path that led directly to West Barton. She had not gone far before she heard the major calling her name. She stopped and turned to see him striding towards her.

'Where are you going?'

'Home.' She waited for him to come up to her.

'It is still early.'

She looked away from his hard, searching gaze.

'I have done enough for today.'

'You are angry with me.'

'Yes.'

'Because I accused you of covering your…charms?'

'It was uncalled for, uncivil and unnecessary.' She added more quietly, 'I thought you knew me better than that.'

He was her employer, he could dismiss her if he objected to her comments, but she did not regret her words.

'You are quite right. I was very rude. What can I do to make amends?'

She did not hesitate.

'I would like you to show a little more interest in your library. I have no idea if you are happy with my work so far, if it meets with your approval. You have not been near the library until today.'

'On the contrary, I visit the library every evening.'

'Oh.'

'Yes, Miss Pentewan. I am taking a close interest in your progress, but I visited West Barton last week, to enquire after Nicky. Your brother-in-law considers your employment at Rooks Tower nothing short of scandalous. I thought by taking myself out of the house every day it would mitigate the impropriety.'

'Some would still consider it improper if you were to take yourself out of the *country* while I am working for you! It is unfortunate that my brother-in-law does not approve but he understands my desire for independence. The fact that he has not thrown me out of the house shows he is prepared to put up with my "scandalous" behaviour, even if he cannot condone it.' She had hoped he might smile at this, but when he did not she added impatiently, 'For heaven's sake, you have some rare books in your collection. Pine's *Horace*, for example, and Hooke's *Micrographia*.' She exhaled through clenched teeth. 'You have engaged me to work for you, Major, and I would much rather discuss matters directly with you than be forever passing messages via Mrs Graddon.'

At last his forbidding frown was lightened. There was a glimmer of understanding in his hard eyes.

'Very well, Miss Pentewan. I will make efforts to be available. Starting tomorrow.'

'Thank you. I will bid you good day, sir.'

'You are still going?'

'Of course.'

'Then I will walk with you.' One side of his mouth quirked at her look of surprise. 'I know what you are thinking: I am now taking too great an interest in my hired staff. You would like to throw my earlier comments in my face.'

'I am not so impolite.'

'Unlike me?'

'Yes, I thought you impolite.'

'Pray do not let yourself be constrained by your good breeding, Miss Pentewan. Rip up at me, if you wish, you have my permission!'

A smile tugged at her mouth.

'It would be no more than you deserve.'

'I am aware of that. So let me make amends now by walking to the edge of my land with you.'

She gave in, nodding her assent, and he fell into step beside her.

'You walk this way every day?'

'Yes. It is much the quickest route.'

'Then you have seen the changes. I have cleared the paths and thinned out the trees—that was what I was doing when I first met you and Nicky in the woods.'

She remembered her first sight of him. A bearded woodsman, his hair long and wild and with a fearsome axe at his side. It was a powerful image that remained with her, even if the major looked so much more civilised now.

'You have done much of the work yourself, I think.'

'Yes. I like to keep active.'

'And it sets your people a good example.'

'There is that, too.'

They were walking through the woods now and Zelah could see the signs of clearance everywhere, but new growth was already appearing, bright splashes of green pushing up from the ground. The Major raised his hand to acknowledge a woman and her children coming through the trees. The woman dipped a slight curtsy, then she murmured a word to the children, who tugged at their forelocks.

'You do not mind the villagers coming here to collect their firewood?'

He shrugged.

'Once we have cut up the logs and taken them away they are welcome to anything that is left, although Phillips, my keeper, tells me there has been a marked increase in the number of people coming into the woods of late.'

'The villagers no longer have access to Prickett Wood,' explained Zelah. 'Reginald tells me the new owner is going to fence it off. Do you know Sir Oswald?'

'A nodding acquaintance only.'

'But I thought his land borders your own.'

'Not quite, so I have had no reason to make contact with Sir Oswald. I told you, I do not socialise, Miss Pentewan.'

'Perhaps you should.' She screwed up her courage. 'People would soon grow accustomed to your...to your scars.'

His short bark of laughter held more than a touch of bitterness.

'I would be accused of frightening the children.'

'No! Think of Nicky.'

'A lonely child, desperate for company. When he is with his new school friends I doubt he will be as keen to acknowledge me.'

'That is not true, he is proud to be acquainted with you.'

'Kind words, ma'am, but I fear you know very little of human nature. But it is not just that.' He paused, and, glancing up, she saw him gazing into the distance, as if looking into another world. 'Spain was a very sobering experience for me, Miss Pentewan. There is no glory in war, in all the death and carnage that takes place, but I found the life infinitely preferable to what I had been before—a rake, a fop, whose only interest was to wear a fashionable coat and flirt with all the prettiest women. That is what society expects of a gentleman, madam, and I want none of it now.'

'But the people here are not fashionably idle, Major Coale. There are many good, hard-working men who want nothing more than to better themselves and their families.'

'Then good luck to them, but they shall not do so on my coat-tails.'

'That is not what I meant—'

'Enough!' They had reached the lane that separated Major Coale's land from the gardens of West Barton. Dominic stopped. 'I am a lost cause, Miss Pentewan. I will live my own life, in my own way. I have no wish to consort with my neighbours, and there's an end to it.' He looked up. 'We part here.'

She said impulsively, 'Even so, there is no reason why you should not treat your wounds. There is a cream, a herbal remedy, it is excellent for softening the skin—'

'I want none of your potions, madam!'

'It is not a potion, but it might help.'

'I hired you as my librarian, not my doctor.' He glowered at her. 'Do not push me too far.'

The implacable look in his eyes told her she must accept defeat. For the moment. As a child she had accompanied her father when he visited his parishioners. They had met with pride and stubbornness many times, but her father's message had always been the same. Where Zelah had been inclined to argue, he would stop her, saying gently, 'Let the matter lie for now, but never give up.' She therefore swallowed any retort and merely inclined her head.

'Thank you, sir, for your company.'

He bowed.

'It was a pleasure. Until tomorrow.'

It was only a step across the lane to the little wicket gate leading to the gardens, but when Zelah turned to latch the gate there was no sign of the major. He had disappeared back into the woods.

Zelah always enjoyed her days at Rooks Tower, but when she awoke the following morning she felt an added sense of anticipation. A blustery wind was blowing the grey clouds across the sky when she set out. It tugged at her skirts and threatened to whip away her bonnet. She arrived at last, windswept but exhilarated, and made her way through the darkened salon to the library. She looked around her with satisfaction. Most of the books were on the shelves now and in a rough order. She had dusted and cleaned each one, putting aside any that required repair. She was engaged in writing the details in the ledgers, in her neat copperplate hand, when the major came in.

'No, no, do not get up.' He waved her back into her seat. 'Carry on with your laborious task. I would not give you an excuse to shirk your duties.'

He perched himself upon the edge of the desk and turned the ledger to inspect the latest entries. She was pleased that he no longer attempted to present only his right side to her and she laughed up at him, barely noticing the jagged line running down his face.

'I am obliged to break off now and again to rest my eyes, so I consider your interruption very timely.'

'If this were my job I would welcome any interruption. It would irk me beyond bearing to sit here all day.'

He pushed the ledger back towards her. 'Do you not long to be out of doors?'

A spatter of rain hit the windows and she chuckled.

'Not when the weather is like this! When the sun is shining I admit it is very tempting to go out, but then I open the windows, and I have my walk home to look forward to.'

'There is that, of course. Now, is there anything you want of me today?'

'Only to look at the books I have set aside, sir, and tell me if you want them repaired or thrown away...'

She directed his attention to the books piled on a side table. The major went through them with the same decisiveness he gave to every other task she had seen him perform.

'So, these are to go to the bookbinder for new covers and the rest...' Zelah paused, picking up a dilapidated copy of Newton's *Principia*. 'Are you quite sure you want me to throw these away?'

'Perfectly. The book you are holding has been ruined by damp and misuse, it is beyond repair.' Reluctantly Zelah put the book down and he gave an impatient sigh. 'Pray do not get sentimental over such an object, madam. There may well be another copy amongst the books from Lydcombe Park. If not, then you can order a new one for me.'

'Yes, sir. May I pass the old ones on to Mr Netherby? Some of his pupils might make use of them.'

'If that is what you wish.' He picked up a small earthenware jar hidden behind a pile of books. 'What is this?'

'That?' Zelah ran her tongue over her lips. 'It is the cream I mentioned to you.' His brows snapped together and she hurried on. 'I, um, I was going to give it to Graddon. I thought he might apply it for you...'

'Did you now? Graddon is no nursemaid.'

She sighed. 'Pity. I am sure it would help—'

He interrupted her with a growl.

'I have told you before, Miss Pentewan, confine yourself to your library duties!'

The jar hit the table top with a thud and he strode off, closing the door behind him with a decided snap.

The jar remained on the side table for three days. It was studiously ignored by the major, although Zelah was sure he knew it was there. Then, just when she was beginning to wonder if she should ask Graddon to try to persuade his master, Major Coale made reference to it.

He had come in for his daily report on her progress and when she had finished he walked over to the side table and picked up the jar.

'What is in this witch's potion of yours?'

'It is no witchcraft, Major, only flowers. Marigold petals, mixed with oil and wax to make a salve. It will help repair the skin and soften the scar tissue. My mother used to prepare it for our parishioners.' She added coaxingly, 'I assure you it will not hurt, sir. I helped Mama to apply it often, once to a group of miners injured in a pit collapse. Their injuries were severe and they said it did not cause any pain, but on the contrary, it was quite soothing.'

His inscrutable gaze rested on her for a moment. 'Very well.' He handed her the pot. 'Let us see.'

She blinked. 'I beg your pardon?'

He perched himself on the edge of the desk.

'Apply your magic potion, and we will see how well it works.'

'Apply it here? Now?' Zelah swallowed. 'I am not sure...'

'Damnation, Delilah, I let you be my barber, surely

you do not balk at touching my face—or is the scar too abhorrent?'

'Not at all, sir.'

She opened the jar and scooped a little of the ointment on to her fingers. She remembered how she had felt when she had cut his hair, standing so close, aware of his latent strength. She felt again as if he was some wild beast allowing her to come near, but at any minute he might turn and savage her. After a very slight hesitation she applied the cream gently to his cheek.

She smoothed it across the skin, working between the hard ridges of his cheekbone and his jaw.

'There, does that feel better?' He grunted and she chuckled. 'Pray do not be ashamed to admit it. A mixture such as this soothes the damaged skin and makes it flexible again, in the same way that wax will soften leather.'

'Are you comparing my face to a boot, madam?'

Zelah laughed as she massaged the ointment into his cheek. 'I would not dare be so impertinent!'

She felt him smile beneath her fingers.

'Oh, I think you would.'

She did not reply, but continued to work her fingers over his skin until all signs of the cream had disappeared.

'The sabre did not only cut my face. It slashed open my body, too.'

Zelah stopped. She said gently, 'May I look?'

He untied his neckcloth and tugged it off, leaving his shirt open at the neck. Zelah pushed aside the material to expose his left shoulder. The skin was golden brown, tanned, she guessed, from working shirtless on the land. It was marred by a wide, uneven white line across his collarbone and cutting down his chest, where it carved a path through the covering of crisp black hair. Her heart lurched at the thought of the pain he must have endured.

She forced back a cry of sympathy, knowing it would not be welcome. Instead she tried to be matter-of-fact, scooping up more cream and spreading it gently across the ragged furrow of the wound.

'It is a pity you did not rub something in this sooner,' she said, absorbed in her task, 'but it is not too late. If you apply this regularly, it will soften the skin and help the scarred tissue to stretch.'

She worked the ointment into his skin, moving over the collarbone and down to his breast. A smattering of black hair curled around her fingers as she stroked the finely toned muscle.

Zelah could not say exactly when the change in the atmosphere occurred, but suddenly the air around her was charged with tension and she realised just what a perilous situation she was in. Not merely the impropriety of being alone with a man who was not her husband, but the dangerous sensations within her own body. She concentrated on the skin that she was covering with ointment, forcing herself to think of that small area of scarring and not the whole body. Not the man. It was impossible. She should stop, move away, but she could not. Of their own accord her fingers followed the scar across the solid breastbone and on, down.

Dominic's hand clamped over hers.

'That will do.' His voice was unsteady. 'Perhaps I should finish this myself. Later.'

Zelah blushed, consumed from head to toe with fiery embarrassment.

'I...um...' She had to take a couple of breaths before she could continue. 'It is best applied every day, and directly after bathing.'

She tried to look up, but could only lift her eyes as

far as his mouth. The faint, upward curve of his lips was some comfort.

He released her hand. 'You are far too innocent to be Delilah, aren't you?'

She dare not meet his eyes. Her cheeks were still burning. She put the lid back on the jar and handed it to him.

'It was never my wish to be such a woman.'

'No, of course not. You are far too bookish.' He pushed himself off the desk and picked up his neckcloth. 'I must go. I want to see Phillips today about restocking the coverts.'

Zelah glanced towards the window as another shower of rain pattered against the glass.

'Should you not wait until the storm passes?'

'Why? It will not harm me. In fact, I think I would welcome a cold shower of rain!'

With a brief nod he strode out of the room and as his hasty footsteps disappeared so the calm and silence settled over the library again.

Zelah sat down at the desk and dropped her head on to her hands. So she was 'too bookish' to be Delilah, the beautiful temptress. She should be pleased that Dominic did not think of her in those terms, and she *was* pleased, wasn't she?

With a sinking heart Zelah realised that she was just a little disappointed.

Zelah's working days had developed a regular pattern. Major Coale would visit the library every morning to discuss the day's tasks. Whenever he was obliged to be out early he would leave her instructions and call in to see her as soon as he had returned to Rooks Tower. Their meetings were brief and businesslike, but Zelah looked forward to them and when, two weeks later, the major left word that he was gone to Exeter and would not be back until the following day, she was surprised at the depth of her dissatisfaction.

The following day saw the delivery of the books from Lydcombe Park. She was reluctant to spoil the space and tidiness of the library and ordered some of the crates to be taken up to the tower room. Unpacking all the new books and arranging for the empty crates to be taken away kept Zelah occupied for most of the day. She was buttoning her pelisse when she heard a familiar step approaching the library and she turned towards the door, her spirits rising. Major Coale came in, his boots still muddy from the journey, and she was unable to keep the smile of welcome from her face.

His first words were not encouraging. 'What, Miss Pentewan, going already? I heard that the books from Lydcombe Park had been delivered. Surely that is a case for working longer.'

'And so I would, sir, but I am walking to Lesserton today, to collect Nicky from his lessons.'

'Then I shall take you there in the curricle.'

'But you have just this minute come in...'

'From riding, madam, a very different exercise. You may show me just what you have done with the books while we wait for my carriage.'

Unable to muster her arguments, Zelah consented and ten minutes later she was sitting beside the major in his sleek, low-slung racing curricle and marvelling at the smooth new road he had built. They had to slow their pace when they joined the Lesserton road, but they still made good time and soon reached the village. They were heading for the main street and, seeing how busy it was, Zelah glanced at the major. He was wearing a

wide-brimmed hat, tilted to shadow the left side of his
face, so that his scarred cheek and chin were barely visible. She was pleased to note that the majority of the men
touched their caps and the women dropped a curtsy as
they bowled past. Some children and one or two of the
adults stopped to stare, but she decided this was due to
the unusual sight of a fashionable carriage with a diminu-
tive groom perched upon the rumble seat.

'Where shall I drop you?' enquired the major.

'Here, if you please. I am still a little early, so I shall
indulge myself by looking in the shops on Market Street
before I collect Nicky. You have no need to hand me out,
I can easily jump down.' She suited the action to the
words as the curricle drew to a stop and gave a friendly
little wave as Major Coale set his team in motion again.

The morning clouds had given way to a warm, sunny
afternoon and when Nicky came running out from the
vicar's rambling house she persuaded him to take a de-
tour before they made their way home. They were just
setting off when Nicky gave a delighted cry.

'Major Coale!'

Zelah looked up to see the major approaching. She
noted with no little satisfaction that there was now only
the faintest irregularity in his purposeful stride.

'Good day to you, Master Nicholas! How do you go
on, how is your leg?'

'Much better now, Major. Zelah wants to see the bluebell woods, so I am going to take her. Will you come
with us?'

'Nicky!'

Her admonition went unheeded. Nicky gazed hopefully at the major, who replied gravely, 'I would be delighted.'

Zelah shook her head vehemently. 'No, no, I am sure you must have more important things to do.'

'As a matter of fact I don't. Sawley noticed that one of the horses has a shoe loose and he is now at the smithy, so I was coming to say if you do not mind waiting a half-hour or so I would take you back to West Barton.'

'You would take us up in your curricle?' demanded Nicky, his eyes wide. 'In your *racing* curricle?'

'I only have the one, I'm afraid, but it is perfectly safe, as your aunt will testify.'

'That is very kind of you, I'm sure, Major Coale,' said Zelah, realising it would be cruel to withhold such a treat from Nicky. 'However, there is no need for you to accompany us on our walk.'

'But Major Coale *wants* to come with us, don't you, sir?'

'I do indeed.'

Zelah looked helplessly from one to the other. Major Coale held out his arm to her.

'Shall we proceed?'

There was no help for it. She laid her hand on the major's sleeve.

'Maria told me about the woods,' she explained as they followed Nicky along the lane that led out of the village. 'She said the bluebells are a picture, but for only a short time each year. I do hope we won't be too late, we are well into May now.'

'We shall soon find out.'

Nicky had scrambled over a stile and the major followed, turning back to help Zelah.

'Careful, there is a ditch on this side and it is a little muddy.'

As Zelah stepped over he reached out and lifted her, putting her down well away from the muddy puddle at the foot of the stile. A hot, fiery blush spread through her, from her head right down to her toes. Whether it was his hands on her waist, or the feeling of helplessness as he held her she did not know and, what was worse, she instinctively gripped his arms, so that when he had placed her on the ground he could not immediately release her, but stood looking down at her with a smile lurking in his grey eyes.

'Are you ready to go on, Miss Pentewan?'

She swallowed. So many new and shocking sensations were coursing through her that she could not think. Her hands were still clutching at his sleeves and, instead of letting go, she wanted to hold on even tighter. It took all her willpower to release him and to step back.

'Y-you startled me,' she stammered. 'I could quite easily have climbed over by myself...'

'I'm sure you could, but my way was much more pleasurable, don't you think?'

His self-possession annoyed her.

'Are you trying to flirt with me, Major Coale?'

'Do you know, I think I am.' He laughed. 'How strange. I used to do it all the time before that damned chasseur tried to cut my face off. I beg your pardon, it was unwittingly done.'

Disarmed by his response, her anger melted away and she chuckled.

'That has pricked the bubble of my self-esteem! What an abominable thing to say.'

'Not at all. It was, in a way, a compliment. I have not felt so at ease in anyone's company since I came back to England.'

'Then I will take it as such, sir.'

She met his eyes, responding to the warm smile in his own and forgetful of everything else until he looked away.

'Nicky is almost out of sight. Shall we continue? Else I fear he will abandon us and we will be left to wander these woods all night.'

Zelah moved on, ignoring his proffered arm. She was shocked to realise just how much she would like to be wandering here all night with Major Coale.

Nicky had stopped at a turn in the path to wait for them and as they reached him Zelah gave a little gasp of pleasure. The woodland stretched before them, the sun filtering through the lacy canopy of leaves onto the floor, which was covered in a thick carpet of bluebells and wild garlic.

'Oh, how beautiful!' She sank down, putting out her hands to brush the delicately nodding bluebells. 'They are at the very peak of their bloom. I think we should pick some for you to take back to your mama, Nicky—make sure you pick them at the bottom of the stem, love.'

She began to collect the tallest flowers and within minutes had a large bunch, then Nicky handed her his contribution.

'Goodness, that was quick!' She rested the delicate blooms more securely on one arm and looked towards the major, who was still standing on the path. 'What do you think, Major, are they not beautiful?' He did not respond, merely stared at her across the dell. 'Oh, I beg your pardon. Perhaps you are wishing to turn back, it must be growing late.'

'We don't have to turn back,' said Nicky. 'The path curves round by Prickett Wood and goes back to the village. It's not far.'

The major cleared his throat.

'Let us go on, then.'

Nicky ran on ahead, but when the major began to stride out Zelah had to hurry to keep up with him.

'I am sorry if we have delayed you, Major.'

'It is not important.'

She frowned at his harsh tone, but said no more, concentrating her energies on hurrying along beside him. They left the wood and found themselves on a wide track running between the trees.

'I remember this,' declared Zelah. 'The road leads into Lesserton and the trees to our left lead into Prickett Wood, so you can be back at the smithy very soon now, sir.'

He did not reply and she gave a mental shrug. The easy camaraderie with which they had started out had gone and she tried to be glad about it, for when Major Coale chose to be charming she found him very hard to resist. She turned her attention to Nicky, running ahead of them, darting in and out of the trees, fighting imaginary foes. He seemed much happier now that he was spending some of his time at Mr Netherby's school. He did not appear to miss her company at all.

Nicky plunged into the undergrowth at the side of the road and she waited for him to reappear, but he had not done so by the time they reached the point where he had dashed off the path. She was about to remark upon this to her companion when they heard a man shouting, as if in anger.

'What the devil—?'

The major followed the narrow overgrown track into the wood and Zelah went after him, a chill of anxiety running down her spine. They heard the man's voice again.

'What in damnation do ye think you're doing here? Trespassin', that's what! I'll give 'ee what for!'

'Take your hands off the boy!'

The major barked out the command as they came into a small clearing. Nicky was wriggling helplessly while a burly man in a brown jacket and buckskins held his collar. The man had raised his fist but he did not strike, instead he glared at them.

'And who the devil might you be?'

'Never mind that. Unhand the boy. Now.'

'That I won't. He's trespassin'. This is Sir Oswald's land and no one's allowed in here.'

'The boy strayed a few yards off the path. He's done no harm.' The major's cool authority had some effect. The man lowered his fist, but he kept a tight grip on Nicky's collar. He said stubbornly, 'He's still trespassin' and so are you. I have me orders, thrash any brats that comes into the wood—'

The major advanced. 'Then you will have to thrash me first.'

The man scowled, his harsh features becoming even more brutish.

'Aye, well, then that's what I'll do.'

'No, please!' Neither man heard Zelah's cry.

There was another shout and a tall, thick-set man pushed through the bushes towards them. He was carrying a shotgun, but Zelah was relieved that he was not threatening anyone with it.

'What is going on here? Miller? Who the devil are these people?'

'Trespassers, Sir Oswald. They—'

The major interrupted him. 'I am Coale, from Rooks Tower. If this is your man, then I'd be pleased if he'd unhand my young friend.'

'Major Coale, aye, of course. Let the boy go, William.'

Reluctantly the man released his grip and Nicky tore himself free and ran over to Zelah, clutching at her skirts. Sir Oswald watched him, then looked at Zelah, giving her a rueful smile.

'I beg your pardon if my bailiff frightened your boy, ma'am, but I have been having a great deal of trouble from the village children running in and out of the woods at all times, causing havoc.'

'Mayhap they dispute your ownership of these woods,' put in Dominic.

'These are ignorant folk, Major. Just because they have been allowed to use the land in the past they think they have a right to it, but it ain't so. I have to keep 'em out.'

'By beating small boys who wander inadvertently onto your land?' The major's lip curled. 'Your methods are a little extreme.'

'But what can I do?' Sir Oswald shrugged. 'We are culling the deer and I would not want to risk shooting anyone.' He looked back at his bailiff. 'It's all right, Miller, you may go back to your work, I'll escort these good people back to the lane.' Sir Oswald stretched out his arm, as if shepherding them along. Zelah took Nicky's hand and led him away. Behind her she could hear Sir Oswald's voice.

'I do not say I like appearing the ogre, Major, but I have to protect my own, and these people are very stubborn. Is it any wonder that Miller has become a little… hardened? But he knows his territory. Believe me, no one will come to any harm as long as they stay off my land.'

'I do believe we have been warned off,' murmured Dominic, when they were once more on the path and making their way back to the village.

'What a horrid man.' Zelah shivered. 'Heaven knows what would have happened to Nicky if we had not been there.'

'He has no right to shoot the deer,' declared Nicky,

who was recovering from his ordeal. 'They have been there for ever, and it's not his land.'

'Well, that is what your papa is trying to prove.' Zelah squeezed his hand. 'I hope he is successful. I do not like to think of Sir Oswald riding roughshod over everyone.'

'There must be documents,' said Dominic. 'Papers stating what belongs to the village.'

'There are, but they are old and not very clear.'

'Robin says it's to do with the boundary stones,' said Nicky.

'Oh?' Zelah glanced down. 'And who is Robin?'

'He's my friend.'

'Another one?' The major's brows lifted. 'I thought I was your friend.'

'Robin is a *different* friend. He lives in the woods.'

'Ah, you mean the crow catcher.' Dominic turned to Zelah to explain. 'There is an old man who is paid to do odd jobs around the village, trapping crows or catching moles, helping out at lambing. In winter I believe he lives with his sister in the village, but during the better weather he has a hut on the edge of the forest. I did not know he was a friend of yours, Nicky.'

'Oh, yes. Sometimes he lets me go hunting with him, sometimes we just follow the deer, to watch them.'

'Well, you had best warn this friend to avoid Sir Oswald Evanshaw's land,' said Zelah. 'I don't think that bailiff of his would think twice about giving an old man a beating.'

'They won't catch Robin,' said Nicky confidently. 'He knows everything about the land here.'

They had reached the village and the major's groom was standing with the curricle outside the smithy, waiting for them. Nicky forgot everything save the excitement of climbing into this elegant equipage, where he sat between

Zelah and the major as they drove back to West Barton. Zelah glanced at the bluebells, still cradled on her arm.

'I almost dropped them all when we ran into Sir Oswald and his horrid bailiff, but I am very glad I did not. They are beginning to droop a little, but I think they will recover, do not you, Major?'

He took his eyes off the road for a moment to look at the mass of nodding bells.

'I am sure they will. You have a knack of reviving wilting spirits, Miss Pentewan.'

It was only natural that Nicky should describe the events in Prickett Wood to his parents. Maria had been outraged at the treatment of her son and Reginald immediately called for his horse and rode off to confront Sir Oswald. The ladies waited anxiously for his return and Maria was just suggesting they should put dinner back an hour when Reginald came in, a frown darkening his usually genial features.

'Oh, my dear, I was beginning to worry that you might have come to blows.' Maria ran to her husband and took his arm, coaxing him to a chair.

'He could not have been more accommodating, damned scoundrel. Apologised profusely, said his man, Miller, was over-zealous.'

'So it will not happen again?' Zelah enquired.

Reginald's scowl darkened. 'Damned rascal had the nerve to say he hoped I'd be able to keep my family away from his land, because he's putting mantraps in Prickett Wood!'

Chapter Six

Zelah was present when Reginald explained the situation to Nicky, impressing upon his son how important it was that he did not stray on to Sir Oswald's land.

'But Prickett Wood isn't his land, it belongs to the village,' Nicky protested vehemently. 'Robin says so!'

'And I hope it is so, but until we can prove it, you must stay away. A mantrap can take a man's leg off, Nicky, it is a barbaric device.'

'But what about Robin, Papa? What about the villagers?'

'Sir Oswald tells me he will post notices in Lesserton and at the edge of the wood. You must not worry about Robin, son, he's too wily an old bird to be caught. As to the rest, well, we have a lawyer coming down from London in a few weeks' time and he is bringing with him a copy of the royal charter. We must hope that settles the matter once and for all.'

Maria declared that if Reginald was not available to take his son to school and back then a servant should accompany him. She tried to insist that Zelah should take a servant with her to Rooks Tower each day, but the suggestion was energetically rebuffed.

'My dear sister, your people have more than enough to do without accompanying me. Besides, my way goes nowhere near Sir Oswald's land. I cross from the gardens directly into Major Coale's woods.'

'Who knows what danger may lurk there?' Maria muttered darkly.

Zelah dismissed her sister's concerns and happily made her way to Rooks Tower the following day, and she was somewhat surprised when Major Coale announced that he intended to accompany her on her homeward journey.

'I assure you there is no need, sir.'

'But I insist, Miss Pentewan.'

'This is absurd,' she challenged him. 'There can be no danger from Sir Oswald or his men on your land.'

Something akin to surprise flashed in his eyes, but it was gone in an instant.

'One never knows,' he replied glibly, falling into step beside her.

'But you are far too busy!'

'Not today. I have spent the day giving instructions for the refurbishment of the orangery. The carpenter knows what to do now and I would only be in the way. Come, Miss Pentewan. Do not look so mutinous. Can you not accept my company with good grace?'

'I suppose I must.'

He laughed. 'A grudging acceptance, ma'am.'

'But this is not treating me as an employee, an independent being who is quite capable of looking after herself.'

He did not respond to her grumbling, but strode across the park and into the woods, describing to her all the improvements he had planned. It was impossible to sulk and Zelah found herself voicing her opinion, telling him her preference for chestnut trees to be planted in the park and suggesting an avenue of limes along the length of the new drive.

'These are long-term plans, Major. Are you planning to settle here?'

'Possibly.'

'Then you should become more involved with the village. You could support my brother-in-law in his efforts to oppose Sir Oswald.'

'I wondered when we would come back to that. I have told you before, Miss Pentewan, one of the reasons I like Rooks Tower is its isolation. I have no desire to become embroiled in local disputes.'

'But—'

He stopped. 'Enough, madam. Sir Oswald may be perfectly entitled to enclose the land, for all we know, and to cover it with mantraps. I will deal with matters that concern me, and no more.'

There was a note of finality in his voice and Zelah firmly closed her lips upon the arguments she wanted to utter.

'Well, at least you could attend the summer assembly. It is looked upon almost as an obligation, you know, to be seen there. Besides, you would become better acquainted with your neighbours.'

He looked so fierce, his lips thinning and his crooked left brow descending so low that for a moment she thought he might shout at her, but he contented himself by saying curtly, 'If I have business with my neighbours I will call upon them. I see no point in social chit-chat.'

They were in the woods now, another few minutes would bring them to the lane, so there really was no point in prolonging the argument.

There was a sudden crashing in the undergrowth and

a hind shot across their path, so close it almost brushed Zelah. It was swiftly followed by a large stag. Startled, Zelah jumped back. The major pulled her into his arms, twisting around to shield her in case another creature should plunge out of the bushes.

He held her tight against him, one hand cradling her head against his chest. She could feel the thud of his heart through the rough wool of his coat. To be held thus was strange, unfamiliar, but she did not find it unpleasant.

Zelah allowed herself to savour the feeling of safety and of refuge as the silence settled around them once more, but as the shock abated she realised her situation and pushed herself away. He released her immediately.

'I beg your pardon. Did I hurt you?'

His curt tone only added to her confusion. Without his arms tight around her she felt quite…vulnerable.

'N-no. I—um—I have never seen a stag at such close quarters before. Magnificent.'

'So it is you!' Nicky's cheerful voice came from the undergrowth at the side of the path. 'We wondered what had startled the deer.'

He emerged from the bushes, followed by a thin man in a faded brown coat and breeches who touched his hat.

'Major.'

'Good day, Robin.' Dominic nodded. 'And to you, young Master Buckland.'

'But, Nicky…' Zelah put her hand on her nephew's shoulder '…why are you out of school?'

'Mr Netherby was called away and he cancelled his classes today, so I joined Robin in the woods. Pray do not worry, Zelah. John the stable boy was in Lesserton and he carried a message back for me, telling Papa that there was no need to send the carriage to collect me. I have been having *such* a good time with Robin, following the deer. We were doing very well until you startled them.'

Zelah gave an uncertain laugh. 'I think they startled *us*.'

'Ah, beggin' yer pardon, ma'am.' Old Robin took off his hat as he nodded to her. 'The hind turned away from yer voices and found us blockin' her way, so she took off across the path and the stag followed.'

'Are they not splendid creatures, Aunt?' Nicky's up-turned face glowed with excitement. 'We have been following them all day.'

'I trust you have not been near Sir Oswald's land.' Zelah frowned, concerned.

'I wouldn't take the boy there, ma'am, you may be sure o' that,' Robin assured her. He turned aside and spat on the ground. 'Not that Sir Oswald owns all the land he's laid claim to, whatever he may say.'

'You know where the boundary runs?' Zelah asked eagerly.

'Aye, that I do. Not that the deer follow boundaries of any man's making.'

Nicky scowled. 'Sir Oswald's told Robin that he'll shoot any animals he finds on his land, but they've been wandering there for years, they don't know any different.'

Dominic shrugged. 'I've no doubt Sir Oswald is trying to make his estate profitable.'

'Aye,' said Robin, rubbing his nose, 'he's cutting down timber above Lydcombe Park and that's his right, on that piece of land. What's going on at Prickett Wood is another matter.'

'If you know something, then you should tell my brother-in-law,' said Zelah. 'Or Sir Arthur, who I think is the magistrate here.'

'Aye, p'rhaps I will.'

His response was too vague to satisfy Zelah, but before she could reply Nicky addressed her.

'I am very glad we met you, Aunt, for I was coming to the Tower to see if you were ready to walk home with me. Robin has some work to do.'

The old man turned to the major, his eyes bright in his weather-beaten face.

'Thought I'd take a look at the moles in yer south lawn, sir, if you still wants 'em gone?'

'I do, Robin. If you wish, you can take yourself off to the Tower now. Tell Mrs Graddon I sent you and she'll make sure there's a meal for you tonight. I shall escort Miss Pentewan and Master Nicky to West Barton.'

It was on the tip of Zelah's tongue to say that was not necessary, but the look of delight on Nicky's face silenced her. They parted from old Robin and set off for the lane. She was not obliged to converse, because Nicky chattered away quite happily to the major, describing his lessons and his friends. The path was narrow and she was content to fall behind, listening to their conversation.

'This is where I shall bid you goodbye.' They had reached the lane and Major Coale stopped.

'Will you not come to the house, sir?' Nick gaze up at him hopefully. 'I know Mama would be happy to offer you some refreshment.'

'Thank you, but no. I have work that needs my attention.'

'But—'

'Do not press him, Nicky,' cautioned Zelah. 'The major sees no point in *social chit-chat.*'

He met her eyes, the glint in his own confirming that he understood her. 'Quite, Miss Pentewan. Good day to you.'

Chapter Seven

'What will you wear to the assembly tomorrow, Maria?'

Zelah was sitting in the drawing room with her sister. Dinner had been a quiet affair, just the two of them since Reginald had not yet returned from his meeting in Lesserton.

'I thought my bronze silk with the matching turban. It has a train, but I will not be dancing, so that will not matter. What think you, Zelah? It is not new but good enough for the summer assembly, I think. After all, it is not a special occasion.'

Zelah sighed.

'It will be very special to *me*. I do so love to dance, but it has been three years since I had the opportunity.'

'Goodness me, yes. I suppose you did not go to the assemblies near Cardinham after…I mean—'

'No, and I have added some new ribbons to my lemon silk for the occasion,' Zelah broke in, speaking quickly to cover her sister's confusion.

'I am sure you will look charming,' agreed Maria, thankful to follow a safer line of thought. 'We will put your hair in rags in the morning to make it curl—'

'No, no, Maria, I shall be at Rooks Tower.'

'What? You cannot work on those horrid books tomorrow, you will have no time to prepare for the assembly.'

Zelah laughed at her sister's horrified look.

'I am not such a great lady, I need only enough time to change my gown.'

'No, no, that will never do. Did you not tell Major Coale about the assembly?'

'I did, but I do not think he attaches much importance to such things.'

'Well, you must send a note over in the morning, telling him you cannot come.'

Zelah shook her head.

'I have not seen him since the day Nicky came to the woods to meet me. I fear he was not best pleased with me then, so I would not wish to antagonise him further. He might turn me off.'

'Oh dear, I never thought, when you decided to earn your own living, that it would come to this. It cannot be right.'

Maria's voice wavered, she drew out her handkerchief to wipe her eyes and Zelah realised that she had scandalised her sister. In Maria's world only her duty to her husband and family would take precedence over a social event. She said gently,

'It is not so very bad, my love. If I was a governess already, I should not be able to dance at all.'

'Oh, Zelah, if only it could be otherwise.' Maria dabbed at her eyes. 'If only you had not—'

Zelah jumped up. 'Let us not think of it,' she said quickly. 'I have a lifetime to regret a moment's madness, but tomorrow I shall go to the assembly, where no one knows my past, and dance to my heart's content.'

* * *

Zelah went off to Rooks Tower the following day, promising Maria that she would return a little earlier to prepare for the assembly, but soon after she arrived Graddon came to inform her that the carter had brought more books for her.

'Seems they were missed off his last consignment.' They watched the crates being carried in and the butler shook his head. 'Looks to me as if you'll have to begin all your work again, miss.'

'Nonsense,' she replied bracingly. 'All that is required is a little reorganisation…well, perhaps rather a lot! But it is not impossible. The first thing is to empty all these boxes.'

The afternoon was well advanced when Major Coale came in to find her surrounded by books.

'You look to be in your element.'

'I am.' She smiled, relieved at his friendly tone. 'This is the remainder of the books you purchased from Lydcombe Park and they are by far the most ancient. There are many more classical texts here—including some in the original Greek and Latin.'

'Can you read them?'

'I know a little, but not enough to work out all these. I shall have to take them to Mr Netherby to translate.'

'Let me have a look…'

He pulled a chair up beside her at the desk and they began deciphering the texts. There was a great deal of hilarity when either of them made a mistake and they continued in perfect harmony until the chiming of the clock proclaimed the hour.

'Goodness, I must go!' cried Zelah. 'It is the assembly this evening. Maria will be wondering where I am.' She laughed. 'Do you know, I almost think I would prefer to stay here, working on these texts?' She added mischievously, 'Is it something about this house that turns one into a recluse? No, no, Major, pray do not fire up, I was only teasing, when I should really thank you, sir, for helping me.'

'So you will go away. You will become a lady for the night.'

She bridled at that.

'I am no less a lady for working here, Major.' She rose and began to move the books off the desk.

'Of course not. So what will you wear and who will you dance with?'

She chuckled as she collected another armful of books from the desk. 'I shall wear my lemon silk robe and as for dancing, why, I will dance with anyone who asks me!'

After Zelah left Rooks Tower the house seemed very quiet. Usually this did not worry Dominic, but for some reason this evening he was restless, unsettled. By God but the chit irked him, prattling on as she did about company, and society and his obligations to his neighbours. He grinned. She had had the nerve to tease him, too, calling him a recluse. It was impossible not to smile at her impertinence. He shut himself in his study and tried to read, but it was no good. He prowled about the room, too restless to sit down. Perhaps he should look in at the assembly. All the local people would be there, and there were a few things that needed to be discussed, small matters that could be dealt with in a moment. With his usual decisiveness he strode out of the room and soon set the household on its ears, calling for an early dinner and sending Graddon to search out his dancing pumps.

* * *

The Lesserton Assembly was crowded and good natured. Sir Oswald Evanshaw's appearance had surprised some and dismayed even more of those gathered in the long room of the White Hart. There were plenty of resentful looks, but mostly everyone ignored him, not wishing to bring their disputes into the ballroom. Zelah was going down the line with a young farmer when his stifled exclamation brought her head up and she saw Major Coale in the doorway. Although he was not wearing regimentals his upright bearing proclaimed the soldier. He was looking grim, but Zelah knew that was merely his defence against the stares of the crowd. Mr Eldridge the MC was bowing, making him welcome, and as soon as the dance ended Zelah hurried over to her brother-in-law.

'I wish you would go and greet Major Coale, Reginald,' she urged him. 'It cannot be easy for him, when he is so new to the area.'

Reginald was inclined to hang back.

'Dash it all, Zelah, I barely know the man myself. If Coale wishes to be introduced, then Eldridge is the man to do it.'

Zelah gave him a little push.

'But you are a relative, Reginald, albeit a distant one. And you are so well acquainted with everyone here that you are much better placed to introduce the major to his neighbours. Please, Reginald. I think it cost Major Coale a great deal to come here this evening. He is not likely to put himself forwards.'

'No, with that hideous scar running down his face I suppose he is not,' Reginald mused. 'Very well, I'll go and talk to him.'

With that Zelah had to be content. She went off to dance again, but found her attention returning constantly to the major. She saw him conversing with Reginald and was relieved when they were joined by several other gentlemen. With some satisfaction she watched the whole group stroll away to the card room and she felt at liberty to give herself up to the enjoyment of the dance.

Some of the young ladies present might bemoan the lack of eligible gentlemen at the Lesserton Assembly, but Zelah was not amongst their number. She wanted only to dance and her sister numbered sufficient married gentlemen amongst her acquaintance to provide Zelah with a partner for almost every set. She was therefore happily engaged on the dance floor for the best part of the evening. She was delighted to see Major Coale take to the floor, partnering Mrs Eldrige, and when the movement of the dance brought them together she gave him a wide smile.

'You came.'

'Yes.'

She wanted to ask him if he was enjoying himself, but there was no time before she was swept off by her next partner. She watched him lead out a couple more partners, both older matrons, and realised that he was avoiding the young ladies who cast surreptitious glances at him and giggled if he went near them. Their insensitive behaviour angered her, but there was little she could do, so when her brother-in-law swept her off to dance again she tried to push the matter from her mind as he whisked her around the floor in a lively jig.

Standing at the side of the room and watching the dancers, Dominic smiled to himself. Everyone was eager to improve their acquaintance with him, but not because he was the son of a viscount, that cut little ice here. They saw him as their landlord, or a fellow land-owner or even a farmer. Phillips, his gamekeeper, would be pleased to know Abraham Judd had trapped the fox that had been terrorising the local bird population and Giles Grundy had suggested digging out the culvert at Rooks Ford, which would benefit them both. All in all it was a successful evening. Not that he would want to make a habit of it, he had grown used to his own company, but Zelah was right, it was a good way to keep in touch with his neighbours. Sir Oswald Evanshaw came up and Dominic returned his bow with a nod.

'Evening, Coale. Surprised to see you here, what with your...' His eyes flickered over Dominic's face and shifted away to the dance floor. 'How are you enjoying the entertainment?' Sir Oswald raised his quizzing glass and surveyed the room, his lip curling slightly. 'A far cry from London, ain't it? In fact it's positively rustic, but it behoves us to make an appearance, what?'

Dominic felt the slight nudge in the ribs from Sir Oswald's elbow and he moved away a little.

'I saw you dancing, too. By Gad, but you are braver than me, Coale. I wouldn't dare to approach any of the dragons lest they devour me!'

'They are more like to refuse you,' murmured Dominic.

Sir Oswald laughed.

'You are right there, of course. It's this demmed court case, they have set me up as the villain of the piece.'

'Can you blame them? They have grazed those fields for years.'

'I know.' Sir Oswald shook his head. 'They have got it into their heads that they can use my land, that it's their right, but it ain't, Coale, and the sooner they learn that the better. They have even paid for a London lawyer to come down to plead their cause at the hearing next week.

I told 'em to save their money, but what can you do? It's ill advised, Major, and I hope you'll support me in that.'

Dominic looked at him, surprised.

'The legal wranglings over grazing rights and the ownership of Prickett Wood is none of my concern, Evanshaw.'

'Not directly, perhaps, but you never know when they might turn on you and begin claiming your land, too. It would be helpful if they knew that you supported my case.'

Dominic regarded him in silence for a long moment. Sir Oswald was smiling, but there was no warmth in his pale eyes, just a cold, calculating look.

'I know nothing of your case,' he said at last, 'and I do not see why you are so concerned, if you are sure the land is legally yours.'

Sir Oswald's eyes snapped with impatience and he chewed his lip.

'At least assure me you won't join with the villagers. It's bad enough that Buckland should lend them his support. The farmers, well, I can understand them fighting me, but Buckland—demme, he's a *gentleman*! It makes the lower sort think they have a chance.'

Dominic did not answer and with a curt nod Sir Oswald lounged away, shouldering his way through the crowd until he disappeared into the card room. An unpleasant fellow, Dominic decided as he strolled around the edge of the room. He found himself hoping that Buckland and the villagers did find some legal loophole that would stop Evanshaw claiming the disputed land.

'You are looking very serious, Major. I hope you are enjoying yourself.'

He looked down at Maria Buckland, sitting on a nearby bench, sipping at a glass of wine. Shaking off his thoughtful mood, he scooped a glass from the tray of a passing waiter and sat down beside her.

'I am, ma'am. More than I expected to do.'

'I am very glad of it. I have always found the society here most friendly. But we were surprised to see you this evening: I understood you had told Mr Eldridge you did not plan to attend.'

Dominic smiled.

'That is correct, ma'am, but I was, er, *persuaded* to change my mind. By your sister.'

'Oh dear, I hope she was not impertinent.'

With some difficulty Dominic prevented the smile from turning into a grin and he resisted the temptation to tell Mrs Buckland exactly what he thought of her sister.

'No, no. Not at all.'

'Do you know, Major, when I think of Zelah spending her life as a governess I am quite cast down.'

Dominic had heard that innocent tone in many a woman's voice, and he was immediately on the alert.

'Indeed?' He sipped his wine, determined to empty the glass and move on as quickly as possible.

'Zelah is extremely accomplished,' Maria continued, still in that thoughtful tone. 'Do you not agree, Major?'

'She certainly seems to be well educated.'

'Oh, she is and her birth is impeccable.' Maria clasped her hands around her glass and gave a huge sigh. 'It is the most tragic waste that her worth—and her charms— are not more widely appreciated. She would make some lucky gentleman the perfect wife.'

Dominic choked in the act of finishing his wine.

'Madam, that is the most blatant propositioning—!'

'Oh heavens, Major, you quite mistake me, I did not mean—' Maria put her hand on his arm to prevent him from rising. 'Oh, my dear sir, I do not mean that *you* should be that gentleman! I beg your pardon. It is just, well, you and Reginald are related, after all.'

'A very distant connection,' he flashed.

Her gracious smile did not falter.

'But it was thanks to Reginald that you heard Rooks Tower was for sale, did you not? So we have been of use to you, I believe.' She leaned a little closer. 'Let me be frank with you.'

He eyed her with some misgiving.

'I'm afraid you have been too frank already.'

'No, no. Pray allow me to explain. Zelah is a charming girl, but this assembly is the nearest she will get to a come-out, and much as I value the local society, you must admit there is no one here worthy of her. It is not that there are not good families living nearby, but you will never find Sir Arthur Andrews, or the Conisbys or the Lulworths attending such an assembly as this. No, what Zelah needs is a benefactor. Someone to hold a ball for her. A splendid affair attended by the best families in the area, so that they may see just what a jewel she is. And so that *Zelah* might see that there is an alternative to becoming a governess.' She gave another sigh. 'I would happily hold a ball for her, if we were in a position to do so, but you have visited West Barton, Major, you know we have no reception rooms suitable for more than a very small gathering.' She fixed her eyes, so like her sister's, upon him. 'I believe Rooks Tower has several excellent reception rooms.'

Despite himself, Dominic's lips twitched.

'Mrs Buckland, you have been very frank with me, let me be equally plain. I will happily acknowledge that your husband and I are related and that it was through our mutual relative that I heard about Rooks Tower. I am very grateful for that, but even so I have no intention of holding a ball, for Miss Pentewan or anyone else.'

She stared at him and he held her gaze unblinking, until finally she nodded.

'Reginald warned me how it would be, that you would not countenance such a thing, but Zelah thinks so highly of you, I thought I might put it to the touch.'

The music had ended and Reginald Buckland was even now bringing Zelah across to them. Dominic rose.

'Well, you have done so and you may now be easy.'

Laughing and breathless, Zelah took Reginald's arm and tripped across the room to join her sister. She immediately noticed the tall figure of the major beside Maria as they left the dance floor. He was standing with his left side turned to the wall so that he was presenting the right, uninjured side of his face to the room. Zelah found herself staring at his profile, the smooth plane of his cheek and the strong, clean line of his jaw. There was just the hint of a smile on the sculpted lips, perhaps it was something Maria had said to him. She was struck again by how handsome he was—had been.

As if aware of her attention he turned to look at her and she saw again the cruel, jagged scar that distorted the left side of his face. She kept her eyes upon him, refusing to glance away. She would not betray any sign of pity, even by a flicker of an eyelid. Whatever happy thoughts he had shared with Maria had gone. There was no hint of a smile in his hard grey eyes. Beside her she could hear Reginald's loud, cheerful banter.

'By Gad, Zelah, you have worn me out! I think I must sit and rest my old bones beside Maria for a while. What say you, will you sit down or shall I find you another partner? Eh, who would you dance with next?'

Her gaze never wavered.

'I will dance with the major, if he will have me.'

It was a bold statement. For a frightening moment she thought he would refuse. Then, unsmiling, he held out his hand. Triumphant, she put up her head and proudly accompanied him to the floor.

The musicians had decided that their audience needed some respite from the energetic dances and now began a slower, much more stately beat. Zelah had time to observe her partner and to be observed. Her own gaze dropped beneath his unwavering scrutiny and she felt herself blushing like any schoolgirl. She would have missed her step, if her partner had not been adept at leading her. His grip tightened and she gave him a little smile, grateful for his support.

'You are a very good dancer, Major.'

'Thank you. I was used to be so, but I am very much out of practice.'

'Ah, but you have been used to dancing in the grandest ballrooms. Your idea of *out of practice* is polished perfection to our little assembly.'

'You flatter me, ma'am.'

'No, I do not.' She met his look, suddenly serious. 'You are not lame when you are dancing.'

'Not when I am dancing with you.'

The sudden and unexpected heat of his glance seared Zelah and a flame of desire threatened to engulf her. She fought it back. That way led only to disaster.

'Nonsense. You have danced several times this evening without any halting step.'

'How can you know that?'

'Because I was watching you.'

The corner of his mouth lifted slightly.

'How very gratifying.'

Too late she realised he had tricked her. Triumph danced in his eyes and drew an answering gleam from her own. She sank her teeth into her bottom lip to prevent the smile that was trying to spill out.

'I was dancing too, so you were often in my sight, I was not deliberately looking out for you.' Her lofty response resulted in a chuckle and she tried to scowl at him. 'Fie, sir, you twist my words to pander to your own vanity!'

'You are twisting your own words. I have said very little.'

'No, but you *looked*—' She laughed. 'You are making May-game of me, Major. Is this how one flirts in the highest circles? I fear I am a very unworthy opponent.'

The music came to an end and she sank into her curtsy. He reached out for her proffered hand to pull her up.

'There is nothing at all unworthy about you, Miss Pentewan,' he murmured and she watched, speechless, as he carried her fingers to his lips.

Once it was seen that Major Coale was no longer confining his attentions to the married ladies, those parents with daughters to marry off began to flock around him and he obliged them all by remaining on the floor for the rest of the night, but Zelah could not quell the little thrill of triumph when he led her out for the last dance of the evening.

'You must be well practised by now, Major.'

'You have done me a great disservice, madam. Since dancing with you I have been besieged with partners.'

'Tell me you did not enjoy it.'

His smile was genuine, softening his face, and again she felt the ache of attraction.

'I have not danced like that since…since I returned from the Peninsula.'

'Then you should do so more often, Major. You look the better for it.'

His hand tightened on her fingers and her body cried out to respond to the warm invitation in his eyes, but she shook her head at him.

'I will not allow you to flirt with me, or to tease me, Major. I have a serious point to make and will not be distracted. You see how everyone accepts you and you are much more at ease with them. I consider this a good night's work.'

'Have I become your charity? Your good cause?'

A quick glance assured her he was not offended and she smiled up at him

'Not at all. But it has done you the power of good to come into society, sir, even if it is only country society!'

Chapter Eight

The early morning sunshine poured in through the windows of the breakfast room at Rooks Tower, sending golden bars of light across the floor. Dominic pushed his plate away and sat back, going over his plans for the day. He had arranged to meet Philips in the West Wood and he knew he would enjoy riding out. Even before sitting down to breakfast he had sent word to the stables to have Cloud saddled, but as he crossed the hall his eyes were drawn to the double doors leading off, his mind flying ahead through the darkened room and into the library beyond. It was the work of a moment to turn aside and stride through the shuttered salon. He pushed open the connecting doors and stepped into the library.

Zelah was already at work, a linen apron fastened over her dark-grey gown as she carefully dusted one of the many piles of books. Her bouncing curls had been ruthlessly drawn back into a knot, exposing the slender curve of her neck and the dainty shell of her ear. She presented a demure picture, cool and elegant. Nothing like the carefree, vibrant creature he had danced with last night, but every bit as alluring. His heart lifted when he remembered Maria Buckland's words—'Zelah thinks so highly of you.'

'I hardly expected you to come today,' he said. 'And here you are, earlier than usual.'

When she turned to smile it brought the golden sunshine into the room.

'I could not sleep. Is that not nonsensical, after dancing into the early hours?' She added shyly, 'I enjoyed myself so much. I hope you did, too, sir?'

'Very much. Do they hold many such assemblies in Lesserton?'

'Oh, I do not think so.' She picked up another book to dust. 'Maria says there will not be another until the harvest.'

He tapped his riding crop idly against his boot. The rest of Mrs Buckland's conversation gnawed away at his brain.

'I do not believe governesses go to balls, Miss Pentewan.'

She looked up at him, her brows raised in surprise at his comment.

'I do not think they do, sir.'

'Then what will you do, since you love to dance?'

'I shall have to teach my charges the basic steps. Then I will skip around the nursery with them!' She finished cleaning the book and put it carefully in place on the bookshelf. 'Have you come to spoil my morning with melancholy thoughts? You will not do it. Last night's music is still running through my head.'

It was still in Dominic's head, too. He wanted to sweep her up in his arms and carry her around the room, breathing in her fresh, flowery scent, making her laugh again.

No. To flirt with a pretty girl in a crowded ballroom was acceptable, to do so with an employee here, under his own roof, would be madness. He gripped the riding crop tighter, felt the sting as it slapped hard against his leg. He said curtly, 'There is still a great deal of work to do here, Miss Pentewan. Do not let last night's amusements interfere with your duties.'

He turned on his heel and marched out, leaving Zelah to gaze after him. Well! Did he think her so inept, so petty minded that she would be distracted from her work by an evening's entertainment? She threw down her duster in disgust. The morning had been so golden, so wonderful that she had been eager to reach Rooks Tower and continue with her work. She had been enjoying herself, carefully cleaning each volume, checking it for damage and putting in its place ready for cataloguing while in her mind she relived the pleasures of the evening, but with a few cold words he had destroyed her pleasure. First he had evoked thoughts of the drudgery that awaited her as a governess, then he had reminded her—quite unnecessarily—of her duties.

With a little huff of anger she stalked across to the window. It would serve him right if she walked out now and left him to organise his own books! Hard on the heels of this mutinous thought was the realisation that Major Coale could quite easily find someone else to take over, possibly someone much more competent that she to do the work. Probably a scholar who understood Greek and Latin and would not need to bother him. Zelah put her hands to her cheeks. If he should turn her off now, before she had secured another position, she would be penniless again, living on her family's charity. It had felt so rewarding to give her advance wages to Reginald, telling him it was for her keep and to pay Nicky's school fees. She needed the second instalment to put aside in case she fell upon hard times in the future.

She must finish her task here, whatever the cost. It shocked her to realise how much she wanted to complete it, to make this a library fit for a gentleman. No, to make it fit for Dominic Coale. She also wanted to see how the seasons played out on this terrace, once the gardeners had tamed the overgrown plants and removed the grass and weeds that invaded the cracked paving.

She clenched her fists.

'I'll show you, Major Coale. I am no poor, bullied soldier to be frightened by your bluster and ill humour.'

With renewed determination she applied herself to her work and returned to West Barton that evening tired, dusty but content.

She tried to be pleased when she heard the next day that Major Coale had gone off on business, but she missed his visits to the library, even when he was being odiously difficult. Now that most of the books were on the shelves, she was working her way through each section, recording, cross-referencing, enjoying the experience of being surrounded by so much knowledge. Her father, she knew, would relish such a wide-ranging collection and in her regular letters to her parents she always included details of her progress at Rooks Tower. It helped her to reinforce her growing sense of pride in her achievement.

'I thought I might accompany Reginald to Lesserton today, for the hearing. I would be very glad of your company.'

Maria was pouring coffee at the breakfast table as she made this request. Zelah glanced at her brother-in-law.

'I have told her it is not necessary, but she insists,' he replied jovially, but Zelah noted the slight shaking of his hand as he took the proffered cup. His was an easy-going nature and she knew he did not relish any sort of confrontation.

'Of course Maria will want to support you,' said Zelah stoutly. 'I shall come with you. Major Coale can spare me for one day, I am sure.'

They travelled to Lesserton in the carriage, Reginald in his best coat of olive superfine and the ladies suitably veiled. The hearing was to take place in the long room at the White Hart, the same room that had been used for the assembly, but now it looked very different, stripped of its garlands and the space filled with desks and benches. The room was already full to overflowing and Maria observed that the whole of Lesserton was represented.

'Which is not surprising,' agreed Reginald, 'since they have all been accustomed to grazing their animals on the land Sir Oswald is claiming.' He looked around the crowded room. 'My dear, I think after all I would prefer you to wait downstairs for me. The proceedings could become boisterous. Come, I will bespeak a private room for you.'

Maria protested, but Zelah could see her objections were half-hearted. They made their way downstairs to a private parlour overlooking the street, where Reginald left them and went to talk to the farmers gathered in a little knot around a tall, saturnine gentleman in a black frock coat and bagwig.

'That is Mr Summerson, the lawyer from London,' whispered Maria, drawing Zelah to the window. 'Reginald was closeted with him for hours yesterday. He has obtained copies of the charters filed with the Crown—' She broke off as another carriage pulled up at the door. She gave a little snort. 'And here is Sir Oswald himself.

The rat-faced little man with him is his lawyer. Look how he follows, bowing and scraping. Ugh, quite repulsive.'

Soon everyone had gone upstairs and the ladies settled down to wait. The landlord sent in coffee and they sat in silence, listening to the tread of feet above them and the occasional rumble as the crowd muttered or protested over something that had been said.

An hour had gone by, two, and still the hearing had continued. There was a cheer at one point, and Maria had looked up hopefully, but it was another full hour before the thunder of movement above them told them that the hearing was over. They waited impatiently, listening to the clatter of feet on the stairs and watching the villagers pour out onto the street.

'They do not look particularly elated,' Zelah observed, not knowing how to interpret the expressions of the crowd.

She turned expectantly towards the door as her brother-in-law came in. Maria ran to him.

'Well?'

He took her outstretched hands and forced a smile. 'All is not lost.'

He guided the ladies back to the table as a servant came in with more coffee and a jug of ale and they sat down, waiting in silence until they were alone once more.

'It was going very well. Mr Summerson brought a charter that describes the common land and mentions the stream that forms the westernmost boundary. The description fits the Lightwater, which runs down from Rooks Ford and to the west of Prickett Wood. I thought we had it then, until Evanshaw's man pointed out that it could just as easily refer to the ditch that runs along the edge of the bluebell wood.' Reginald shook his head.

'Evanshaw then produced a map, which clearly shows the ditch as the boundary.'

Maria snorted.

'A forgery!'

'Very likely, my dear, but with that and the charter, Sir Arthur is minded to agree that Prickett Wood and the hill grazing does belong to Sir Oswald.' He sighed. 'Some of the older villagers claim their parents told them of a boundary stone, but it hasn't been seen in living memory, and Sir Oswald's man claims it will have been removed when the lane at the edge of bluebell wood was widened.'

'Oh dear,' said Zelah. 'Then the villagers have lost their fight. No wonder they were looking so downcast.'

'Well, not quite. Sir Arthur is not wholly convinced, and he has given us until the end of June to find more evidence to prove our case.'

'And must Sir Oswald allow the villagers access until then?'

'I'm afraid not. Evanshaw's lawyer argued most successfully against it. However, Sir Arthur has ordered that he remove the mantraps, but he has conceded that Evanshaw has the right to shoot any deer that wander into the wood, since they damage his valuable woodland.'

'It would seem Sir Arthur is well nigh convinced the land belongs to Lydcombe Park,' sighed Zelah.

'If that is the case, can we afford to fight it?' asked Maria. 'I know how hard it was for everyone to find the money to pay for the lawyer to come down for just this one visit.'

'You can perhaps find someone local,' suggested Zelah.

Maria looked doubtful. 'Perhaps, but it will still be costly.'

Reginald took his wife's hands. 'Perhaps I should have discussed this with you first, my love, but I have pledged that I will bear the costs for the next hearing. If we win then the farmers and villagers will pay me back, if we lose… I know that would leave us sadly short,' he said quickly, seeing the dismay in her face, 'but we shall come about, with a little economy. We have to try.'

'What is the alternative?' asked Zelah. 'What will happen if the villagers lose the hill grazing and the right to forage in Prickett Wood?'

Reginald shrugged. 'Many of them will not be able to survive. Some of them are our tenants and if they cannot pay their rents then that will affect us, too.'

'Then of course we must do what we can to avoid that,' said Maria. She glanced at the little bracket clock on the shelf. 'Pray order more refreshments, Reginald. If we wait another hour, we can collect Nicky from Mr Netherby's on our way home.'

When Dominic walked into the taproom of the White Hart that evening he found the mood distinctly sombre. He was on his way back from Exeter and had made good time, but the warm weather had left him parched and he decided to slake his thirst in Lesserton before the final stage of his journey.

He entered the inn, his coat collar turned up and his hat pulled down to shade the left side of his face, as was his habit, but several of the locals recognised him and nodded. Giles Grundy was sitting at one end of the bench beside the long central table and he shifted up to make room. Dominic hesitated, but he knew it would be churlish to ignore this small sign of friendship so he went over to join him, saying as he sat down, 'How went the hearing today?'

Giles grunted and after taking a long draught from his tankard he gave Dominic a brief account.

'Ah, 'tis all over,' grunted Abraham Judd, puffing morosely on his pipe at the other end of the table. 'Even Mr Buckland bringing down a fine Lunnon lawyer didn't make no difference. Evanshaw claims the ditch is the boundary stream and Sir Arthur do believe ''un.' He turned to spit into the fireplace at his back. 'Stream! There's more water in my pisspot than that there ditch, and allus has been!'

He stopped and glared at the doorway. Dominic felt the tension around him and looked up to see Miller, Sir Oswald's bailiff, had entered. His glance at the long table was met with sullen stares. With a scowl he turned away, then thought better of it and came over to the long table.

'Drownin' yer sorrows?' His lip curled. 'I heard how it went today, so here's a warnin' to you all to keep off Sir Oswald's land.'

'But 'tedn't his land yet, Miller,' growled Giles Grundy. 'Not fer another month.'

Miller shrugged.

'As near as damn it, an' I'll be out with me gun every night, as will my men. Should any of 'ee want to argue the point, we'd be only too pleased to shoot ye.'

'I really don't think Sir Arthur would approve of that,' remarked Dominic. He raised his head as he spoke and saw the bailiff's eyes widen slightly as he recognised the face beneath the wide-brimmed hat.

'Beggin' yer pardon, Major. I'm merely passin' on a message from my master. Besides, we're permitted to shoot the deer, and how are we to know what's man and what's beast in the dark?'

'Aye, well now you've passed on yer message, get yerself back to the Three Tuns with the rest of yer cronies,' muttered Abraham Judd. 'You bain't welcome here.'

Miller scowled, and with a reluctant tug at his forelock towards Dominic he slouched off to the corner, nursing his mug of ale. The men around the table looked at each other.

'Well, 'tedn't too bad at the moment,' remarked one, shaking his head, 'but come summer we needs the high pasture for grazing. And in the autumn we'll need to be collectin' firewood. You've been very good, Major, lettin' us forage in your own grounds, but that won't be enough to keep us all going.'

'Then we must hope you find the evidence you need to win your case.' Dominic finished his ale and rose. 'Now I'll bid you goodnight.'

He strode out of the door, buttoning his coat, ready to continue his journey. Since the assembly he had been making a conscious effort not to drag his right leg and his stride was becoming easier. Perhaps the doctors were right, after all. There was nothing wrong with his leg. He grinned to himself. He had not been prepared to make the effort for the sawbones, but to please an impertinent slip of a girl...

'Ooomph!'

As he stepped out of the inn a shambling, unsteady figure cannoned into him and collapsed on to the ground, cursing roundly. Dominic grinned as he recognised the ragged heap.

'Old Robin.' He held out his hand. 'Up you come, man, and look where you are going next time.'

As he pulled the old man to his feet he turned his head away, grimacing at the stench of beer and onions on his breath.

'Major Coale,' he hiccupped and swayed alarmingly. 'Just goin' to wet me whistle...'

'You should be going home, man.'

Robin gave a grunt. 'A fine night like this, I'll be sleepin' in the woods.'

Dominic laid a hand on his shoulder. 'Then take care where you lay your head. Evanshaw has armed men patrolling Prickett Wood.'

'That's very kind o' you, Major, but I've been followin' the deer into Prickett Wood since I was a boy an' I don't plan to stop now. It'll take more'n Sir Oswald's men to keep me out!'

With a nod he shuffled off into the inn, singing roisterously as he bounced from wall to wall.

Shaking his head, Dominic went off to collect his horse.

Summer was nearly here. Zelah could smell it in the air as she walked across the lawn towards Rooks Tower. Even in the few weeks she had been coming to the house she could see the changes Major Coale had wrought. The new road was only one of the improvements he had made—clinging ivy had been stripped away from the windows, which had been cleaned and painted and gleamed in the morning sunshine. The gates from the new road had been repaired and oiled and now opened easily on to the freshly gravelled drive. The house stood proudly amid its scythed lawns and seemed to welcome her. The weather was so glorious that Zelah was reluctant to go indoors and once she had reached the library she lost no time in throwing up the windows.

There was no sign of the major. Zelah assumed he had not yet returned from Exeter. A pity, she thought, since the oppressive, sultry air hinted that the good weather would soon break and she would have liked him to see his house on such a beautiful day.

Even with the windows open it was very warm in the

library and she decided against emptying the last two crates that stood in one corner. She had peeked in them upon their arrival and knew they held large, ancient manuscripts that would require some exertion to move. Instead she settled down at her desk to continue cataloguing the books she had already sorted.

When the pretty ormolu clock on the mantelshelf chimed noon she looked up, surprised at how quickly the morning had gone. She got up and stretched. The still air was heavy and oppressive. She went to the double doors and threw them open, but the dark stillness of the shuttered salon did nothing to dispel the humid atmosphere. She stood for a moment, listening. The house was hushed, expectant, as if it was waiting for her to act. Zelah crossed to the first window and after a short struggle with the catch she folded back the shutters and threw up the sash. She went to the next window, and the next. As the fresh air and sunlight flooded in the room seemed to sigh and relax, like a woman released from her confining stays. Zelah chuckled at the image. The room was decorated in yellow and white with the ornate plasterwork of the ceiling and the magnificent chimneypiece picked out in gold and reflected in the straw-coloured sofas and chairs. She took up a cushion and hugged it, revelling in the glowing opulence of the salon.

'What in damnation do you think you are doing?'

Zelah dropped the cushion and spun around. Major Coale was standing in the doorway, his scarred face pale with anger.

'Well?' he demanded. 'What are you doing in here?'

'N-nothing. That is…I thought this room could use a little air.'

'I gave express instructions that this room is to remain shuttered. I hate this salon. It is not a room for levity.'

'Oh, but it is,' cried Zelah, throwing her arms wide and spinning around. 'Just look at the colours and the space. Can you not feel it? The happiness? It is a room for children, and laughter and lo—'

She stopped.

'Love? Marriage? A happy family?' His face twisted into a bitter grimace, making the livid scar even more noticeable. 'You are far too romantic, Miss Pentewan. In future you will confine your work to the library.'

He turned and stalked out. Zelah frowned, but even as she strove to understand his anger she saw what she had not noticed before, that between each of the windows was a pier glass, paired with its equal on the opposite wall. Wherever she went, whichever way she turned, she could not escape her reflection.

'Oh goodness. Major!' Picking up her skirts she flew after him. 'Major Coale, wait, please.'

He was crossing the hall and she caught up with him just as he opened the study door. She put out her hands to stop him closing it in her face.

'Please,' she begged him. 'Please let me apologise.'

He glared at her, eyes blazing, his chest rising and falling as he fought to contain his rage. She held her ground and after a moment he turned and walked away. Silently she followed him into the room and shut the door.

'I did not understand, until I saw the mirrors.' He was standing with his back to her, staring down into the empty fireplace. She said quietly, 'Forgive me, Major. I did not mean to make you angry.'

'So now you will go back and close the room up again.'

'Must I?'

'Yes! I do not wish to be reminded of the monster I have become.'

'You are *not* a monster!' Angrily she caught his arm

and turned him towards her. 'You are a man, a soldier with a scarred face. Is that so very bad? You went to the assembly—'

'That was an aberration, a moment of madness.'

'Perhaps it was so, for you, but you were not shunned. One or two were shocked, of course, people who had not seen you before, but the majority—those who know and respect you—they accept you for what you are.'

'What I am is a *freak*.'

'Now you are just being foolish! There are many men with worse disfigurements than this, many whose wits are addled.'

'And there are many who lost their lives!' he flashed. 'Do you think I am not aware of that? Do you think I do not *know*? Every time I see this scarred face it is a reminder of all those men that died, good men, with more right to live than I will ever have—' He broke off and swung away towards the window. 'From the moment we crossed into Spain I was writing letters of condolence. To wives, fathers, mothers, as more and more comrades perished. And still they died, those poor souls, never to see their homeland again. You have no idea of what it's like to wake up at night asking, *why me?* Why should I live when all around me perished—Graddon was a fool to bring me back. And the others who helped him. They should have left me to die like the rest at Cacabelos—'

'No!' Zelah grabbed his arm and pulled him round again. 'How dare you say such a thing. Any life lost is a tragedy, yes, but a life *saved*—it shows the love and respect in which you were held that so many put themselves out to bring you home! So your scars remind you of your fallen comrades. Is that so very bad? You are not the only one to have bitter regrets about the past. Perhaps instead of wallowing in your self-pity every time you look in a mirror you should feel proud to have fought beside those men.' She stepped closer and put up her hand to touch his face. 'These marks are not so very bad—'

He grabbed her wrist and whipped her hand behind her back. They were so close that her breast brushed his waistcoat. Immediately her body tensed. She could see every detail of the long black lashes that fringed his eyes, the fine lines etched into his skin. She dropped her eyes to his mouth, the curve of his lips, the slight droop on the left where the scar ran close. In her mind she put her arms about his neck and gently touched her lips to the livid scar, kissing his brow, his cheek, his mouth, making him forget his injuries and remember that he was a man, like any other.

'You go too far, madam.' His voice was rough, not quite steady.

Not far enough. The words were on the tip of her tongue. She felt her body softening, yielding to the magnetic power of the man. She felt naked under his scorching glance. It had been so long since any man had held her thus, but the desire for that first youthful love had not been as strong as this, as unconfined. She had never wanted a man as she wanted Dominic. His eyes wandered to her mouth and nervously she ran her tongue over her lips. Surely he would kiss her now, or she would die.

He released her so suddenly that Zelah swayed.

Dominic turned away from her, rubbing his eyes. This would not do. Only by an extraordinary effort of will had he resisted the temptation to kiss her. She was willing enough, he knew that look; the darkening lustre of the eyes, the soft flushing of the lips. He could have taken her, made love to her there and then in this very room, but what then? To have her working in his library was giving rise to scandalous rumour, but while it remained only that, she could still become a governess and maintain her independence. If he took her as his mistress it would outrage the neighbourhood and ruin her reputation for ever. When they grew tired of each other what would there be for her, save another man, another protector, until her looks had quite gone.

'I b-beg your pardon,' she said quietly. 'I…perhaps I should leave. You could find another archivist.'

He swung round. She was very pale, but outwardly composed.

'Is that what you want?' She shook her head and Dominic realised he had been holding his breath for her reply. He nodded. 'Very well. We shall say no more of this. Go back to work, now, Miss Pentewan.'

She clasped her hands in front of her, twisting her fingers together and running the tip of her tongue over her lips. Dear God, if she continued to do that it would be his ruin! He said roughly, 'Well, madam?'

'The salon. May I…will you allow the shutters to remain open?'

A smile tugged at the corner of his mouth.

'You are nothing if not persistent, madam. If it is your wish.'

'Thank you. You might of course remove the pier glasses.'

'No, let them stay. The room is designed for them.'

He was surprised by his response and took a moment to consider how he felt. Exhausted, drained, but somehow calmer than he had felt for years. Somehow his outburst had been a catharsis. He had spoken to no one of his guilt and it had built inside him, reaching such proportions that it had distorted everything, even, he suspected, his view of his own disfigurement. When he looked up Zelah was still standing before him, uncertainty in her hazel eyes.

'Will—will it prevent you coming to the library?'

He thought about it. 'I do not know. Shall we put it to the test?'

He walked to the door and stood there, looking at her. After a brief hesitation she accompanied him back across the hall. The doors to the salon still stood wide. Beyond, the room glowed with the afternoon sunlight. It glinted off the gilded plasterwork, twinkled from the mirrors. His step slowed at the threshold and he held out his arm.

'Will you do me the honour?'

She placed her fingers on his sleeve and they processed slowly through the salon.

'I had no idea you had returned from Exeter, Major.'

'Evidently, or you would not have turned my house upside down.' She shook her head, refusing to respond to his teasing. He continued. 'I have ordered a carpet for the library. It will mirror the pattern on the ceiling, I hope you will approve.'

She looked up quickly, surprise and pleasure in her eyes.

'I am sure it will add the finishing touch.'

They had gone more than halfway across the long room before Dominic realised that he had held out his left arm to her, so that when he looked to the left his eyes were drawn to her reflection rather than his own. And there was something else. The man in the mirror was walking with a sure, steady gait. He was no longer dragging his right leg.

Dominic stretched and rubbed his eyes. He had slept well again, untroubled by dreams or nightmares. That was three nights in a row. He put his hands behind his head, thinking about the change in him. It was due to Zelah. She had accused him of wallowing in self-pity.

He could not deny it. She had coaxed and bullied and nagged him until finally he had erupted, his pain, anger and guilt spilling out and the relief, to finally confess it all to someone, had been overwhelming. That was three days ago and now he felt purged, ready to rebuild his life, to face the world.

And it was all due to his little librarian.

Graddon brought his shaving water and Dominic considered how best he could reward her. Money? The razor rasped over his cheek. No. He knew her well enough now to know her proud independent spirit would never accept such a gift, or any gift. Damnation, then how was he to thank her? One thing was certain, he would not let her become a governess. She deserved to be her own mistress, with her own servants to command. But how was he to engineer such a change in her life? It must not look as if he had any hand in the affair. He could set up an annuity and have his lawyer tell her it was from some long-lost relative, but that would mean taking her family into his confidence, and if her father was the upright clergyman she had described then he might not be happy to collude in such a lie. Besides, there was not much time. The work in the library was almost complete. Every day he dreaded that Zelah might come to him and say she had accepted another post. And once she had left her sister's house—

'Marriage!'

Of course. He dropped his razor and dried his face quickly. Maria Buckland had already thought of an excellent plan. It was up to him now to carry it out.

When Zelah set off for another day at Rooks Tower, the sky was a blanket of unbroken grey and a freshening wind promised rain later. Spring was refusing to give way to summer. However, the lowering weather did not affect

her spirits. When she thought of what she had achieved
in the library she was pleased, but when she reached the
house and walked through the salon, its window shutters now folded away to allow the light to fill the elegant
space, her heart swelled with pride. She was pleased to
think she was playing some part in Major Coale's reha-
bilitation, encouraging him to see that he need not lock
himself away and live a solitary existence.

She must face up to the fact that she had grown fond of
the major. Too fond. He could be overbearing and irasci-
ble, but she knew much of his ill temper sprang from the
horrific injuries he had suffered, not just to his face, but
to his mind. She had seen a softer side to his character
and now her day was not complete unless she saw him—
Zelah shook her head. Heavens, what was she thinking?
She must not allow herself to become attached to Dominic Coale. It would be foolish to dwell upon his many
kindnesses to her. They meant nothing, and if she should
betray her feelings—she knew only too well how easily
a man could succumb to temptation. It had almost destroyed her once, it must not happen again.

It was therefore a very cool and formal greeting that
she gave the major when he marched into the library the
following morning, before returning her attention to her
work. He appeared not to notice.

'You will leave off your interminable cataloguing,
Miss Pentewan. I have another job for you.' He strode
about the room as he spoke, his hands clasped behind
his back. 'I want you to compile a list of all the families in the county. Those with the rank of gentlemen and
above, naturally.'

She paused, her pen caught in mid-air.

'A list, sir? Very well, if that is what you want…'

'It is, and I want it complete by tomorrow. You may need to consult your sister on this.'

'Yes, I think I shall have to do that.'

She stared at his broad back, wondering if she dare ask him why he wanted these names. He swung round, catching her glance.

'I am going to hold a ball.'

Zelah dropped her pen.

'A—a *ball*?' She hurriedly blotted the ink that had splashed on to the ledger.

'Yes. Now we have opened up the salon it seems a pity not to use it.' He began to pace up and down the room. 'My sister will be coming down to play hostess. I have already written to her. You and I will compile a list and then you will write to everyone, inviting them to attend.'

'And…and when is this ball to be?'

'At midsummer. Three weeks from now.'

'Three weeks! So little time.'

'I know, but it cannot be helped. I have asked Mrs Graddon to let me know what is required to make all the bedrooms habitable and I will be sending someone to buy what is necessary—give me a list of your require-ments, pens, paper, seals and so on and they shall be fetched for you.'

'Th-thank you,' said Zelah, her head reeling. She lis-tened as he explained the steps he had already taken to prepare for the event and drew a sheet of paper towards her to write down a few notes.

'I think that is all,' he said at last, rubbing his chin. 'I must be off to find Phillips and ask him if Old Robin has been back yet to finish removing the moles from the south lawn.' He strode towards the door and stopped. 'Oh, and remember to put your own name on the list. You and your sister and brother-in-law will be my guests at dinner beforehand.'

'Me? Oh, I do not think I could—'

He turned to glower at her. 'You will do as you are bid, Miss Pentewan. If I am going to all this trouble, then I expect you to make a little effort, too!'

Chapter Nine

Zelah was still dazed when she returned to West Barton that evening and it was a relief to unburden herself to her sister.

'Do you not think it odd,' she mused, 'that a man who so very recently lived as a recluse should suddenly take it into his head to hold a ball?'

Maria was inclined to be complacent. 'That is the life he has been used to.'

'But up until a few days ago he could not bear to look at himself in the mirror. He kept the salon in darkness.'

'Yes, until you showed him how nonsensical it was. You are a beneficial influence, Zelah. Think how much he has changed since he has met you.'

'He would have come about, even without me, but a ball! That is most unexpected.'

'He appeared to be enjoying himself at the assembly,' returned Maria, her eyes twinkling. 'Perhaps someone gave him the hint.'

'Yes, but the worst thing is, he insists that I should be there. I suppose that he feels he cannot leave me out, since you and Reginald are invited. We are all to dine there, too, beforehand. And I am to tell you, sister, that he will have a suite prepared for you and the children, because he knows you will not stay away long from Baby.'

'Well, I consider that to be exceedingly kind, and beyond anything I was expecting.' She cast a shrewd look at Zelah. 'Major Coale must think very highly of you, my dear.'

'I think he values the work I am doing.'

'Are you sure that is all?'

'Of course. What else should a viscount's son think of a parson's daughter?' Zelah forced herself to speak lightly and she was glad to see the speculation fade from Maria's eyes.

'Oh well, at least this will give you the opportunity to mix in society.'

Zelah shook her head. 'But I don't *want* to mix.'

'Well, you should. Who knows? There will be many gentlemen there, and dancing has been known to lead to greater things, like an offer of marriage.'

'Maria, you know that is impossible.'

'Not so,' said Maria stoutly. 'You have many qualities that an honest man would look for in a wife—'

'Not if he knows of my past. Would you have me deceive an honest man?' Zelah bit her lip and fixed her eyes upon her sister's dismayed countenance. She said gently, 'I should not be attending this ball at all. I am a fallen woman, Maria. If anyone should discover that—'

'They won't. No one outside Cardinham knows what happened to you—why, even Reginald and I don't know the whole!'

No, thought Zelah, sadly, she had never told anyone about the man who had stolen her heart and her virtue. She thought back to that halcyon summer. She had been in love and thought herself loved in return. She stifled a sigh.

'Well,' she said brightly, 'at least it will give me the opportunity to find out if anyone requires a governess.'

Two weeks before the ball, the major's sister arrived. A handsome travelling carriage bowled up the drive and Zelah, watching from the tower room, saw a lady alight. She was elegantly attired in a travelling dress of olive green, her dark hair caught up under a stylish cap from which a number of curling ostrich feathers nodded in the breeze. Even as she shook out her skirts Dominic came striding out of the house and caught her up in his arms, swinging her around. Zelah turned back to her books. She had no right to feel jealous of the major's lovely sister.

Down on the drive, Dominic hugged his sister. 'It is good to see you, Sal. How was your journey?'

'Tiresome. If only all the roads on Exmoor were as good as this last mile!' She pushed herself free of his arms and stood looking him over. 'Hmm, a vast improvement, Dom, I would not have recognised you. The last time I saw you was at Markham and I thought then you bore a strong resemblance to a bear. And you are no longer limping.'

He grinned. 'The Exmoor air agrees with me. Come inside. We will drink a glass of wine while they take your baggage to your room.' He kept his arm around her as he swept her inside.

'So this is your new home.' She gazed up at the impressive roof of the hall as they passed through. 'A touch Gothic for you, Dom.'

'This side of the house is the original, but do not despair, the bedrooms have every comfort, including new windows that do not rattle in the night. Later I will show you the salon and the library, more recent additions to the building.'

'Ah, yes, the library. You wrote to tell me you had a home at last for all your books!'

'Yes.' He looked down to brush a speck of dust from his sleeve before continuing in a casual tone, 'I have found a librarian to put them in order for me.'

'Ah, good.'

'A woman.'

The choking sound from his sister made him smile inwardly, but his look was all innocent concern. Sally was not deceived.

'The devil you have,' she said rudely. 'She is a beauty, I suppose.'

'Not particularly. She is kin to the Bucklands and I took her on because she lives at West Barton, so I did not need to have her living here.' His lips curved upward. 'Actually, she has done an excellent job of creating order from the chaos that was the library. But that is not important—we have a ball to organise.'

He pulled out the list of names Zelah had written out and handed it to Sally, who perused it carefully.

'Well, you can add Jasper to the list. He will come, if he can. He is currently in town and waiting to see what changes Prinny will make now he is Regent.'

Dominic nodded. It would be good to see his twin again. 'What about Ben?'

'My darling husband is in the Peninsula and the last I heard he was with the army at Albuerra.'

Dom gave a mirthless laugh. 'Ah, yes, our so-called victory. The losses were terrible, I hear.'

'I know. It is very sad. I think Ben is safer as an intelligence officer.'

He nodded, then said abruptly, 'Do you worry about him?'

'Of course.' Sally's smile softened and her eyes took

on a dreamy, faraway look. 'I cannot wait until he comes back again.'

Something twisted deep in his gut and Dominic found himself wondering if any woman would ever have such a look for him.

'You have finished your wine, Sal. Would you like more, or can I take you to meet my librarian? I fear if we wait until you have changed your gown she will have left.'

'Take me to her,' said Sally immediately. 'I am agog to see the woman you will trust with your precious books.'

Sally's tone was light, but her interest in the unknown employee was very real. She followed him across the hall, not knowing what she would find. Some harpy, perhaps bent on securing a wealthy husband. Or an eccentric blue-stocking. What she did not expect was a slender girl with sun-streaked brown hair and golden skin. She would be looked upon askance at Almack's, where pale skin was so fashionable and even the odd freckle was frowned upon. Not a harpy, then. Her high-necked grey gown was plain to the point of severity and with her hair strained back into a knot at the nape of her neck, Sally thought the girl was doing her best *not* to attract any man's attention.

Observing Dominic's constraint as he made the intro-duction, and Miss Pentewan's faint blush, Sally was even more intrigued. She gave Zelah her most friendly smile.

'Dominic tells me you are making excellent progress with his wretched books. Why he had to collect so many I really cannot think! I do hope you will be able to spare some time to help me organise this ball.'

'Yes, ma'am, if you wish it.'

Her voice was soft, musical even and the smile lurk-ing in her hazel eyes hinted at a mischievous sense of humour. A pleasant enough child, but nothing to attract her brother. When he had been on the town, his flirts had always been diamonds of the first water and even his mistresses—of whom she was supposed to know nothing—had been ripe beauties. What he saw in this unremarkable young woman she did not know.

'You are free to give Mrs Hensley as much assistance as she needs,' barked Dominic, as if impatient to be gone. 'The library can wait until after the ball.'

Sally inclined her head. 'That is very kind of you, Dominic.'

'Not at all. There is still a deal of work to be done out of doors and I shall not be able to give you as much attention as I would like.'

'Ah, I see now. You are shuffling off your responsibilities, brother. Very well, Miss Pentewan, we shall begin tomorrow by looking at the lists you have drawn up and seeing how many have replied. But that will have to be in the afternoon. Tomorrow morning I want to be shown around the estate.' She turned to Zelah. 'Do you ride, Miss Pentewan?'

'I was used to, but not any more. There are no mounts suitable for a lady at West Barton.'

'Oh, if that is all then I will provide you with a mount. I brought two of my own hacks, because Dom warned me how bad the roads can be. Do you have a riding habit?'

'Yes, but—'

'Then that is settled. We will go riding tomorrow, if the weather holds.'

She paused, raising her brows at Zelah, who clasped her hands together, saying, 'I am very grateful for the offer, but I am afraid I cannot ride out with you. I am a librarian—'

'Hell and damnation,' growled Dominic, 'you will be whatever I pay you to be!'

Zelah's head went up.

'I am no bondservant! If that is what you think, then I am sorry to disappoint you and we will part now.'

Sally put up her hands. 'Of course he does not think that, Miss Pentewan. Shame on you, Dominic, did you leave your manners behind when you moved here?'

After a tense interlude he shook his head. 'I beg your pardon, Miss Pentewan,' he ground out. 'I would be *much obliged* if you would accompany my sister when she rides out tomorrow. Since I cannot go with her myself, I would feel happier knowing she did not go with only a groom for company.'

There was a proud tilt to Zelah's chin and the stormy look was still in her eyes as she met Dominic's fiery glare. So the drab little librarian had steel in her soul.

Good for her, thought Sally appreciatively, *but is she a match for Dominic?*

She waited silently and saw the anger fade from her brother's eyes. His tone was quite cordial as he posed his next question.

'Do you *dislike* riding, Miss Pentewan?'

'On the contrary, but there is no place for it in my life now.'

'Not even if it will assist me?'

'Dominic, do not press her,' Sally began, but he waved his hand and continued in a coaxing tone,

'Come, are you so eager to finish working in my library that you cannot leave it for another day?'

A soft blush suffused Zelah's cheeks. 'It—it is not that,' she stammered. 'I really do not think it is my place...'

'My dear Miss Pentewan, I really would be most grateful for your company,' said Sally. 'I shall keep you away from your work for no more than two hours—three at the most. Do say you will come.'

'I would enjoy it very much, ma'am, but I do not think

it possible. I could not sit down in here in all my dirt, and to go home and change would severely curtail my day...'

'Then take the whole day off, madam. I am not such an ogre that I will prevent you having any pleasure.'

'There you are,' said Sally triumphantly, 'You are to take a day's holiday, Miss Pentewan!'

'My dear, you will wear out the carpet!'

Maria's laughing protest halted Zelah as she paced up and down the morning room and she dropped into a chair, albeit one with a view of the drive.

They were in the morning room at West Barton. Breakfast was finished, Zelah had donned her riding habit and was waiting for Sally Hensley to arrive. She could not deny she was looking forward to riding out. She had enjoyed riding her father's hack at Cardinham and she had brought her riding habit with her to West Barton. However, Maria had explained to Zelah that she had sold her horse, for there would not be any opportunity for her to ride until little Reginald was older. What Zelah knew, although it remained unspoken, was that there was no money to spare for such a luxury. Zelah had resigned herself to the fact that she would never ride again, but now Major Coale's delightful sister had not only invited her to ride, but was willing to provide a mount, too.

Zelah had spent some little time wondering if she should have held fast and refused to go. But it had been far too tempting an offer and when Sally eventually arrived, and Zelah was at last mounted upon the spirited bay mare, she could not regret her decision. The mare tossed her head and snorted, playfully sidestepping across the drive while Zelah kept control with the lightest hold on the reins.

'She is very lively, but you have her measure.' Sally

nodded approvingly as Zelah brought her mount along-side Sally's glossy black horse.

'She is delightful.' Zelah laughed. 'What is her name?'

'Portia. After Shakespeare.' Sally chuckled. 'Dom and Jasper had taken me to see *The Merchant of Venice* as half of my birthday treat. Portia was the other half. She is a delightful ride and can cover miles without flagging, but then my husband bought Ebony for me.' She leaned forwards and stroked her horse's gleaming neck. 'Poor Portia was ousted.'

'I do not know how you can choose between them,' commented Zelah as they rode out into the lane.

'Ebony was a present from my darling Ben. When you have a much-loved husband you too will value any gift he gives you.'

'I do not intend to marry. I am going to be a governess.'

'Goodness. Wouldn't you rather have a husband?'

'No.' Realising this bald answer might be a little rude, she added, 'I would rather be independent than marry the wrong man.'

'Very true, but if you could marry *any man* you wanted…?'

Zelah was silent. There was no possibility of her being able to marry the man of her choice, so she would rather not think about it. She said carefully, 'It is all too easy to be deceived by a charming man.' They followed Sawley into a field and she took the opportunity to change the subject. 'The land is well drained here, shall we gallop the fidgets out of these horses?'

After racing across the open ground they settled down to follow the groom as he pointed out to them the extent of the land belonging to Rooks Tower. It was impossible for Zelah to keep up her reserve when Sally was so naturally friendly. She could not, of course, agree that they should do away with formality completely and while she was happy for Sally to use her first name she was resolved never to call her companion anything other than Mrs Hensley.

They had finished their tour with another gallop across the moors and were about to turn back when a lone rider appeared in the distance. Zelah's heart skipped a beat. She instantly recognised the upright rider on the huge grey horse.

'Here is my brother now,' declared Sally. She waved. 'Just in time to escort us home.'

The major spotted them and raised his hand. The grey mare broke into a canter and very soon he had caught up with them. He did not smile in response to Sally's greeting and the downward turn of the left side of his mouth was more pronounced than ever. Zelah regarded him anxiously.

'Is anything the matter, Major?'

'It's Old Robin. They found his body in the Lightwater today.' His voice, his whole manner, was terse.

'Oh, good heavens!'

'Who is this Robin?' demanded Sally, her frowning glance moving between them.

'An old man from the village who spent most of his time living wild in the woods. He earned a little money doing odd jobs for me or the other landowners. There was nothing he didn't know about this land. A useful fellow.'

'He will be sorely missed,' added Zelah, thinking of Nicky. 'Who found him?'

'Buckland was out with Giles Grundy early this morning, trying to prove that the Lightwater is the river referred to in the charter. They came upon him just where the Lightwater enters Prickett Wood.'

She shuddered. 'Poor man. How long...?'

He shook his head. 'No one knows. I saw him outside the White Hart on the night of the hearing. He was drunk, then. No one seems to have seen him since that night.'

'Perhaps that was it, then,' suggested Sally. 'He lost his footing and slipped into the stream and drowned. How sad. Has he any family?'

'A sister. Buckland has gone to see her.'

'Is there anything to be done?'

'No. Buckland and Sir Arthur, the local magistrate, have everything in hand. Let me escort you home.'

The little party was subdued as it cantered back across the fields to Rooks Tower. When they reached the fork in the path which led to West Barton, Zelah drew rein.

'This is where I must leave you. My brother-in-law will send someone over with the mare tomorrow, if you wish, or Sawley can come with me now.'

'I would not hear of you going home alone,' said Sally. 'Dominic shall accompany you.'

'No, please,' cried Zelah, alarmed. 'There is no need for that!'

'It is the least he can do when you have given up your time for me this morning. And we must do it again—I have enjoyed it so much. I know! We will keep your riding habit at Rooks Tower, then when we want to go riding you only have to change into it, and can go back to your work in the library afterwards. What do you think, Dom?'

'I think you are imposing upon Miss Pentewan's good nature, Sal.'

'Nonsense. You enjoyed riding out with me, did you not, Zelah?'

'Very much, but—'

'Then it is settled. Dom shall send the carriage over

for you in the morning, so that you can bring everything with you. Is that agreed?'

Overwhelmed, Zelah could only nod and earned a beaming smile from Sally.

'Good. That is settled. Now, see her home safely, Dominic. I should come too, but I fear the journey yesterday tired me more than I first thought.'

'Very well,' said Dominic. 'Take Sawley with you, Sal. I will see Miss Pentewan home.'

Once they had watched Sally and the groom cantering off towards Rooks Tower, Zelah turned her horse towards West Barton, the major bringing the big grey into line beside her. He said quietly,

'You will have to explain to Nicky about Robin.'

'I was thinking of that. Nicky has seen much less of Robin since he has been attending classes with Mr Netherby, but he will still be upset, I think.'

'Would you like me to come with you?'

She looked up, surprised. 'Th-that is very kind of you, Major, but I think I can manage.' She gave a little smile. 'After all, I need to learn to handle things like this, if I am to make a good governess.'

He gave an impatient huff. 'You still hold by your absurd plan?'

'Of course.' Zelah blinked. 'Why not?'

'You are attending the ball. It is not impossible that you will meet some gentleman—'

'Not you, too!' she exclaimed bitterly. 'I do not *want* to meet some gentleman. I can never marry.'

'*Can* never marry?' He jumped on the word. 'Is there some impediment then?'

Her hands jerked on the reins and Portia sidled nervously.

'N-no, of course not,' she stammered, aware that her

cheeks were hot and most likely very red. 'I am merely determined to maintain my independence. In fact...' she put up her chin, suddenly remembering a letter that had been delivered yesterday '...I have received an enquiry for a very good situation as a governess. In Bath. I have to send references.'

'Do not look to me for that.' His tone made her frown and he gave an exasperated sigh. 'However good your work has been, you must be all about in your head if you think any respectable family will consider you upon *my* recommendation.'

'Then I shall find others to recommend me,' she said stiffly. 'I cannot afford to miss this opportunity.'

'But you will still come to the ball.'

'If you wish it, sir.'

'Damnation, it has nothing to do with my wishes!' he exclaimed wrathfully. 'I want you to come and dance. I want you to enjoy yourself. As you did at the assembly.'

She turned an indignant glance upon Dominic. 'You cannot order me to enjoy myself!'

'I can, and do.'

The glinting smile in his eyes set her heart bounding in her chest as if desperate to break out. Her mouth was dry. Somehow she tore her eyes away. Somehow she found the strength to speak. 'Absurd, Major. What an arrogant thing to say.'

When they reached West Barton he jumped down and ordered Cloud to stand. He reached up and plucked Zelah from the saddle. For one dizzy moment she was suspended in mid-air, then she slid down into his arms. Her eyes were level with his mouth and she found herself wondering what it would be like to be kissed by him, to have those firm lips gliding over her skin. Her body went hot at the thought. She pushed away from him and thrust the reins into his hand.

'I must go. Thank you for allowing me this holiday, Major Coale. I shall work extra hard tomorrow, to make up for it. There is one final crate of books from Lydcombe that I must unpack, ancient books that might be of interest.'

She knew she was gabbling but she dare not stop, fearing a silence between them. Looking anywhere but in his face, she gave a little nod, picked up her skirts and ran into the house.

Since Reginald was still in Lesserton, Maria had not heard of Robin's death and Zelah passed on the few details she knew. Nicky had been invited to spend the day with one of his school friends and when he returned the news had already reached him. He had been sad, of course, but, as Zelah had predicted, school and his newfound friends occupied so much of his time that he had not seemed overly disturbed and when she peeped into his bedroom before retiring for the night she was relieved to see that he was sleeping peacefully.

Zelah envied Nicky's slumber when she eventually lay down in her own bed, for sleep eluded her. She had enjoyed her day, but riding out with Sally Hensley only served to highlight what she was giving up. But what choice was there? She could not marry any man unless he knew of her past, and what honest man would want her then?

Tossing restlessly in her bed, she glanced towards the window. There was no moonlight to disturb her sleep, but a star twinkled brightly and she remembered just how she had felt all those years ago, dishonoured, betrayed, her life in ruins. She had been fooled by one man—who was to say it couldn't happen twice? Gazing out at the distant star, Zelah renewed her vow never to put herself in any man's power.

Chapter Ten

Life at Rooks Tower was very different with Sally Hensley in residence. She carried Zelah off for long walks or
to go riding with her and set the household by the ears
with her arrangements for the forthcoming ball.

'We really must use the orangery, now it has been
painted and reglazed,' mused Sally, as she toured the
gardens with Zelah. 'I will leave that to you, my dear.'

'We will need lamps, then. Perhaps a few coloured
ones would look pretty—I could paint some of the glass
lanterns.'

'You could? How clever you are, Zelah! We will move
some of the statues in there from the house, too, and you
can arrange them. And that reminds me,' Sally continued.
'We will need to use the tower room as a bedchamber.'

'No!' Zelah stopped, appalled. 'Surely that is not necessary? It—it is far removed from the rest of the accommodation.'

'Well, I have thought and thought about it, but we have
invited so many cousins and uncles that even if we send
the servants into Lesserton we will be overflowing, and
I need to keep a room spare for Jasper.'

'But I moved all the clutter from the library up there

when you said we would need to open up the library,' objected Zelah. 'I can work up there while all the guests are in residence without being in anyone's way.'

Sally took her arm and urged her to walk on. 'There is one solution...' she said thoughtfully.

'Yes?' Zelah looked at her eagerly.

'We could use it as your bedroom. That would free up another bedchamber.'

'If that is all, we could make up a truckle bed for me in Maria and Reginald's suite.'

'No, that will not do. I have already crammed in a bed for the children's nurse. It will have to be the tower room.' She laughed suddenly. 'Do not look so downcast, Zelah. It will only be for the one night and you will not object to being surrounded by your books and ledgers, I am sure.'

'All this effort for one night,' exclaimed Zelah. 'I wish to goodness I did not have to attend.'

'Nonsense.' Sally patted her arm. 'It will be quite delightful. Now let us go indoors and we will decide which of the marble statues we should move to the orangery.'

With three days to go to the Rooks Tower ball it seemed that the event was all anyone could talk about. Nicky was thrilled when he was told they would all be staying at the house overnight and Maria spent hours deciding which gown she would wear. Only Zelah refused to show any enthusiasm. She declined a new gown, declaring that she would not waste her money on something she would never wear again.

It was almost impossible to think of working when everywhere was in such upheaval, but Zelah did her best. When she arrived at Rooks Tower the following day she was informed that Mrs Hensley had gone into Lesserton and would not be returning until dinnertime, so she hurried off to the tower room, determined to catch up on some of her work. The room was far more cluttered than when she had left it. The small writing desk and the remaining crate of books still stood by the window, but the rest of the furniture had been moved up to make room for an oak tester bed, one of several old beds Sally had discovered dismantled and stored in the nether regions of the house. There were no fluted footposts, no light-as-air draperies. The headboard and canopy were elaborately carved and the two supporting posts were as thick as young trees. She was thankful that the bed-hangings had long ago disappeared and when she peeped beneath the scarlet-and-gold bedcover and cotton sheets, the mattress looked to be quite new. Sally had thoughtfully provided a stepping stool and Zelah climbed up on to the bed. She gazed out through the leaded windows and felt a little *frisson* of excitement at the thought of waking up there and seeing the moors in the early morning light.

Another memory to be locked away.

Zelah slipped off the bed. She must not worry about the future. Her work here was as yet unfinished.

Having windows on three sides made the tower room very light, it also made it very warm with the June sun beating down. Zelah opened all the windows before setting to work, listing another set of books in the ledger. She was writing in details of the last volume when she heard a hasty step on the wooden stairs. She smiled. It was Major Coale. There was no longer any hesitation or unevenness in his step, but no one else moved about the house so quickly, or entered any room with such a burst of energy. He came in now, wearing boots and buckskins and the old jacket she had seen on him the first time they had met, his restless presence filling every corner of the room.

'So this is where you are hiding yourself.'

'Not hiding, sir. The library has been prepared in readiness for your guests' arrival tomorrow. I can as easily work up here.'

'The devil you can.'

She laughed.

'It is true. I bring a few books up here, enter the details, then return them to their place on the shelves. It takes a little longer, but it means I am not in the way.'

'Hmmph.'

He looked around the room, his eyes coming to rest upon the bed.

'Good God, where did that monstrosity come from?'

'Mrs Hensley said it was in storage. Presumably left here by the last owners.'

'More likely abandoned by the builders! It is a relic of the last century at least. It should have been thrown out.'

'Fie, Major, if that had happened then I should have had nothing to sleep on.'

'You are sleeping here?'

'Why, yes, sir. For the night of the ball. Did your sister not tell you?'

'No, she did not,' he replied grimly. 'It is out of the question. It is too remote. There is no accommodation for a maid—'

'I do not have a maid, sir.'

'That is not the point. What was Sal thinking of to put you here?'

'Mrs Hensley needed one last room and if anyone had to have this room I would much rather it was me.' She waved her hand in the direction of the desk. 'For anyone else all this would have to be removed. Believe me, sir, I shall be quite comfortable.'

'As you wish.' He shrugged, as if tired of the conversation.

'Did you want to talk to me, sir?'

'Mmm? No, I just wanted to know where you were. I am going out. There is a dead beech tree in the woods that needs felling and my sister has seen fit to set all my best men to prettifying the grounds ready for this damned ball.'

She said, hoping to mollify him, '*My* sister says it will be the most magnificent event in the county this year.'

'Is that supposed to please me?'

'Yes, it is. Why else are you holding the ball?'

She waited for his answer, her head tilted on one side. His eyes narrowed.

'Another momentary aberration, Miss Pentewan. They are becoming quite common since I met you!'

He swept out again and Zelah returned to her work.

Mrs Graddon brought her a glass of wine and a little bread and ham at noon and while she enjoyed her solitary meal, Zelah considered the final crate of books. She would empty it now and have Graddon take the box away. That would be a little less clutter in the room.

She lifted out the books, three large volumes each in panelled calf. Carefully she opened the first one and read the inscription. It was the first volume of *Vitruvius Britannicus*. She had never seen Lydcombe Park, but she had heard that it was a delightful Palladian mansion. Its owner was quite likely to have taken the design from one of these volumes. Sir Oswald would be quite sorry not to have them, if that was the case. She picked up her duster and carefully ran it over the book before putting it to one side and wiping down the next volume. The cloth snagged on something between the pages. Fearful that she had damaged a loose page she carefully opened the book.

'Have you seen Major Coale? Is he back?'

Zelah asked the question of a startled footman as she hurried across the great hall. The man stuttered out that he thought he had seen the master crossing the lawn from the woods towards the stables some ten minutes ago. The stables were situated in a block beyond the north-west corner of the house, as far from the library as it was possible to be. With scarcely a pause Zelah set off through the twisting passages to the back of the house, hoping that her quarry did not enter by some other door unknown to her, or walk around to the front entrance and miss her altogether.

Outside the sun was blazing down, and the heat was intense after the shady corridors of the house, disastrous for a lady's complexion, but Zelah did not waste time going back for her bonnet. She set off towards the stables, nearly running in her haste to find Dominic. As she rushed through the arch into the yard she heard voices mixed with the creak of the pump handle and the splash and gurgle of water. The sight that met her eyes made her stop in her tracks, open-mouthed.

Dominic was bowed down with his head under the pump while one of the stable lads worked the handle, drenching his head and shoulders with clear, cold water. He straightened and shook himself like a dog, sending diamond droplets of water flying in every direction. Zelah was unable to look away. He was naked to the waist and she could plainly see the white line of the sabre slash running from his left shoulder and across the dark shadow of hair on his chest. But it was not the jagged scar that held her spellbound, after all she had seen that before. It was the sight of his powerful torso, tanned from working out of doors, the muscles flexing as he grabbed a cloth and began to dry himself. She stared, taking in the broad shoulders, the flat stomach with its tapering line of hair that disappeared into his breeches. A powerful ache tore at her insides. Even the man who had taken her virginity had not roused such a powerful physical longing.

Dominic stilled when he saw her, slowly lowering the cloth. He resisted the temptation to hold the towel against his chest, covering the scar. She continued to stare at him in silence. What the devil was she doing in the yard? He threw the drying cloth at the grinning stable hand and barked out a command which sent the lad scurrying away. The movement woke Zelah from her trance and she blinked, a hot flush flooding her cheeks.

'I—um—I came to find you.'

He spread his hands. 'Well, here I am.' Her confusion angered him and he said roughly, 'I am sorry if the sight of me disturbs you.'

He picked up his shirt and threw it over his head. His shoulders were still damp and the soft linen stuck to his skin, but at least he was covered.

'No, no...' She trailed off, then her flush deepened as the meaning of his words hit her. 'Oh heavens, please do not think I was upset by the scar! I hardly noticed. That is, I was looking...' Her eyes were still fixed on his chest, but the look in them was not horror, or revulsion. It was something he had not seen in a woman's eyes for a long time. Desire. His heart swelled and he stood a little taller. Drawing a deep breath, she started again. 'I have found something—a paper—in the tower room. I think you should see it.'

He picked up his discarded waistcoat and jacket and came towards her.

'Propriety would suggest I should dress first, but there seems to be some urgency in your coming to find me.'

'I *do* want you to see this as soon as possible.'

His lips quirked. 'Are you sure you can cope with my, er, informal attire?'

She saw the glinting smile in his eyes and her chin went up. 'I am sure it is no concern to me!'

He laughed. 'Perhaps not, but I will change, all the same. Give me five minutes and I will follow you.'

She stood for a moment, uncertain how to respond to his teasing. Then she picked up her skirts and swept ahead of him back to the house.

Zelah went back to the tower room, wishing she could lock the door against the major. She had been shocked by her reaction to seeing his naked body. She had allowed herself to be carried away once before, but then she had thought herself in love, and if she was honest she had been more anxious to please her lover than herself. Their love-making had consisted of one fumbling, disappointing night and the consequences for Zelah had been disastrous. She had had no difficulty after that in eschewing all men and could honestly say that she was content to lead a celibate life—until now.

She pressed her hands to her stomach. Her body felt strangely light and out of balance. She looked around in a panic, her eyes alighting on the huge bed. She could not see him here, in this room!

Zelah ran to the desk and was about to pick up the manuscript and carry it to the library when she heard him coming up the stairs. It was too late to remove, she must concentrate on her news. He was hardly through the door before she began to speak.

'I emptied the final crate from Lydcombe Park this

morning. It contained all three volumes of Campbell's *Vitruvius Britannicus*.'

'Are you suggesting I should remodel Rooks Tower into a Palladian mansion?'

She threw him a scornful glance but was grateful for his tone—she could deal with his light banter.

'It is what is inside the second volume that is important.'

Carefully she opened the book to display a single sheet of parchment, covered with closely packed rows of bold, black handwriting.

'It is a contract for the sale of Lydcombe Park.' Zelah could hardly keep the excitement out of her voice.

'But not a recent one. It is dated 1779.'

'I know, but it describes in detail the eastern boundary of the park and look here—it says that the easternmost point of the boundary is marked with a large stone in Prickett Wood. The charter that was produced at the hearing mentioned a boundary stone and everyone thought it was the marker that used to be on the lane running past the bluebell wood.'

'And that was removed over fifty years ago,' said Dominic slowly. 'At least twenty years before this document was written.'

'So there must be another marker stone, in the wood itself. Could we go and look? If we could find it—'

'No. We must proceed cautiously. Evanshaw may well know about the marker. That may be why he has his men patrolling the wood, but they are more likely to shoot you than ask what you are doing there. We should take this document to Buckland. He will be able to verify it and then he can ask Sir Arthur to authorise a search.' He carefully rolled up the manuscript and tied it with a ribbon. 'Sally has taken my curricle, but I expect her back any time now. Once she is returned I will take you and this document to West Barton.'

Zelah frowned. 'Could I not take it now? I could walk...'

'Are you so keen to get this to your brother-in-law?'

'Well, most likely he will not even be at home, but I will not rest until he has seen it.'

Dominic hesitated, then shook his head. 'No. It is too hot for such exertion. I will take you in the curricle.'

His autocratic tone made her long to retort, but she closed her lips firmly together. Dominic saw her response and his mouth quirked upwards.

'You must have patience, madam. Your family would berate me soundly if I allowed you to walk home in this heat.'

He was right, she knew it. She looked at the manuscript.

'I suppose it would be foolish to set off yet. But after finding this I do not think I can sit down and work.'

She risked looking at him and immediately realised her mistake. Once he had captured her glance she could not look away. She was trapped. The smile in his eyes deepened. He lifted one hand and gently rubbed the backs of his fingers over her cheek.

'There is one way to pass the time.'

His eyes dropped to her mouth and she responded by running her tongue over her lips. She should step back, but her wayward limbs refused to move. She was drawn like a magnet to the man in front of her. He had changed into a clean shirt, waistcoat and buckskins, but without a jacket the white sleeves billowed out, making the breadth of his shoulders even more impressive. He dominated the space before her and she could not look away.

Very slowly he lowered his head and kissed her. It

was the gentlest of touches, his lips gliding across her mouth. She closed her eyes, almost swooning as desire swamped her. His kiss deepened as he sensed her reaction, his mouth working on her lips until they parted and his tongue flickered, seeking her own. She wound her free hand around his neck, pulling him closer while he plundered her mouth, his tongue dipping, diving, driving her senses wild. She responded by pushing against him, returning kiss for kiss. When he released her mouth and raised his head she gave a whimper, turning her face up, standing on tiptoe as she reached up for him.

He put his hands on her shoulders, holding her away from him, his eyes hard and bright.

'You are not…repelled by my disfigurement?'

'Repelled? No.' She reached out one hand and gently placed her fingers on his ragged cheek, then she brought up the other hand to pull his head down until she could kiss his scarred brow, his cheek, his jaw.

Dominic put up his hand to cover hers and dragged it to his mouth, pressing a kiss into the palm before pulling her into his arms again. She lifted her face, inviting his kiss and eagerly returning it as he pushed aside the muslin scarf that covered her neck and shoulders, his thumbs gently rubbing along her collarbones. She threw back her head as his mouth grazed her throat and moved on to kiss the soft swell of her breasts. Zelah trembled, the desire that had been smouldering inside her bursting into a flame that threatened to consume her, but even as she felt her body slipping out of control she began to fight. She pushed against Dominic and immediately he let her go.

With a sob she turned away. 'Oh, what have I done?'

'Zelah.'

'Oh, do not call me that! I am—must be—Miss Pentewan to you.'

'Of course.' His voice was harsh. 'I should have known. You were merely taking pity—'

'No!' She spun round, saying indignantly, 'What I feel for you is *not* pity.'

'Then why push me away?'

She put her hands to her burning cheeks, forcing herself to tell him the truth.

'I was afraid that if I did not stop you now I would not be able to do so. You—you arouse such feelings in me as I have never known.'

As she spoke she fumbled to straighten her neckerchief. Dominic pushed her hands aside and carefully rearranged the folds of muslin decorously across her shoulders.

He said quietly, 'Such feelings are natural between a man and a woman.'

'Not to me! I cannot afford such a luxury.'

'It is not a luxury, it is a blessing.' He slid his hands down her arms and grasped her fingers. 'Believe me, I would not have kissed you if I didn't think you wanted it, too. I saw the way you looked at me in the yard.'

She pulled away, confused and embarrassed. 'Fine words, sir. It is very easy for you to return to your rakish ways!'

'Hell and confound it, madam, do you think I am toying with you?'

'Of course you are. But it is partly my fault, for coming here to work, putting myself in your power.'

'My power!' He laughed savagely. 'You make me sound like the villain of a melodrama.'

'And that is just what you are,' she flashed. 'With your black scowls and tortured looks—' She stopped, her hands flying to her mouth. 'Oh, I should not have said that, I am so sorry—'

'Nay, why should you hold back? I cannot deny that I have the physiognomy for a rogue!'

'That is not what I meant.'

'Isn't it? Do I not feature as the villain in your fantasy, a grotesque being who has ensnared you, drawing you in against your will? Do I not exert an evil fascination?'

'No, no,' she said unhappily. 'You wilfully misunderstand me. I will not stay here—I shall walk home now and never return.'

At that moment a sudden crack of thunder ripped the air. Zelah gave a little cry of fright and shrank towards Dominic. Instinctively his arms closed around her.

'So,' he muttered, 'the thunder frightens you more than I do.'

Zelah extricated herself from his embrace and said with as much dignity as she could muster, 'I never said you frightened me. I merely wish to quit this house—and you!—as soon as possible.'

The quiet patter of raindrops intensified to a roar. Dominic went over to close the window.

'Well, you can hardly walk to West Barton now.' He glanced back and saw that she was looking out at the rain sheeting down, her bottom lip caught between her teeth. He said coldly, 'Do not fret, madam. I will not inflict my presence on you a moment longer than necessary. Once my sister returns, Sawley shall drive you to West Barton.'

He turned on his heel and stormed out. Damn the woman! Did she think he was made of stone? He was no saint, but she would turn him into a veritable Lothario. He had not meant to kiss her, but she had looked so damned alluring with the flush on her cheeks and those sparkling eyes.

And she had wanted him to kiss her, he would stake his life on that. She had been right to stop him, another few moments and he would have made good use of that ancient bed. But why had she ripped up at him? Why was she so afraid to admit the attraction?

He had reached the yellow salon by this time and saw the answer in the mirrors. A dozen reflections of his scarred face. Gritting his teeth, he strode through the room. She had touched that scar, kissed it, but in the end the thought of his disfigured body was too much for her. Well, the sooner she was removed from Rooks Tower the better!

It was another hour before Sally returned in the curricle. Dominic took an umbrella out as the carriage pulled up on the drive, but when he informed his groom that he was to take Miss Pentewan to West Barton, Sawley shook his head.

'Not with this team, sir. I've nursed 'em this far, but I don't want to take 'em any farther.'

'We had a slight mishap as we were leaving Lesserton.' Sally took Dominic's proffered hand and alighted. 'The doctor's hack broke loose from the smithy and charged into us. The off-side horse took a blow to his thigh.'

'Aye, and t'other's started limping,' added Sawley. 'I think he might've taken a kick on his fetlock.'

Dominic handed the umbrella to Sally and went to inspect the horse, running his hands gently over the suspect leg.

'You are right. It's beginning to swell.'

'Pray don't blame Sawley,' Sally implored him, observing his black frown. 'He did well to avoid overturning us. You can imagine that everything was confusion, until the blacksmith's apprentice managed to quieten the poor runaway creature.'

Dominic straightened, exhaling. Just his luck for this to happen today. He waved Sawley away.

'Take the team round to the stables and look after them, Jem, and have my match greys harnessed to the curricle. I shall drive to West Barton myself.'

Thus when Zelah presented herself at the front door it was to find Major Coale holding the reins. Briefly he explained the situation, adding when he observed her hesitation, 'I am afraid Sawley must stay here to look after the horses and I will allow no one else to drive my greys.'

For a moment Zelah thought it might be a ploy, but Dominic looked as dissatisfied with the arrangement as she was, so she allowed herself to be handed up into the carriage.

'You have the manuscript?'

'Yes.' She held up the rolled parchment, safely wrapped in oilskin.

They set off, Dominic holding the greys to a sedate trot along the drive. The rain had eased, but the grey clouds were still threatening and Zelah hoped they would not have to stop to put up the hood. It was bad enough to have to sit next to a man whose whole demeanour was one of barely controlled anger, she had no wish to be trapped in a confined space with him. She stared ahead, trying to maintain a dignified silence, but her conscience was making her uncomfortable. The tension between them was palpable and they had not gone far before she could no longer bear the strained atmosphere.

'Major Coale!' She clasped and unclasped her hands, forcing herself to speak. 'What happened earlier, it was as much my fault as yours. For me to say such terrible things to you—I am ashamed. It was unjust and...and I beg your pardon.'

His countenance did not change. Not by the flicker of an eye did he acknowledge that she had spoken. Zelah's spirits sank. He could not forgive her.

She ought not to be surprised. She had intended to wound him and had done so magnificently. She was mortified now even to think of it and to be barred from Rooks Tower—and its owner—for ever would be a fitting punishment. A silent tear slid down her cheek.

'My own conduct was reprehensible.' Dominic spoke without taking his eyes from the road. She sucked in a ragged breath.

'Oh, if you only knew how much I wish my words unspoken!'

'That is impossible, but if we both regret what happened this afternoon, if we admit that we were both at fault, could we not put it behind us?'

She looked down. 'I had determined never to come back to Rooks Tower.'

'That would be sad indeed. Is that what you really want?'

She blinked back the tears. 'Not at all.'

He took one hand from the reins and reached out to cover hers. 'Then let us cry friends, Zelah.'

'Do…do you think we can?'

He turned his head to smile at her. 'I have a damnable temper, my dear, but if my black scowls don't frighten you…'

'They do not. They never have.'

'Then, yes, I think we can be friends.'

Her fingers twisted under his and she clasped his hand. She said shyly, 'Then I would like that very much, Major.'

'Dominic.'

'Dominic.' The name rolled off her tongue. She relished each syllable.

The sun breaking through the clouds lifted her spirits, so much so that when Dominic mentioned the forthcoming ball she was able to reply with perfect candour.

'I am glad I am not to be excluded, I am looking forward to it, very much.'

'And will you save one dance for me?'

'As many as you wish,' she replied recklessly. 'I am unlikely to have many partners, I know so few people.'

'You underrate yourself, my dear—' He broke off to guide the curricle through the gates of West Barton. A closed carriage was already standing at the door.

'Well, that is very good timing,' declared Zelah. 'Here is Reginald just arrived home. Now you will be able to give him the charter yourself.'

Dominic brought his team to a stop and a groom ran out to hold the greys. Zelah climbed down and shook out her skirts, glancing towards the carriage where her brother-in-law had alighted and was waiting while another gentleman clambered out.

'Reginald has brought a guest home,' she murmured, as Dominic came round to join her. She handed him the manuscript. 'It makes no odds, you can still give this to him, it is too important to wait and I am sure he will be...'

Her words trailed away. The fashionably dressed gentleman beside Reginald smiled, lifting his hat from his carefully arranged blond curls.

'Zelah, my dear. How good to see you again.'

Chapter Eleven

Zelah could not speak. She did not resist when the gentleman picked up her hand and pressed a kiss upon her fingers, holding them for far longer than was polite. He looked up and smiled into her eyes and the years fell away. She was eighteen again, gauche and tongue-tied. Dominic shifted impatiently at her side and she pulled her hand free, giving only the slightest nod of recognition.

Reginald was beaming.

'What a stroke of luck, my dear. I met Lerryn at the White Hart. Major Coale, let me present Mr Timothy Lerryn to you. His father is the squire in my wife's home town of Cardinham.'

Timothy's eyes flickered over Dominic's scarred face, but his smile never wavered.

'I am travelling to Bristol and I thought, since it is on my way, that I would call upon Mrs Buckland at West Barton. When Buckland told me that Miss Zelah Pentewan was staying here too, I could hardly believe my good fortune.'

His smile had turned to a caress, but it only made her shiver. Reginald laughed and patted him on the shoulder.

'What could I do but invite him to join us for dinner. And you too, Major, if you are free.'

'Thank you, I regret that I cannot stay. I came only to give you this.' He handed Reginald the manuscript. 'It relates to the dispute with Sir Oswald. Miss Pentewan will explain it all.'

Reginald's eyes lit up.

'Another charter, is it? This could be important. Come along to my study now and tell me everything. My man will look after your horses. Lerryn, you will not object if I leave you with Zelah?'

'On the contrary.' Timothy Lerryn held out his arm to her. 'We are such old friends I am delighted to have her to myself.'

Zelah wanted to say that *she* objected, but Reginald bore Dominic away, leaving her with Timothy Lerryn. His blue eyes roved over her.

'You have not changed one jot.'

She had thought the same of him, but now that he was closer she could see that he was different. He was still a handsome man, in a florid way, but the last four years had added inches to his waist and tiny lines at the sides of his mouth and around his eyes. Lines of dissipation, she thought.

'What do you want here?'

He looked pained. 'I came to find you. I heard you were visiting your sister.'

Once such words would have delighted her. She would have given anything to hear them. Now her lip curled.

'You can have nothing to say to me.'

'How can you speak so?' He followed her into the empty hall. 'Remember what we were to each other.'

She stopped. 'No one here knows of that!' she hissed at him. 'I do not want them to know.'

'And nor shall they. I did not come here to make trouble for you, Zelah. I wanted merely to see you.' He lowered his voice. 'I have missed you.'

'You are a married man.'

'That was a mistake. I see that now.'

'Ha!' She turned from him. 'I will take you to my sister. You shall have dinner here, but then you must go, do you understand?'

Head high, she led the way into the drawing room. Maria was reading to Nicky, but she stopped when they came in, regarding Mr Lerryn with a polite, questioning air. She listened to his explanation, flattered if a little bemused that he should break his journey to see them.

Zelah made her excuses and went off to change her gown. Her nerves were jangling, not only from the events at Rooks Tower but also from the unexpected appearance of Timothy Lerryn. He said he had come to find her and that could only mean trouble.

She tarried as long as she dared, but when she returned to the drawing room she was surprised to find Major Coale taking wine there. The sight of Dominic and Timothy Lerryn talking together did nothing to calm her nerves. She could not help comparing the two men— Dominic no longer turned the injured side of his face away from the room, but the sight of his terrible scars only added to his dark, powerful presence. By comparison she thought Timothy's tightly waisted coat and fashionable blond locks looked positively effete.

She had to steel herself not to run away as Timothy crossed the room to her.

'My dear Zelah—Miss Pentewan,' he corrected himself smoothly, seeing the flash of anger in her eyes. 'Your brother-in-law was explaining to me about the current land dispute going on in Lesserton. I understand you were instrumental in finding a new document that will help the villagers' case.'

'Yes. I certainly hope that will be so.'

She went to leave, but he put his hand under her elbow. 'Will you allow me to escort you to a chair?'

She quickly pulled her arm free. A swift glance assured her that Maria and Reginald were engaged in conversation with Dominic so she walked to the bay window where they would not be overheard. Timothy followed her, as she knew he would.

'Let me make one thing plain,' she began. 'I am not your dear anything and I do not wish to renew our acquaintance. After tonight I never want to see you again.'

'I am very sorry to hear that.'

'Are you? I should have thought you would be pleased to know that I am making a new life for myself, that does not involve you.'

'Ah, yes, your sister told me you are working for Major Coale, as his librarian. Are you sure that is wise?'

She eyed him coldly. 'I do not know what you mean.'

'With your, er, history.'

She fought down the blaze of anger at his words and the knowing look that went with them. 'No one knows about my *history* here and my employment at Rooks Tower is perfectly respectable.'

'People might not think so, if they were to know the truth about you…'

'Which they never will,' she flashed, 'unless you tell them!'

He put his hand on his heart. 'My dear Zelah, it is not my intention to say a word.' He reached for her hand, but she snatched it away. His eyes hardened. 'Of course, if you are unfriendly I might inadvertently let something slip.'

His hand remained outstretched, the challenge in his eyes unmistakable. Reluctantly she gave him her fingers. He lifted them to his lips.

'There, that is not so bad, is it? Now, as long as you are sweet to me, your secret is safe.'

She put up her chin. 'It is *our* secret, Mr Lerryn, and if it was to become public then you would not appear in any very honourable light.'

His grip tightened. 'True, but a man's reputation will survive the odd scandal—a woman's good name is a very different matter.'

Zelah clamped her lips closed upon the angry retort that rose within her and with a slight nod she moved off, inwardly seething.

Disinclined to join the others, she moved to the piano on the pretext of tidying the pile of music, but Dominic soon followed, carrying two glasses of wine. He held one out to her.

'You look troubled. I am sorry if you did not wish me to stay. I merely came to pay my respects to your sister and see how Nicky goes on.'

The roughness of his tone rubbed at her raw nerves.

'Your presence does not trouble me.' She forced herself to smile. 'I have a headache. The weather…'

Her gaze shifted to Tim Lerryn, who had come up. She kept the smile fixed on her lips as she hid her dismay at his interruption.

'Poor Zelah never could endure thunder. The storm this afternoon was particularly bad, was it not? However, the sky is clearing now and I am in hopes that the weather will improve for the remainder of my visit.'

'How long are you staying in Lesserton?' Dominic enquired.

'Oh, a few days more, at least. Having caught up with

my friends again we have a great deal to talk about, do we not, my dear?'

Zelah felt her cheeks burn with anger and embarrassment at his familiar tone. She dare not risk her voice, so she turned her attention to straightening the sleeve of her gown.

'I shall not see much of them tomorrow, I fear,' Timothy continued. 'Mrs Buckland tells me the family are joining you at Rooks Tower for your summer ball, Major Coale. I hope the weather holds for you.'

'You are welcome to join us for the dancing, if you wish, Mr Lerryn. My sister has already sent out all the invitations, but I will see to it you are not turned away if you present yourself at the door.'

Zelah froze.

'Why, that is exceedingly kind of you, sir, most obliging, is it not, Zelah?' Timothy beamed with pleasure. 'It means I shall have the opportunity to dance with you again, my dear. By heaven, that will bring back some memories, eh?'

She murmured something incoherent. After listening to Timothy repeat his gratitude, Dominic gave a little nod and walked away. He exchanged a few words with Maria and took his leave. Beside her, Timothy expelled a hissing breath.

'Dashed ugly brute, ain't he? Didn't know where to look when we was first introduced, my eyes kept going back to that damned scar.'

'One hardly notices it after a while.'

'*You* might not, but others will, take my word for it. I heard about this Major Coale of yours in Lesserton. Allowing villagers grazing rights, letting them forage in his woods—trying to buy his way into their favours, I don't doubt.'

'You know nothing about him,' snapped Zelah.

His brows rose. 'Oho, and you do? I hope you are not growing too attached to the Major, my dear. He won't be interested in the likes of you, at least not in any honourable way.' He leaned closer. 'Better to let me look after you...'

She hunched a shoulder and turned away, just as Reginald came up to escort her to dinner. Zelah placed her fingers on his arm, steeling herself for an interminable evening.

'Ah. I did not expect to see you here today, Miss Pentewan.'

Zelah looked up as Dominic strode into the library. His formal address did not escape her notice. After Timothy's remarks yesterday perhaps it was for the best. She could be formal, too.

'Good morning, Major Coale. I wanted to finish listing the books on mathematics today. I understood you and your guests were going riding, so the library would be empty.'

He spread his hands, looking down at the buckskins. She wished he had not drawn her attention to them, for they clung to his powerful thighs in a way that made her feel quite weak. 'I am dressed for riding, as you see. I was on my way to the stables when I heard a noise in here and came to investigate. Your devotion to your work is admirable, but it is the summer ball this evening.'

'I am aware of it. My sister is bringing my ball gown. I shall go upstairs and change when she arrives.' She was quick to note his frowning look and added, 'Mrs Hensley has no objection to my working here today.'

'Hmm.' The major walked over to the window while

Zelah continued to pull the books off the shelf. She was about to take them upstairs to the tower room when he spoke again. 'I thought you would spend the day with your friend Mr Lerryn.'

She stopped. 'Mr Lerryn is not my friend.'

'Oh?' He turned to face her. 'I thought he was damned friendly towards you yesterday.'

'Mr Lerryn is an old acquaintance, nothing more. He is a married man.'

'Married! His behaviour towards you did not give me that impression.'

Zelah had no answer to that. Silently she started towards the door. In two strides he had crossed the room and blocked her way.

'And you were not exactly spurning his advances.'

The accusation hurt her, but she could not deny it. She merely gave him a scorching look and went to walk past him. He caught her arm.

'Let me warn you to be careful, madam. I'll not have an employee of mine embroiled in a scandal.'

Her face flamed. Anger, indignation and dismay warred within her breast. Silently she shook off his arm and stalked off. Only when she reached the seclusion of the tower room did she allow her self-possession to crumble. She dropped the books on to the desk and sank down on the chair, shaking.

Scandal.

How could it be avoided? If she allowed Timothy Lerryn to dance with her, to flirt with her this evening, she risked Dominic's wrath, possibly even dismissal. If she followed her inclination and refused to have anything to do with him, she knew Timothy would not hesitate to make her past known to everyone.

* * *

She tried to get on with her work, doggedly listing details of each book in her ledger, but Dominic's uncompromising words kept coming back to her. He would not tolerate a scandal. Perhaps she should not go to the ball, but then Dominic would know she was avoiding Timothy Lerryn and draw his own conclusions. Even worse, Timothy might decide he had nothing to lose by exposing her. At length she admitted defeat, put down her pen and dropped her head in her hands. Whatever happened she was ruined.

Eventually the heat roused her from her reverie and she went to open the window, looking down at the gardens shimmering in the summer heat, while beyond the park she could see the ragged outline of the moor, bare but majestic above the trees. She stared about her, trying to memorise every detail. It might be the last time she ever enjoyed this view. She had been a fool to think the past could be so easily left behind.

A party of riders crossed the park, cantering towards the house. Dominic was easily recognisable on his grey mare and she spotted Sally Hensley beside him, tall and elegant in the saddle. The rest of the party were the relatives and friends invited to stay for the summer ball and she knew none of them. Zelah had begged Sally to wait until this evening's dinner to introduce her, not wanting the other guests to see her in her role as librarian. Now her caution seemed laughable. If she did not dance to Tim Lerryn's tune, then they would soon know her as something far worse and how embarrassing that would be for Dominic, when he discovered she had deceived him.

Yesterday Dominic had asked her to cry friends with him. What sort of friend was it that kept secrets? She squared her shoulders. What was it her father had always said? Tell the truth and shame the devil. If Dominic was to learn the truth about her, then she would tell him herself.

She ran down the stairs and made her way to the great hall, where the riding party was milling around, chattering and laughing. As she hoped, no one spared a second glance for the dowdy little figure in her grey gown and linen apron hovering in the doorway of the yellow salon, but she managed to catch Dominic's eye. With a word here, a smile there, he left his guests and made his way across the hall. It occurred to her that he looked very much at home amongst his friends. He was no longer the surly recluse she had first met. Surely she could take some credit for that? The thought gave her courage as he approached, even though his eyes were as hard and cold as the stone on the moor.

'If I might beg a word with you, Major?'

He did not disappoint her. With a slight nod he led her to his study.

'Well?' He closed the door, shutting out the laughing, chattering crowd. 'I perceive it must be important for you to come down from your eyrie to seek me out.'

'It is.' She dared not stop to think of the consequences now.

'Then will you not sit down?'

He gestured to the armchair beside the empty fireplace and once she was seated he pulled up a chair to face her. She would have preferred him to keep his distance, to stand over her, looking down in judgement like some omnipotent deity.

'You said this morning that you would not countenance a scandal.' She looked down at her hands clasped in her lap. 'Before I sit at your table for dinner tonight there is something you should know about me.' She stopped.

How would he react? Would he have her escorted from the house immediately? 'I wanted to tell you about myself, before you heard it from anyone else.'

He sat back in his chair. 'Then tell me.' His expression was cold, his tone indifferent. Her courage faltered. He said brusquely, 'Go on.'

Zelah's hands were clasped so tightly her knuckles went white. There was no going back now.

'There was a man, in Cardinham. He called himself a gentleman. He was handsome and so very, very charming. I suppose I was flattered by his attentions.' She screwed up her courage to continue. 'When he said he would marry me I believed him. I allowed him to… to bed me. It happened only once, but that was enough to get me with child.'

'And then I suppose he disowned you.'

His dispassionate tone made it easier for her to continue.

'Yes. My parents were deeply hurt, but they refused to abandon me, even though I would not tell them who the father was. I thought it best that everyone should think it was a stranger, a traveller from the annual fair that passed through our town each summer. I wanted no repercussions. It was my mistake and I would suffer the consequences. I was sent away to live with an aunt until my confinement.'

She stopped. She felt physically sick, but there would be no relief until she had finished her story.

'The baby was stillborn—a just punishment for my wickedness, I suppose. After a period of recuperation I returned to Cardinham. Everyone was told I had gone away for my health, but you know what villages are, I doubt if anyone really believed that. There were sly glances, whispers. No possibility of finding work with any local family.' She risked a quick glance at him. He had not moved, his face remained inscrutable. 'Reginald met Maria while she was on a visit to Bath two years ago and married her immediately. He knows my…unfortunate history, but he is very good and agreed to my coming to live with them for a short while. I hoped I would be able to make a new life for myself. I thought I could be respectable.' She lifted her chin. 'I *am* respectable. That is why, when you kissed me yesterday, I could not let it go on.'

The silence that followed was unnerving. She dared not look up again, but threaded her handkerchief through her fingers, over and over.

'And why are you telling me this now? Ah, but you said, did you not, someone else is likely to tell me?'

'Yes.'

'Mr Lerryn.'

'Yes.'

'He was your lover.'

She flinched. 'How did you know?'

'From what you told me this morning, and what I observed yesterday. He has threatened to expose you, I suppose?'

She flushed. He made it sound so sordid. 'Yes.'

He rose and paced the room once, twice. Zelah remained in her seat, her head bowed. He said abruptly, 'Do you still love him?'

'No. I doubt if I ever did. It was a foolish infatuation. I was very young and he was very…experienced.'

'What does he want for his silence?'

'My…co-operation.'

His angry snort told her he knew just what that would involve.

'Damnation, if I had known I would not have invited him to come here this evening.'

She raised her head. 'Why *did* you invite him?'

He scowled. 'Your sister wants you to marry, and I, too, consider it would be the best thing for you,' he said bluntly. 'I thought...Lerryn seemed to be keen to fix his interest with you. I did not know yesterday that he was married!'

Zelah stared at him. 'So you thought to promote his suit?'

'And why not? He is a squire's son.'

A cold hand wrapped itself around her heart. She jumped to her feet. 'Oh, why is everyone so keen to marry me off?'

'Because it would be a better future for you than a governess. Good God, there is no knowing what might befall you. Believe me, I know this world. There are many men, outwardly respectable, who would not hesitate to seduce a servant. If you marry a man of means you will have the protection of his name, servants, a carriage. A family.'

'No.' She shook her head, tears starting to her eyes.

He caught her arms. 'So you have been hurt once and lost a baby, but that need not be the end. There are other men than Lerryn. Good men.' His grip tightened.

She closed her eyes, but the tears squeezed out and made hot tracks down her cheeks. She heard him sigh. He put one arm about her shoulders, holding her to him while he pulled a clean white handkerchief from his pocket.

'You should not be anyone's drudge, Zelah.' He wiped her cheeks gently. 'You should be respected, loved.'

He put his fingers under her chin and forced her to look up at him. His grey eyes were no longer hard rock, but something hotter, darker. Her head was thrown back against his arm, he had only to lower his head and their lips would meet. Her heart was beating such a heavy tattoo she thought he must hear it. Her breasts had tightened and ached for his touch. She placed her hand on his chest and felt the powerful thud of his own heart against her palm. With sudden, startling clarity she knew she wanted him to kiss her, more than anything in the world.

'No.' The heat faded from his eyes. Gently he released her.

Unable to speak, she watched him walk away from her, his shoulders straight, his back rigidly upright as he continued. 'You need not fear Lerryn. I will not turn him away tonight, that would give rise to the type of gossip we are trying to avoid, but I will make sure he does not trouble you. Now, I have detained you long enough. It wants but a few hours to dinner, so I suggest you finish your work. I have given orders that the library is to be opened to my guests tonight, so perhaps you will make sure it is looking its best before you go off to change your gown.'

He turned back, smiling, urbane, his face shuttered. She was dismissed.

Chapter Twelve

Zelah made her way back to the library. She kept her head up as she passed through the salon where an army of servants were fitting fresh candles to the chandeliers and polishing the mirrors. The carpet had already been rolled away and the floor cleared for dancing. The double doors to the library would be thrown open once the ball commenced, but now she closed them, preferring to be alone with her thoughts. Not that they were very coherent. Dominic would protect her from Timothy Lerryn's threats, she was sure, but he had made it plain that he had no interest in her. She had known that all along, of course. He liked her, he respected her work and he was anxious for her happiness, which he thought would be best achieved by marriage. To someone else. In all likelihood he was right, but this foolish heart of hers had decided otherwise, and Zelah knew that if she could not have Dominic Coale she would have no one.

'Well, you had your plans, you were determined to earn your own living.' She spoke aloud as she walked around the empty library. 'You should be happy. Nothing has changed.'

But in her heart Zelah knew that nothing could ever be the same again.

A burst of laughter from the salon reminded her of the servants next door. She hurried off to the tower room, where she made a few last entries into the ledger and began gathering together the books to be returned to the library. She was soon joined by a harassed-looking Hannah bearing a tray.

'Mrs Graddon thought you might like some lemonade, miss, seeing as how she has made plenty for this evening.' She wiped her hand across her brow. 'My, 'tis hot, miss. I've opened the windows in the library, to let in some air.'

'Thank you, this is very welcome.' Zelah took the lemonade and sipped it. 'This must be a great upheaval for you, after living so quietly.'

'Aye, it's all at sixes and sevens. We have hired more girls from the village, though, the master insisting that Mrs Graddon should have all the help she needs, as well as the grand French chef who is come down from Lunnon to take over the kitchen. But 'tis good to see the master taking his rightful place,' Hannah continued. 'And I hear that Master Nicky is coming to stay and his little brother, too, so I hopes I might be allowed to wait on them, dear little mites.'

She bustled away, leaving Zelah feeling slightly more cheerful. There was a definite buzz of excitement around Rooks Tower. The old house had come alive with so many people in residence.

Zelah took her empty glass back to the kitchens and begged a piece of lemon to clean the ink from her fingers. Once she had done that she checked the clock. There was a good hour yet before she needed to disappear and transform herself from employee to house guest and there were still a dozen or more books in the tower room that needed to be returned to the library. She ran to fetch them. She found it was still possible to lose herself in her work, matching up books, wondering if Ehret's botanical prints should be placed beside the works of philosophy and science rather than with the book entitled *Modern Voyages and Travels*. As she straightened the volumes of *Vitruvius Britannicus* she remembered the paper she had found and wondered if it would prove useful to the villagers in fighting Sir Oswald Evanshaw's claims.

Sir Oswald would be at the ball that evening. Zelah had been present when Sally and Dominic had discussed it. Zelah remembered how flattered she had been when Dominic asked her what she thought. She had agreed with Sally that it would be impolitic to exclude him.

Now, standing alone in the library, a little flush of pleasure nudged through her depression. Dominic valued her opinion. Despite everything, he clearly wanted her to be present at the ball, so perhaps he would dance with her as he had at the assembly. The thought cheered her immensely and, determined to remain cheerful, she began to sing as she placed the last few books on the shelves.

'Well now. Minerva, in her element.'

The deep, warm voice held a laugh and she swung around, smiling when she saw Dominic. He was sitting astride the open window, his back against the jamb with one booted foot upon the sill. Her smile wavered. It *was* Dominic, and yet…he looked slightly more modish than usual. The top-boots seemed to fit more snugly, the buckskins were a shade lighter. His riding jacket was just as tightly fitting, but the buttons were larger and his neckcloth was a froth of white folds. His dark hair glowed like a raven's wing in the sunlight, but it had obviously been cut by a master. The eyes were a shade lighter, more blue than grey, and his face, that beautiful face with its smooth planes and lean jawline, was just too perfect. On both sides. Her hands flew to her mouth.

'You must be Lord Markham.'

With a laugh he swung himself into the room and came towards her, tossing his hat, gloves and crop on to a chair. 'How do you do—no, no, none of that.' He reached out and caught her hand, pulling her up as she sank into a curtsy. 'I should be saluting *you*, fair Minerva!'

He bowed over her hand and she chuckled, even as he placed a kiss upon her fingers.

'I am merely the librarian, my lord.'

'You are not merely anything. You are important enough to be invited to the ball.' His eyes were laughing at her, joyous, carefree, with none of the sadness she detected in his brother. He continued. 'You are Miss Pentewan, are you not? My sister told me all about you when she wrote.'

Her cheeks grew hot. 'There is nothing to tell.'

'No?'

It was impossible not to warm to the viscount. His likeness to Dominic would have endeared him to her in any event, but she found his charm irresistible and she responded, quite at her ease, 'No. I am merely going about my business here.'

'That in itself is unusual. A female in the library.'

'I am very grateful to Major Coale for the opportunity.'

'Sal speaks very highly of you.'

'She is most kind.'

She could think of nothing more to say, and with a little smile of apology she went back to tidying away the books.

'I hear my brother is improved a great deal.'

'You have not seen him yet?'

'No. I have only just arrived and was taking a look around the house when I heard you singing.'

'Then I beg your pardon for distracting you.'

'I was not distracted, I was enchanted.'

The compliment came easily to his lips and she giggled. 'I think you are trying to charm me, my lord.'

'Would you object to that?'

She considered the question. 'That depends upon your reason for doing so. If it is purely to put me at my ease, then, no, but if your intention is more mischievous then I do object, most strongly.'

His brows lifted. 'Straight talking, madam.'

'But necessary, sir. I may be an employee, but I am not to be imposed upon. I would not want to fall out with you.'

He laughed. 'Nor I with you, Miss Pentewan. I shall treat you with the utmost respect.'

Her lips twitched. 'Very well, my lord, then I beg you will leave me to finish tidying this library.'

'Oho, am I to be dismissed summarily?'

Zelah could not suppress a smile. She was beginning to enjoy herself. 'You are indeed, sir. You said yourself you have only this minute arrived. You should make your presence known to Major Coale. You will find your way lies through those doors, which lead to the salon and then to the great hall.'

He was laughing down at her, not at all offended by her dismissal. She was struck again by the similarity between the brothers, both tall, broad-shouldered and dark-haired, and although there was more laughter in the viscount's eyes she was reminded of Dominic every time she looked at him. Perhaps that was why she felt so little restraint with the viscount. He gave a little bow.

'Very well, Miss Pentewan, I shall leave you to your books.'

He sauntered off, whistling, and Zelah went back to work, her spirits lifted even further.

When the party from West Barton arrived Zelah made her way to the suite of rooms set aside for her sister and brother-in-law, where she received a warm welcome. A footman was despatched to the tower with the small trunk containing Zelah's evening clothes, but she did not immediately follow and instead asked Reginald about the charter.

'I think it proves the case for the villagers, but I don't plan to tell anyone about it until we get to the hearing next week. Sir Oswald's lawyer is as cunning as a fox.' He frowned. 'I understand Evanshaw is expected here tonight. I don't deny it goes against the grain to meet the fellow on friendly terms.'

'Well, I don't know how I shall look at the man,' exclaimed Maria, 'when I think how roughly he has treated anyone wandering into Prickett Wood, even catching Nicky—'

'That was his bailiff, Mama, and I came to no harm.' Nicky came running in at that moment and threw his arms around Zelah, who hugged him back.

'No, because your aunt and the major were on hand to rescue you,' retorted Maria, who could not bear the thought of any danger to her child.

'Now, now, my love, if Evanshaw thinks people are trespassing he is perfectly entitled to put a stop to it,' said Reginald mildly. 'I admit I cannot like the man, but I do agree with Coale, it does not do to fall out with a neighbour if it can be avoided.'

Zelah could not listen to more because Nicky demanded that she come and look at the room that had been allocated to him and his baby brother.

'Major Coale says I can watch the dancing from the landing,' he told her. 'And he is going to send up supper for me.'

'The major has been very kind,' declared Maria. 'Having this apartment means I will be able to slip away and feed the baby and then return for the dancing.'

'Will there be ices, do you think?' asked Nicky, his eyes wide.

'Alas, no,' laughed Zelah. 'However, there will be little pastries and definitely lemonade, because I have already had some.'

'So you will have a little party all of your own,' said Maria, scooping up Nicky and kissing him soundly. 'Now we must not keep Zelah, she has to change. I have already sent Bess to your room, my love. She will help you get ready.'

Zelah protested, but only half-heartedly. She wanted to look her best tonight and she knew that Bess would be able to dress her hair far better than she would be able to manage alone.

By the time she arrived back at the tower room the maid had emptied the trunk and laid out everything upon the bed.

'Oh.' Zelah stopped. 'That is not my dress.'

Bess curtsied. 'The mistress bought it for you, miss. She said this ball is the biggest event of the summer and she wanted you to have something new. It's Indian muslin,' she added, helping Zelah out of her grey gown. 'And madam thought the green bodice would suit your colouring. I hope you aren't displeased?'

'How could I be?' She fingered the filmy skirts, then,

looking up, her eyes fell upon a little cup full of rosebuds on the desk. 'Oh!'

'The mistress picked them from the garden today,' explained Bess. 'She sent them over specially for me to put in amongst your curls.'

Zelah wondered if she should protest at such frivolity. After all, if she was going to be a governess should she not put herself above such worldly considerations? But her doubts were quickly suppressed. Her work at Rooks Tower was coming to an end and this might be her last opportunity to dance. And besides, she wanted to see if she would win a look of warm admiration from a pair of sombre grey eyes.

She looked at her maid and allowed a smile to burst forth. 'Well, Bess, will you help me to get ready?'

The chiming of a distant clock reminded Zelah that it was time for the dinner guests to meet in the drawing room. She left her temporary bedchamber and made her way downstairs. Her route lay through the empty salon and she could not avoid seeing her reflection in the mirrors as she crossed the room. She stopped and moved closer to one of the mirrors. There was no hint of the bookish librarian in the elegant stranger she saw there, with her hair piled up and white rosebuds nestling amongst the curls. Her neck and shoulders rose gracefully from a short green velvet bodice that was ornamented at the neck and wrist with twisted white-and-gold braid. The low neckline fell to a point at the centre of the bosom and the braid continued down the front of the muslin skirts. It gave the illusion of height and she smiled to herself. She looked almost as willowy as the elegant models on the fashionplates. She flicked open her new spangled fan and held it before her, experimenting with different poses. When she held it across the lower part of her face her eyes appeared to sparkle invitingly.

The sound of the door opening made her jump and a guilty flush heated her cheeks.

'I beg your pardon, I did not mean to startle you.' Dominic stood in the doorway.

'I—there is no mirror in the tower room....' Her words trailed off. She knew she must sound very conceited.

'You look very well.' He cleared his throat. 'Everyone else is in the drawing room. I was merely coming to check that the salon and the library were in order. The orchestra will be setting up in here while we are at dinner.'

He seemed ill at ease, whereas Zelah's fine new clothes gave her an added confidence.

'I have just come through the library, Major, and I can assure you there is not a book out of place.'

'No, of course.' He seemed to battle with himself for a moment before meeting her eyes. 'Very well, then, shall we join the others?'

He held out his arm to her. Zelah placed her fingers on his sleeve. She could feel the ribbing of the wool-and-silk fabric through her glove. Expensive. Everything about his coat—the sheen of the material, the fit, the exquisite cut—it all shouted quality. Tonight he was every inch a viscount's son.

And she was a parson's daughter, an encumbrance that he was trying to marry off by inviting her to his ball. Had he not said as much?

The silence was uncomfortable and she searched for something to say as they crossed the hall.

'I met your brother earlier. He came into the library.'

'I know. He said you had given him his marching orders.'

'I hope he did not think me uncivil. I tried very hard not to be.'

'No, but you surprised him.' A glancing smile touched his lips. 'He is not accustomed to being turned away.'

As the footman jumped to open the door, Dominic released her arm and allowed her to precede him into the drawing room. It was filled with a chattering, glittering crowd and Zelah knew a moment's panic, but it subsided when Sally Hensley came forward to meet her.

'My dear, how charming you look. I have just been talking to your sister. She is over there by the window, but you can find her later. First I want to introduce you to everyone....'

It was not to be a large dinner, a mere ten couples were sitting down, but that was more than a dozen new people for Zelah to meet and remember their names. She realised Sally had chosen the company with care, they were all close friends of Dominic or family. No one to stare or comment upon his scarred face.

At dinner she found herself beside one of Dominic's army colleagues. Colonel Deakin was a jovial, bewhiskered gentleman who lost no time in telling her that he had served with Dominic in the Peninsula. He patted his empty sleeve.

'Wasn't long in following him home, too! I'll not complain, though, my wife and I have settled into a nice little house in Taunton and she says she's glad to have me under her feet all day, even if I only have the one good arm.' He raised his glass at the plump little woman sitting opposite, who twinkled back at him and addressed herself to Zelah.

'I'm lucky to have him and I thank the Lord for it, every day.'

Colonel Deakin chuckled. He leaned a little closer to

Zelah, lowering his voice. 'And I'm pleased to see Coale looking so well. He was a good officer. Thought we might lose him, y'know.'

'Was he very badly injured?'

'Barely recognisable,' replied the colonel, cheerfully helping himself to a large slice of raised pie. 'Fortunately we had a good sawbones who patched him up pretty well, but even then when we sent him off to England I never really expected to see him again. Pity about his face, of course. He was a dashed handsome fellow.'

Zelah glanced to the head of the table, where Dominic was engaged in conversation with his brother. With the two of them together she had no need to try to imagine how Dominic had looked before he went to war, but the scars mattered very little to her now.

By the time the guests left the dining room the first carriages were pulling up on the drive. Zelah and Maria went off to tidy themselves before the ball and Zelah took the opportunity of thanking Maria for her gown.

'With the fan, and new shoes and gloves—it is all too much. How I wish you had not spent your money on me, Maria.'

'Oh, tush! If you will not think of yourself, then please think of what my feelings must be on the occasion. Reginald is highly respected here and I would not have it thought that we could not afford to dress you.'

Zelah hugged her sister, tears starting to her eyes. 'Then I will accept it all very gratefully, my love. Thank you, dearest sister!'

Maria had to stay to feed the baby, so Zelah made her way back downstairs alone. The great hall and the salon were already full and she saw Dominic greeting his guests. She thought she had never seen him look better.

His black frock coat, tight-fitting breeches and stockings only accentuated his powerful physique. Now he was no longer limping his movements were graceful and assured, those of a man at the peak of his physical power. Dragging her eyes away, she spotted Reginald talking to Sir Arthur Andrews and on the far side of the room stood Sir Oswald Evanshaw, resplendent in a lime-green coat. She descended the final few steps and was caught up in the crowd. Almost immediately Dominic was at her side.

'I was looking out for you.'

'You were?'

Her spirits soared, only to plummet at his next words.

'Yes. Lerryn has not arrived yet. I have given instructions that if he turns up he is not to come in until I have had a word with him.' He touched her arm. 'Do not worry. He will do nothing to harm you.'

She murmured her thanks and watched him walk away. The harm was already done. Dominic knew what she was. Sally came up and took her hand.

'You are looking very pensive, Zelah. I hope everyone is being kind to you?'

'Oh, yes, in all the noise and confusion no one has time or inclination to question too deeply why Major Coale should invite his librarian to the summer ball. Indeed, most have no idea of my identity, and I think the guests who were at dinner merely look upon me as a poor little dab of a girl who is on the receiving end of the major's charity.'

Sally laughed. 'Oh, no, my dear, you are much more important than that! All Dom's friends know he was becoming a positive recluse. When he moved to Rooks Tower we thought we had lost him but now, barely six months later, he is holding the most important local gathering of the summer.'

'But I had nothing to do with this—' Zelah protested.

'You taught him that he is still a person worthy of note,' Sally cut in. 'He told me as much. We all owe you a great deal.'

Zelah saw her chance. 'Then perhaps I could ask a favour of you,' she said. 'Would you be kind enough to supply me with a reference? I am sure a good word from yourself would mean a great deal to any future employer.'

'Oh, my dear, you are looking so lovely tonight that I am sure you will have no need of a *reference*—'

'But I *will*.' A note of desperation crept into Zelah's voice. 'My work here is almost done and I have had a very favourable enquiry from a widow in Bath. She has three children in need of a governess and has asked me to provide references. My father has offered one, and Reginald, but they are family and therefore not as valuable... I would be most obliged if you would provide one for me.'

Sally squeezed her hands. 'I will, of course, Zelah, if that is what you wish. But on one condition.'

'Anything!' was Zelah's grateful response.

'That you forget all about being a governess for tonight and enjoy yourself!' Bestowing an airy kiss upon Zelah's cheek, she dashed off to greet more guests.

When the music began Zelah moved to one side of the room. She knew so few people that she had little expectation of dancing, although, with Sally's words still ringing in her head she did hope that Dominic might claim her hand later in the evening. That could not be for some time, of course, because there were many ladies with whom he must stand up first. She watched him from the side of the room. He strode proudly through the crowds, seemingly unaware of his scarred face and because he took no note of it, most of his guests did the same. She was aware of one or two sly looks, the odd hesitation when someone was introduced to him, but she saw no signs of the repulsion Dominic had feared would mar his return to society. She was glad, for his sake.

'Zelah.' Timothy Lerryn was beside her. 'You need not look daggers at me,' he muttered savagely. 'I have already been warned not to importune you.'

'Then there is no reason why we should not be civil to one another.'

'Will you dance with me?'

'Thank you, I would rather not.'

His face darkened. They were surrounded by people and she did not wish to quarrel openly with him. She said pointedly, 'My sister tells me your wife is expecting a happy event soon. That must be cause for celebration.'

'Yes. Thank you. It will be our third child.' His smile remained, but there was a spiteful note in his voice as he added, 'My wife breeds like a sow. We expect no still births in *our* family.'

Zelah's hands went immediately to her stomach, as if to protect herself from the cruel blow. Feeling sick and disgusted, she turned away, grateful to hear her brother-in-law's cheerful voice close at hand.

'There you are, my dear. Maria is not yet downstairs so I shall carry you off to dance in her stead.'

'I'll dance with you, Reginald, with pleasure!' Zelah accepted with alacrity and went off, determined to forget Timothy Lerryn.

Despite his duties as host, Dominic found his eyes drawn constantly to Zelah. He watched her dance with her brother-in-law, then Colonel Deakin led her out, and finally Jasper.

Dominic watched his brother taking Zelah down the dance. How had he ever thought her an insignificant little thing? She was the most elegant woman in the room. Her only ornament was the string of fine pearls around her neck, but she outshone the other ladies with their flashing jewels. He was standing beside Lady Andrews, who saw his concentrated gaze and gave a little chuckle.

'Lord Markham appears quite taken with young Miss Pentewan. I am not well acquainted with her, but she seems a pleasant, well-mannered gel.' There was a pause. 'She is employed here, I understand, as your archivist?'

'That is correct, ma'am.'

'How unusual. And, may I say, very daring.'

'Oh?' He frowned. 'How is that? Why do you call it daring?'

Lady Andrews fluttered her fan nervously. 'Oh well, perhaps I am old-fashioned,' she tittered. 'Sir Arthur says he sees no objection, but to have an unmarried lady employed in a bachelor's establishment...'

'I have several housemaids working here. They are unmarried—do you consider them at risk, too?' he countered bluntly.

'Oh, no, no, Major, of course not—' She broke off, flustered, then gathered herself and came back to say brightly, 'And you have your sister staying here, so there can be no objection, can there?'

Dominic forced himself to smile before he moved away. He had known from the outset there would be gossip, but he had ignored the voice of caution and hired the girl, wanting only to help her. He had thought only the meanest of tabbies would consider there was anything improper in the situation. After all, she did not live at Rooks Tower and he had a house full of female servants, so there should be no question of impropriety. Yet if he was honest with himself, Dominic knew that he had failed to keep a proper distance between himself and his employee. By God, if anyone found out he had kissed her! He knew his world, it fed upon sordid intrigue and gossip—that was the reason he had refused to give her a reference: the more glowing his recommendation, the greater the belief that she was his mistress.

Dominic nodded to one acquaintance, threw a brief word to another, but continued to move through the crowd, his thoughts distracted. Hell and damnation, he had no wish to ruin the chit. The work in the library was all but complete now. He would end her employment before Sally left Rooks Tower.

Chapter Thirteen

Dancing with Lord Markham set the seal on Zelah's success at the ball. After that there was no shortage of young gentlemen begging for the pleasure of leading her out. She whirled from one partner to the next in a heady round of gaiety, but her enjoyment was cut short when she left the floor at the end of one dance to find her way blocked by Timothy Lerryn. He bowed elegantly and held out his hand.

'Dance with me once,' he coaxed her. 'For old time's sake.'

There was no escape. The matrons on the nearby benches were all smiling and nodding encouragement, pleased to see the young people so enjoying themselves.

She could declare that she would dance no more that evening, but Dominic had not yet asked her to dance, and she desperately hoped he would do so before the end of the ball. Putting up her chin, she gave Timothy a challenging look. 'One dance,' she told him. 'No more.'

Triumph gleamed in his eyes as he led her back to the floor. While they waited for the other couples to take their place in the set he leaned towards her.

'Have I told you how well you are looking tonight, my dear? Quite beautiful.'

She ignored his compliment and returned only short answers to his remarks as they went down the dance, impatient for the ordeal to end. But even when she made him a final curtsy he took her hand and placed it on his arm.

'You sister and her husband are over there, I shall escort you to them.'

Zelah merely inclined her head, keeping as much distance as she could between them. A moment later he spoke again.

'By heaven.' He raised his quizzing glass. 'Who is that fellow in the lime-green coat, talking to Buckland?'

Zelah shifted her gaze. Reginald was standing beside Maria's chair, looking very much like a terrier guarding a bone.

'That is Sir Oswald Evanshaw.'

Even as they watched, Maria rose from her chair and Reginald swept her off towards the door.

'Well, well, they have cut him dead!' He stopped. 'No point in taking you over there now, your sister and brother have gone off to the supper room, I suppose. So what do you say to one more dance?'

'No.' She tried to pull her hand free. 'Release me, if you please.'

'If you will not dance, then I shall escort you in to supper.'

She could smell the brandy on his breath as he leaned closer. She tugged again at her hand. 'Let me go,' she hissed. 'You have been warned.'

He leered at her, a reckless look in his eyes. 'Coale can do nothing to me if you come with me willingly.'

'But the lady does not want your company.' With relief she heard Dominic's voice behind her. 'I suggest you leave now, Mr Lerryn.'

Dominic spoke very softly, but there was no mistaking the menace in his tone.

Lerryn glared at him for a moment, his jaw working, then he flung himself away, shouldering his way through the crowd.

Zelah closed her eyes and released a long, grateful sigh. 'Thank you.' She put out her hand and he took it in a warm, reassuring grip.

'I did not expect him to stay so long. His attachment to you must be stronger than you thought.'

She shuddered. 'His attachment is nothing more than pique, the desire to have the unobtainable.'

'We are all guilty of that,' muttered Dominic. He pulled her hand on to his sleeve. 'Come. Let us go to supper. My sister is waiting for you there.'

Timothy Lerryn lounged out of the salon. Damn the chit, who was she to set herself up against him? He would show her! He had half a mind to tell her story now, to anyone who would listen. But his brain was not so befuddled that he had forgotten Major Coale's quiet threats when he had arrived. They had been issued in a cold, matter-of-fact tone that was much more effective than any blustering arguments and he did not doubt that if word of Zelah's past got out the major would indeed hunt him down and ruin him. Well, the slut was not worth the risk. Seething with frustration he set off across the great hall.

He had almost reached the door when a flash of bright green caught his eye and another idea came into his sly brain. He stopped, stepping back and across to put himself in the way of his quarry.

'Sir Oswald.' He bowed. 'Timothy Lerryn, at your

service. I wonder if I might have a word with you. There is something I think you should know...'

In the supper room Zelah found her sister sitting with Sally Hensley while Reginald paced up and down behind them.

'He is still fretting over his words with Sir Oswald,' Maria explained when Zelah came up with Dominic.

'Aye, blast his eyes, the man came bang up to me to say that his men had found Giles Grundy on his land and sent him home with a broken arm. Then he had the effrontery to suggest the hearing next week was as good as settled!' Reginald scowled blackly. 'He thinks he has Sir Arthur in his pocket, but when I show them that new document—!'

'Yes, dear, now sit down, do and calm yourself.' Maria shook her head at him. 'The man is indeed a scoundrel, but we will not stoop to his level. I will visit the Grundys tomorrow and offer what help I can and you will use the law against Sir Oswald.'

'I'll ride over, too,' said Dominic, holding a chair for Zelah. 'I can spare some of my men from the woodcutting if Grundy needs help on his farm. Now if you will excuse me—'

'Are you not going to eat with us?' asked Sally.

Dominic shook his head. 'I promised a certain young man he would have some supper. So I am going to take it to him!'

The last dance had ended and the salon was rapidly clearing. Dominic looked for Zelah, but she was nowhere to be seen. Perhaps she had gone off with Jasper to the drawing room. He and his twin had made a habit of that in their younger days, seeking out the prettiest girls and carrying them off at the end of the evening to engage in a desperate flirtation.

Dominic tugged at his neckcloth. It was all he could do not to go storming off to find them. Instead he forced himself to remain outwardly calm as the last of his guests took their leave. He escorted them out to the drive and watched the final carriages rattle away until the silence of the summer night was restored. For once there was no wind to freshen the balmy air, the moon rode high in the cloudless sky, dimming the stars and bathing everything in a silver blue light. After the clamour of the evening, the peaceful calm was soothing and he did not want to return to the house immediately. He set off across the grass rather than have the scrunching of the gravel under his feet disturb the night.

Even before the ball was over, Maria was congratulating Zelah on her success. She began to talk of having a small gathering at West Barton.

'Nothing as grand as this of course, but we could perhaps invite one or two of the gentlemen who danced with you...'

Zelah stopped her. 'I know what is in your mind, Maria, you think to persuade one of those eligible gentlemen to offer for me.' Timothy Lerryn's scowling image rose up before her. 'I do not *want* a husband.'

She read the determination in her sister's face and made her excuses to walk away. The orchestra was playing the last dance of the evening and she could see Dominic partnering his sister. There was no chance now that he would dance with her and Zelah slipped quietly away to her room.

There were no curtains or shutters on the windows and the moonlight flooded in on all sides, making candles unnecessary, but it was oppressively hot. She wanted to be out of doors, but that was impossible. It was the middle of the night and not safe for anyone to be wandering around alone, especially a young lady. She remembered the flat roof above her. That surely would be safe enough. Quickly she slipped out of the room and up the stairs.

Zelah stepped out on to the roof. She gazed about her, entranced. It was a magical world, all grey and blue moonshadows. She paced around, her slippered feet making no sound on the stone slabs. It was easier to think up here, for the rest of the world seemed very far away and somehow less important. There had been no lack of partners this evening, she had enjoyed the dancing and for a short time she had felt like a carefree girl again. That was what she had hoped for, wasn't it? A few hours of enjoyment before she settled down to the sober existence of a governess.

She gazed out at the distant moors, silver under the moonlight. She would not deceive herself, she had hoped for more. She had wanted Dominic to dance with her. It was too much to hope that he would flirt with her, as his brother had done, bringing a flush to her cheeks with his cheerful nonsense, but she had thought perhaps he might compliment her upon her appearance.

She wrapped her arms across her chest as a huge wave of anger and futility welled up. She wished there had been no summer ball, that the world had remained shut out of Dominic's life.

That she could have kept him to herself.

It was a despicable thought and she quickly dismissed it. She did not want Dominic to be a sad, lonely recluse. He needed to take his place in society, even if that meant he had little time for her.

And what did that matter? She would not be here much

longer. The books were all in order now and in another few weeks the cataloguing would be finished. She really must remind Sally to write her a reference and make efforts to secure another position, although she knew that nothing could compare to being at Rooks Tower.

'What the devil are you doing here?'

She jumped as Dominic's angry words cut through the night. 'I—I beg your pardon. I did not think there could be any harm...'

'Harm? Foolish girl, you know the stonework is unsound. Come away from that wall.'

His anger sliced into her like a knife. Not for her the soft, civil tone he used for his guests. Just because she had been allowed to attend his summer ball she must not think herself anything other than a servant. The unhappiness within her tightened into a hard knot.

'I had not forgotten. I am sorry. I shall not come here again—'

She ran for the stairs, but as she passed him his hand shot out, gripping her arm. He was not wearing gloves and she could feel the heat of his fingers through the thin sleeve.

'Wait. There are tears on your cheek.'

She turned her head away from him. 'Please, let me go.'

Instead he pulled her closer, putting one hand under her chin and forcing her to look up at him. The moonlight glinted in his eyes, twin devils sent to mock her. Gently he wiped her tears away with his thumb.

'Has someone been unkind to you tonight?'

'N-no.' It was a struggle to speak with more tears ready to fall.

He said roughly, 'Perhaps you are regretting sending Lerryn away.'

'You know that is not so!'

'Then why are you crying?'

'I—um—I am just…very tired.'

How could she tell him the truth? His eyes bored into her and she prayed he would not read her thoughts. At last he looked up at the moon, letting his breath go in a long sigh.

'Yes, it has been a long day.' He pulled her close and enfolded her in his arms. She did not resist, it was the most natural thing in the world to allow herself to lean against him. 'It has been quite exhausting, having so many people in the house.'

'Did you not enjoy it?' she murmured the words into his coat.

'I did, after a fashion. It is good to know I am not a pariah, a social outcast.' His arms tightened. 'And it is you I have to thank for that, Zelah. You made me see that all was not lost.'

'Then…then you are not angry with me?'

'Angry? No. I was worried lest you lean on the parapet and the stonework should give way.'

'Oh.'

It was a spark of comfort. The tiny flame warmed her heart. She let herself relax against him, her cheek against his shoulder. His breath ruffled her curls, softer than the night breeze.

'I am pleased I could help,' she murmured.

'And now I shall do something for you. Sally told me you had asked her to recommend you. With her support I have no doubt that we can find you a suitable post. I was talking to her earlier—are you set upon becoming a governess? Because we thought perhaps you might find the role of companion more to your taste. Sally has many contacts.'

The little flame flickered and died.

'You are very kind, Major.' Steeling herself, she pushed away from him. 'I should go in now.'

Dominic caught her fingers. His body was alive, aroused and he wanted to succumb to the attraction he felt for her, to seduce her here on this moonlit terrace far above the everyday world. He could do it, too. She had responded to him before, and here, with the darkness to hide his face, why should it not happen again? But she was pulling away from him and he could still see the trace of tears on her cheeks. He buried his own desires and squeezed her hands.

'Of course. It is very late.'

For a brief moment her fingers clung to his. Perhaps she wanted comfort, but he was not the one to give it. He would do nothing that she might regret in the morning. He said formally, 'Goodnight, Miss Pentewan.'

Without a word she walked away, her figure a pale blur on the stairs before she disappeared from his sight. There. It was done. He had saved her. From himself, possibly from her own weakness.

Why, then, did he feel no pleasure in his chivalrous deed?

Zelah did not sleep well and was relieved when the morning came and she could leave the tower room and go in search of her sister and brother-in-law. She found them at breakfast, being entertained by Sally and Lord Markham.

'Dominic has already gone out,' explained the viscount, rising to escort her to her chair. 'Taking his duties far too seriously, if you ask me. He should be here looking after his guests.'

'But he knows he can rely upon us for that.' Sally beamed at Zelah across the table. 'So you are to leave us this morning and go back to West Barton. What shall I do without my little companion?'

'Any number of things, I should imagine.' Zelah had lost all her shyness with Sally and treated her in the same friendly manner as her own sister. 'But perhaps before I leave this morning you will write a reference for me, as we agreed?'

'By all means, if that is what you wish.'

Zelah nodded, saying firmly. 'It is, madam.'

'I have a great deal to do before the hearing next Friday,' said Reginald. 'How soon can you be ready to travel, Zelah?'

'Hannah has already packed for me.' She pushed her plate away. 'I can leave as soon as Mrs Hensley has furnished me with my reference.'

'Then I shall go off and write it now,' said Sally, smiling.

'Well, I need to feed Baby before we can set off,' put in Maria. 'It will be at least another hour.'

A sudden burst of sunlight filled the room, making everything jewel bright and sending glittering rays bouncing off the breakfast silver.

'Ah, the sun is making an appearance.' The viscount put down his napkin and looked at Zelah. 'Perhaps Miss Pentewan would care to take a stroll around the grounds with me until the carriage is called?'

Zelah assented readily. The viscount was an entertaining companion and, knowing her heart was in no danger, Zelah could relax and enjoy his company. She encouraged him to talk about his brother, hoarding each little nugget of information. Jasper's revelations only confirmed her impression of Dominic. Honest, loyal and honourable, a man determined to do his duty.

'And now he is throwing his energies into Rooks Tower,' said Jasper as they reached the orangery. He opened the double doors and stood back for her to enter. 'I thought at first he wanted it merely as a retreat, to hide away from the world, but his holding a ball has made me think again. Perhaps he is intending this as a family home. What do you think, Miss Pentewan, is my brother on the look-out for a wife?'

The thought was a body blow to Zelah, robbing her of breath. She hoped it did not show in her face and she pretended to give her attention to looking about the summer house, admiring the arrangements of plants and marble while she considered her response. At last she said carefully, 'There were several very eligible young ladies here last night.'

'I know, I danced with them all,' he replied promptly. 'Dominic, on the other hand, danced with none. But perhaps he was just being cautious. He is not the sort to raise false hopes.'

'No. He is far too chivalrous for that.'

Jasper did not notice the bleak note in her voice. He merely nodded, gazing around him in admiration.

'Now, madam, you are to be congratulated. You have created here the perfect trysting place. Do you not find it most romantic?'

Zelah summoned up a smile. 'Not in the daylight, sir, I see only the empty glasses that the servants failed to clear away because they were hidden behind the plants.'

He looked pained. 'You are far too practical, my dear.'

'My besetting sin,' she told him cheerfully.

'You puzzle me, Miss Pentewan. Why do you resist all my attempts to flirt with you?'

His worried tone amused her and she gave him a mischievous look.

'Since you attempt to flirt with every young lady, my lord, it will do you no harm to be rebuffed occasionally.' She moved towards the door. 'Shall we go back to the house?'

Jasper was in no way discomposed by her response and they strolled back across the lawn in perfect accord. The entrance door was standing open and as they approached Dominic came out.

'Good morning, brother,' Jasper hailed him cheerfully. 'You were up and out before I had even shaved this morning!'

'I went to see Giles Grundy,' he replied shortly.

'Ah, yes, how is he?' asked Zelah.

'A little bruised, but he will mend. Doctor Pannell has set his arm—he says it is a clean break and should heal well.'

'And while you have been busy with your tenant, you have left me with the very agreeable business of entertaining your guests,' Jasper responded, putting his free hand over Zelah's where it rested on his sleeve.

Dominic shifted his stony gaze to Zelah. 'I have just ordered the carriage for your sister.'

She knew him well enough now to know he was angry about something, but she said calmly, 'Then I shall fetch my wrap.'

She moved past him into the great hall, wondering if he had received bad tidings. Poachers, perhaps, or news that Sir Oswald had destroyed more deer. She had not quite reached the top of the stairs when his gruff, furious words echoed off the walls.

'By heaven, Jasper, it is bad enough that you flirt with every woman you see. Must you also attempt to charm my librarian?'

Chapter Fourteen

~~~~~~~~~~~~

Librarian. Yes, that is all she was to him, thought Zelah as she sat in the tower room the next day, working at her ledgers. She tried to ignore the huge bed that still dominated the room, a constant reminder of her attendance at the summer ball. The weather had broken and the rain had fallen steadily all day. She saw no one save Mrs Graddon, who brought her a tray at noon, along with an invitation from Mrs Hensley to join the other guests in the drawing room later to play charades.

Zelah sent back her apologies. She had lost too much time already. She wanted to finish her work at Rooks Tower and be ready to take up the post in Bath, should her application be successful. Dominic had told her that Sally could find her a position with someone of her acquaintance, but Zelah wanted to sever all ties with Major Coale's family and had already sent off the required references to Bath.

She was relieved when at last she could return to West Barton, but even there the talk was still of the ball. Learning that Maria was in the nursery, she ran upstairs to find Nicky telling Nurse how exciting it had been.

'Major Coale brought me supper, and by sitting on the

edge of the landing I could hear what people said when they came into that little spot beneath the stairs.'

Maria threw up her hands. 'Lud, my son is an eaves-dropper! He now knows all the secrets of the village.'

'Devil a bit, Mama,' grinned Nicky. 'It was only Lord Markham telling one of the ladies that her eyes reminded him of the stars, and then Sir Oswald came over with—'

'Enough!' Maria put up her hand. 'It was very naughty of you to be listening, Nicholas, and you must say no more about it. Eavesdroppers will never hear any good of them-selves.' She turned her attention to her sister. 'Good eve-ning, Zelah. Did you get very wet walking home? I had hoped Major Coale or his sister would have the goodness to send you home in the carriage.'

'I slipped away without telling them.' Zelah recalled the shouts and laughter coming from the drawing room when she had crossed the empty hall. She raised her chin a little. 'It was never part of the agreement that the major should provide a carriage for me.'

'It was never part of the agreement that you should catch a chill,' retorted Maria. 'But never mind, it is done now and you are here safe. Mr Lerryn has sent word that he is resuming his journey to Bristol so we shall be able to enjoy a quiet family dinner together.'

Zelah uttered up a silent prayer. Dominic had assured her that she was safe from Timothy Lerryn, but it was still a relief to know he had quit Lesserton. It was one less problem to worry her.

When Zelah arrived at Rooks Tower the next morning her spirits were as leaden as the overcast sky. Two more weeks, three at the most, and she would be finished here. The library was just as she had left it, no sign that the major had been there to check her progress. She had the lowering suspicion that he was avoiding her.

She had not been working long before Sally Hensley burst into the room, saying impetuously, 'Oh good, you are here! I have come to say goodbye!'

'G-goodbye?' Zelah rose from her seat and was immediately enveloped in a scented embrace.

'Yes! I had planned to stay another two weeks at least, but I have today had a letter from my darling husband! Ben is well, and in England, and on his way to our house at Fellbridge. He may already be there, because his letter went to Markham and they have sent it on to me. I must go home immediately. I only hope this rain does not slow my journey. Oh, I cannot *wait* to see him again.'

'Yes, yes, of course. I am very happy for you.' Zelah barely had time to murmur her words before she was caught up again in another fierce hug.

'Thank you. I count you very much my friend now and I am very sorry to be leaving, but I shall write to you at West Barton—'

'I—I doubt I shall be there for much longer. My work here is almost finished. I hope to hear soon about the post in Bath.'

Sally regarded her for a moment, as if she would protest, but in the end she merely nodded. 'Very well, but if you take it you must let me know where you are. I do not want to lose touch with you now.'

Then, like a whirlwind, Sally was gone, leaving only silence and the faintest hint of perfume behind her.

Zelah resumed her seat and picked up her pen. It was unlikely they would ever meet again. Sally would be preoccupied with her husband for the next few weeks and by the time she was able to think about her new friend, Zelah hoped to be far away from Exmoor.

*   *   *

The rain persisted well into the afternoon, but about five o'clock there was a break in the weather. The sky was still a thick grey blanket, but Zelah decided she should set off for West Barton before there was another shower. She was just crossing the hall when she heard her name. Dominic was standing in the doorway of his study.

'Perhaps you will grant me a few minutes of your time before you go?'

'Yes, of course.'

He stood aside and allowed her to enter. The hearth was empty although the smell of wood smoke lingered in the air. There was a large desk by the window and two glass-fronted cupboards that housed the estate's papers. Everything was orderly, businesslike, as was the major's tone when he spoke.

'You have done an excellent job, organising my library. You are to be congratulated.'

'Thank you, sir. The catalogue of titles is almost complete, I shall begin the final section tomorrow—'

'That will not be necessary.'

She frowned. 'I do not understand you.'

He turned on his heel and walked across to the window. 'You have done enough, thank you. I will arrange for your final payment to be made. It will be brought to West Barton tomorrow.'

She blinked. 'You do not wish me to return to Rooks Tower?'

'That is correct.'

'But I have not finished!'

'You have done enough.'

She clutched her hands together. 'Are you—are you dissatisfied with me, with my work?'

'I have already said that is not the case.'

'But that does not make sense. It will take only a few more weeks—'

'No!' He swung back. 'Don't you understand? I am trying to protect your reputation. While my sister was here, there was a modicum of propriety, but now—'

'You never worried about that before.'

'That was an error. I should never have allowed you to work here.'

'You *invited* me to come here,' she retorted, anger beginning to mount.

'I know. It was wrong of me. I admit it.'

Beneath Zelah's annoyance was another emotion. Panic. He was sending her away. She would never see him again.

'Please,' she said quietly. 'Let me finish what I have started. If you are anxious for my reputation, I could have a maid in the library at all times—let Hannah attend me!'

'No. My mind is made up. This will be the last time you come to Rooks Tower.'

Her eyes searched his face, but his eyes were shuttered, withdrawn. He would not be moved.

The rumble of voices filtered through the door, but she barely noticed.

'Then will you not shake hands with me?' He looked as if her outstretched hand was a poisoned chalice and a strangled cry was wrenched from her. 'I thought we were friends!'

The stony look fled. 'Friends. We could never be that.' He reached for her. 'Zelah—' He broke off as the door opened and Reginald burst in.

'Coale—and Zelah. Thank God. Have you seen Nicky?'

Chapter Fifteen

Dominic's hands fell. He stared uncomprehending at Reginald Buckland, who had stormed into his study without so much as a knock. Then he saw the look of strain in the other man's face and he said sharply, 'What is it?'

'My son. He has gone missing. Because of the rain I sent my man to collect him from Netherby's house today, but the boy had already gone. The other boys said he had set off for home, but my man did not pass him on the road. I thought he might have come here.'

'I have not seen him, but he could have gone straight to the kitchens.' Dominic strode out of the room and barked an order, sending a footman scurrying away. A few minutes later he returned and Dominic went back to the study, frowning.

'No one has seen him. Could he have stopped off with friends?'

Reginald shook his head. 'I have checked that. I beg your pardon, if he is not here then I must get back…'

'Yes, let us get home with all speed,' said Zelah quickly.

'Wait.' Dominic caught Reginald's sleeve. 'You are on horseback?'

'Yes.'

'Then we will follow in my curricle.' He glanced at Zelah's pale face. 'I know it is a greater distance, but it will be almost as quick as walking and will leave you in a better state to support Mrs Buckland.'

His heart lurched. She looked utterly bewildered, and little wonder. A few moments' earlier he had been telling her he wanted nothing more to do with her.

He sent Reginald on his way and ordered his curricle to be brought round. When he returned to the study Zelah was still standing in the middle of the floor, clasping and unclasping her hands. He pushed her gently into a chair.

'Try not to worry, Nicky might well be home by now.'

'Yes, yes, of course.'

The curricle was soon at the door and Dominic drove his horses hard, praying that they would not meet anything in the narrow lanes. He stopped only once, to drop his groom off in Lesserton, with instructions to make enquiries at the local inns. Then it was off again at a breakneck pace. A swift glance showed him that Zelah was hanging on to the side of the carriage with one hand, the other clamped firmly over her bonnet. 'My apologies for the bumpy ride, ma'am.'

'Do not slow down on my account,' she told him. 'I, too, want to get to West Barton as soon as possible.'

When they reached West Barton a servant ran out to grab the horses' heads. Zelah jumped down before Dominic could run round to help. He followed her into the house, where the butler's careworn expression told them that the boy had not come home.

They were shown into the drawing room. Reginald was pacing up and down and Maria sat on a sofa with her head in her hands. When the door opened she flew out of her seat and threw herself into Zelah's arms, sobbing wildly.

Dominic looked at Reginald, who shook his head.

'No one has seen him. I have sent my people into the village to ask questions, but the answer is always the same. He was seen leaving the vicarage and walking out of the village in this direction, but then he disappeared.'

'I left orders for my woods to be searched,' said Dominic. 'Everyone at Rooks Tower is fond of the boy, they will make every effort to find him.'

'Oh, my poor child,' cried Maria. 'Where can he be?'

They sat in silence, until Maria pushed herself out of Zelah's arms.

'I am forgetting my duty,' she sniffed, taking out her handkerchief and wiping her eyes. 'You would like some refreshment, Major Coale. Tea, perhaps?'

'I think brandy might be preferable,' suggested Reginald.

When Dominic assented he rang the bell.

'I would like tea,' said Zelah, hoping her sister would find some comfort in the well-rehearsed ritual.

Conversation had been stilted as they waited for news. Every knock on the door heralded the return of another search party, but each time they had to report failure. The dinner hour had come and a place was laid for Dominic, but no one had much appetite. The hours passed. Maria dragged herself up, saying she must feed the baby and Dominic announced he would go.

'No, please, Major, stay,' Maria beseeched him. 'Stay at least until I return.'

He could not refuse, but the inaction irked him. By the

time Maria came back to the drawing room it was growing dark. He rose.

'I must get back, my groom is waiting for me in Lesserton. I will come over again in the morning, and if there is still no news we will work out a plan...'

There was a scratching at the door and the butler entered. He crossed the room, holding out a folded piece of paper to his master.

'Someone slipped this under the door, sir. I looked outside, but I could see no one.'

'Then go out and search the grounds,' barked Reginald, taking the note.

'Too late,' muttered Dominic, peering out of the window. 'They'll have gone away immediately.' He returned to the hearth and waited. Reginald's usually cheerful countenance became increasingly grim. 'Well?'

'What is it?' demanded Maria, her hands clasped to her breast. 'Tell us!'

Silently Reginald handed Dominic the note. 'Read it out, Coale, if you please.'

'If the Parents of a certain Young Man want to see him Alive again, then they will not be presenting any new evidence at the White Hart on Friday next. Neither will they make any effort to find him. If they comply with these instructions, the Young Man in question will be delivered to them, unharmed, on Sunday next.'

'Oh!' Maria's hands flew to her mouth.

'Evanshaw,' ground out Reginald. 'It has to be.' He drove his fist into his palm. 'But how did he know? He came up to me at the ball and mentioned the hearing. He was bragging that he could not lose, crowing so hard that I cannot believe he knew about the new document.'

'You told no one about it?' asked Dominic, pacing the room.

'No, of course not. I told you I wanted to keep it from that rascally lawyer Evanshaw has engaged.'

'And I mentioned it to no one at Rooks Tower,' muttered Dominic. 'No one outside this room knew of it.'

'Mr Lerryn.' Zelah put her hands to her white cheeks. 'Timothy Lerryn was here when we brought over the manuscript.'

'By heaven, you are right,' declared Reginald, horror dawning in his eyes. 'He asked me about the case, while we took brandy together after dinner.'

'And I pointed out Sir Oswald to him at the ball,' whispered Zelah. 'He must have warned him.' She turned her eyes, dark with horror, towards Dominic. 'It is all my fault. This is his revenge upon me...'

Dominic saw the bewildered looks bent on Zelah and he said abruptly, 'Lerryn tried to impose upon Zelah. I sent him packing. If it is anyone's fault, it is mine for allowing him into my house in the first place!'

Reginald shook his head. 'Never mind that now, what are we going to do?'

Maria jumped up and gripped his arm. 'You must go to Sir Arthur now, Reginald. He is the magistrate, he can get a party together and go to Lydcombe Park—'

'That will not work,' put in Dominic. 'Sir Oswald will deny everything.'

'But it *must* be his doing,' protested Zelah. 'We could search Lydcombe—'

Dominic shook his head. 'You may be sure the boy will not be hidden anywhere on Evanshaw's land.'

Maria looked at each of them in turn, her eyes wide with apprehension. 'Will he keep his word, do you think? Will he return Nicky to us if we do as he says?'

Reginald rubbed a hand across his brow. 'Why should

he not? Once the hearing is concluded it will be too late to change anything.'

'But we cannot just sit here,' declared Zelah.

Reginald snatched the note from Dominic's hand and waved it at her, his eyes bleak with despair. 'It says if we try to find him—' He broke off, swallowing. 'I dare not do anything.'

The sound of voices in the hall caught their attention. Maria leapt up as the door opened, only to slump back again when she saw Jasper. He was dressed for riding, his spurs jingling cheerfully as he walked in.

'Lord Markham!' Reginald sounded more hopeful.

Jasper nodded to the assembled company as he began to strip off his gloves.

'I was out looking for your boy when I came across Sawley.' He glanced round as the groom followed him into the room, having stopped to wipe his boots thoroughly before entering the house. Jasper fixed his eyes on Dominic. 'He was rushing here on foot, so I thought it might be important and took him up behind me.'

Jem dragged his hat off and twisted it between his hands.

'I thought to see you on the road, sir, seein' as you hadn't got to the White Hart an' I wanted to tell you as soon as maybe.' No one spoke, no one even moved while he paused to wipe his face with a red handkerchief. 'I did what you said, sir, and took myself off to the Three Tuns for some home-brewed.' He grimaced. 'Rough place, it is, but I pulled me cap down over me face and settled in a corner of the taproom. Anyway, one or two of Sir Oswald's people was in there, drinking, when a man comes in looking for Miller, the bailiff. Said he had some gaming cocks for him. "He's gone off to see 'is brother," says one, only to have 'is foot stamped on by his mate, which shut him up. "Well, that's odd," says the man. "When I saw 'im the night afore last he said he'd be 'ere to take these birds off me hands." Well, there was some mutterings and shifty looks, and it struck me as a pretty rum do.' Jem rubbed his nose, his brow wrinkled in concentration. 'They all left soon after, so I took meself off to the High Street to see old Mother Tawton, the washerwoman. Regular gossip, she is, and knows everything about everyone around Lesserton. It being a warm evening I found her sitting in her doorway, smoking her pipe. She told me that Miller's brother runs a tavern down at Beston Quay. And according to Mother Tawton, that's who supplies Sir Oswald with his brandy and tea.'

'Smugglers,' declared Reginald.

'Most likely they wouldn't be above aiding a kidnap, too,' muttered Dominic.

Reginald rubbed his chin. 'But that is what, thirty... forty miles away. Would they take the boy that far?'

'If Evanshaw is involved, he wouldn't risk hiding the boy locally,' said Jasper. 'We should take a look.'

'Yes, yes!' cried Maria. 'You must go there this minute, Reginald.'

'Yes, we—' Reginald stopped, his animated look replaced by one of wretchedness. 'But it won't work. You saw the note, Coale. He threatens the boy if we try to find him. Our hands are tied.'

Dominic handed the paper to Jasper.

'*Yours* may be,' he said slowly, 'but mine are not. No one will be any the wiser if I am gone from Rooks Tower for a day or two, and you can make sure you are seen in Lesserton, to allay suspicion.'

Jasper immediately spoke up. 'I shall come with you, Brother.'

Reginald shook his head. 'No, no, I cannot let you do it. If Evanshaw finds out—'

Zelah put her hand on his arm. 'What is the alternative?'

His shoulders drooped. 'We let Evanshaw redraw the boundary. The villagers lose their land. And I will have spent a great deal of money I could not afford bringing the lawyer down from London for nothing.'

'But we will have our son back.' Maria's voice broke and she dropped her face in her hands again.

'But if he is at Beston,' said Dominic, 'and we can bring him back safe before the hearing?'

'I think it is worth an attempt.' Jasper nodded.

'But it is not your son's life at stake,' retorted Reginald, strain beginning to take its toll of his nerves.

'True,' said Dominic, 'but what guarantee do you have that Evanshaw will keep his word and return the boy?' The awful reality of his words hung in the silence. He continued urgently, 'Let us try this, Buckland. If Nicky is not there, we have lost nothing. If he is…'

'Oh, yes,' sobbed Maria. 'Yes, Major, please try. I only wish I could go with you. My poor little boy will be so frightened.'

'I will go, if you will provide me with a horse.'

Zelah's words were quietly spoken and Dominic thought he had misheard until Jasper protested.

'No, Miss Pentewan, there is no call for that.'

'Nicky may need me,' she said simply. 'He is a little boy, snatched away from his home and everything he knows. He will be very frightened.'

Dominic shook his head. 'Out of the question,' he said curtly. 'It is far too dangerous.'

He found Zelah's agonised gaze fixed upon him.

'Please,' she whispered, 'let me do this. Nicky is like my own son. To lose him…'

He read the anguish in her eyes and suddenly he understood: she was racked with guilt. About Lerryn, Nicky's disappearance—about her own stillborn child. His judgement said she should not go, but he could not deny her.

'We will be riding hard,' he warned.

She returned his look, her own hazel eyes now steady and unafraid. 'I am used to that, and thanks to your sister I have had some practice these past weeks.'

She looked pale but resolute and Dominic's heart swelled. Her spirit was indomitable.

'Sal has left Portia at Rooks Tower,' put in Jasper. 'I will have her saddled up for you. And we will need to leave at dawn.'

Zelah nodded.

'My habit is still at Rooks Tower, I will come back with you now.' She went to her sister. 'You and Reginald must convince Sir Oswald that you are complying with his demands, Maria. Do not worry, if Nicky is at Beston Quay we will find him.'

Maria hugged her tightly. 'Bring him back safely, Zelah.'

Dominic felt better now that they had a plan. He turned to Reginald. 'Can you trust your servants, Buckland?'

'Aye, they've all been with me for years.'

'Very well, then, impress upon them that no one must know what we are doing. And put it about that Miss Pentewan is confined to her room.'

She met his eyes in a fleeting glance that held the hint of a smile.

'I am of course exhausted after the ball.'

'Can you do it?' asked Reginald. 'It is Thursday tomorrow. Can you get to Beston and back before the hearing?'

'We will do our level best.' Dominic held out his hand to him. 'Keep that paper ready to produce at the hearing, Buckland. With luck we will beat Evanshaw at this!'

By the time they arrived back at Rooks Tower Zelah could not see anything in front of the horses and she wondered just how Dominic kept the curricle on the road. Jasper had stabled his horse and was waiting to hand her down.

'All our guests have retired, so we do not need to offer any explanations yet,' he said, escorting her into the hall. 'I took the liberty of asking Mrs Graddon to make up a bed for you, Miss Pentewan. She tells me the tower room is ready. And I have ordered refreshments to be served in the morning room. I hope you don't mind, Dom?'

'Of course not.'

His tone was curt, but she was used to that. She did not think he was angry with her, merely that he did not want to take her to Beston Quay. When Jasper excused himself and went off to change out of his muddy clothes, Zelah followed Dominic into the morning room.

'I promise I shall not hold you up,' she said, 'if that is worrying you.'

He walked over to the window and closed the shutters. 'I know that. I have seen you ride, Miss Pentewan.'

She winced at his formality. 'You had begun to call me Zelah,' she reminded him gently.

With a smothered oath he swung round. 'I am doing my best to protect you, madam, and at every turn you thwart me!'

She raised her brows. 'Do you think I am doing this to thwart you?'

He looked up at the ceiling, exhaling. 'No, of course

not. But this could leave you open to gossip, when it becomes known.'

She lifted her shoulders. 'It does not matter. I will soon be gone from here.' He did not contradict her. Another blow, but she shut her mind to it and said fiercely, 'Besides, rescuing Nicky is far more important than any reputation.'

They set off at sunrise, riding away from the moor, through wooded valleys towards the Devon border. Zelah rode between Dominic and his brother, Jem Sawley following behind on a large dappled roan. Jasper had laughed when the groom had brought it into the yard.

'Good God, Dom, do you have only ugly horses in your stable?'

'Aye.' Dominic grinned. 'They are a good match for their master!'

Jasper winked at Zelah before scrambling up on to his handsome bay gelding. The exchange had lightened the mood a little—until then Dominic had behaved with numbing politeness and she was relieved that he had now returned to his usual habit of barking orders at everyone.

On they rode, mile after mile, down ancient tracks and across open land, following the route Dominic and Jasper had memorised the previous night. They skirted towns and villages for the first part of their journey, only coming on to the main routes to cross the rivers. The last major crossing was at Torrington, and as they trotted across the bridge Dominic gave Zelah an encouraging smile.

'Not long now.'

She nodded, easing her aching thighs on the saddle. At any other time she would have relished the challenge, but for now her mind was fixed on rescuing Nicky.

They followed a narrow lane and soon found themselves travelling across a desolate plateau of bare fields and scrubland. Ahead of them was the sea, a deep grey line between the edge of the land and the heavy grey cloud bank on the horizon. Zelah could taste the salt in the fresh breeze as they rode on, skirting the village itself and heading directly towards the quay, which was a mile or so to the west. Then, suddenly, their goal was in sight and they reined in their horses as the ground fell away sharply before them. On each side the black, ragged cliffs dropped into the choppy grey waters, while directly below them a haphazard collection of buildings straggled across a promontory. The inn was easily identified, a low stone building with its blue sign and a row of barrels standing against the wall.

'I think it best if I go down alone first,' said Jasper. 'It is possible that some of Evanshaw's people might be there and they could recognise one of you.'

Zelah gazed down at the little hamlet.

'It looks a very poor, isolated sort of place. What will you say?'

Jasper grinned. 'No need to worry, I am quite adept at playing the eccentric traveller.' He pointed to a small stand of trees. 'Wait for me over there, where you will not be seen.'

While Jasper set off down the winding track, the others moved back into the trees, where only the sighing wind and the distant cry of the gulls broke the silence. It was impossible to ride into the small wood because the overhanging branches were too low, so they dismounted and Sawley led their horses along a narrow path. Zelah was thankful that the thick canopy of leaves sheltered them from the hot sun. Their path led to a small clearing.

The groom took the horses to one side while Zelah and Dominic found a convenient tree stump and sat down.

'This reminds me of the first time I saw you,' said Zelah, removing her bonnet and wiping her hand across her hot brow. 'You had been working in the woods and you were carrying a fearsome axe.'

'With my wild appearance I must have been very frightening.'

She considered for a moment. 'No, I was never really frightened of you.'

'Not even when you attacked me with that tree branch?'

She laughed. 'A mere stick, which you disposed of quite summarily!'

He looked at her, the faint smile in his eyes causing her heart to beat a little faster. 'You were very brave, you know, to stand your ground against me. You did not know who I was, or what I might do.'

'But I could not leave Nicky.'

'No, you are very fond of him, are you not?'

'He is like my...' She stopped, shaking her head a little.

'Go on,' Dominic urged her gently.

Zelah drew in a long, steadying breath.

'He is like my son, the baby that n-never lived, that I never held in my arms. I shut it out, all the pain and loss, until I came to West Barton and met my sister's little stepson. He was so bright, so very much alive—I could do nothing else but love him.'

Dominic gave a short laugh. 'I know what you mean. He soon found his way past my defences!'

'And now he has been snatched away—' She gripped her hands together tightly in her lap. 'Do you think Jasper will find him?'

Dominic's heart lurched when she spoke his twin's

name. Were they on such good terms already? He tried to dismiss the thought and concentrate upon her question.

'I doubt it will be quite so easy. If they have the boy, you may be sure they will keep him out of sight. But he may glean some useful information. Then we will act.' She shivered, instinctively leaning closer. Dominic put his arm around her shoulders. 'Try not to worry. If the boy is here we will find him.'

She leaned against him and he lowered his head until her honey-brown curls brushed his chin. Desire stirred, but Dominic knew it was more than that. He wanted to protect her, to wipe away the anxious frown that creased her brow. It was a jolt to realise that her happiness was the most important thing in the world to him. With a sigh she reached for his hand, twining her fingers with his.

'Thank you. It is such a comfort to have you here. You really are a true friend to me.'

The knot in Dominic's stomach hardened. There was that word again. Friend. She kept insisting it was what they should be, but it was a million miles away from what he wanted from her.

They sat thus for a long time, each lost in their own thoughts. Behind them was the quiet snuffle and chomping as their horses nibbled at the tender young shoots pushing up through the ground.

Chapter Sixteen

'Listen!'

Dominic's soft hiss brought Zelah's head up. She sat very still, straining to hear. Someone was approaching, whistling a jaunty tune that mingled with the sighing of the gentle breeze through the leaves. Minutes later Jasper appeared, leading his horse through the trees. Dominic jumped up to meet him.

'What did you discover?'

'There's the usual customs house, some warehouses and a few cottages down by the quay, and the inn of course. The Anchor. It's a rundown tavern used mainly by the fishermen, so it's pretty quiet at the moment because all the boats are out.' He stripped off his gloves, grinning. 'Landlord's name is Miller—'

'The bailiff's brother!' declared Zelah.

Jasper nodded. 'Very likely. He and his wife run the place, but they were not very welcoming, told me they had no rooms to spare and suggested I should try the Ship in Beston village.'

'You saw no sign of Nicky?' Zelah questioned him anxiously.

'No, but I thought I heard a child's voice coming from one of the upper rooms.'

'Then we must go back immediately,' she said quickly. 'If Nicky is there we must rescue him—'

'I intend to,' replied Dominic, 'but we won't go rushing in.' He nodded towards the coast. 'We are less likely to be seen once the rain sets in.'

A bank of cloud was rolling in from the west. The minutes dragged by but at last it had enveloped the fields and as it crept ever closer to the trees, the gentlemen unstrapped their greatcoats from the saddles and prepared themselves for bad weather. Jasper and Dominic pushed their cuffs out of sight and each wrapped a muffler around his neck to conceal the white linen. Zelah, shrouded in her enveloping cloak and with the capacious hood hiding her face, thought they would look like grey wraiths riding out into the swirling mist that had swept in from the sea.

Zelah picked up Portia's reins. 'Will one of you help me to mount?'

'It would be best for you to wait here with Jem,' stated Dominic.

'I am coming with you.'

'You are not!'

'But—'

He flung up his arm. 'I do not have time to argue, Zelah. We need to concentrate on finding Nicky and getting him away safely, not protecting you from danger.'

She opened her mouth to protest, but Jasper put his hand on her arm.

'Dominic is right,' he said quietly. 'You would distract us. We would both be far too anxious for your safety if you come with us. Let Dom and me rescue the boy. Besides, if anything should go wrong, you and Sawley will be free to raise the alarm.'

She closed her lips against further protest—it would only add to their belief that she was a distraction, she thought bitterly. With a nod Jasper began to lead the big bay out of the clearing. Dominic stepped in front of her, hesitated, then briefly placed his hands on her shoulders.

'Don't worry, if the boy is there we will find him and bring him back to you.'

Silently she nodded. *I am a distraction*, she thought, and fought down the desire to throw her arms about his neck and kiss him, to wish him good luck and urge him to be careful. Instead she tried to keep her worries hidden as she watched them walk away. They were soon swallowed up by the mist and she was left with only Jem Sawley for company.

Dominic followed Jasper down the narrow track. The drizzle and mist enveloped them and within minutes their outer clothes were dusted with tiny water droplets. When they reached the small promontory Jasper led the way to a derelict barn. The door had disappeared, but the roof was almost intact.

'We'll leave the horses here,' said Jasper. 'The inn lies at the other side of the quay, but it's not far.'

'Good.' Dominic drew his pistol from its saddle holster. 'You go to the inn and call for service, I'll slip in the back way and search the rooms.'

'I shall go to the front door and make a lordly fuss.' Jasper looked at Dominic, his eyes unusually sombre. 'Be careful, Brother.'

He slipped away and was soon lost to sight between the straggling buildings. Dominic waited a few minutes, then set off after him. The whole area was deserted, no fishing boats were tied up at the quay, the houses and outbuildings were empty and an air of quiet desolation hung over everything. He kept close to the buildings, the rain splashing from the roof tiles onto his hat and shoulders as he hurried along the muddy lane and into the narrow alley that led to the rear of the inn. The long, low building formed an L-shape around a cobbled yard. On one side the roof was extended to form a covered way, which looked as if it had once been a skittle alley, but was now filled with empty beer barrels stacked untidily against the back wall.

He could hear Jasper's voice, loud and bombastic as he shouted for the landlord. Dominic moved cautiously towards the open doorway. He found himself in a narrow passage. An open door immediately on his right led to the kitchen and a set of narrow stairs ran up to his left. He slipped up the stairs, which mercifully did not creak. A series of doors led off the landing. Boldly he put his hand on the latch of the first one and walked in, prepared to apologise and retreat if it was occupied, as if he was a genuine guest.

The room was empty, shabby but clean with the bed made up and ready for use. The second and third attempts revealed similar empty rooms.

'Hmm,' he muttered to himself, 'that gives the lie to their being full.'

The next door was locked and a heavy bolt had been fastened to the outside, the freshly splintered wood evidence that it had been fitted very recently. He knocked softly and heard a sobbing whimper.

Dominic took out a pocket knife and set to work on the old lock, which soon gave way.

Cautiously he opened the door. The room was as sparsely furnished as the others, but Nicky was there, alone, sitting disconsolately on the edge of the narrow bed. As soon as he saw Dominic he threw himself at him.

'Thank God,' muttered Dominic, laying a hand on the boy's shoulder. 'Come now, let us get out of here—'

'Not so fast, my fine friends.'

The rolling West Country vowels made Dominic's head snap around. The landlord was at the door, a shotgun held menacingly in his hands.

'Ah. I thought I heard a noise up 'ere.'

Dominic stepped in front of Nicky. 'Don't be a fool, man. Put the gun down. The game is up now, unless you mean to murder us.'

The landlord shrugged. 'Murder, abduction, it makes no odds. We'd hang anyway if we was found out—and keep yer hands where I can see 'em,' he ordered, as Dominic reached for the pistol in his pocket.

'Dan'l, what're you doin'...?' the landlady's shrill tones preceded her up the stairs. A slatternly looking woman with untidy hair and a greasy apron appeared beside her husband, who sniffed.

'We got a visitor, Martha. Come to get the boy. Do you check 'is pockets, and see if he's carryin' a weapon.'

The landlady wiped her hands nervously on her apron and approached Dominic, keeping well to the side so there was no possibility of blocking her husband's aim. She lifted the pistol from his pocket and the man called Daniel gave a satisfied nod.

'I thought as much.'

'So are you going to shoot 'im, Dan'l?'

'No!' cried Nicky, clinging to Dominic.

'It's all right, Nicky,' said Dom quickly. 'Don't worry, lad.'

'Aye, that's right, you tell 'im,' leered the landlord, waving the shotgun menacingly. 'If you are wise, you'll both behave yerselves.'

'And if *you* are wise, you will let them go.' Jasper's cool drawl came from the landing, a pistol in his hand.

'Is that right?' The landlord spat on the floor. 'Seems to me that pop gun o' yers might get me, but not afore I've pulled the trigger, and one blast from this would send the nipper *and* yer friend to kingdom come. And it's not to say that Martha here might not loose off yer friend's shooter, too.'

A cold chill ran down Dominic's spine. He wondered how quickly he could drop down and shield the boy. If he was quick enough, he could take the force of the blast and Nicky might survive.

'So what's it t'be?' the landlord demanded. 'I ain't gonna stand here all day. Either you comes in here with yer friend and the boy, or I'll shoot 'em both.'

'Don't 'ee be too hasty, Dan'l.' The woman placed her hand on the landlord's arm. 'If we has trouble here then we'll have the Revenue men crawling all over the place.'

'She's right,' agreed Jasper. 'You cannot fire that thing without an almighty disturbance that will bring every Revenue man for miles down upon you.'

The landlord shrugged. 'No matter. They ain't found nothing yet so I reckons I'll tek my chances, if I 'as to. And as to shooting anybody...' his lip curled, displaying a mouth full of yellow, rotted teeth '...a man's entitled to defend his property. No, my fine buck, I thinks you'd better give that pretty pop o' yours to my good lady, afore my finger gets itchy on this trigger and I shoots the boy.'

Through the open doorway Dominic met Jasper's eyes and read the message there. The risk was too great. Jasper lowered his pistol.

'Well, fellow, it seems you have me there.'

The landlord stood away from the door. 'You come

on in here, then, where I can see thee. And, Martha, you go and fetch some cord to tie up these fine gennlemen!'

'I'm sorry, brother,' murmured Jasper as he came to stand beside Dominic. 'Perhaps we will have another chance.'

'Perhaps.' Dominic shrugged.

Faced with the shotgun pointing at them, they could do nothing but wait until the landlady returned with a length of thin rope, with which she proceeded to bind their hands behind their back.

'Tight, mind,' ordered Daniel. 'They's big divils and I don't want no messin with 'em.'

'Aye, but what now?' said Martha, when she had finished. 'Do you want to leave 'em all here?'

'No, the boy can stay—the lock's bust, but the bolt on the door will hold'n.' He looked up suddenly. 'Where's your horses?'

'Back at the village,' said Dominic. 'At the inn.'

'Aye,' added Jasper. 'We told them we were here to paint the landscape.'

The landlord's face twisted into a cruel grin. 'Well, then, they won't think nothing of it if you takes a tumble off the cliff into the sea. We'll put you in the cellar 'til nightfall, then tek you out to sea an'—'

'No!' shouted Nicky, 'You shan't hurt them, you shan't.'

The landlady pulled him against her greasy skirts. 'No, no, they won't be 'armed, my babby.' She glared at her husband. 'Do you want to have the nipper bawling and troublesome all night? Will said we was to keep 'im safe—no marks, 'e said.' She looked down at the little boy. 'Don't 'ee worry, me lad. We're jus gonna put yer friends into the cellar for a while, till William comes to take you all home, ain't that right, Dan'l?'

'Aye,' growled Daniel. 'So you two get yerselves down-stairs, now, and don't try anything, I ain't afraid to deal with you.'

'No, of course not, now we have our hands tied behind our backs!' retorted Dominic. He turned and nodded at Nicky. 'We will see you later, Nicky.'

Daniel waved the shotgun again. 'That's enough, now get yerselves down them stairs.'

The landlord kept a safe distance behind them and the landlady, waving Jasper's pistol in her hand, informed them that she was quite prepared to use it.

A door under the stairs led to the cellar. The landlord waved them forwards, waited until they were both on the stairs, then kicked his foot into Jasper's back, send-ing them crashing down into the darkness.

Zelah paced up and down the clearing. The light within the trees had faded to a grey dusk. Surely Dominic and Jasper should have returned by now? It was still raining, but the mist had lifted a little and she could see where the lane dropped away to the quay. There was no one in sight. She felt quite sick with apprehension, imagining the most horrendous scenes. It was almost too dark to see now and with grim determination Zelah made her way back to where the groom was sitting with the horses.

'Help me to mount, Sawley. We will go and find out what has happened.'

'Nay, madam, the major said—'

'The major should have been back by now,' she re-torted fiercely. 'Now it is up to you—either you come with me, or I shall go to the quay alone!'

Chapter Seventeen

⁓⤠⤡⤢⤣⁓

The darkness was complete. Dominic and Jasper sat back to back on the cellar floor, each in turn trying to untie the other's wrists. Dominic ran his tongue over his lips, tasting blood. He guessed he had cut his face when the landlord had pushed them down the stairs, but that was a minor concern. He thought of Nicky locked in the room upstairs and his anger grew. He would give everything he had if he could save him, not only for his own sake, but because of what the boy meant to Zelah.

Jasper swore softly. 'It's no good, Dom. That damned fishwife has tied the ropes too well.'

'We'll rest for a moment, then I'll try again,' muttered Dominic. He leaned against his twin. 'How long do you think we have?'

'Heaven knows. I wouldn't think he would try to get rid of us while he has any customers, and by the sound of it the inn's pretty full tonight.'

'A couple of hours at most, then.'

'Our best chance would be when they take us to the ship,' said Jasper. 'We might be able to make a run for it then, perhaps get help at the customs house from the Revenue officer.'

Dominic said nothing. They both knew it was a slim chance, but neither was willing to admit defeat.

'We'll just have to conserve our energy and—'

'Hush!' Dominic whispered urgently. 'Someone's coming.'

They struggled to their feet and waited, tense and expectant. They heard the soft rasp of bolts being drawn back from the door at the top of the stairs. Dominic swallowed the bitter bile of frustration. If only his hands were free he would punish that damned landlord—

'Nicky!'

Jasper's exclamation mirrored his own surprise. The soft glow of candles appeared at the top of the steps and Nicky came racing down towards them, Jem Sawley following quickly, but it was the figure behind the groom that caused Dominic's heart to stand still.

'Zelah! By heaven, what are you doing here?'

She closed the door carefully behind her before descending, holding her candle high to give as much light as possible.

'We guessed something had gone wrong and came to find you. Here, Nicky, hold the candle for me.'

'Did you call at the customs house for help?' Dominic demanded, looking past her.

'No,' she said. 'Everything was in darkness and we did not want to waste time.'

With a furious oath Dominic turned to his groom. 'Hell and damnation, Jem, you should not have brought her here!'

Zelah did not wait for the hapless groom to muster his arguments.

'He could not very well leave me behind!' She pulled a long-bladed knife from the folds of her cloak. 'I found this in the kitchen and thought it might be useful. Turn about, if you please, and I will cut you free.'

It was the work of moments to cut through their bonds. Dominic stood for a moment, rubbing his sore wrists. His relief at being free was tempered by anger. He wanted to rail at Zelah for putting herself into such danger, but because he knew it was foolish and unjustified he kept silent. Jasper knew no such reticence. He put his arm about Zelah and kissed her soundly on the cheek.

'Well done, my dear!' He looked across at Dominic and grinned. 'I don't know about you, brother, but I have had enough of this inn's hospitality. Shall we go?'

'Yes, immediately,' returned Zelah. 'We left our horses with yours, at the old barn.'

The three men went first, cautiously opening the cellar door. The laughter and chatter from the taproom filtered through the narrow passage, but there was no one in sight as they crept out.

They had almost reached the doorway when the landlord appeared from the courtyard. His eyes bulged when he found his way blocked by the men he thought safely trussed up in his cellar, but Jasper's fist caught him squarely on the chin and laid him low. Hurriedly Dominic and Jem dragged the landlord's unconscious body into the shadow of the building and signalled to Zelah and Nicky to come out into the wet twilight.

Once in the yard Zelah found her breathing easier: it was good to be outside again, even though the mist was thicker than ever. She held Nicky's hand as they followed Jasper out of the yard, Dominic and Jem hovering protectively behind them. Her spine tingled. She was fearful of hearing the alarm raised, or, even worse, a shot ringing out. Even when they reached the horses she could not relax. Jasper threw her up into the saddle while Dominic took Nicky up before him and they left the village at a canter, not slowing up until they were up on the plateau again, with only the mist and the rain for company. Zelah glanced nervously over her shoulder.

'Do you think they will follow us?'

'It's possible,' said Dominic. 'We should get as far away as we can while there is some light.'

Jasper nodded.

'I agree, although it pains me to lose two good pistols to the villains. But we may yet recover them. I do not intend to let that rascally landlord and his wife get away with this. But first we have to return Nicky to his parents, and before tomorrow's hearing, if that's possible. Let's press on, if you feel up to it, Miss Pentewan?'

Zelah nodded and Nicky, cocooned inside the front of Dominic's greatcoat, raised his head.

'Yes, please,' he said, his voice breaking. 'I w-want to go home.'

They had ridden hard until it was too dark to travel, then broken their journey at a coaching inn, where all Jasper's considerable address and his full purse had been required before the landlord was persuaded to admit them. They had set off again at dawn, but heavy rain hampered their progress and they had to divert several times to avoid the swollen streams that blocked their route. There was no time to go to West Barton before the hearing started at ten o'clock so they made directly for Lesserton, where the church clock was already striking the hour when they reached the White Hart.

'Your brother is here,' observed Dominic, nodding towards the carriage pulled up across the street.

'Good, I hope Maria is with him too, I cannot think

she will be sitting at home on such an important day,' declared Zelah, as Jasper helped her dismount.

He pulled her hand on to his arm. 'Come along, then, we will all go in together.'

Their entrance caused immediate confusion. Sir Oswald, facing the door, saw them first. His eyes narrowed and a dull, angry colour mottled his cheeks. Maria gave a little scream and Reginald, who was sitting beside Mr Summerson, his lawyer, jumped up, gazing at his son and unable to speak for some moments. Maria ran forwards to take Nicky in her arms while the rest of the crowd muttered in surprise, knowing nothing of what had ensued.

Dominic stepped into the centre of the room and addressed the magistrate.

'I beg your pardon for the intrusion,' he announced. 'We came to tell Mr Buckland his son is safe.'

'Aye,' declared Reginald, his eyes bright with anger. 'He was abducted, Sir Arthur, and this note was sent to me, warning me not to present my new evidence to this hearing!'

The surprised mutterings around the room swelled as Reginald handed the paper to the magistrate. Sir Arthur hammered on the desk again, then looked at the little boy, now held safely in his mother's arms.

'You were taken, young man, against your will?'

Nicky nodded solemnly. 'Yes, sir.'

'And do you know who it was who did this to you?'

'Yes, sir. He's there.' Nicky pointed towards Sir Oswald's bailiff. 'It was Mr Miller, the man who is trying to leave.'

The villagers raised their voices in a howl of outrage and those nearest Miller held him fast as he edged past them. The bailiff swore and tried to shake them off, but found himself trapped.

'It weren't my idea to take the boy!' he cried. 'Sir Oswald ordered me to do it.'

Sir Oswald jumped to his feet. 'Be quiet, you fool!'

Mr Summerson rose and directed a stern look at the bailiff. 'If you know anything more you should tell us now, Mr Miller. The charge against you is a serious one.'

'He told me to do it!' Miller was gabbling now, fear loosening his tongue. 'Just like he told me to get rid of Old Robin, to stop'n talking.'

There was a moment of shocked silence, then fresh cries of fury filled the room. Giles Grundy rose to his feet, his broken arm strapped up securely across his chest.

'We found Old Robin drowned in the Lightwater,' he said slowly. 'But his head was bashed open fearsome bad.'

'Sir Oswald said I was to frighten 'im,' said Miller, still trying to free himself. 'Said I was to get him to leave the area, but the old man were stubborn. Drunk, he was, and we came to blows.'

'So you knocked him unconscious and threw him in the Lightwater,' pursued Sir Arthur.

Maria gasped and Zelah saw that her sister was holding Nicky tight to her and covering his ears.

'He'd have fallen in anyway, like as not,' muttered Miller sullenly.

Sir Arthur hammered on the desk to regain order. 'Take him away and lock him up,' he commanded. 'We will deal with this later.' He turned to Sir Oswald. 'I find it hard to believe, sir, that you would resort to abduction to prevent new evidence being put to the court.'

'Of course I would not,' declared Sir Oswald impatiently. 'I knew nothing about any new evidence.'

'Oh, yes, you did.'

Silence fell over the room as Nicky's young voice rang out. All eyes turned towards him and he flushed, shrinking closer to his stepmother. Sir Arthur turned to him.

'And how do you know anything about this, young man?'

Nicky swallowed hard. 'It was at the ball at Rooks Tower. I was on the landing. Major Coale said I might stay up and watch.' He turned his eyes towards Dominic, who nodded. Encouraged, Nicky continued. 'I heard Mr Lerryn tell Sir Oswald that Papa had a new document that would win the case for the villagers.'

'Utter nonsense,' blustered Sir Oswald. 'The child is dreaming.'

Sir Arthur put up his hand and directed his solemn stare at Nicky. 'I was at the ball, young man, and I know how crowded it was. How could you have possibly heard what was said?'

'It was supper time, and there weren't many people in the hall. Mr Lerryn brought Sir Oswald over to the corner of the hall, beside the stairs. Directly below where I was sitting.'

'And you are sure that is what was said?' Sir Arthur asked him.

'Yes, sir,' affirmed Nicky. 'When Sir Oswald asked him how he knew about it, Mr Lerryn said he was there when Papa received the paper and that he wanted to...to *put a spoke in Buckland's wheel*. He said he knew Papa meant to keep the paper a secret until the hearing.'

The murmur amongst the crowd swelled again. Sir Oswald jumped up, banging his fist upon the table.

'You will never take that child's word over mine, Andrews!'

'It explains why you thought it necessary to abduct my son!' roared Reginald.

Shouts and cries of 'shame' filled the air. Sir Arthur hammered on his bench.

'I will have order!' he bellowed. He fixed a stern gaze upon Sir Oswald. 'I will question you about the matter of abduction later, but first I am obliged to finish this hearing. I charge you, therefore, not to go out of my sight.'

'Don't 'ee worry, sir, we'll keep'n safe for 'ee,' shouted someone in the crowd, amid much cheering.

Reginald murmured something to his lawyer, who handed the magistrate a rolled parchment.

'My client informs me this paper was found amongst the books Major Coale recently purchased from the Lydcombe Park estate. You will see, Sir Arthur, that it is a contract of sale for Lydcombe Park, a transaction that took place some thirty years ago, and it describes the boundary between the village land and Lydcombe Park in great detail, placing it quite clearly on the Lightwater, which flows along the western edge of Prickett Wood, and marked by a white boundary stone.'

'And you were not going to declare this?' demanded Sir Arthur, frowning heavily.

'I think, in the circumstances, we can understand my client's reluctance,' stated Mr Summerson. 'But this contract is quite precise in the boundary's location.'

'Aye, but rivers can change their course over the years,' cried Sir Oswald, his face still alarmingly red. 'And I tell you there is no stone in Prickett Wood. If there was, then surely someone would know of it.' He glared at the packed courtroom. 'Well, have any of you ever seen it?'

'It would appear not,' mused Sir Arthur, shaking his head. 'In the absence of a boundary stone...'

'But there *is* one,' cried Nicky, his high young voice piping clearly over the hubbub. 'There is a white stone in Prickett Wood. I've seen it!'

'The boy's deranged,' Sir Oswald sneered, but when Sir Arthur had again called for order Dominic stepped up and placed his hand on Nicky's shoulder.

'Let the boy tell us what he knows.'

'I've seen it,' Nicky said again, his eyes wide. 'Old Robin took me following the deer and we often tracked them into Prickett Wood, and the pricketts always use the white stone.'

'Pricketts are the young bucks,' Reginald explained to Mr Summerson. 'They like to rub their new antlers against favourite trees and rocks.'

Dominic's contemptuous gaze fell upon Sir Oswald. 'So that is why you were killing the deer.'

Sir Oswald glared at Nicky, fury etched into every line of his face. 'By God, you young devil, I should have told Miller to dispose of you rather than—' He broke off, realising what he had said.

'The boy has certainly got the better of you, Evanshaw,' said Dominic with grim satisfaction.

Sir Arthur turned again to Nicky. 'Can you show us where to find this stone, young man?'

'Yes, sir.'

'No, no, not today,' cried Maria. 'My son has suffered far too much. He needs to rest.'

'Devil a bit, Mama,' retorted Nicky, stoutly. His courage faltered slightly and he cast a quick beseeching look at Dominic. 'Will you come with me, sir, you and Papa?'

'Of course. And your mother and aunt. Lord Markham, too. We will all be there for you.'

'Well, that is most satisfactory,' declared Reginald as he walked back to the High Street with Maria on his arm. 'It was delightful to see everyone from the courtroom traipse off to Prickett Wood like that. No one can be in any doubt now of where the boundary stone is situated. The villagers have won their dispute and Evanshaw and Miller have been locked up to await trial. All in all a good day's work. But now, my love, I think you should take Nicky and Zelah home; they look exhausted.'

'Of course,' said Maria. 'I have to get back for Baby, too. You will come home as soon as you can?'

'I will follow on, once I have instructed Summerson to conclude the business of the boundary with Sir Arthur.'

He turned and hailed Dominic and Jasper as they passed. Zelah stepped back behind her sister. She felt as drawn and exhausted as Reginald had said and did not want to face anyone, especially Dominic.

'How can we ever thank you, gentlemen, for returning my boy safely to us?'

'I am pleased we could be of service,' returned Jasper with his cheerful grin. 'Sir Oswald should not bother you any more, I do not see how he can explain away the evidence against him.'

Maria put out her hand first to Dominic, then to his brother. 'I know you must be very tired,' she said, smiling mistily up at them, 'but you are very welcome to come to West Barton. Join us for dinner—it is the least we can do after all you have done for us.'

'And do not forget Miss Pentewan's efforts, too,' put in Dominic, his words and the trace of a smile that accompanied them making Zelah feel as if she might cry at any moment. 'But, no, thank you. We will stay until Sir Arthur has concluded the hearing, then we must go back to Rooks Tower. I still have guests there. I shall send Sawley ahead to tell them what has occurred, but I know they will be anxious to hear the story from us.'

'Of course.' Maria nodded. 'I quite understand, but

pray believe me when I say that you are both welcome to take pot luck with us at any time.'

'Thank you, ma'am.'

Jasper bowed over her hand and Zelah's before ruffling Nicky's hair. 'Good day to you, Master Nick. Do not frighten your mama too much with the tales of your adventures!'

Zelah stood by, smiling, supposedly listening to Nicky's reply, but all the time she was painfully aware of Dominic, standing beside Reginald. He would be taking his leave any moment. She would give him her hand for the last time. There would be no 'until tomorrow' because she no longer worked at Rooks Tower.

Dominic stood outside the little circle, watching. Jasper found it easy to converse, to do the pretty and bow over the ladies' hands, but Dominic held back. What was wrong with him? His manners could be every bit as polished as his brother's, but somehow today he could not push himself forwards. If Zelah had given him the slightest encouragement, a mere look, then he would have stepped up, taken her hand, but she had been avoiding him ever since they had arrived in Lesserton this morning. Now he watched the way she smiled up at Jasper when he took her hand and the demon jealousy tore at his gut so that he could manage no more than a curt nod of farewell before he turned away.

Zelah's heart sank. After all they had done together, all they had been through, he could not wait to get away. Bitterly disappointed, she climbed quickly into the carriage.

Dominic cursed himself for a fool. How could he leave her without a word? He owed her more than that. Quickly he turned back, but she was already in the carriage. The moment was lost.

* * *

'Well, we did it, Brother,' declared Jasper once they had collected their horses and were trotting out of the village. 'We brought the boy home safely, the principal villains have been locked up and a party is even now on its way to Beston Quay to apprehend the innkeeper and his wife. Everything has worked out very well.' Jasper laughed. 'By Gad, I never thought Exmoor would prove so interesting! You are the hero of the hour, Dom. And Miss Pentewan is the heroine.' When Dominic was silent he continued. 'By Gad, what a woman. Came into the inn, cool as you please, and cut us free. Heaven knows what would have happened if she hadn't come looking for us.'

'Utter recklessness,' retorted Dominic, chilled at the thought of what might have happened. 'To put herself in danger like that! If she'd had any sense she would have gone to Beston village for help.'

'And that might have come too late. Admit it, man, she's a damned fine woman. I thought so the first time I met her in your library. Not one to say yea and nay because she thinks you want to hear it.'

'Certainly not,' agreed Dominic with feeling. She had challenged him from the first moment they had met.

'Graddon says Rooks Tower has been transformed since she first entered it.'

'Aye,' growled Dominic, 'if you call setting the place on its head, opening up rooms and encouraging me to hold a ball—a ball, mark you!—a transformation then, yes, she has changed it out of all recognition.'

'And you too, Dom. When Sal wrote and told me how you had recovered I could scarcely believe it, but it is true.' His shrewd gaze slid to Dominic, who strained every muscle to keep his countenance impassive. 'How much of that is due to your little librarian?'

'I agree she was a civilising influence,' Dominic said carefully, 'but any woman would have been the same.'

'It takes more than just any woman to put up with your moods and your curst temper,' retorted his fond brother. 'You know you have been the very devil to live with since you came back from the Peninsula. And with good reason, I admit. The state you were in, we were surprised you survived at all. What you suffered would have tried the patience of a saint. But from what I've heard Miss Pentewan has been more than a match for you.'

Exhaling in frustration, Dominic kicked his horse into a canter, relieved that they had reached a stretch of open ground, but when they drew rein to make their way onto the road he found his brother had not finished with the subject of Zelah Pentewan.

'And the way she kept up with us all the way to Beston Quay and back. Never a murmur of complaint. Pluck to the backbone. Do you know, brother, I think I am in love.'

A short laugh escaped Dominic. 'Again! How many times has that been this year?

'No, this time I am serious.' Jasper brought his horse to a stand, a look of dawning wonder on his face. 'Zelah Pentewan is intelligent, courageous, generous—not a beauty, perhaps, but very lovely. There is something quite out of the ordinary about her.'

Dominic swung round in the saddle, scowling fiercely. 'Devil take you, Jasper, Zelah is not one of your sophisticated society ladies. She has no more guile about her than a kitten! I'll not have you break her heart with your flirting!'

'Flirting?' Jasper looked genuinely shocked. 'Dom, I have no intention of flirting with her. I want to *marry* her!'

Chapter Eighteen

If he had taken a blow to the solar plexus Dominic could not have been more winded. For a full minute he stared at his brother, and his stunned countenance brought a rueful flush to Jasper's handsome face.

'Oh, I know I have thought myself in love before, but this time I am convinced it is for real. It has been coming on ever since I danced with her at your summer ball. She was so graceful and with such a natural wit that she completely bowled me off my feet. Of course, I don't know if she'll have me, but I'd like to put it to the touch. What do you think, Dom, do you think I have a chance?'

Looking at Jasper with his perfect features, his clear brow and the smooth, unblemished planes of his face, Dominic knew he was looking at one of the most handsome men in the country. Add to that a generous nature, a noble title and enough charm to bring the birds out of the trees, and it was inconceivable that his offer should not be accepted.

'Damn you, I do not see how you can fail.'

Jasper's black brows snapped together and he subjected his brother to a searching scrutiny.

'Dominic? Do you have an interest there yourself? Because if that is so...'

Dominic wished he had bitten off his tongue rather than have Jasper guess his secret. In his mind's eye he compared himself with his twin. What woman would want a scarred wreck with a comfortable income when she could have the exceedingly rich and handsome Viscount Markham? Not only that, but Jasper's unfailingly cheerful disposition was a stark contrast to his own foul temper. It was time to be honest with himself. He had held the ball for Zelah's sake, had he not? So that she might find a prospective husband. Now it seemed he had succeeded only too well, for she had won the biggest prize on the matrimonial market. He forced himself to laugh.

'I?' He spoke with all the ease and nonchalance he could muster. 'Good God, man, what makes you think that? No, I merely want her to be happy. Go to it, Jasper, and I wish you every success. She is indeed a diamond.'

'Thank you, Brother!' Jasper reached across to slap his shoulder. 'Do you know, I think I should put it to the touch today, before I lose my nerve. Mrs Buckland invited us to take pot luck at any time, did she not? Very well, then, I'll ride over there now. Pray make my excuses to everyone—if I am in luck then I will not be back for dinner.'

Dom found it more and more difficult to maintain his smile. He managed a nod. 'Aye, go on then. Take your lovesick sighs to West Barton and leave me in peace!'

Dominic took out his watch. Nine o'clock and no sign of Jasper. The faint, barely acknowledged hope that Zelah would refuse him had finally died. How he had managed to get through dinner without his guests realising that he was totally preoccupied was a mystery. He remembered nothing of the meal, prepared by the London chef Sally had sent down to relieve Mrs Graddon, but as soon as the ladies had withdrawn he excused himself from the table. It had not taken long for the events of the past two days to become known to his guests. They were being discussed at Rooks Tower even before Dominic returned, so his male friends and relatives were happy to send him off, declaring he must be exhausted after his heroic efforts.

Dominic *was* tired, but he did not go to his bedchamber. Instead he had come here, to the tower room, where the last flare of the setting sun beamed in through the windows and bathed everything in a rosy-golden light. Now even that was gone, replaced by grey twilight that robbed even the bed's garish cover of its colour. It was just as she had left it, the books and ledgers on the desk beside the inkwell and the freshly trimmed pens. As orderly and neat as the woman herself. He heard a light scratching on the door and Graddon entered.

'I thought you might like some refreshment, sir.' He brought in a tray laden with glasses, decanters and water plus a lighted taper.

'No.' Dominic stopped him after he had touched the taper to only two candles. 'Leave them. And make sure I am not disturbed again!'

His rough tone earned him an affronted look from the butler, but without a word Graddon left the room, closing the door carefully behind him.

Impatiently Dominic pushed his fingers through his hair. It was unreasonable of him to vent his ill humour on a servant, especially one as loyal as Graddon. He unstoppered the brandy and poured himself a generous measure. He would have to beg his pardon, of course, but he could do that tomorrow, when hopefully this black cloud would have lifted from his spirits.

Dominic carried his brandy over to the window, warming the glass between his hands before tasting it. He could get riotously drunk. That would bring him some measure of relief, but he would pay for it in the morning, and so would his guests, if he was surly and uncommunicative. Damn his sense of duty that obliged him to act the perfect host. He put his arm against the window and rested his forehead on his sleeve.

It was that same sense of duty that made him hold back from informing Jasper of Zelah's past. She had told him in confidence and he thought it likely that she would tell Jasper, too—he understood his twin well enough to know that the story of her seduction and the lost baby would elicit nothing but sympathy, but if she chose not to do so, he would not expose her. And what of his own connection with Zelah, the kisses, the passion that had threatened to overwhelm them? Would she tell Jasper of those? He guessed not. She was too honourable, too generous to want to cause a rift between brothers. And if she could put those precious moments behind her, then he could too. He would do nothing to spoil her happiness.

A movement on the drive caught his attention. There were shadows on the lawn, two riders approaching the house. Even in the dim light there was no mistaking them. As he watched they looked up at the tower. Dominic jumped back, cursing. What in hell's name was Jasper doing, bringing Zelah to Rooks Tower? It was late—did he mean to make sure of her tonight? Could he not wait until they had exchanged their vows before he took her to his bed? Dominic dragged the chair over to the side table and threw himself down, reaching for the brandy. Let them do what they wished, Zelah Pentewan was no longer any concern of his.

He leaned back in the chair and stretched out his legs, wondering how soon it would be safe to cross the great hall to his study. He had no wish to see Zelah. Would Jasper take her into the drawing room where family and friends would be gathered now, or would he take her straight to his room?

He shook his head to dispel the unwelcome images that thought brought forth. He heard a soft knock and turned towards the door, snarling, 'Damn you, Graddon, I told you not to come back tonight!'

'I do not recall you doing so.' Zelah stepped into the room, unperturbed by his ill humour. With a smothered oath he jumped to his feet, sending the chair crashing behind him.

'What are you doing here?'

'I saw the light and came to find you.'

'Well, now you have found me you can take yourself off again!'

'You are not very polite, sir.' She came closer, stripping off her gloves.

'I don't feel very polite,' he retorted. 'If you want me to bestow my blessing upon the match, I will do so to-morrow.'

'If you wish.' She pointed to the decanters. 'Is that Madeira? Perhaps I could have a small glass? I have had quite an exhausting day.'

He scowled, but automatically filled a glass for her. 'You should not be here.'

She took the glass from him, her clear eyes upon his face. 'Why should I not? I have quite come to look upon this room as my own.'

He concentrated on refilling his own glass and deliberately avoided looking at her. 'You will soon have much bigger properties than this at your disposal.'

'Ah. You mean when I am Viscountess Markham.'

She moved closer, so near he could have reached out and embraced her. He had to force himself not to do so.

'Jasper is very rich, isn't he?' she said, sipping at her Madeira.

'Exceedingly.'

'Handsome, too, and charming.'

'Yes.' Dominic ground his teeth. Damn him. He took a mouthful of brandy, impatient for the powerful spirit to begin clouding his brain.

'I turned him down.'

Dominic choked. Carefully he put down his glass. Zelah put hers beside it.

'I am very sorry to hear that,' he said cautiously.

'Are you?'

'Of course. He could give you everything your heart desires.'

She shook her head. 'No, that is not possible. You see, I do not love him.'

'If you are still pining for Lerryn, then you are a fool,' he said bluntly.

She waved her hand impatiently. 'No, of course I am not. Oh, Dominic, you are so, so *dull-witted* tonight!'

'Well, I, too, have had a difficult day. Give Jasper time to win your heart. You will come to see that there is not a better man in England—'

'That may be true. Jasper is very charming and I was very sorry to cause him pain, but I am not the woman to make him happy, and he is not the man for me. He is not you.' She stepped up to him and raised her hand to caress his left cheek, her palm cradling the scarred tissue. 'There is only one man who has ever held my heart,' she said softly, her eyes shining into his and filling his soul with light. 'Only one man that I could imagine spending the rest of my life with, and that is you, Dominic.'

There. She had said it.

'And what of Jasper? How did he take your refusal?'

'Like the true gentleman he is. I do not think he is truly heartbroken, but even if that was the case, I could not act differently.'

Zelah waited breathlessly, her eyes fixed on his face. Jasper had guessed her reason for refusing him. He had told her Dominic was very much in love, and all she had to do was to make him admit it. Now, as the minutes ticked by and she could discern nothing in his hard impassive gaze, Zelah wondered if Jasper had been wrong about his twin. Her hand dropped and she turned away, blinking back the hot tears.

'So there it is,' she said lightly. 'I am a hopeless case. I have heard nothing back from the widow in Bath, so I must surmise I was unsuccessful there, too. Do—do you think your sister will write me another ref—'

An iron hand gripped her arm and swung her round. The collision with Dominic's unyielding chest winded her, but the glow she saw in his eyes set her heart pounding.

'You would take me, rather than Jasper?'

'I will take no other,' she answered him solemnly.

She saw the desire leap in his eyes, but also uncertainty. She prayed he would not reject her now.

'Are you sure this is not just…pity?' His voice was harsh, the words edged with bitterness.

Summoning all her courage she slipped her hands about his neck. 'No, not pity. Love. I love you, Dominic. Let me show you how much.'

She pulled him down towards her and kissed his mouth. His touch was cool, wary, and she closed her eyes, willing him to respond. She felt rather than heard him growl, or was it a sigh? His arms went round her and he kissed her, working her mouth hungrily beneath his, forcing her lips apart, his tongue invading, demanding. Zelah gave way to her passion.

Her hands scrabbled with his jacket, pushing it off his shoulders. The waistcoat followed, but she had to break away to see how to untie the intricate knot of his neck-cloth. Impatiently he pushed her hands aside and ripped off the muslin. He was breathing heavily and the crisp dark hair of his chest was visible at the shirt opening. Her hands shook a little as she tugged his shirt free from his breeches. He was far too tall and she could only gather it up and allow him to pull it off. The sight of his naked chest enthralled her. A dark cloud of hair ran down the centre of his chest and the shadows from the candlelight enhanced the rippling muscle. She leaned forwards to press her lips to the ragged scar that crossed his body, trailing kisses down its length as it passed across his breast and the hard undulations of his ribs to the soft, flat plain of his stomach while her hands unfastened the flap of his breeches, her heart jumping with pleasure and anticipation when she noticed how hard and aroused he was beneath the soft buckskin.

She pushed aside the material and began to kneel, intending to follow that wicked scar its full length, but Dominic stopped her.

'This is unfair,' he muttered, pulling her to her feet. 'Let us take this slowly.'

Her body sang with anticipation as he undressed her, pausing to kiss each new area of skin as he exposed it. She gasped when he reached her breasts. She reached out for him, but he caught her arms, pinning them to her sides while his mouth circled and teased her exposed flesh until she was almost begging him to stop. Only then did he raise his head, a devilish gleam in his eyes.

'Now you know how I feel when you touch me.'

As soon as he released her she threw herself at him, kissing him hungrily, tangling her tongue with his and pressing herself against him. It was not enough. There were too many layers of fabric between their bodies. In silent accord they hurriedly shed the remainder of their clothes until they stood before each other, naked and breathless. The glow in Dominic's eyes burned into Zelah. She felt beautiful, powerful. Glorious.

With a growl he swept her up and carried her to the bed. The silk was cold as he laid her naked body down upon the cover, but only for an instant, and it was soon forgotten as he knelt beside her.

'Now,' he said softly, 'where were we?'

She sat up and reached out to touch him, just below his navel. 'I was about there.'

'Hmm.' He cupped her breasts, which tightened immediately beneath his hands. 'You are a little ahead of me, but I will catch you up.'

She shifted around until she could place her lips on his abdomen, steadying herself by placing her hands on his hips, revelling in the feel of his smooth skin beneath her fingers, her mouth, her senses enhanced by the attention he was giving to her own body. Even as she made him groan with pleasure he was moving lower, his lips burning a trail across her body while his hands, the vanguard of his exquisite assault, caressed her thighs, preparing her for his most intimate kiss.

She wanted to please him, to worship his body as he was worshipping hers, but he was sapping her control. She tried to move her hips away from his pleasuring tongue, but his hands gripped her, holding her firm while he continued his relentless onslaught, rousing her to a bucking, crying frenzy that left her almost sobbing with the pleasure of it.

Dominic gathered her to him and she lay for a few moments in the shelter of his arms. Her senses were still heightened, she could feel his soft breathing, hear the stir of the breeze through the distant trees. The fragrance of lavender from the sheets filled her head, mixed with the musky male scent of the man beside her. The candles had guttered and died and they had only the moonlight now, casting its silver gleam over the tower room. She stirred a little, but when Dominic tried to pull the covers over them she stopped him.

'No, I have not satisfied *you* yet.'

He chuckled. 'There is plenty of time for that.'

Zelah sat up. 'No, let me do this.'

He was still aroused, but she was pleased, and slightly awed, by the way his body reacted to her touch. It excited her and she could feel her body responding again. Dominic groaned and pulled her to him, his mouth seeking hers. His kiss reignited the fire and her body was soon burning with desire. He rolled over her and she opened for him, tilting her hips, inviting him to enter.

He pushed against her, deep and satisfying. She matched his rhythm as he gradually increased the momentum, each thrust carrying her closer to the uncontrollable excitement that was so alarming and yet so exhilarating. She clung on tightly, digging her fingers into his back, afraid she might faint with sheer pleasure. Then, just when she thought she could stand no more, he cried out. She felt him tense. Her whole body gripped him. He shuddered and her own body answered with a tremor of its own. It was a climax, a tipping point and she clung tightly, as if to let go would plunge her into some black and endless abyss.

* * *

Exhausted, they sank down together beneath the covers, Dominic wrapping himself around Zelah in a way that made her feel safe, cherished.

'I hope you are going to marry me after that,' he whispered, nuzzling her neck.

'If that is what you want, Dominic.'

'I have no choice. I love you too much to risk losing you.'

'Oh.' She struggled to sit up. 'Oh, please, say that again.'

'Say what?'

'That you love me.' Suddenly she felt very shy. 'I have wanted you to say that for such a long time.'

'Have you? Then I will say it every day from now on.' He drew her towards him. 'I love you, Zelah, with all my heart. No, you *are* my heart. You are my reason for living.'

He kissed her gently and, smiling, Zelah gave a contented sigh and snuggled down in his arms to sleep.

She awoke the next morning to birdsong. It was not yet dawn, but the lack of curtains or shutters in the tower room gave them no shelter from the grey light. She opened her eyes and found Dominic propped up on his elbow, watching her. The sight of his naked torso was enough to bring memories of the night's activities flooding back. She put her hand up to his cheek and he turned to plant a kiss in the palm.

With a little shiver of pleasure, she slipped her arms around him. 'Oh, I am such a lucky woman!'

He gathered her against him. 'No regrets, then?'

'Not one.' She turned her face up and he obliged her with a long, lingering kiss. 'Mmm.' She snuggled closer.

'I feel quite dizzy. Perhaps I should not have drunk that Madeira last night.'

'You need some water.' He slipped out of bed and went to the cupboard. Zelah watched him, enjoying the sight of his bare, athletic body moving effortlessly as he crossed the floor.

'How did you know to come back?' he asked her, pouring water into two glasses. 'I thought I had done everything I could to keep you away, damned fool that I was.'

Zelah scrambled off the bed, but she paused to find her chemise from the tumble of clothes on the floor before she joined him, not quite comfortable yet to stand naked before him, except when she was in the grip of passion.

'Jasper told me how angry you were when you thought that he was merely toying with me.' She took the proffered glass. 'He said you wanted me to be happy.' The water was sweet as nectar. 'So I told him what would make me happy. Pray do not frown so, Dominic. I thought if anyone could tell me if there was any hope, it would be your twin.'

'And what did he say?'

'He had guessed you were not...indifferent to me, but we agreed that you were—how did he put it?—*too damned noble for your own good.*'

He scowled at her, his look promising retribution for her mockery. It sent a pleasurable shiver of anticipation down her spine. She continued.

'Jasper consented to bring me back with him, so that I might try to discover how you felt about me.'

'Damned foolishness,' he said explosively. 'What if I had turned you away? Worse, what if I had taken you to my bed and then cast you aside?'

Her stomach tightened in horror at the thought, but

she merely shrugged, turning to put down her glass as an old quotation came to her mind. 'Then *I would build me a willow cabin at your gate…*'

'Ah, don't, love!' He pulled her into his arms. 'I don't deserve you,' he muttered, covering her hair and her face with kisses. The now-familiar flame of desire began to burn inside, but she tried to quell it.

'You are right, of course,' she murmured, her head against his chest. 'As I shall endeavour to remind you at every opportunity.'

He put an end to her teasing by forcing her chin up and kissing her ruthlessly.

'When all our visitors have gone,' he growled once he had reduced her to shivering, adoring silence, 'which I hope will be very soon now, I plan to make love to you in every room in Rooks Tower. But for now, we will have to confine ourselves to this one.'

As his mouth covered hers, his arms tightened and he lifted her off the floor, carrying her backwards until she felt the solid edge of the desk against her thighs. The kiss deepened as her lips parted and his tongue invaded her, hinting at the pleasures to come. Her pulse was racing, control slipping away as he pushed her back on the desk. Her wayward body began to sing, straining for his touch. She made one last conscious effort to be rational.

'Dominic, the books!' she muttered against his mouth as he swept everything from the desk and laid her down on its unyielding surface. His mouth ceased the tender exploration of her lips and he raised his head a fraction to gaze down at her. The intense look in his eyes was so dark, so dangerously seductive that she shivered pleasurably beneath him.

'Damn the books,' he growled, before lowering his

head again and continuing his meticulous inch-by-inch kissing of her body that taught her more about her anatomy than all her reading had ever achieved.

* * * * *

Behind the Rake's Wicked Wager

Chapter One

'Well, well, Lord Markham, have you ever seen such a bonny child?'

Jasper Coale, Viscount Markham, looked down at the baby lying in its crib and was at a loss for words. Thankfully, his sister-in-law came to his aid.

'Fie now, Lady Andrews, when was a man ever interested in babies? I suspect the viscount is merely glad that his little godson is not screaming the house down, as he was doing during the ceremony.' Zelah gazed down fondly at her baby son. 'Fortunately the journey back from the church has rocked him off to sleep.'

The christening of Dominic and Zelah's second child had been a major event and the little church at Lesserton was crowded for the ceremony. Afterwards, Dominic laid on a feast at the White Hart for the tenants and villagers to enjoy, while family and close friends were invited to Rooks Tower for an elegant and substantial repast. Zelah had the satisfaction of seeing her rooms overflowing with guests, despite the threat of snow which was always a concern during the early months of the year. She suspected no small part of the inducement to the local families to leave their firesides was the knowledge that no lesser person than Viscount Markham would be present.

Jasper had been unable to attend the christening of his niece Arabella some eighteen months earlier, but Zelah and Dominic had asked him to stand godfather for their new-born son, and only the direst winter weather would have kept him away.

The fires at Rooks Tower were banked up, the table almost groaned with the banquet it was required to support and the wine flowed freely. Jasper was sure the neighbourhood would be talking about the Coales' hospitality for months to come. Most of the guests were gathered in the yellow salon, but Jasper had wandered across to join Zelah in the study where the baby was sleeping, watched over by his devoted nurse. Sir Arthur and Lady Andrews had followed him into the room, brimming with good humour thanks to the abundant quantities of wine and food.

'I admit I have nothing but praise for my godson while he is sleeping,' said Jasper, glancing down into the crib.

'It makes me quite broody,' declared Lady Andrews, causing her husband to guffaw loudly.

'Now, now, my dear, our breeding days are well past, thank the Lord!'

'I am well aware of that, sir.' The lady turned her bright gaze upon Jasper. 'But what of you, Lord Markham? I am sure, seeing your brother's felicity, you must envy him his happy state.'

Jasper's smile froze. Glancing across the crib, he saw the sudden alarm in Zelah's dark eyes. He must respond quickly, lest they notice how pale she had grown. But even as he sought for the words his sister-in-law recovered with a laughing rejoinder.

'Having spent the past two weeks here with his niece and godson, Lord Markham is more likely to value his freedom!' She tucked her hand in his arm. 'If you will excuse us, Sir Arthur, Lady Andrews, I must carry the viscount away now to speak to my sister before she leaves us…'

'I commend your quick thinking,' he murmured as they crossed the hall.

'I had to do something,' she responded quietly. 'I did not want you to snub them for their impertinence. They are good people, and mean well.'

'Mean well—!' He smothered an exclamation and after a moment continued, 'I beg your pardon, but it seems these days the whole world is eager to marry me off. I cannot look at a woman without her family hearing wedding bells.'

She chuckled. 'Surely it has always been thus. 'Tis merely that you are more aware of it now.'

'Perhaps you are right. I thought by leaving London I should have some respite from the incessant gossip and conjecture.'

Zelah gave a soft laugh and squeezed his arm.

'You are nigh on thirty years old, my lord. Society considers it time you settled down and produced an heir.'

'Society can go hang. I will not marry without love, and you know you are the only woman—'

Zelah stopped. 'Hush, Jasper, someone may hear you.'

'What if they do?' He smiled down at her. 'Dominic knows you refused me, it matters not what anyone else thinks.'

Zelah shook her head at him, trying to joke him out of his uncharacteristic seriousness.

'For shame, my lord, what of your reputation as the wicked flirt no woman can resist? It would be sadly dented if word got out that you had been rejected.'

He looked down at her, wondering how it was that of all the women he had met, the only one he had ever wanted to marry should prefer his twin.

'So it would,' he said, raising her fingers to his lips. 'Then let it be our secret, that you are the woman who broke my heart.'

Zelah blushed and shook her head at him.

'Fie, Jasper, I may have bruised your heart a little, but it is not broken, I am sure. I am not the woman for you. I believe there is another, somewhere, far more suited to you, my lord.'

'Well, I have not found her yet, and it is not for want of looking,' he quipped lightly.

'Mayhap love will come upon you when you least expect it,' she responded. 'As it did with me and Dominic.'

Jasper's heart clenched at the soft light that shone in her eyes when she spoke of his brother. It tightened even more as he observed her delighted smile at the sound of her husband's voice.

'What is this, sir, dallying with my wife again?'

She turned, in no way discomposed at being discovered tête-à-tête with the irresistible viscount, but that was because she knew herself innocent of any impropriety. She had never succumbed to his charms, thought Jasper, with a rueful inward smile. That had always been part of the attraction. She held out her hand to her husband.

Marriage suited Dominic. The damaged soldier who had returned from the Peninsula, barely alive, was now a contented family man and respected landowner, the horrific scars on his face and body lessened by the constant application of the salves and soothing balms Zelah prepared for him.

'Lady Andrews has been telling Jasper it is time he married,' said Zelah, her laughing glance flicking between them.

'Aye, so it is,' growled Dominic, the smile in his hard eyes belying his gruff tone. 'Put the female population out of its misery. My friends in town tell me at least three more silly chits sank into a decline when you left London at the end of the Season.'

Jasper spread his hands. 'If they wish to flirt with me, Dom, who am I to say them nay? As for marriage, I have no plans to settle down yet.'

'Well, you should,' retorted his twin bluntly. 'You need an heir. *I* do not want the title. I am happy enough here at Rooks Tower.' His arm slid around Zelah and he pulled her close. 'Come, love. Your sister is about to set off for West Barton and wishes to take her leave of you.'

'Ah, yes, we were on our way to say goodbye to Maria and Reginald, and little Nicky, too. I doubt we shall see my nephew again before he goes off to school in Exeter.' She sighed. 'We shall miss him dreadfully, shall we not, Dom?'

'*Little Nicky* is now a strapping eleven-year-old and so full of mischief he is in serious danger of being throttled by my gamekeeper,' retorted her fond husband.

'Ripe and ready for a spree, is he?' Jasper grinned, remembering his own boyhood, shared with his twin. 'Then by all means pack him off to school.'

He allowed Zelah to take his arm again.

'So you intend to leave us tomorrow,' she remarked as they walked towards the yellow salon. 'Back to London?'

'No, Bristol. To Hotwells.'

'Hotwells?' Dominic gave a bark of laughter. 'Never tell me you are going to visit Gloriana Barnabus.'

'I am indeed,' replied Jasper. 'I had a letter from her before Christmas, begging me to call upon her.'

'What a splendid name,' declared Zelah. 'Is she as colourful as she sounds?'

'No,' growled Dominic. 'She is some sort of distant cousin, a fading widow who enjoys the poorest of health. Did she say why she is so anxious to see you after all these years?'

'Not a word, though I suspect it is to do with her son Gerald. Probably wants me to sponsor his entry into Parliament, or some such.'

Dominic shrugged as he stood back for his twin and his wife to enter the yellow salon.

'Well, dancing attendance upon Gloriana will keep you out of mischief for a while.'

Zelah cast a considering glance up at her brother-in-law.

'I am not so sure, my love. With that handsome face and his wicked charm, I fear Lord Markham will get into mischief anywhere!'

Jasper set off from Rooks Tower the following morning, driving himself in his curricle with only his groom beside him and his trunk securely strapped behind. Dominic and Zelah were there to see him off, looking the picture of domestic felicity. He did not begrudge his twin his happiness, but despite Zelah's words he could not believe he would ever be so fortunate. He had met so many women, flirted with hundreds, but not one save Zelah had ever touched his heart. With a sigh he settled himself more comfortably in the seat and concentrated on the winding road. He would have to marry at some point and provide an heir, but not yet, not yet.

Miss Susannah Prentess wandered into the morning room of her Bath residence to find her aunt sitting at a small gilded table whose top was littered with papers. She had a pen in hand and was currently engaged in adding up a column of figures, so she did not look up when her niece addressed her.

'How much did we make last night, ma'am?'

Mrs Wilby finished her calculations and wrote a neat tally at the bottom of the sheet before replying.

'Almost two hundred pounds, and once we have taken off the costs, supper, candles and the like, I think we shall clear one-fifty easily. Very satisfying, when one thinks it is not yet March.'

Susannah regarded her with admiration.

'How glad I am you discovered a talent for business, Aunt Maude.'

A blush tinted Mrs Wilby's faded cheek.

'Nonsense, it is merely common sense and a grasp of figures, my love, something which you have inherited, also.'

'And thank goodness for that. It certainly helps when it comes to fleecing our guests.'

'Susannah, we do not *fleece* anyone! It is merely that we are better at measuring the odds.' The blush was replaced by a more indignant rose. 'You make it sound as if we run a gaming house, which is something I could *never* condone.'

Susannah was quick to reassure her.

'No, no, of course not, I was teasing you. We merely invite our friends here for an evening of cards, and if they lose a few shillings—'

'Or guineas!'

'Or guineas,' she conceded, her eyes twinkling, 'then so much the better for us.'

Aunt Maude looked at her uncertainly, then clasped her hands and burst out, 'But I cannot like it, my love. To be making money in such a way—'

'We do not make very much, Aunt, and *some* of our guests go away the richer for the evening.'

'Yes, but overall—oh, my dear, I cannot think that it is right, and I know our neighbours here in the Royal Crescent do not approve.'

'Pho, a few valetudinarian spoil-sports. Our card parties are very select.' She sank down on to a sofa. 'I agree, Royal Crescent would not be my first choice of a place to live, but Uncle's will was quite explicit, I cannot touch my fortune or sell this house until I am five and twenty. Another two years.'

'You could let it out, and we could find something smaller...'

The wistful note was not lost on Susannah, but she shook her head, saying firmly, 'No, this house suits my requirements very well. The location lends our parties a certain distinction.' She added mischievously, 'Besides, I am a great heiress, and Royal Crescent is perfectly in keeping with my status.'

Aunt Maude looked down, gazing intently at the nails of one white hand.

'I thought, when you asked me to come and live with you, it was so that you could go about a little.'

'But I do go about, Aunt. Why, what with the Pump Room and the theatre, the balls and assemblies, we go about a great deal.'

'But I thought you wanted to find a husband.'

Susannah laughed at that.

'No, no, that was never my intention. I am very happy with my single state, thank you.'

'But at three-and-twenty you are in danger of becoming an old maid.'

'Then that is what I shall do,' she replied, amused. 'Or mayhap I shall accept an offer from one of the charming young men who grace our card parties.'

'If only you would,' sighed Mrs Wilby.

'Mr Barnabus proposed to me yesterday.' She saw her aunt's hopeful look and quickly shook her head. 'I refused him, of course. I tried very hard not to let it come to a proposal, but he would not be gainsaid.'

'Oh dear, was he very disappointed?'

'Yes, but he will get over it.'

'I hope to goodness he does not try to end it all, like poor Mr Edmonds.'

Susannah laughed.

'I hope you do not think my refusing Jamie Edmonds had anything to do with his falling into the river.'

'I heard he jumped from Bath Bridge…'

'My dear Aunt, he was drinking in some low tavern near the quay, as young men are wont to do, and then tried to walk the parapet on the bridge, missed his footing and tumbled off on to a coal barge.' Her lips twitched at the look of disappointment on her aunt's face. 'I know it to be true, Aunt, because Jamie told me himself, when I next saw him in Milsom Street.'

'But everyone said—'

'I know what everyone *said*, but that particular rumour was spread by one of Mr Edmonds's friends, Mr Warwick. He was angry because I would not take an IOU from him last week and sent him home before supper.'

'Ay, yes, I remember Mr Warwick.' Mrs Wilby nodded.

'It was quite clear that he was drinking too much and was in no fit state to be in a respectable establishment.'

'And in no fit state to play at cards, which is more to the point,' added Susannah. 'But he did make me a very handsome apology later, so he is forgiven.' She jumped up. 'But enough of this. I am for the Pump Room, then back via Duffields, to find something to read. Will you come with me?'

'Gladly. I hope we shall find old friends at the Pump Room to converse with.'

Susannah's eyes twinkled wickedly.

'And *I* hope we shall find new friends to invite to our next card party!'

Chapter Two

The damp February weather made for a dirty journey north, but Jasper spent only one night on the road and arrived at Mrs Barnabus's house at Hotwells shortly after mid-day. He was ushered in by a butler whose sombre mien led him to wonder if he had maligned his relative, and she was in fact at death's door. However, when he was shown into the elegant drawing room, Mrs Barnabus appeared to be in her usual state of health. She came forwards to meet him, hands held out and shawls trailing from her thin shoulders.

'Markham, my dear cousin, how good of you to call.' Her voice was as frail as her person, but Jasper knew there was a will of iron inside the waif-like body. He took the hand held out to him and kissed it punctiliously. The fingers curled around his hand like claws. 'So good of you to come out of your way, when you know I have no room to put you up here.'

'Yes, wasn't it?' he replied cheerfully.

She sank on to the sofa, trying to pull him down with her, but he freed himself and drew up a chair.

'You are on your way back to London, Markham?'

'Yes. I hope to reach Corsham tonight. Well, Gloriana, what can I do for you?'

Her sigh was audible.

'So like your dear father.'

'Devil a bit, madam. He wouldn't have put himself out to come here at all. He would have sent a servant to find out what it was you wanted.'

Gloriana looked a trifle discomposed at this but she recovered quickly and gave him a wan smile.

'In looks, my dear boy, in looks. And how is your poor, scarred soldier-brother?'

The epithet grated on Jasper but he concealed it.

'Dominic is prospering. And very happy with his growing family. Now, Gloriana, tell me why you have summoned me here.'

The widow wrung her hands and uttered dramatically, 'It is Gerald.'

'I thought as much. What has the boy done?'

This cool response drew a reproachful look from the widow.

'So charming yet so implacable.' She sighed. 'No wonder you break so many hearts.'

'Not intentionally, ma'am, I assure you.' He took out his watch. 'I am sorry to hurry you, Gloriana, but my curricle is waiting and I do not want to keep the horses standing too long in this cold weather. Tell me about Gerald.'

'Your manners, Markham, leave a lot to be desired.'

'But a moment ago you were telling me I was charming.'

Mrs Barnabus struggled with herself. She would have liked to give the viscount a sharp set-down but she wanted his help, and she was very much afraid if she ordered him to apologise or be on his way, he would choose the latter option. The fact that he was well aware of her inner turmoil did nothing to improve her temper. She forgot her plaintive tone and spoke curtly.

'He has formed a disastrous attachment.'

Jasper's black brows rose.

'Really? That does not sound like Gerald. When I've met him in town I have always thought him a level-headed young buck.'

Apart from a faint moue of distaste she ignored his description of her beloved son.

'That is why I am so concerned. He came to see me before Christmas, extolling the virtues of this woman— a very paragon she sounded!—but I took little notice. He has always been a sensible boy and I thought his infatuation would soon burn itself out. Then one of my acquaintances wrote to tell me that this…this *female* holds regular card parties. I am told she won a considerable sum of money from Gerald. Two hundred guineas!'

'A mere nothing. He could lose more than that in a sitting at White's.'

'Perhaps, but my acquaintance says all Bath was talking of it.'

'Bath!' Jasper laughed. 'He has become enamoured of a lady from *Bath*? Is she an invalid or old enough to be his grandmama?'

'It may not be quite as fashionable as it was, but there are still any number of people who like to visit there,' replied Mrs Barnabus, affronted by his humour. 'I should go there myself, if the waters here were not more beneficial for those like myself who are prone to consumptive symptoms.'

'Well perhaps you should go there anyway, to find out just what Gerald is about.'

'He will not listen to me. He is one-and-twenty now,

and in charge of his own fortune. Besides, I could not possibly travel such a distance.'

'It is barely fifteen miles, Cousin.'

'And I would be so knocked up I should be in no fit state to help my poor son.' She sank back on the sofa and waved her vinaigrette under her nose, weakened merely by the thought of such a journey. 'No, Markham, as head of the family, it is up to you to rescue Gerald from the clutches of this—this harpy.'

'My dear ma'am, we have no evidence that there is anything wrong with the woman at all, save that she has beaten Gerald at cards. And even that is not to be wondered at. If I remember rightly he was never that sharp.'

Gloriana's eyes snapped angrily.

'You are too cruel, Markham. The boy is almost ten years your junior and lacks your worldly experience. And now, when I ask, nay, *beg* you to help him, you can do nothing but jest.' She broke off, dragging a wisp of lace from her pocket and dabbing at her eyes.

Jasper regarded her in exasperation as he saw his dinner at the Hare and Hounds slipping away. However, beneath his insouciant exterior he was quite fond of Gerald, so he gave in with a faint shrug.

'Very well, ma'am, I can as easily stop at Bath tonight as at Corsham. I will seek out Gerald and find out just what is afoot.'

Gently brushing aside her grateful effusions and the belated offer of a glass of ratafia, Jasper took his leave of Gloriana and headed for York House.

He arrived at the busy Bath hotel before five o'clock, in good time to bespeak rooms and dinner. Then, having changed his travel clothes for the coat and knee-breeches that were still the required evening dress for Bath, he sallied forth in search of Gerald Barnabus.

Susannah looked around the drawing room with satisfaction. It was filling up nicely and most of the little card tables were occupied.

'Another good turn-out.'

Susannah heard the murmur and found Kate Logan at her side. Kate was a widow and past her thirtieth year, although she looked younger and her stylish gown of bronze satin with its matching turban drew many a gentleman's eye. Susannah knew Kate was well aware of her attraction and used it to advantage at the card table, although she never succumbed to any gentleman's advances. She continued now in her habitual slow drawl, 'There is a ball at the Lower Rooms tonight, so doubtless many will take themselves off there at ten and then we can get down to business.'

Susannah shushed her with a look and said in a voice of mock severity, 'There is no *business* here, Mrs Logan. We merely invite a few friends to enjoy a game of cards.'

Kate gave a knowing smile.

'That is what I meant, Susannah.'

'Of course,' added Susannah innocently, 'some of our guests might lose a few guineas at our tables, but that is hardly to be wondered at, after all.' She glanced at her friend, trying to keep her countenance, but failed miserably, and her peal of laughter made several heads turn. 'Oh dear, now I have made people stare. Go away, Kate, before I forget myself again. Look, my aunt is waving to you to make a fourth at whist.'

'And she is sitting down with Mr and Mrs Anstruther, who spend so much time bickering that they invariably lose. Very well, I shall go, and I see old Major Crommelly is coming over, no doubt to engage you for a game of picquet, which is his pretext to get you to himself and subject you to the most fulsome compliments.'

'He may positively shower me with compliments as long as he is happy to play for pound points,' chuckled Susannah, turning to greet the elderly gentleman who was approaching her.

It was well over an hour later that she rose from the table, refusing the major's suggestion that they should play another hand.

'But, my dear Miss Prentess, the night is yet young.'

'It is indeed, but I have other guests to attend, Major, and cannot let you monopolise me.' She softened her words with a smile and went off to join her aunt, whom she found bubbling with excitement.

'Susannah, I am so glad you are come, I was determined to interrupt your game if you had not finished when you did.'

'My dear ma'am, what has occurred to put you into a spin?'

'Mr Barnabus has arrived—'

'Is that all? How did he look? I hope he is not too downhearted—'

'No, that is, I did not notice.' Aunt Maude flapped her hands in excitement. 'Did you see the stranger he brought with him?'

'No, I was paying picquet with the major and had my back to the door.' Susannah looked around. 'Has Mr Barnabus brought another gentleman, then? That is good of him, and shows he has not taken umbrage at my refusal.'

'No, not a gentleman, Susannah. A *viscount*. There, I knew that would make you stare.'

'It does indeed. We have had nothing more prestigious than a baron here before, although I suppose General Sanstead is pretty high…'

Mrs Wilby tapped her niece's arm with her closed fan.

'Pray be serious, Susannah, his presence here adds distinction! You must let me make you known to him at once.'

'By all means, Aunt. Lead on.'

'No need, here he comes now,' Mrs Wilby responded in a shrill whisper, and Susannah looked around to see two gentlemen approaching. The first, a stocky young man with an open, boyish countenance beneath a thatch of fair hair, was Gerald Barnabus, and after a brief smile of welcome she turned her attention to his companion. The contrast with Mr Barnabus was striking. Gerald looked neat—even smart—in his evening dress, but the viscount's black coat bore all the hallmarks of a London tailor. It fitted perfectly across his shoulders and followed the tapering line of the body to his waist. Satin knee-breeches stretched over muscled thighs that hinted at the athlete, while the startling white of his quilted waistcoat and impeccable linen of his shirt and neckcloth proclaimed a level of sartorial elegance not often seen in Bath.

The man himself was tall and lean, with hair as dark as midnight. The golden, flickering candlelight accentuated the strong lines of his handsome face. When she met his eyes a little tremor ran down her spine. She was used to seeing admiration in a man's look, but the viscount's gaze was coolly appraising.

'Ah, there you are, Miss Prentess,' Gerald greeted

her cheerfully. 'I have brought a friend with me; I made sure you would not object to it. Well, I say friend, but he is some sort of cousin, actually...'

'Come, Gerald, you are taking far too long about this.'

The viscount's voice was low and pleasant, with just a hint of laughter. He turned to Susannah, the cool look in his eyes replaced by a glinting smile.

'I am Markham.' He gave a little bow. 'How do you do?'

'I am very well, my lord, thank you. And of course there can be no objection to your coming here with Mr Barnabus.'

'Aye, I knew you would be pleased,' said Gerald, grinning.

Susannah barely heard Gerald's words for the viscount had reached for her hand and lifted it to his lips.

'Are you making a long stay in Bath, my lord?' She struggled to ignore the fluttering inside, like the soft beating of birds' wings against her ribcage. The pad of his thumb had rubbed gently over her knuckles before he gave up her hand and her skin still tingled with the memory.

'I am on my way to town. I merely stopped off to look in on my cousin.'

'Aye, which is why I persuaded him to take pot luck here with me tonight,' added Gerald.

'And we are delighted to have you join us.' Mrs Wilby spread her fan and looked about her while Susannah stood mute at her side, trying to make sense of her reaction to this stranger. 'What would you care to play, my lord? There is macao, or loo, or euchre...or if you care to wait a little I am sure we can set you up with a rubber of whist—'

'You are too kind, ma'am, but if you have no ob-jection I shall walk about a little.' He bestowed such a charming smile upon Aunt Maude that Susannah was not at all surprised to see her simpering like a school-room miss. 'I like to gauge the opposition before I com-mit myself to the game.'

'You will find no deep play here, my lord,' Susannah responded. 'And no hardened gamesters.'

'No?' His brows lifted. 'Not even yourself, Miss Prentess?'

Again that flutter down her spine. She was close enough to see his eyes now. Blue-grey, and hard as slate.

She shook her head. 'I am no gamester, my lord.'

'But she *is* good,' said Gerald. 'I'd wager she could match you, Cousin.'

'Indeed? Perhaps we should put it to the test.'

His voice was silky, but she heard the note of con-tempt in his tone. To her dismay she felt the blush ris-ing to her cheeks. She could do nothing to hide it, so she put up her chin and replied to Gerald with a smile.

'You are too kind, Mr Barnabus. I have no wish to pit myself against one who is no doubt a master.'

She excused herself and walked away. As she passed the table where Mrs Logan was presiding at a noisy game of *vingt-et-un,* Kate stretched out her hand to detain her.

'You seem to have netted a big fish there, Susannah,' she murmured. 'Who is he?'

'Viscount Markham, Gerald's cousin.'

'Indeed? A very big fish then.' Kate's eyes flickered over the viscount, then came back to her friend. 'He does not please you?'

'He seems inclined to sneer at our little party.' Susannah shrugged. 'Let my aunt deal with him. If we are not to his taste I hope he will not stay long.'

A shout recalled Kate's attention to the game and Susannah moved on. She sat down with a large group who were playing loo and tried to give her attention to the cards, but all the time she was aware of the viscount's tall figure wandering around the room. Then, suddenly, she could not see him and wondered if he had been persuaded to sit down at one of the other tables, or if he had taken his leave. The unease she had felt in his presence made her hope it was the latter.

As the evening wore on and the crowd in the room thinned, Susannah noticed the familiar, subtle change in the card party. The chatter and laughter died away as those who were left concentrated on their game. Two young gentlemen challenged her to take them on at ombre and she was busily engaged with them until the supper gong sounded at midnight.

'*Sacardo* again, Miss Prentess,' laughed one of the young men, throwing down his cards in mock disgust. 'You are unbeatable tonight.'

'Aye, she has won almost every trick,' declared the other, watching as Susannah swept the small pile of coins from the table into her reticule. 'I hope you will allow Warwick and me the chance to take our revenge later?'

'More to the point, Farthing, I hope Miss Prentess will allow me to escort her down to supper,' added Mr Warwick, looking hopefully across at Susannah.

'Nay, as to that, surely the honour should fall to me?' said Mr Farthing. 'I at least won *codille*, sir, so it can be said I bested you!'

Susannah threw up her hands, laughing.

'Gentlemen, pray, do not fight over such a trifle.'

'Especially when the trick is already won,' said a deep, amused voice. 'I have come to escort you down to supper, Miss Prentess.'

Susannah looked round to find Lord Markham standing behind her, his hand on the back of her chair.

'Indeed, my lord?' His self-assurance rattled her. 'I rather think these gentlemen might oppose you.'

A glance back showed Susannah that the two young men might have been prepared to fight each other for the pleasure of taking her to supper, but they were far too in awe of a viscount to raise an objection. She was disappointed when they scrambled to their feet, uttering disjointed phrases.

'L-Lord Markham! N-no, no objections at all, my lord.'

'Only too happy...'

'There, you see? No opposition at all.' The humour glinting in Lord Markham's eyes did nothing to appease Susannah, but it would not do to show her displeasure, so with a smile of acquiescence she took his hand and allowed him to lead her off. As they moved through the room she looked around her.

'Ah, my aunt is setting up another game of loo. Perhaps she would like me to help her—'

'No, it was she who suggested I should take you downstairs.' When Susannah hesitated he added, 'You can see, Miss Prentess, that everyone is perfectly content. You may take a little time now to enjoy yourself. These parties are designed to be enjoyed. After all, it is not as if you are running a gaming hell here.'

She looked at him sharply, but could read nothing from his smile. His manners were perfectly polite, but she had the distinct feeling he was on his guard, that he was assessing her. Susannah gave an inward shrug. What did it matter? He was not staying in Bath.

She accompanied him to the supper room, where a selection of cold meats, fruits and sweets was laid out on the table. Susannah chose sparingly from the selection before her, but she was surprised when her escort showed no interest in the food.

'I am sorry I cannot offer you soup or ramekins, Lord Markham. Our guests make do with a cold collation, even in winter, although there is warm wine for anyone who wishes it.'

'I require nothing, thank you.'

They found an empty table and sat down. Susannah took a little minced chicken, but found she had no appetite with the viscount sitting opposite her.

'You work very hard at your...entertainments, Miss Prentess.'

'I help my aunt as best I can, sir.'

'And how often do you hold these little parties?'

'Every Tuesday.'

'Indeed? You must be prodigious fond of cards, ma'am.'

'My aunt enjoys them, yes.'

'I stand corrected.'

She looked up at him, understanding dawning.

'Ah, I see what it is,' she said, smiling. 'You are concerned for your cousin.'

'Should I not be?'

'Mr Barnabus will come to no harm here.'

'But you have already taken two hundred guineas from him in one night.'

She stared at him. 'How do you know that? Did Mr Barnabus tell you?'

'He did not need to. Such deep play excites comment.'

'Deep play?' She laughed. 'I am sure in your London club such a sum would be considered insignificant.'

He leaned forwards.

'But we are not in my London club, Miss Prentess.'

The unease she had been feeling all evening intensified. She put down her fork.

'It was unfortunate. I have not allowed it to happen again.' She met his eyes, returning his gaze steadily. 'I am not trying to entrap your cousin.'

'No?'

'Of course not.' She hesitated. 'You may not know it, but he made me an offer of marriage and I refused him. Does that not tell you I have no designs upon him?'

'Perhaps you are hoping to catch a bigger prize.'

Some of the tension eased and she laughed at the absurdity of his claim.

'My lord, you have seen the guests my aunt invites. Couples, mainly, like General Sanstead and his wife, intent upon an evening's sport. And as for the single gentlemen, they are either too old to be looking for a wife or they have yet to make their way in the world.'

'And such men are very susceptible to the, ah, blandishments of a pretty woman.'

Susannah's brows snapped together.

'I find the implication insulting, sir.' She pushed her plate away. 'I must go back upstairs.'

'As you wish.'

What she *wished* was to order him from the house, but she could hardly eject a viscount from her aunt's card party without good reason, and it would not do to stir up gossip. Instead she contented herself with returning to the drawing room and quitting his company with no more than a nod of her head.

A rubber of whist with Kate as her partner did much to restore her spirits and later she took her turn at playing *vingt-et-un*, drawing a crowd of gentlemen, as usual. She concentrated hard on the game. This was her aunt's party, after all, so it was not for her to keep an eye on who was leaving. However, the game was over and the players dispersing when Gerald approached her, so she could not avoid him.

'Are you leaving us, Mr Barnabus?' She put aside her cards and rose to meet him.

'Aye, my cousin has invited me to take my brandy with him tonight, if you will give me leave?'

From the corner of her eye Susannah saw Lord Markham standing a little way behind his cousin. It would have given her great pleasure to tell Gerald that she would not release him. He would stay, she was sure of it from his look and the warm note in his voice. But that might raise his hopes that she felt something stronger for him than friendship, and she would not serve him such a trick. Instead she contented herself with giving him her warmest smile as he bowed over her fingers, and a murmur—loud enough for the viscount to hear—that she hoped to see him again *very* soon.

'I saw the viscount take you off to supper.' Mrs Logan came up as Susannah watched the two men leave the room. 'Another conquest, do you think?'

'Hardly.' She chuckled. 'The viscount is more inclined to think me a gold-digger. I have no doubt that he will warn his cousin off.'

'Pity. He would have been a rich pigeon for the plucking.'

'I wish you wouldn't use such cant terms, Kate.'

'I am a soldier's widow, love. I know a lot worse than that.'

'I am sure you do, and I am pleased you have left that life behind.'

'Aye, and with it the need for a husband.'

'Come, Kate. You are still young, and I have seen how the men flock to you—are you sure you do not wish to marry again?'

'Put myself in the power of one man, when as a widow I can flirt and enjoy myself with anyone I wish?' Kate shook her head. 'Never. Never again. You know as well as I what monsters men can be, if one allows them dominance.'

Susannah shivered.

'Let us not think of that, Kate. It is all in the past.' She gave her friend a quick hug. 'Now, let us see what we can do to hurry these few remaining guests on their way. I need to get to bed since I have to be up early in the morning.' She lowered her voice. 'Odesse sent me a note. We have another client.'

Kate's eyes widened. 'Word is spreading,' she murmured.

Susannah nodded. 'As we knew it would. I shall drive out tomorrow to make sure she is settled in.'

'That is not necessary,' said Kate. 'Mrs Gifford—'

'Is a dear soul, but I like to talk to each of our—er—clients myself, it reassures them.' She laughed. 'Pray do not look so disapproving, Kate. This was as much your idea as mine.'

'I know, but it was never my intention that you should be so personally involved.'

Susannah's laughter deserted her.

'Why not? It is my reason for living, Kate.'

The walk back to George Street was not a long one, but the icy blast that hit them as they stepped out on to the Crescent prompted Gerald to ask Jasper if they would not be better to go back indoors and send a servant for a cab.

'By no means,' he replied. 'The fresh air will do us good. Unless you mean to imply I am too old for such a journey…'

Gerald laughed.

'I would not dare. Let us walk, by all means.' He tucked his hand into Jasper's arm as they set off at a good pace towards the Circus. 'Tell me what you thought of Susannah.'

'Miss Prentess? At first glance, a beauty.'

'She *is* beautiful, isn't she? A golden goddess! But it is not just her looks, Jasper, it is her spirit, too. She is so good, so charitable.'

'Not so charitable that she won't take your money at the card table.'

'No, no, a mere trifle. She will not countenance anyone losing more than fifty guineas at a sitting.'

'That is not what I have heard.'

'Ah.' Gerald gave a self-conscious laugh. 'You said you had called upon my mother. I suppose she told you I had lost more, and asked you to come and rescue me.'

'Not in so many words.'

Gerald swore under his breath.

'Damn the Bath tabbies that report my every move! That was a single occurrence, and entirely my own doing. Susannah did not wish to take my money, I assure you—I had to almost beg her to do so. And I had thought hard beforehand. It was money I could afford to lose.'

'That is what all gamesters will tell you.'

Gerald stopped and pulled away.

'I am no gambler, Jasper. If I was I would be sporting my blunt in some hell, rather than in Mrs Wilby's drawing room!'

The flare of a nearby street lamp showed the boy's face to be serious. Jasper put a hand on his shoulder.

'No, I had not thought it of you, until now. I take it that Miss Prentess is the attraction, rather than the cards?'

'Of course. You must have noticed how many young bucks were there tonight.'

'And old roués,' added Jasper.

'It is all the rage to be in love with her.' Gerald began to walk on, his good humour quite restored. 'She is beautiful, and an heiress.'

'Indeed?'

'Aye. She is old Middlemass's heir, don't you know.'

'What, the nabob?'

'That's right.'

'Well, that explains the house in Royal Crescent.'

'Aye, the old man bought it when he returned from India, but rarely used it. Susannah was his only relative. She was living with him at his place in Westbury when he died, and he left everything to her in trust until she is five-and-twenty.'

'Then I am no longer surprised all Bath is at her feet. Yet why should Gloriana call it a disastrous attachment?'

'Not everyone in Bath is enamoured of Miss Prentess.'

'I would have thought her fortune would make her universally admired.'

'Yes, well, Bath is not London, Jasper. Respectability is everything here, don't you know. And there are some high sticklers in Bath, including those who write to my mother. And Miss Prentess does not go out of her way to flatter them.'

'So what do they have against the lady?'

'For one thing they do not approve of her setting herself up in Royal Crescent with her aunt—if the truth were told I suspect they are jealous that she can afford to do so. Then there is her birth. Her father was a soldier and her mother an officer's daughter. Perfectly respectable,' he added quickly. 'I ascertained as much before I—'

'Yes?' Jasper prompted him.

'I offered her my hand.'

There was no mistaking the rather belligerent note in Gerald's voice. He clearly expected Jasper to be outraged. Instead Jasper said merely, 'I am glad you had so much presence of mind. When one is…head over heels, one is inclined to forget such things.'

Gerald relaxed again and aimed a playful punch at his ribs.

'Well, I didn't! I am not such a looby.' He sighed. 'I made sure the fortune would reconcile Mama to her, and I am sure it would have done, if Susannah had accepted me.'

'Does that matter now? Since the lady has refused you…'

'I hope she will be persuaded to change her mind.' They had reached George Street and the entrance to York House. Jasper stood back for Gerald to precede him but the young man turned to him, saying earnestly,

'You have met her, Jasper. You could speak to Mama for me. Susannah—Miss Prentess—is infinitely superior to every other woman I have ever met, you must see that.'

'Ah...' Jasper gave him a rueful smile '...but I have met rather more women than you, Cousin. Now, shall we go in out of the cold?'

Gerald took his leave a couple of hours later, but instead of retiring immediately, Jasper poured himself another brandy and settled himself into the chair beside the fire. He had done his duty by his cousin and warned him against proposing marriage again without careful thought, but Gerald had merely laughed at his concerns and asked him what fault he could find with Susannah Prentess. And indeed, Jasper could not find any, but something nagged at him.

He had spent the evening in Royal Crescent, watching and listening. The card party appeared to be quite innocuous and everyone enjoyed themselves, especially the numerous gentlemen who vied with each other for the opportunity to play cards with Miss Prentess, but he would be surprised if many of them left the house richer than they entered it. Both his hostess and her niece were excellent card players. He had observed them closely during the evening—their assessment of their opponents' hands was shrewd and the play was as clever as anything he had seen in town. Then there was the widow, Mrs Logan. She appeared to be very thick with Miss Prentess, and when the two ladies sat down together at the whist table they were unbeatable.

Jasper frowned, cupping his brandy glass between his hands. He had seen no evidence of sharp practice, and he noted that Miss Prentess kept the stakes deliberately low and gently turned away any gentleman who was losing too much. She was very clever, winning small amounts, not enough to cause the loser distress, or to arouse suspicion. And as Gerald said, they were safer playing there than in some gambling hell. But there were at least a dozen gentlemen present, and fifty guineas from each....

'Hell and confound it, she is an heiress,' he muttered. 'She cannot want the money!'

Perhaps they needed the extra funds for their lifestyle. But there had been nothing too lavish about the supper provided for the guests and Miss Prentess's gown of figured muslin showed quality rather than ostentation.

He finished his brandy in one gulp and set down the glass. He had fulfilled his promise. He could write to Gloriana and tell her that Miss Prentess was no harpy, but something still rankled. Gerald had laughed off his words of caution and was obviously too infatuated with the lady to make a rational judgement, so it behooved his older and more worldly-wise cousin to do it for him.

He would remain in Bath.

Chapter Three

'My dear, are you sure you want to go to the ball to-night? You are almost asleep there.'

Susannah looked up with a start. She and her aunt were sitting in the morning room, where the welcome heat from the fire had made her quite drowsy.

'Of course, ma'am. I shall be very well, once I have had dinner.' Susannah brushed aside her aunt's concerns with a smile.

'But you have been sitting there this past half-hour without saying a word.'

'Then I beg your pardon, I am a little tired after my travelling today.'

'You were gone for so long I was beginning to worry.'

'There was no need, Aunt. You know I had Dorcas with me.'

'But I *do* worry, my love. I can never be easy when you are…visiting. One never knows what you might pick up.'

Susannah smiled. 'My dear aunt, I assure you there is no danger of contamination.'

'Not of the *body*, perhaps, but—'

'Please, Aunt, you know we have discussed this often

and often. There is no danger at all in what I do, so let us not pursue it.' She looked across as the door opened. 'Ah, here is Gatley to tell us dinner is ready. Shall we go down?'

Susannah did her best to entertain her aunt at dinner and to hide all signs of fatigue, but she had to admit to herself that she *was* tired. It had been three o'clock before the last of the guests had left and she could fall into bed that morning. She should not complain, for it proved how successful their little card parties had become. But she had been up and out of the house before ten o'clock, not returning to the Crescent until late in the afternoon. Her aunt would argue that there was no need for her to go out, that she could entrust such errands to a servant, but Susannah's independent spirit baulked at that. She had set herself a task and she would see it through. And that included going to the ball tonight.

The Upper Rooms were already crowded when Susannah and her aunt arrived. Their chairmen weaved through the press of carriages and deposited them under the entrance portico, where the music from the ballroom could be faintly heard. It was ten o'clock, the hour when the fashionable would leave their private parties and proceed to the ball, so the entrance was buzzing with activity. There were many acquaintances to be greeted once the ladies had removed their cloaks and straightened their shawls.

Susannah waved to Mrs Logan, who had just arrived, then turned back to greet a turbaned matron who sailed up to her with two marriageable daughters in her wake.

'Oh, Miss Prentess—another new gown? You are always so beautifully turned out.' The matron sighed ecstatically as she regarded Susannah's flowered muslin. 'So fine, my dear. And the lace edging, quite, quite exquisite. Is it Brussels?'

Susannah smiled and shook her head. 'No, ma'am, it is made locally, and it is exclusive to Odesse, the new modiste in Henrietta Street.'

'Indeed? I thought you had ordered it from London, so fine as it is.'

'Thank you, Mrs Bulstrode. I find Odesse excellent. And she has excelled herself; I did not expect to have this gown for another week at least.'

The matron's eyes brightened. 'And in Henrietta Street, you say?'

'Yes, her prices are very reasonable.' Susanna dropped her voice a little. 'Especially when one considers what one has to pay for gowns in Milsom Street. Not that one objects to the price, of course, but Odesse does seem to have a certain style...'

'Indeed she does, Miss Prentess. That gown is quite superb. Well, well, I shall look her up.' With a smile Mrs Bulstrode gathered her daughters and went off, leaving Susannah to smile after her.

'Excellent,' murmured Kate, coming up. 'That could not have been better timed. Amelia Bulstrode is such a gabble-monger that our new modiste's name will be on every woman's lips by the end of the evening.'

'And her gowns will be on a good many ladies' backs by the end of the month,' added Susannah. 'I have achieved what I wanted to do without even entering the ballroom.' She noted the startled look in Mrs Wilby's eye and shook her head, laughing. 'You need not fear, Aunt, I do not intend to go home yet. I hope to drum up even more business for the new modiste before the evening is out.'

'Don't!' hissed Mrs Wilby in an urgent whisper. 'Pray, Susannah, do *not* mention the word business. It is not at all becoming.'

'Quite right,' agreed Kate, her lips twitching. 'Susannah is a lady and should know nothing about such matters. She is here merely to look beautiful and to stir up such envy that the other ladies will all want to know where she buys her gowns.'

'Kate!'

Susannah's protest evoked nothing more than a shake of the head from her friend.

'It is true, Susannah, and you know it. And I like the new way you have put up your hair,' she added. 'Quite in the classical style. What is it Mr Barnabus christened you? The golden goddess. Well tonight you could as well be called a Greek goddess.'

'Thank you, but enough of your nonsense,' said Susannah, trying to ignore the heat that burned her cheeks. 'Let us go in, shall we?'

They moved on to the ballroom. Heads turned as Susannah entered, but she was used to that. As Bath's richest heiress it was only to be expected that she would be pointed out wherever she went, and tonight it suited her purpose to be noticed.

The dancing was already in progress and the floor was a mass of bodies, swirling and skipping in time to the music. There were a good number of acquaintances present, including many of the gentlemen who had attended the card party the previous evening. As soon as she entered she was surrounded by hopeful suitors, all begging for the honour of a dance. Laughing, Kate carried Mrs Wilby off to the benches at the side of the room, leaving Susannah with her admirers.

The country dances were lively and in such a crowd

it was necessary to concentrate to avoid jostling the other dancers. Nevertheless, Susannah enjoyed herself, and was happy to join a second and even a third set as the gentlemen lined up to partner her. She was hot and not a little dizzy by the time Mr Edmonds swung her through the final steps of a particularly lively country dance. He invited her to stand up again even as the last notes were fading.

'You are very kind, sir, but I am going to sit down now,' she said, half-gasping, half-laughing as she rose from her curtsy. 'I really do not think I could dance another reel for quite a while, but thank you—oh!'

As she turned to leave the dance floor she found her way blocked by a wall of black. A second glance showed her it was not a wall, but a gentleman's evening coat, and when she allowed her eyes to travel up from the broad chest they were dazzled by the snowy white linen of an intricately tied neckcloth.

'I am very pleased to hear it, Miss Prentess, for I have brought you a glass of wine.'

She stepped back and lifted her gaze even further, to the smiling face of Lord Markham.

Jasper noted with satisfaction Susannah's start of surprise. There was no denying she looked quite beautiful with her golden hair piled up on her head and a soft flush of exertion mantling her cheeks. And she used her looks to good effect, for most of the men he had seen at the Crescent last night were in the ballroom. He had watched the young pups—and some of the older ones—flock around her as she entered and he had no doubt that they had engaged her for every dance, which was why he had decided upon more subtle tactics.

'Oh,' she said again, the blush on her cheek deepening. He held out a wineglass and she took it. As she sipped gratefully at her wine he cast a swift, appraising glance over her.

'Madras muslin,' he said, displaying his knowledge of ladies' fashion. 'Is that in deference to your late uncle, the nabob?'

Immediately she was on the defensive.

'No, but I am not ashamed of the source of my fortune, Lord Markham.'

'I am glad to hear it.'

They stood in silence, watching the dancers, but Susannah was very much aware of the man beside her. His evening clothes were simple, a plain coat of black superfine with black knee-breeches of Florentine silk, but they were superbly cut and he wore them with an air of assurance. He was a man used to commanding attention, and she could not deny that he had hers. They were standing side by side, inches apart, and the skin on her arm tingled at his proximity. Her whole body was aware of him, of the power in that long, lean frame. No man had ever affected her like this before. Swallowing nervously, she sought for something to say.

'I thought you had left Bath, my lord.'

'Not yet. My cousin appears very happy with the attractions here and I decided to stay and—er—sample them for myself.'

A wary look appeared in her hazel eyes.

'For one used to the delights of London, I fear you will find it sadly flat.'

'Are you trying to discourage me, Miss Prentess?'

'Not at all. But I believe our entertainment is nothing to London.'

'And how long have you lived here?'

'We moved into Bath about a year ago.'

'Then you shall advise me on the entertainments available.'

'I am sure your cousin can do that, sir.'

'But I would value a different perspective.'

'I would be only too happy to help you, sir, if I had the time, but I regret I am too busy at present.'

'Busy? With what?'

She ignored his question.

'But here is someone who may be able to help you.' She looked past him. 'You know Mrs Logan, I think?'

'We met last night.' Jasper bowed. 'Madam.'

'Ah, yes, Viscount Markham.' The widow held out her hand to him. 'We played at euchre together. How could I forget?'

'The viscount is planning to remain in Bath for a while, Kate.'

Jasper's keen eye did not miss the look of appeal Susannah gave her friend.

'Indeed? How delightful.'

'Yes, and he is anxious to know what entertainments the city offers. Perhaps, Kate, you can assist the viscount? You must excuse me, but I see my next dance partner is looking for me…'

With a gracious smile she hastened away. Jasper watched her go, his eyes narrowing. Outmanoeuvred, by gad, and by a slip of a girl. He told himself he was amused by her antics, but to one more accustomed to being toadied to and courted wherever he went, Jasper could not deny a small element of annoyance.

'Well, my lord?' Mrs Logan's voice cut through his thoughts and he turned back to her, his urbane smile firmly in place.

'Yes, madam, pray tell me the delights I might expect to find in Bath…'

* * *

Susannah hurried away to join her partner for the next dance set. She found her encounters with the viscount strangely unsettling. He was undoubtedly handsome and charming, but her impression upon meeting him for the first time was that he was suspicious of her. He had as good as accused her of having designs upon his cousin, but she hoped she had reassured him on that point. He did not like her, she was sure of that. There was no warmth in his eyes when he looked at her. Why, then, was he singling her out?

'Wrong way, Miss Prentess!'

Her partner's urgent whisper brought Susannah back to the dance and she tried to concentrate upon her steps, but even as she twirled and passed and skipped she was aware that the viscount was watching her from the side of the room. Perhaps he was looking out for a rich wife. Another pass, another skip and she gave her hands to her partner to swing her around. She also gave the young gentleman her warmest smile. If Lord Markham thought he only had to parade his title before her and she would fall at his feet, then he was very much in error.

Susannah danced and laughed until her feet and her cheeks ached. Her partners had never known her so vivacious, nor so encouraging. She never once looked for the viscount, but when the ball ended she was disappointed to learn from Mrs Logan that he had left soon after speaking to her.

'He was less interested in knowing about Bath than learning about you,' Kate told her as they waited for their cloaks.

'Oh?' Susannah tried not to be intrigued and failed miserably. 'What did he say?'

'He asked about your parents.' Kate's cynical smile dawned. 'If he is looking for a rich bride he could do worse.'

'No, he could not.' Susannah shivered. 'He is wasting his time with me. I do not want a husband, and certainly not one who looks down his aristocratic nose at me.'

'But you must admit he is devilishly handsome,' murmured Kate.

Susannah thought of those hard eyes boring into her. Something inside fluttered again when she thought of Viscount Markham, but she would not admit it to be attraction.

'Devilish, yes, I'll agree to that.'

'Well, for my part I like him,' declared Mrs Wilby, coming up. She cast an anxious look at her niece. 'That is, he has never been anything but charming to me.'

'Hah!' Susannah found two pairs of eyes upon her. Her aunt's held merely a question at her vehement exclamation, but Kate Logan's glance was brimful of merriment and a knowing look that brought an angry flush to Susannah's cheek. She said haughtily, 'Charm is the viscount's second nature, but it will not work with me!'

Thus, when she spied Lord Markham approaching in Milsom Street the following morning she determined to give him no more than a distant nod. She said as much to her companion, Mrs Logan, who gave a tiny shake of her head.

'I fear you will catch cold at that, Susannah. You see he has Mr Barnabus with him, and *he* will hardly be fobbed off with so slight a greeting.'

She was right. Gerald hailed them cheerfully and immediately enquired their direction. Kate responded even while Susannah was trying to frame an answer that would send the gentlemen in the opposite direction.

'We are going to the Pump Room to meet up with Mrs Wilby.'

'Then we will accompany you, will we not, Jasper?'

'Oh, but we do not want to take you out of your way.' Susannah's protest was overruled.

'It is no trouble,' replied Gerald. 'I dragged my cousin from his bed for an early walk before breakfast, and we may as well go to the Pump Room as anywhere. Come, now, let us be moving!'

She was not sure how it happened, but moments later Susannah found the viscount beside her. He had said very little, but such was his address that somehow he had inveigled Gerald into escorting Kate and Susannah was left with no option but to accept his arm. She placed her fingers carefully on his sleeve, as if afraid the contact might burn.

'I remember you telling me how busy you are, Miss Prentess.'

'I am.'

Nerves made her respond more curtly than she intended.

'And is this the nature of your busyness, to be shopping all day?'

Her sense of the ridiculous put flight to her tension and a laugh escaped her.

'Not *all* day, my lord.' She held up her free hand, displaying the tight-fitting covering of fine kid leather. 'Besides, a lady always needs new gloves.'

'Undoubtedly. How did you enjoy the ball last night?'

'Very much. I suspect the company was a little provincial for you, sir, since you did not dance.'

'You noticed.'

The laughter in his voice brought a tell-tale flush to her cheeks, but she recovered quickly.

'No, my aunt told me as much. I take no interest in you at all.'

Too late she realised she should not have added those final words. She waited for him to tease her and could only be grateful that he changed the subject.

'Mrs Logan tells me you spent your early years following the drum.'

'Yes, my father was a captain in an infantry regiment.'

'You lived in Gibraltar, I believe.'

'Yes. That is where I met Mrs Logan.'

'And did she accompany you home to England?'

'No. I returned here when my father died nine years ago. Mama brought us back to live with her sister. Mrs Logan and I met again when I came to Bath last year. I was fortunate to find her here. She has been a good friend to me.' She added, in response to the question in his eyes, 'She is a soldier's widow, I am a soldier's daughter. We have similar interests.'

'And why did you come to Bath, Miss Prentess?'

'Why not?' she countered.

'It seems an odd choice for a young lady of means.'

'My Uncle Middlemass left me the house in the Crescent. It is not within my power to sell it.'

'But it is such a choice property, you could let it out and go where you will. Why not London?'

There was a heartbeat's hesitation before she replied.

'Bath suits me very well. And my aunt, too. She likes to take the waters. Ah, we are here.'

Susannah was never more glad to reach her destination. She was finding it far too easy to talk to the viscount, but it did not suit her to share her history with him. She released his arm as they entered the Pump Room and led the way towards Mrs Wilby. Her aunt was part of a lively group standing in the curved recess at one end of the room but as Susannah approached the crowd dispersed, leaving Aunt Maude alone to receive them.

'There you are, Aunt. I hope we have not kept you waiting.'

'In no wise.' Mrs Wilby's smile encompassed them all. 'I have had a delightful time with my friends.'

'And drinking the waters, ma'am?' suggested the viscount.

Mrs Wilby made a face.

'Ugh, nasty stuff. I never touch it. Tea is my favoured drink here, my lord.'

'Indeed?' Lord Markham raised his brows as his glance flickered over Susannah. 'I thought—'

'Oh heavens, is that the time?' Susannah interrupted him hurriedly, looking at the long-case clock by the wall. 'I hope I do not rush you, Aunt, but Kate and I have an appointment in Henrietta Street later, so we should be on our way back to the Crescent to take breakfast. It is quite a long walk.'

'We will accompany you!' declared Gerald promptly.

'No, no, I will not hear of it,' replied Susannah firmly. 'There can be no need of a gentleman's escort when there are three of us and besides,' she added with an arch look, 'how are we to discuss our little secrets if you come with us?' She held out her hand. 'We will say goodbye here, if you please.'

'But I have barely had time to exchange a word with you,' objected Gerald.

'Nor have you,' agreed Mrs Wilby, her kind heart touched by the young man's despondent look. 'Perhaps you would like to join us for tea tomorrow afternoon? It is nothing special, of course. We stand on no ceremony, just a few close friends who drop by for a comfortable coze, but you are very welcome to come. And Lord Markham, too, if he would like.'

'Lord Markham would like, very much,' said Jasper, amused by Susannah's obvious disapproval. Those hazel eyes of hers darkened to brown and he read objection in every line of her body, although of course she could not contradict her aunt. He took her hand. *'Adieu,* Miss Prentess. I shall look forward to taking tea with you tomorrow.'

'Not if you are going to cut me out,' declared Gerald, half-laughing, half-serious.

'He will not do that, you may be sure, Ger...Mr Barnabus.' Susannah's soft words and warm look killed Jasper's amusement in an instant. He was still holding her hand and his fingers tightened angrily. She looked up at him, her eyes wide and innocent. 'My lord?'

Jasper caught his breath. That remark was not for Gerald's benefit but for *his.* So the minx wanted to cross swords, did she? A touch of uncertainty entered her gaze. Jasper bowed over her hand in his most courtly style. As his lips brushed her fingers they trembled in his grasp. The lady was not as confident as she would have him believe.

Jasper waited for the spurt of triumph to accompany the thought. It did not come. Instead he was aware of a sudden tenderness, a desire to press that little hand against his heart and assure her of his protection. Shaken, he straightened and released her.

'That worked out very well,' commented Gerald, as they watched the ladies walk away. 'This must be down to you, Jasper. Mrs Wilby has never invited me to take tea before.'

'Then I hope you are satisfied.'

'Very. Only, it makes it pretty clear that Mrs Wilby would prefer you as a match for Susannah.'

'Would that matter to you?' Jasper asked him. 'Have you set your heart on marrying her?'

'Oh, well, you know, she has already told me that she can never think of me as anything other than a friend, but I hope that when she comes to know me better— but she is so good, she is not one to raise false hopes in a fellow.'

'You know, Gerald, I wonder if Miss Prentess is quite the paragon you make her out to be.'

His cousin laughed at that.

'Oh but she is, Jasper. Good, kind—a veritable angel. She is quite, quite perfect.'

Jasper shook his head.

'My poor deluded boy, when you know as much about women as I do you will know there is no such thing!'

'My mother is convinced of that, certainly. Which reminds me, I had a note from her, asking me to visit. It is still early, I could go today, riding cross country would be a pleasure.' He put his hand on Jasper's shoulder. 'And you can come with me. You will be able to support me when I tell her about Susannah.'

'Why not, if we can hire a hack for me?' Jasper swallowed his misgivings. 'When I left Rooks Tower I sent my horses on to Markham, not expecting to need them in Bath. However—and forgive me if this pains you,

Gerald—your mother is not famed for her hospitality, so let us have breakfast first!'

After they had eaten, Jasper and Gerald rode over to Hotwells. Gloriana received them joyfully enough, but when Gerald happily disclosed that he was to take tea in Royal Crescent the following day, the look she threw at Jasper left him in no doubt that she was seriously disappointed in him. She despatched Gerald on an errand to fetch a further supply of tonic from her doctor and as soon as he was out of the door she turned on Jasper.

'I thought you were going to Bath to save my poor son from this woman?'

'I was going to look into the matter,' he corrected her. 'Having done so, I have given up all plans of returning to Markham for the time being.'

'Aha. Then you admit my son is ensnared.'

'Miss Prentess is an heiress, Gloriana. Does that not please you?'

'If that is the case why did she take his money from him? Besides, she is a nobody, and she is too old for him.' Gloriana was determined not to be appeased. 'She is three-and-twenty if she is a day. And her birth—who knows anything about the girl, save that she is heir to the Middlemass fortune?'

He smiled slightly.

'That would be enough for most mothers.'

Gloriana looked at him and for a moment her guard dropped.

'I only want his happiness, Markham. If you could assure me of that I could be reconciled.'

'I wish that were possible, but I cannot believe it.' He frowned. 'You know he has offered her marriage, and she refused him?'

'He wrote to tell me. I hoped that would be the end of it, but today he seems as beguiled as ever.'

'I know, ma'am. I have failed to find anything against the lady. However, my enquiries about her friend Mrs Logan have proved far more interesting. She is the widow of a soldier and the story goes that he quit the army to open a gambling house in Portsmouth. When Logan died, his widow sold up and came to Bath, where she now lives in respectable retirement. I am not in the habit of listening to the gossip-mongers, but having watched the lady at work at one of Mrs Wilby's little parties I know that she is very good with the cards. Good enough to be a professional.' He strode to the window and stood for a moment, looking out. 'Add that to the skill shown by both Miss Prentess and her aunt and I cannot help thinking that there is more to their little card parties than mere social entertainment. I would wager that at the end of the evening the three ladies come away from the tables considerably richer than they started.'

'A gaming hell. Oh my heavens.' Gloriana resorted to her handkerchief. 'To think my poor boy should be caught in the tangles of such women.'

Jasper shook his head.

'By London standards the stakes are trivial, and the play is certainly not deep enough to cause concern. There is no faro bank, something which attracted a great deal of criticism when employed by several high-born ladies in London twenty years ago. But the suspicion persists that they run their little parties at the Crescent for profit. Not that there is anything wrong with that, if they would but own it.'

'In Royal Crescent? It would never be permitted!'

'No, ma'am, I suppose you are right.'

'And you have spoken to Gerald about this? You have told him the sort of woman he has given his heart to?'

'I have tried, but he is deaf to any criticism of Miss Prentess.' He turned away from the window, his jaw set. 'My cousin is seriously besotted with the woman. I think he would have to witness the lady's fall from grace for himself before he would see her for what she really is.'

'Then that is what must happen.'

There was such an air of grim determination behind the words that the corners of Jasper's mouth lifted a trifle.

'I'm afraid wishing won't make it happen, ma'am.'

'No, but *you* could,' came the confident reply. 'You have a reputation with the ladies, Markham, your flirtations are forever gracing the society pages. *You* must seduce Susannah Prentess!'

Chapter Four

Whatever startled response Jasper would have made was silenced by Gerald's coming back into the room at that moment. Nor was there opportunity to discuss the matter again, for very soon afterwards the gentlemen took their leave. Gloriana squeezed Jasper's fingers as he bowed over her hand, and the speaking look in her eyes told him that she relied upon him to comply with her outrageous suggestion.

But was it so outrageous? Jasper pondered the matter as he rode back to Bath beside Gerald, the setting sun casting long shadows before them and the chill wind cutting through their coats. If he succeeded in turning the lady's head then it would destroy his young cousin's infatuation at a stroke. Many men would not hesitate, but for all his reputation Jasper had never yet set out to make any woman fall in love with him. He might have done so with Zelah, if it had not become plain to him that she was head over heels in love with his brother. She was the only woman he had ever loved, the only woman he had ever considered taking as his wife, so there was no danger that he would succumb to Miss

Prentess's charms. He could flirt with her, court her, even seduce her without risk to himself.

He shifted in the saddle. What of the risk to the lady? If he went that far it would ruin her reputation and she would lose her good name. He hardened his heart. She had every young man in Bath at her feet and from what he had seen at her aunt's card party she was fleecing them quite ruthlessly. The amounts might be small, but over the weeks they would mount up to a considerable sum. Enough to live quite comfortably. Dammit, the woman was running a gaming hell, she deserved no good name!

'Eh, what's that?' Gerald looked round. 'Did you say something?'

Jasper glanced at the young man riding beside him.

'Aye. I was wondering about those little card parties of Mrs Wilby's. Do you think they profit from them?'

Gerald shrugged.

'A hundred or two, perhaps. I doubt it is ever more than a monkey.'

'I should hope not.' He paused. 'Does it not concern you that they are making money out of these parties?'

Gerald looked at him.

'No, why? The sums are negligible.' He laughed. 'Mother told me that when she was young the London hostesses made thousands in an evening, especially those who ran a faro bank. *And* they charged their guests card money, to cover the cost of the new packs. Mrs Wilby does nothing like that. Her parties are for friends to gather together and enjoy themselves.'

'And lose money.'

'Not everyone loses.'

'But enough to make it a worthwhile evening for the hostess.'

'And why not?' countered Gerald. 'We might all go elsewhere and lose a great deal more.' He shook his head. 'Let be, Jasper. Those of us who go there choose to do so, and if we lose a few guineas, well, what does it matter? I would lose twice as much to Miss Prentess and think it money well spent.'

Jasper said no more and the subject was not mentioned again during their ride back to Bath. It irked him that Susannah Prentess, with her charming smile and beautiful face, had quite beguiled his cousin, and if he had to make her fall in love with him to free Gerald from her clutches he would do it. He would even risk ruining her good name, if that was the only option, though his innate sense of honour balked at such a course. But it would be a cruel trick to play upon his young cousin. If it was at all possible he would find another way to prove to Gerald that the lady was not the angel he thought her to be.

As soon as they had left the Pump Room, Mrs Wilby made clear her disapproval at being dragged away so precipitately.

'What will everyone think of you, Susannah? To dash away so suddenly, with Mr Barnabus and the viscount only just arrived.'

'They will think nothing of it, Aunt. And besides, I am quite out of sympathy with you for inviting them to join us tomorrow.'

'But why? What possible objection can there be?'

'None, to Mr Barnabus, but the viscount…' She bit her lip, wondering how to explain her reluctance to see more of Lord Markham. 'I think he suspects something.'

Mrs Wilby stopped.

'Oh heavens, never say so! Oh, Susannah—'

'No, no, he can have no inkling of the truth, and Gerald would never tell him, I am sure.' She took Aunt Maude's arm and gently urged her on. 'It is just the comments he made to me, as if he thinks we run some sort of gambling den.'

'All the more reason, then, for him to take tea with us and see that it is not the case,' declared Mrs Wilby. 'A gambling den! How perfectly ridiculous.'

Her aunt's outraged dignity made Susannah chuckle.

'But if he *is* suspicious of you,' continued Mrs Wilby, 'perhaps it would be best if you curtailed your visits to…'

'My dear aunt, I will do nothing of the sort. In fact, I am going there tomorrow morning. Really, I did not realise, when I started this, this *project*, that there would be so much to do, or that it would cost so much.'

''If people knew of it, Susannah, they would be quite scandalised.'

'I am an heiress, Aunt,' she said drily. 'They would merely think me eccentric. If only I had control of my fortune now there would be no problem over money, but my uncle has bound it all up so tight I cannot even borrow upon the expectation, unless I go to a money-lender.'

'Oh heavens, child, pray do not even think of it!'

'I don't. But we will need to find extra money soon.' She sighed. 'My dependence is upon you and Kate to win a little more at our next card party.'

'Which will make Lord Markham even more suspicious,' said Mrs Wilby bitterly. 'I have a mind not to take tea with anyone tomorrow. I shall write and tell them all I have been laid low with a fever.'

'No, no, dear Aunt, let them all come. 'Pon reflection, I think you are quite right. Nothing could be more respectable than the guests you have invited. Lord Markham is most likely to be bored to death and will beat a speedy retreat!'

It was a cold, clear afternoon, but a biting wind made Susannah glad she had ordered her carriage to take her and Kate to Henrietta Street. They drew up on the gentle curve of the street outside one of the elegant three-storey houses, where only the array of fabrics displayed in the window gave an indication that this was not a private residence. A young woman in a plain dark gown opened the door to them.

'Good day to you, Mabel. Is Odesse upstairs?'

'Good day, Miss Prentess, Mrs Logan. Yes, Madame Odesse is in the showroom with Mrs Anstruther.'

'And how is little James?' murmured Susannah as she followed the girl up the stairs.

'Oh, he is doing very well, miss, putting on weight just as he should, and sleeping through the night now.' Mabel cast her a quick, shy smile. 'It is so good to have him close, where I can keep an eye on him.'

They had reached the landing and Mabel showed them into the large reception room, where a dark-haired woman wearing a plain but exquisitely sewn round gown was talking with a formidable matron in a Pomona-green redingote and matching turban, assuring *madame* in a lilting foreign accent that her new gown would be completed *tout de suite*.

She looked up as her new visitors came in, but Susannah waved her hand.

'No, no, *madame*, please continue serving Mrs Anstruther. We are happy to browse amongst these new fabrics.' Her smile included the matron, who quickly looked away.

'Thank you, I have finished here.' Mrs Anstruther hastily pulled on her gloves and headed for the door. 'If you will have the new gown delivered to me this afternoon, *madame*...'

She hurried out and Madame Odesse shut the door carefully behind her.

'Miss Prentess, Mrs Logan, how good of you to call. Will you not be seated?'

Susannah noted with a smile that all trace of the vague European accent had disappeared from the modiste's tone.

'This continuing cold weather has made it necessary for me to order a new redingote, and I have persuaded Mrs Logan it is time she bought a new gown. We have brought with us a length of silk especially for the purpose.' Susannah smiled. 'I trust everything goes well here?'

'Very well, thank you, we have made some changes.' Odesse paused. 'Would you like to come and see?'

'We would indeed!'

She took them back down the stairs and through a door on the ground floor. The room was alive with quiet chatter, which stopped as they went in. Four young women were present, sitting near the large window. Each one was engaged in sewing the swathe of material spread over her knees, while a nearby table was covered in a confusion of brightly coloured material and threads. Madame Odesse waved an expressive hand

'This is now our sewing room.'

Susannah smiled at the young ladies but hastily begged them not to get up or stop their work. She was acquainted with them all and knew that each one had a baby to look after. The absence of cribs and crying was noticeable.

'Where are the children?' she asked.

'We take it in turns now to stay in the nursery with the babes,' offered one of the girls in a shy voice. She added, indicating the cloud of pale-blue woollen fabric on her lap, 'I am sewing the final seam of your walking dress now, Miss Prentess.'

'My girls find they prefer to work away from the babies,' added the modiste. 'We have six seamstresses living here now, and Mabel, of course, who is proving herself a valuable assistant to me. Two of my girls stay in the nursery while the others get on with the sewing.'

'And the lace-makers?' asked Kate. 'How do they go on?'

'Very well.' Madame Odesse's dark eyes twinkled. 'The fashion for extensive trimming on gowns could not have come at a better time. Demand is growing for our exclusive lace, and I hope they will be able to train up a few more girls soon.'

'And have you room for more seamstresses?'

'Certainly,' agreed Odesse. 'If we keep getting new customers then I shall have work for them, too.'

She led them down another flight of stairs to the nursery, where two young women were looking after the babies in a large, comfortably warm room. Susannah and Kate spent some time in the nursery before making their way back upstairs, Susannah declaring herself very satisfied with the arrangements.

'It appears to be working out very well,' she re-marked, when they were once again in the reception room. 'The children are content and their mothers seem happy.'

The modiste took her hands and pressed them, saying

earnestly, 'We all appreciate your giving us this chance to keep our babies *and* earn a living, Miss Prentess.'

'I am glad to do it, and the gowns you have made for me are very much admired, Olive—I mean Odesse,' Susannah corrected herself hastily. 'I beg your pardon!'

The seamstress laughed and shook her head.

'I would not have you beg my pardon for anything. When I consider what might have happened, to all of us....' There was a moment's uneasy silence before she shook off her reflective mood and said brightly, 'The new apricot silk you ordered arrived this morning, and I know just the design I would like to make for you...'

An hour later the ladies were on their way back to Royal Crescent, a number of packages on the seat beside them and the prospect of more new gowns to follow.

'I must say, I never thought charity would be so pleasurable,' declared Kate, smiling. 'Your idea of setting the girls up in their own establishment was a very good one, Susannah.'

'I merely made use of Olive's talent for sewing. She has such a shrewd eye for design, too.'

'But it is unlikely she would have succeeded alone, and with a young baby to support.' Kate reached out and squeezed her arm. 'You should be very proud of yourself, my dear.'

'I am very proud of my ladies,' replied Susannah. 'I have merely provided the means. It is their hard work that is making it such a success.'

'If only the starched matrons of Bath knew that their gowns were being made by unmarried mothers they might not be so keen to patronise Odesse.'

'I do not think they care who makes their clothes as long as they are fashionable and a good price,' retorted

Susannah. 'Florence House, however, is a different matter. News of that establishment will scandalise the sober matrons, so I hope we can keep it a secret, at least until I have control of my fortune and can support it without the aid of Aunt Maude's card parties.'

Winter would not release its grip and when Jasper rose at his usual early hour the following morning, there was a hint of frost glistening on the Bath rooftops. He decided to take a long walk before breakfast. Enquiries of the waiter in the near-empty coffee room elicited the information that the view from Beechen Cliff was well worth the effort, so he set out, heading south through streets where only the tradespeople were yet in evidence. Striding out, he soon came to the quay and the bridge that took him across the river, and he could begin the climb to Beechen Cliff.

When he reached the heights he considered himself well rewarded. Looking north, Bath was spread out in all its glory below him. Smoke was beginning to rise from the chimneys of the honey-coloured terraces but it was not yet sufficient to cloud his view and his gaze moved past the Abbey until it reached the sweeping curve of the Royal Crescent. Immediately his thoughts turned to Miss Prentess and Gerald. If it wasn't for those damned card parties he would be inclined to tell Gloriana to give Gerald her blessing and let nature take its course. After all, the lady had refused him once. He would wager that if he was left alone, Gerald would recover from his infatuation and settle down with a suitable young bride in a year or so.

But it was Susannah Prentess who set the alarm bells ringing in his head. Why did a rich young woman need to engage in card parties to raise money? If she was looking for a brilliant match then why was she not in London? With her good looks and her fortune there were plenty of eligible bachelors who would be eager to win her hand. Clearly there was something more to the lady than met the eye, and he was determined to discover it.

The icy wind cut his cheeks, reminding him of his exposed position and a sudden hunger made him eager for his breakfast. Jasper set off on the return journey at a good pace. The streets were busier now with a constant stream of carts and wagons making their way across the bridge. He heard the jingle of harness behind him and looked round. The equipage was quite the smartest to pass him that morning and clearly a private carriage, although there was no liveried footman standing on the back. The sun's reflection from the river shone through the carriage window and illuminated the interior so that Jasper could see its occupant quite clearly. There could be no mistaking Susannah Prentess's perfect profile, nor the guinea-gold curls peeping out beneath her silk bonnet. Jasper raised his hat but even as he did so he knew she had not seen him. The lady appeared to be deep in thought. However, Jasper had to own that to see her out and about so early in the day, when most of her kind would be still at their dressing table, did her no disservice in his eyes. His spirits, lifted by the exercise, rose a little higher, and he found himself looking forward to the forthcoming visit to Royal Crescent.

'Ah, my lord, Mr Barnabus, I am so pleased you could join us.'

Mrs Wilby came forwards as the butler ushered them into the drawing room. There were already a dozen or so people present, grouped around little tables, the same ones that had been used for cards, but they now held nothing more exciting than teacups. Gerald immediately headed for Susannah, who was sitting near the fireplace, dispensing tea. Jasper would have followed, but Mrs Wilby, conscious of her duties as a hostess, gently drew him aside, intent upon introductions. The stares and whispers that had greeted his entrance made it clear that the appearance of a viscount was an occurrence of rare importance. It was therefore some time before he was free to approach Susannah.

Gerald was beside her, and hailed him cheerfully.

'Come and join us, Markham. I was just telling Miss Prentess how we rode over to Bristol yesterday.'

'I suspect you wish you were out riding now, my lord.' There was laughter in her eyes as she regarded him, as well as a hint of an apology. 'Some of my aunt's friends appeared to be fawning over you quite disgracefully. And Mr Barnabus assures me that is *not* something you enjoy.'

'Aye, I've told Miss Prentess that even if you are a viscount you are not at all high in the instep,' added Gerald, grinning.

'Very good of you,' retorted Jasper.

'Bath is now the home of a great many retired people,' said Susannah, keeping her voice low. 'Perfectly genteel, but not the highest ranks of society. I'm afraid some of those present are rather overwhelmed to have a viscount in their midst.'

'Not overwhelmed enough to be tongue-tied, unfortunately,' murmured Jasper. 'The lady in green was particularly garrulous.'

'Amelia Bulstrode.' She gave a gurgle of laughter. 'And her friend, Mrs Farthing. When my aunt told them you were expected they were exceedingly put out. They have sent their girls to dancing class today, you see. But it is no matter. Now they can claim acquaintance they will make their daughters known to you at the first opportunity. But you need not be alarmed,' she added kindly. 'They are very well-mannered girls, albeit inclined to giggle.'

'Nothing wrong with that,' remarked Gerald nobly. 'They are very pleasant, cheerful young ladies.'

'And one of their pleasant, cheerful mothers is approaching,' muttered Jasper. 'I shall retreat to that corner, where I see my old friend General Sanstead and his wife. I must pay my respects, you know.'

Susannah's eyes were brim full of mirth and she mouthed the word 'coward' at him before turning to greet Mrs Bulstrode. Jasper made good his escape, but behind him he heard the matron's carrying voice.

'If there is more tea, Miss Prentess, I would be happy to refill my cup. So refreshing, is it not? I do not believe those who say it does you no good. Why, they have only to look at you. A picture of health, if I may say so.'

'Thank you, Mrs Bulstrode. This is a particularly pleasant blend...'

He smiled to himself, appreciating the way she dealt with the overpowering matron. Enjoying, too, that warm, laughing note in her voice.

'And you are a wonderful advocate for the benefits of tea drinking,' continued Mrs Bulstrode. 'You have so much *energy*, always out and about, like this morning, for example. I saw your carriage at the Borough Walls—'

Jasper halted, under the pretence of removing a speck of dirt from his coat. Perhaps now he might find out what she was doing so early in the day.

'No, no, ma'am, you are mistaken. I have not been abroad today.'

He turned. Susannah was smiling serenely as she poured more tea for the matron.

'No? But I made sure it was your carriage…'

'Very likely,' returned Susannah, handing her the cup. 'I believe my aunt sent Edwards to collect some purchases for her. Is that not right, Aunt?'

'What's that, dear? Oh, oh, yes—yes, that's it.'

Mrs Wilby's flustered response was in itself suspicious, yet if he had not seen Susannah in the carriage with his own eyes Jasper would be as ready as Mrs Bulstrode to believe her story.

Schooling himself, he continued towards General Sanstead. It was clearly not the time to question Miss Prentess, but he would get to the bottom of this. Later.

The General, an old friend, was delighted to see Jasper and kept him talking for some time, asking after the family. The viscount responded suitably and once he had fetched more tea for Mrs Sanstead, he sat down and engaged them in conversation for the next half-hour while he observed the company.

Jasper realised this was a very different gathering from the discreet little card party he had attended. Gerald was staying close to Susannah and Jasper couldn't blame him, they were by far the youngest people in the room. Apart from Gerald, Jasper could see he was the only unmarried man present and for the most part the visitors were older matrons, who moved about the room, forming groups to gossip and disperse again.

Jasper played his part and was much sought out by the other guests, who were all eager to claim acquaintance with a viscount. No one could have faulted his manners, but he was all the time watching Susannah, and when at last he found her alone beside the tea-table he moved across to join her.

'No, thank you.' He put up his hand as she offered him tea. 'Are your rooms never empty, Miss Prentess?'

'My aunt enjoys entertaining.'

'And you?

'Of course.'

He looked about the room.

'But this company is not worthy of you, madam.' She looked at him, her hazel eyes puzzled and he continued. 'Apart from Barnabus and myself it is all matrons and married couples'

'This is my aunt's party, sir.'

'Perhaps your milieu is the cardroom.'

She looked down, smiling.

'No, I do not think so.'

Jasper hesitated, wondering if he should mention seeing her on the bridge that morning and into the lull came Mrs Sanstead's voice as she moved across to join the other married ladies.

'We are missing Mrs Anstruther today, Mrs Wilby. Is she not well?'

Immediately Miss Prentess was on the alert. Jasper could not fail to notice the way she grew still, nor the wary look in her eye. There was some coughing and shuffling and from the furtive looks in his direction it was clear this was not a subject for his hearing. He turned away, pretending to interest himself in a pleasant landscape on the wall, but not before he had seen Mrs Bulstrode turn quickly in her seat, setting the tassels on her green turban swinging wildly.

'Lord, Mrs Sanstead, have you not heard? The Anstruthers have retired to Shropshire. They left Bath this morning.'

'Heavens, that was sudden. When do they mean to return?'

'Who can tell? Their daughter...'

He could not make out the next words, but he heard Mrs Sanstead sigh.

'Oh, you mean she is with child? Poor gel.'

'Yes. I understand she refused to say who the father might be and Anstruther has banished her.' Mrs Bulstrode's whisper was easily audible to Jasper's keen ears. 'Thrown her out of the house in disgrace.'

'Flighty piece, I always said so,' muttered Mrs Farthing with a disdainful sniff. 'My son William showed a preference for her at one time, but I am glad it came to nought. She has obviously been far too free with her favours.'

'Whatever she has done she does not deserve to be cast off,' murmured Mrs Wilby. 'And what of the father? Do we have any idea who he might be?'

'No one will say, although there are rumours.' Mrs Farthing dropped her voice a little and ended in a conspiratorial whisper that somehow managed to carry around the whole room. 'Mr Warwick.'

'What? Not the young man we met here the other night?' exclaimed Mrs Sanstead. 'Why, he made a fourth at whist, and seemed so charming.'

'The very same.' Mrs Farthing nodded. 'He denies it of course.'

'Naturally,' muttered Susannah.

She had not joined the matrons, but she was listening as intently as Jasper. Now he heard her utterance, and saw the angry frown that passed across her brow.

'But what of Anstruther?' barked the General, with

a total disregard for the fact that the ladies considered their gossip confidential. 'If it was my gel I'd have it out with the rascal, and if 'tis true I would make him marry her.'

'That certainly would be preferable to her being cast out and having to fend for herself,' sighed Mrs Wilby.

Susannah's lip curled. 'An unenviable choice,' she said, *sotto voce*. 'Marriage to a scoundrel, or destitution.'

'You do not agree, Miss Prentess?' Jasper kept his voice low, so that only she could hear him. 'You would rather he did *not* marry her?'

'If there is resentment on either side, the match is doomed to failure. But having said that, he should know the damage he has caused. Too many men think that women are put on earth purely for their pleasure.' She looked up, a challenge in her eyes. 'I would have the father face up to the consequences of his actions. But whoever he may be he will not do so, and the poor girl is cast off to make her own way as best she can.'

'She will no doubt find her way to Walcot Street,' said Mrs Farthing, overhearing. 'It is a Magdalen Hospital, after all, and the right place for such women, though heaven knows there are more entrants than we can accommodate at the present.'

Mrs Bulstrode fluttered her hands in agitation.

'My dear Mrs Farthing, I am not sure we should be discussing this here, now…'

Her eyes darted about the room, and Jasper quickly moved to the mirror to adjust his neckcloth. He saw her glance flit over Gerald, who was studiously brushing a fleck of dust from his sleeve and avoiding everyone's eyes. Susannah was not so reticent. She stepped into the group.

'If you fear for my sensibilities then pray do not be anxious,' she replied, her head up. 'I am no innocent miss fresh from the schoolroom and I think this is a subject that should be discussed in *every* lady's drawing room.' She turned her challenging eyes upon Mrs Farthing. 'I believe you are on the committee for Walcot Street Penitentiary, are you not, ma'am?'

'I am. We do our best to teach the inmates the folly of their ways...'

'Inmates. Yes, I believe the young women there are more prisoners than patients.'

Mrs Farthing's thin lips curved into a patronising smile.

'My dear Miss Prentess, these young women come to us in desperation and we look after them. In return, of course we demand their compliance. They arrive sick, often with child. We look after them, train them in an occupation and put them out to service where we can.'

'We?' Susannah's voice was deceptively sweet. 'You take an active interest in these poor women, do you, ma'am? Perhaps you take your daughters to visit them.'

'Heavens, my dear, what can you be thinking of?' declared Mrs Bulstrode with a nervous laugh. 'Mrs Farthing didn't mean *that*, I am sure.'

'Of course not. Why, Mr Farthing would never allow me to set foot in such a place, let alone our daughters. It would be to risk physical and moral contagion.'

Jasper saw the light of battle in Susannah's eyes, but before she could reply Mrs Wilby swept forwards.

'Dear me, where is that girl with the water? Mrs Sanstead, I am sure you would like more tea, and the General, too. This cold weather we are having is very drying on the throat, don't you find?' She bustled towards the tea-table. 'Susannah, dearest, ring the bell again, if you please. We cannot have our guests go thirsty...'

Jasper sauntered over to Gerald.

'A skilful interruption,' he murmured appreciatively. 'Pity. The conversation was becoming interesting. Far better than the usual dull inanities.'

Gerald gave him a distracted smile.

'Indeed, but some of the guests are uncomfortable with the subject in mixed company.'

'But not all.' Jasper fixed his eyes on Susannah, who had approached with a cup of tea for Gerald. 'Miss Prentess advocates more discussion about the Magdalen Hospital, do you not, madam?'

She handed the cup to Gerald, saying as she did so, 'It would do no harm for young women to be a little more informed on these matters. If they knew the risks of flirting with gentlemen they would be more cautious.'

'You disapprove of flirting?'

'It can be very dangerous.'

'It can also be very enjoyable.'

Susannah turned her head to find him regarding her, that familiar, disturbing glint in his eye. She discovered that her breathing was restricted, as if Dorcas had laced her corsets too tightly. Yet the sensation was not unpleasant. Enjoyable.

He is flirting with me.

Sudden panic filled her, turning her bones to water so that she was unable to move. Those intense, blue-grey eyes held her gaze. She felt like a small animal in thrall to some predator. She swallowed, desperately trying to regain her composure. The glint in his eyes deepened to pure amusement and a sudden spurt of anger released her.

She stepped back, distancing herself. She could excuse herself and move away, but such was her perverse nature that she preferred to make a retort.

'Enjoyable? Yes, if both parties know it is nothing more than a game.'

'So you do not disapprove.'

She forced herself to hold his gaze.

Walk away, Susannah. Walk away now. Instead, she lifted her chin.

'I disapprove of gentlemen who take advantage of innocent young women.'

He moved closer, filling the space she had made between them and setting her skin tingling with anticipation.

'But you are no innocent miss,' he murmured provocatively. 'You said so yourself.'

'Jasper, do not tease her so!' Gerald's laughing protest hardly registered.

Susannah's brows lifted. She continued to give Jasper look for look.

'Then you will not be able to take advantage of me, my lord.'

'No?' The gleam in his eyes became even more pronounced. If she was fanciful she could imagine twin devils dancing there.

Devilishly handsome, Kate had called him. The faint, upward curve to his mouth brought the words rushing back to her.

'Is that a challenge, Miss Prentess?' His voice was low, sliding over her skin like cool silk and raising the hairs at the back of her neck.

Gerald was watching them, his smile uncertain and a faint crease in his brow. Common sense reasserted itself, yet Susannah's stubborn pride would not let her bow her head and move away. Instead she gave the viscount a haughty smile.

'Of course not. I would not have you waste your time.'

She excused herself and walked off, head high, hoping her knees would not buckle beneath her. What was she doing, responding to him in that way? As well tease a wild animal! The last thing she needed was to have him paying attention to her.

Jasper watched her walk away and realised he was smiling. The blood thrummed through his body, a sure sign that he had enjoyed the interchange.

'Jasper?'

He looked up to find Gerald regarding him.

'Jasper, I won't have you pursuing Miss Prentess if you mean nothing but mischief. She is too good, too honourable, to deserve that.'

He observed the slightly anxious look in Gerald's eyes. Good? Honourable? Perhaps she was, but why then should she lie about being abroad in her carriage that morning? He still wanted an answer to that one, but he was experienced enough to know that he would not get it today. He shrugged.

'Believe me, Gerald, I have never intended mischief towards any young lady. Let us take our leave. I have had enough tea for one day.'

'Oh heavens, I have never been so uncomfortable in all my life.'

Mrs Wilby sank back in her chair and fanned herself vigorously once the last of their visitors was shown out. Susannah was standing by the window but she turned at this.

'No, ma'am, and why should that be?'

'My dear, I never thought to hear such things in our drawing room. The talk of, of fallen women and by-blows—and with gentlemen present, too! I am sure General Sanstead did not know where to look.'

'I thought the General took it rather well,' mused Susannah.

'But what of Mr Barnabus, and Lord Markham? I am sure they must have overheard the conversation.'

Susannah frowned.

'If it were not for *gentlemen* such as they, many of these girls would not be in such dire straits, and girls like Miss Anstruther would not be thrown on to the streets.'

'Ah, yes.' Mrs Wilby sighed. 'That poor child. I do hope she is safe.'

'There at least I can put your mind at rest.' Susannah came away from the window, smiling slightly as Mrs Wilby's mouth dropped open.

'What! Never say she is…'

'Yes, she is our newest client. I took her to Florence House this morning.'

Chapter Five

Jasper spent the following week doing everything he could to distract his cousin's thoughts from Susannah. It seemed to work—he even persuaded Gerald to accompany him to the theatre rather than attend the card party in Royal Crescent. Gerald was happy enough to go with him and he never once mentioned Miss Prentess. Perversely, she was rarely out of Jasper's thoughts. He told himself it was the unanswered questions he had about the woman and nothing to do with their last exchange, the way she had boldly returned his gaze, challenged him to flirt with her. That merely showed how dangerous she was to innocents like Gerald.

He sent his valet off to make discreet enquiries about Miss Prentess. Peters was a loyal, intelligent employee who had proved his worth over the years in ferreting out secrets others would prefer to keep hidden. But on this occasion he was unsuccessful.

'No one will say a word against the lady,' he reported back. 'The men know nothing, and the women—the maidservants I have spoken with—they have nothing but praise for her.' The valet shook his head. 'Odd, very odd, if you asks me, m'lord. There's usually some juicy gossip to be had.' He coughed. 'There was one thing, though.'

'Yes?'

'Friday morning, my lord. You asked me to lay out your riding dress because you was going riding with Mr Barnabus, but then you had a message from the young gentleman, sir, saying as how he was indisposed.'

'Yes, I remember that,' said Jasper, a touch impatiently. 'What of it?'

Peters fixed his eyes on some spot on the wall and said woodenly, 'I saw him walking with Miss Prentess that self-same morning. They was in Henrietta Street. I didn't think anything of it at the time, and wouldn't have mentioned it, only you wanted to know about the young lady, and I thought that mighty odd...'

Yes, very odd indeed, thought Jasper, and when he had tackled Gerald, his cousin looked sheepish and laughed it off.

'Oh, well, you know how it is, cos,' he said. 'I thought you'd be a trifle vexed if you knew why I had cried off, but Miss Prentess asked me particularly to come with her.'

Gerald apologised and they left it at that, but Jasper didn't like to think his cousin was keeping secrets from him, and even less did he like the thought that Susannah was encouraging him to do so.

Jasper had even taken to walking out every morning and keeping a watch for Miss Prentess's carriage. He had been rewarded just once, on a misty morning when he saw the vehicle bowling along Horse Street. He had quickened his pace and was just in time to see it sweep across the bridge and turn on to the Wells Road. He did not know if Miss Prentess was inside on that occasion, nor did he have any idea of its destination. All he knew was that both Miss Prentess and her aunt were in Bath for the concert the same evening.

He had seen her almost as soon as he entered the Assembly Rooms. Her gown of kingfisher-blue satin was an unusual choice for an unmarried lady, but he had to admit it suited her, contrasting with the gleaming golden curls piled around her head. He tried to approach her at the interval, but she was at the centre of a crowd and not all Jasper's considerable address could separate Miss Prentess from her friends and admirers. Instead he escorted Mrs Wilby out of the concert room in search of refreshment.

'We have not seen you since the afternoon at Royal Crescent,' she remarked, encouraged to speak by his silence.

'No, I have been rather busy,' he handed her a glass of wine. 'I thought I saw Miss Prentess, however. Early this morning, heading out of Bath.'

If he had not been watching closely he would have missed the slight tremor of the widow's hand as she held the wine to her lips. Her answer, when it came, was composed.

'You are mistaken, my lord. That was merely our carriage, going off to collect provisions.'

'You send your servants in your own carriage, ma'am? Is that not rather extravagant? How far do they have to travel?' He added helpfully, 'I saw it heading off on the Wells Road.'

The hunted look in the widow's eyes convinced him he was on to something.

'N-not far, but the vegetables are so much better, you know, from out of town.' Her fan fluttered nervously. 'We should be going back, my lord. The concert will be starting again soon and I do so dislike latecomers...'

He escorted her back to her seat and as soon as he moved away she had her head close to her niece and was talking animatedly. Jasper stood watching, until Susannah looked up and met his eyes. Her face was impassive but he was close enough to read a frown in her clear gaze. He smiled and inclined his head, but she immediately looked away, and when the concert ended she whisked her aunt out of the building before he could approach them.

'If mine was a suspicious nature I should say Miss Prentess was avoiding me,' he murmured, thinking back to that concert as he strode along High Street a few days later. It was Tuesday. Gerald was intent upon going to Royal Crescent that evening and Jasper could offer no good reason why he should not do so. 'Well, I shall accompany Gerald this evening. She can hardly avoid me in her own drawing room.'

A familiar figure on the other side of the road caught his eye.

'Charles!' As the man stopped, Jasper crossed the road to greet him. 'What the devil are you doing in Bath?'

'I might ask you the same thing,' retorted Charles Camerton, taking Jasper's hand in a friendly grip.

'Family matters,' said Jasper vaguely. 'Are you staying at the York or the Christopher?'

'Devil a bit, they are too far above my touch,' replied Charles. 'I am at the White Hart. I have been visiting my godmother in Radstock. Doing the pretty, you know, in the hopes that she will die soon and leave me her fortune.'

Since Jasper knew Charles to be very fond of his godmother, he grinned at this.

'Then what are you doing in Bath?' he asked again.

'She thinks that a treatment at the hot baths will do her good. I am here to seek out lodgings for her.' He glanced up at the lowering sky. 'Although I have persuaded her she should not attempt the journey for another month at least. We are barely out of February and it looks like snow is on the way.'

'So you are here for a few days?' Jasper said, an idea growing in his mind. 'Will you dine with me this evening?'

'With pleasure,' returned Charles, promptly. 'There is little else to do in a watering place populated by the old and the infirm.'

Jasper smiled. 'Oh, I think I can find you some entertainment. You are fond of cards, I believe...'

'Miss Prentess!'

Susannah gave her hand to Gerald and he raised it to his lips.

'Welcome, sir.' She looked behind him. 'You are alone?'

'Yes. I am sorry I missed your last party.'

She smiled at him as she gently withdrew her fingers from his grasp.

'I do not expect you to attend us every week.'

'But I like to come.' He glanced around the drawing room and lowered his voice. 'I like to help where I can, Susannah, which is why I was so pleased you allowed me to escort you to see Odesse the other day.'

'I hope your mama will like the lace you ordered for her.'

'I am sure she will, and if she tells her friends that may bring in more orders.'

Susannah smiled at him.

'It may indeed. You see, you have been a great help, Mr Barnabus—'

'Gerald,' he corrected her. 'Are we not friends enough now to dispense with formalities?'

'Gerald, then.' She shook off the twinge of guilt at allowing such familiarity. She had made it plain they could only ever be friends, after all. Then, hating herself for succumbing, she asked the question that had been in her mind ever since he arrived. 'Has Lord Markham left Bath?'

'No, he is still here and means to look in presently. But enough of this. Are you free? Will you play picquet with me?'

She shook her head.

'You know you always lose.'

'Tonight I feel lucky,' he declared. 'And I have improved vastly since we last played. Mrs Logan said so.'

She laughed at that.

'Very well, then, but do not expect me to hold back. I shall show you no mercy!'

In the event, mercy was not necessary. Susannah had chosen a table where she could watch the door, and such was her distraction that Gerald won the first game. The second was closer, but the entrance of more visitors caused her to lose track of the discards and she was defeated again.

'I told you I had improved,' chortled Gerald, sweeping the coins from the table.

'You are very right,' agreed Susannah, getting up. 'But perhaps you will oblige me by taking your winnings to the loo table and giving my aunt a chance to recoup.'

With a smile she excused herself, glancing at the

clock. It was gone ten, there would be very few visitors arriving now. Even as she thought this the door opened and Lord Markham walked in. His appearance made her spirits leap most shamefully. Susannah could not deny that she had been looking out for him, as she had done in vain the previous week. He might be suspicious of her, and cause her nerves to flutter alarmingly, but any party where he was not present was an insipid affair. When she had seen him at the concert she had wanted so much to speak to him, but Aunt Maude had warned her that he had asked awkward questions, and she knew it would be folly to linger and risk further interrogation. All such thoughts were bundled into the back of her mind now as she moved forwards to greet him, wondering why it was that he was not charmed by her smile like every other man in the room.

'Lord Markham.'

She held out her hand but, despite steeling herself, his touch still sent a tremor of excitement running up her arm, and when his lips brushed her fingers the excitement flooded through her before settling into an indescribable ache somewhere low in her body.

'Your servant, Miss Prentess. I have brought someone to meet you. May I present Mr Charles Camerton? He is an avid card player.'

'Indeed?' She subjected the newcomer to a swift appraisal. He looked genial enough, some years older than the viscount, she guessed. His figure was good, his clothes elegant and his curling brown hair was fashionably short. A man used to the London salons, perhaps. 'I hope we will not disappoint you, sir. This is merely a friendly little gathering.'

'Those are the best sort, Miss Prentess. I am here with every intention of enjoying myself.'

'Then what will you play, sir? I could find two more players, if you and Lord Markham would like to play whist, or…'

Mr Camerton looked around the room until his eyes came to rest upon Kate, who was at that moment opening two fresh packs of cards.

'*Vingt-et-un*,' offered Susannah, following his gaze. 'It is very popular.'

'And it is my favourite game. If you will excuse me?'

With a practised smile and a bow he moved off towards Kate's table.

'Which leaves you with me.'

The viscount's low murmur was like a feather on her skin. She glanced at her arm to see if it was covered in tell-tale goose-bumps. Thankfully there were none.

'I am sure we can find something—'

'I thought we might play picquet. You and I,' he added, so there should be no misunderstanding.

'Thank you, sir, but I think not.'

'Afraid?'

She would not rise to his taunt. Instead she replied frankly, 'Your cousin tells me you are an expert at the game. I will not risk it.'

She looked about her, hoping to distract him. 'My aunt is playing macao and there is room at her table…'

'If you were a true gambler you would not be able to resist the challenge.'

Her chin went up.

'If you were a true gentleman you would not press me so.'

That only made him smile more.

'Is it the game that frightens you, or me?'

Her cheeks flamed at his quiet words. She could feel the heat flooding through her and her heart was beating wildly, making her breathless. Her senses were heightened, as if by a sudden danger. She was enveloped by his closeness. She wanted to flee, but was rooted to the spot. She must be rational. This was her drawing room, they were surrounded by people. What possible harm could come to her here? Yet everything around them was muted. It was as if they were alone, shut off from the world. She could smell the tangy scent of him, sandalwood and lemon and a faint, indefinable fragrance that she now recognised was his alone.

Her eyes were fixed on his chin, on that mobile mouth with its finely sculpted lips and the faint creases at each side that deepened when he smiled. She dare not look higher and instead dragged her eyes down and stared at the diamond winking from the folds of his neck cloth.

'Well, Miss Prentess?'

He was so close she felt his breath on her brow, soft as a caress.

This must stop. Now. Gathering all her strength she drew herself up and forced herself to look him in the face.

Well, she fixed her eyes somewhere around his left temple.

'It is not fear, Lord Markham,' she said coolly. 'It is common sense. One should never take unnecessary risks.'

She turned to walk away and he touched her arm.

'One more thing. You were seen with Gerald on Friday morning.'

She spun back, quickly schooling her features into a look of haughty unconcern.

'What is so wrong about that, my lord?'

'He cried off from an appointment with me to accompany you.'

She had not known that, and regretted it, but she was determined the viscount should not know it. She summoned a glittering smile, as if it was her victory.

'That is unfortunate, of course, but it is no concern of mine.'

The tightening of his jaw told her he was angry. With a slight nod she turned and walked away from him, the knowledge that he was watching her sending a ripple of unease along the length of her spine.

'Well, Camerton, what did you think of Bath's latest hell?' asked Jasper.

They were walking away from Royal Crescent, keeping up a brisk pace to offset the icy wind that whipped around them, tugging at their coats. Charles Camerton laughed at Jasper's description.

'Mrs Wilby's soirée is no hell, my friend. The stakes are so low they would be ridiculed in town.'

'True, they are unlikely to arouse the interest of the magistrates,' agreed Jasper. 'You saw no instances of foul play?'

'None. Mrs Wilby and her niece are canny players, as sharp as any females I have ever encountered.'

'Aye, and they favour the games where skill and a good memory will aid them. What of Mrs Logan? I noticed you spent a great deal of time at her table.'

Camerton grinned.

'With such paltry sums at stake I had to find something to entertain me! She is different and I like that. I suspect she was a professional gamester at some time. She gave me a run for my money. However...' he patted his pocket '…I came away the richer, so I am not complaining.'

'Nor do the other men that play there, but I am convinced they rarely win.'

'Ah, but they are not there for the cards. They are there to worship at the feet of La Prentess.'

'You noticed that?'

'Of course. She is a diamond. Your cousin Barnabus is most definitely enamoured.' Jasper frowned. That was not what he wanted to hear. He dragged his thoughts back to Charles, who was still speaking. 'And you say she is an heiress? Interesting. With her looks she should be in town. She could make a brilliant alliance.'

'That is what I thought,' agreed Jasper, frowning. 'I believe her family come from London. Dammit, Charles, there is some mystery here.'

'And you have an interest in La Prentess so you want to know what it might be?'

Jasper was quick to disclaim.

'I am only interested in saving my cousin from a disastrous liaison.'

'Don't see that marriage to an heiress would be that much of a disaster.'

Jasper had said very much the same to Gloriana, but now it was important to him that Susannah Prentess should not marry Gerald.

'You know,' mused Charles, 'I might even have a touch at La Prentess myself.'

'I beg you won't!'

Charles laughed. 'No, I won't. Her friend Mrs Logan is much more to my taste. I shall leave La Prentess to you, Jasper.'

They had reached the top of Milsom Street and Jasper was relieved to part from his friend. Their conversation was becoming far too uncomfortable.

A week of chill winds and snow flurries kept all but the most hardy indoors. Servants scattered cinders over the footpaths to prevent pedestrians from slipping and Aunt Maude insisted they take chairs to the Assembly Rooms the following Monday, rather than risk the horses on the icy cobbles.

Susannah expected the rooms to be very thin of company, but the Dress Ball was incentive enough for Bath's residents to turn out in force. Susannah was wearing another new gown from Odesse, a cream silk with a finely frilled hem and short puff sleeves, the rose-coloured decoration set off by matching long gloves. She carried a silk shawl embroidered with tiny rosebuds to combat the icy air that she knew would penetrate even the building, at least until the ballroom filled up and everyone was dancing.

Gerald was looking out for her and immediately led her away to join a country dance. Susannah was surprised to find Kate was already on the floor, partnered by Charles Camerton.

'You, Kate, dancing?' she teased when the movement of the dance brought them together.

The widow's self-conscious look surprised Susannah even more and when there was a break in the dancing she sought out her friend.

'I do not think I have ever known you to dance here,' she remarked. 'And with Mr Camerton, too.'

Kate shrugged one white shoulder and busied herself with her fan.

'He seems keen to dance with me. And after the way

he fleeced me so unmercifully on Tuesday I thought it might help to find out what he is about.'

Susannah sighed, momentarily diverted.

'Our losses last week were very disappointing. Aunt Maude went down a couple of hundred pounds to Lord Markham and I even lost at picquet to Gerald Barnabus.'

'I am beginning to suspect it was a concerted effort by those three gentlemen.'

'By Mr Camerton and the viscount, perhaps, but not Gerald, that was entirely my own fault. I was... distracted.'

'Well, we must be on our guard,' said Kate. 'Such losses cannot be sustained for long.'

'Perhaps we should refuse to admit Mr Camerton and the viscount in future.'

Kate's response was swift.

'Oh, no, we must hope they keep coming.' She added airily, 'That is why I am going to dance again with Mr Camerton now. I hope to lull him into complacency, so that when we play again I will catch him off-guard.'

Kate sailed off in search of her prey. She was clearly enjoying herself and Susannah was not convinced by the reasons she had given for dancing with Mr Camerton.

'Something amuses you, Miss Prentess?'

The viscount's voice at her shoulder was warm and seductive, like being wrapped in sables. Susannah scolded herself for being fanciful.

'I have been talking to Mrs Logan. She always amuses me.'

He glanced across the room.

'She certainly seems to be on the best of terms with Charles Camerton. He is leading her out for another dance.' He held out his arm. 'Shall we join them?'

Susannah had already made up her mind that she

would avoid the viscount whenever possible, but surely Kate's arguments had some merit. Perhaps instead of alienating Lord Markham she should try harder to charm him. In that case, it was clearly her duty to dance with him.

She placed her fingers on his arm and accompanied him on to the dance floor. It was a lively affair and Susannah enjoyed it immensely. She was surprised when the music ended—surely the orchestra had stopped too soon? Lord Markham invited her to remain on the floor for a second set and she thought it would be churlish to refuse him.

When he finally led her from the floor she was happy to stand with him at the side of the room, watching the dancing. Even when he mentioned seeing her carriage on the Wells Road again she was not discomposed.

'Surely it is no one's business if my servants use my carriage for their errands?'

'True.' He guided her to an empty bench and sat down beside her. 'It is, however, unusual. But in an heiress such extravagance will not be criticised.'

It was on the tip of her tongue to explain that for the next couple of years she had no access to anything more than an allowance, but that would undermine her explanation. She held her peace.

Sitting with the viscount was causing some comment. Brows were raised, Susannah saw one or two of the matrons whispering behind their fans, but when one particularly haughty lady smiled and inclined her head towards Susannah, a chuckle escaped her.

The viscount's brows went up.

'Being seen in your company is proving most useful for me,' she explained, her eyes twinkling. 'There are several very high sticklers here tonight and I have never known them to look upon me with such approval.'

'Why should they not approve of you?'

'Oh, well…' she waved her hand '…because my father was a mere captain. Because my uncle was a nabob.'

'A very rich nabob,' he corrected her.

'True.' She sipped at her wine. 'But birth is every-thing.'

'Is it?' He shifted his position to face her. 'You are a gentleman's daughter, and heir to a fortune. I should have thought that would open every door in Bath to you.'

'Perhaps it would, if I would conform and toady up to those matrons who think themselves so superior.'

'From what I know of you, I cannot imagine you doing that.'

His sudden smile flashed and for a moment she was dazzled by his charm, as if someone had knocked all the breath out of her body. She looked away quickly. She was meant to be charming *him*.

Jasper felt rather than saw her sudden withdrawal. She had been relaxed, prepared to confide in him and he was reluctant to let the moment go. He remembered something Gerald had said to him.

'Living in the Crescent, in such an elevated position, could be seen as having pretensions.'

'Perhaps.'

He smiled. 'But you don't really care for their good opinion, do you?'

He read the answer in her face.

'To have their approval could be very useful,' she said carefully.

'To enhance your little card parties?'

'Of course. Imagine how much I would like to have a dowager duchess in my drawing room.'

Her eyes twinkled wickedly. She was teasing him again and Jasper was surprised how much he enjoyed that.

'No doubt you would not refuse to play picquet with her.'

'Of course not.'

'But you will not play with a mere viscount.'

'Not with you, my lord.'

'Why not? You have played picquet with my cousin on more than one occasion.'

'That is different.'

'Why, because you are going to marry him?'

'No!'

He cursed inwardly as soon as he uttered the question, but the tone of her denial and the serious look in her eye reassured him. She was sincere.

She gave a sigh. 'Can you not content yourself with winning two hundred pounds from my aunt last week?'

'A mere trifle. Two games of picquet for pound points would recover that.'

'Or double the loss.'

'True.' He leaned forwards. 'What would it take, Miss Prentess, to make you play with me?'

He saw the shutters come down. He had pressed her too hard. She laughed and shook her head at him.

'Fie, my lord, I have no doubt you are used to playing in the London clubs, to losing thousands at a sitting. Do you expect me to risk my pin-money against you?' She rose. 'You may come to Royal Crescent, my lord, and I will play with you at *vingt-et-un*, or loo, where there are others at the table.'

'You consider me too dangerous an opponent to play alone?'

Jasper was standing, too. The top of her head, crowned by those guinea-gold curls, was level with his eyes. She was the perfect height for kissing. He shrugged off the distracting thought as he held her gaze. She returned look for look, but there was no sign of laughter now in those hazel eyes. Suddenly all Jasper's senses were on the alert, aware that they were not speaking merely about playing cards.

'I think you could be extremely dangerous, my lord.' Her words fell softly between them before she turned and walked away.

'The lady seems displeased with you, Markham.' Charles Camerton came up to him. 'What did you say to her?'

'I asked her to play cards with me.' He did not take his eyes off the retreating figure. 'She refused me.'

Camerton chuckled.

'You must be losing your touch, old friend.'

The comment rankled, but Jasper tried to ignore it.

'Or perhaps,' mused Charles, 'she is playing with you, to excite your interest.'

'Perhaps.' Jasper kept his tone light, but in his heart he didn't want to think that Susannah was toying with him.

'Good morning, Miss. I've brought your hot chocolate.'

Susannah groaned. After tossing and turning all night, she had only just dropped into a deep slumber when Dorcas's cheerful voice disturbed her. The curtains were thrown back and the feeble light of a grey winter morning filled the room. Susannah groaned again and pulled the covers over her head. Her maid responded with a tut.

'Come on now, mistress. You ordered the carriage to be here in an hour. That doesn't give us long to get you ready...or shall I tell Edwards to go away again?'

'No, no, I will get up.'

Susannah sat up and rubbed her eyes. She stared at the flames blazing merrily in the hearth. She had not heard the maid come in to light the fire, so she must have had some sleep, even if it had been disturbed by dreams. She sipped at her cup of chocolate while Dorcas bustled about the room.

'It's a cold morning, miss, will you wear the high-collar spencer?'

She held out the short, rose-coloured jacket with its fur trim.

'Yes, yes, that will do.' Susannah cast an eye at the bleak, overcast sky outside the window. 'And you had better look out my old travelling cloak as well.'

The clock was just chiming the hour as Susannah descended the stairs. Gatley informed her that the carriage was ready, but instead of opening the front door for her, he accompanied his mistress to the lower floor and let her out of the door leading into the garden. Susannah was enveloped in her serviceable cloak and with the hood pulled over her curls she hoped she might pass for a servant as she sped through the garden and into the narrow alley that led between the stables fronting Crescent Lane, where her carriage was waiting. Before settling into her seat she drew down the blinds. If Lord Markham was abroad again this morning she would not risk being seen, even if she did have Lucas, her footman, standing at the back to give her countenance.

She stifled a yawn. It was thoughts of the viscount that had disturbed her sleep. She had gone to bed after the ball with her head spinning. When she closed her eyes she was once again dancing with Lord Markham, fingers tingling from his touch, heart singing from the caress of his smile. Yet no sooner did she relax in his company than he began to talk of the card parties and she would be on the defensive, suspicious of every remark. She rubbed her arms, suddenly chilled, despite the thick cloak and the warm brick her servants had placed in the carriage for her feet to rest upon. If Lord Markham would only leave Bath then she could be easy again.

But how dull life would be without him.

Susannah gave herself a mental shake. These megrims were unlike her, brought on by lack of sleep and travelling in this gloomy half-light. She pulled at the side of the blind and peeped out. They were well out of Bath now, and she thought she might safely put up the shades. The carriage rattled along through the country lanes, up hill and down dale until at last the carriage slowed and turned off the main road towards the village of Priston. Susannah sat forwards, knowing that very soon now she would have her first, clear view of her destination.

The carriage picked up speed as it followed the road that curled around the side of the valley and there, nestling against the hill on the far side of the valley, was a rambling Jacobean mansion built of the local Ham stone which glowed warmly, even in the pale wintry sunlight. It was not as grand as the other properties she had inherited from her Uncle Middlemass and it was in dire need of repair, as witnessed by the scaffolding surrounding the east wing, but she thought it by far the most charming. She was impatient to reach five-and-twenty, when she would have control of her fortune and would be able to fully renovate the building. Until then she must make do with what little money she could spare from her allowance, and the profits from the weekly card parties.

The carriage slowed again to negotiate the turning and her heart swelled with pride when she saw the newly painted sign fixed to the stone gatepost: Florence House. They bumped along the drive and on to the weed-strewn carriage circle in front of the house. They came to a stand before the canopied front door and Lucas jumped down and ran around to let down the steps.

As she descended, a motherly figure in a black stuff gown came hurrying out to meet her, the white lappets from her lace cap bouncing on her shoulders.

'Miss Prentess, welcome, my dear. Pray come you in and do not be standing out here in this cold wind.'

'Thank you, Mrs Gifford.'

The older lady ushered her indoors to a small parlour off the hall, where a welcome fire was burning.

'Has our builder arrived yet?'

'Not yet, ma'am, but you have made very good time—I do not expect him for another half-hour yet. You have time for a little refreshment. Jane is bringing a glass of mulled wine for you.'

'Thank you, that is very welcome.'

Susannah untied the strings of her cloak and looked about her. She had always thought this parlour a very comfortable room. With its low, plastered ceiling and panelled walls it was certainly one of the easiest to keep warm. A door on the far side led to a much larger dining room, but that needed refurbishment and was currently not in use, the occupants of the house finding the smaller apartment sufficient for their needs. A padded armchair and sofa were arranged before the fireplace while under the window a small table and chairs provided a surface for dining or working. At present the table was littered with writing materials and a large ledger, indicating that the housekeeper had been at work on the accounts. Susannah draped her cloak over one of the chairs and went to the fire to warm her hands. She turned as the door opened and a heavily pregnant young woman entered, carrying a tray. She walked slowly, holding the tray well out in front to avoid her extended belly. Susannah straightened immediately.

'Jane, let me take that, you should not be waiting upon me—'

'Thank you, but I can manage perfectly well. And it is a pleasure to bring your wine for you.'

Susannah sat down, recognising that to insist upon taking the tray would hurt the girl's pride. 'Thank you, Jane, that is very kind of you.' She watched her place the tray carefully on a side table. 'When is the baby due?'

'The midwife thinks it won't be for a week or two yet.' Jane smiled and rubbed her hands against her swollen stomach. 'It cannot come soon enough for me now, Miss Prentess.'

'Call me Susannah, please. There is small difference in our stations.'

Jane's smile disappeared.

'Perhaps there was not, at one time, but now—' She looked down at her body. 'I am a fallen woman.'

'I will not have that term used here,' Susannah replied fiercely. 'You have been unfortunate. 'Tis the same for all the ladies we bring in.'

'And if it was not for your kindness we would be even more unfortunate,' replied Jane. 'We would have to go to Walcot Street, and we would not be called ladies there,' she added drily.

'Will you not sit down?' Susannah indicated a chair, but Jane shook her head.

'If you will excuse me, I will go back to my room now and rest. The midwife might say this little one isn't ready to be born, but it seems pretty impatient to me.'

'She is a dear girl,' said Mrs Gifford, when Jane had gone. 'Her stitching is so neat that Odesse says she will be happy to take her on, once the babe is born.'

'Good.' Susannah sipped at her wine. 'Since we have a little time perhaps you would like to give me your report now, rather than wait until after I have spoken to Mr Tyler.'

Mrs Gifford sat down and folded her hands in her lap.

'I have had to move everything out of the east wing because the chimney is unsafe and we fear it might come crashing through the roof if we have a storm. Then there is the leak on the south gable, which is getting worse. But this section of the house is reasonably sound, and I have been able to find dry bedchambers for each of our guests. Miss Anstruther—Violet—is settling in well, although she is still very despondent and keeps to her room.'

'That is to be expected, having been cast off by her family,' replied Susannah. 'I will go up to her later, if she will see me.'

'If?' uttered Mrs Gifford. 'Of course she will see you. 'Tis you who made it possible for her to be looked after. She has much cause to be grateful to you, as do all the others…'

Susannah shook her head.

'I will not trade on their gratitude,' she said quietly. 'Everyone here is a guest, and I want to treat them with the same respect I would like for myself. But enough of that. Do go on.'

'We have only three ladies here at present: Lizzie Burns, Jane and Miss Anstruther.'

'And how is Lizzie? When I was here last she was not well.'

'I think we have avoided the fever, but the doctor says she should keep to her bed for another week. However, her baby is now three weeks old and doing well.'

'That is some good news then. And what of you, Mrs Gifford? How is your sister?'

The older lady's face was grave.

'Very poorly, I'm afraid.'

'Then you must go to her as soon as maybe. The woman we interviewed to replace you—Mrs Jennings—how soon can she be here?'

'She is moving in this afternoon. I hope to get away this evening.'

'Good. And you have enough money for your journey?'

'Yes, thank you.' The old woman blinked rapidly. 'Bless you, Miss Prentess, you have been very good. I do not expect to be away for long, I fear my sister's end is very near.'

'You must take as long as you need,' Susannah told her softly. 'We shall manage here. Now—' she looked towards the window '—if I am not mistaken, the builder has arrived, and we will find out just what work is needed.'

Chapter Six

Susannah's cheerful, business-like manner did not desert her until she was alone in her carriage on the way back to Bath. Mr Tyler was a tradesman she had used before, and she trusted him not to mislead her, but his report on the house was not encouraging. He had already carried out some of the most urgent repairs but needed payment for the materials he had used before he could continue. He had pleaded his case with her. He was a family man, with debts of his own, and if she couldn't pay him something now he would have to remove his scaffolding and his men, and once he had left the site he would not be able to return until late summer. She had promised to send him something by the morning, but her concern now was where to find the money.

When she had first embarked upon this project she had approached her uncle's lawyer, now her own man of business. He had politely but firmly rejected her requests for an advance upon her inheritance. She was allowed sufficient funds to run the house in Bath and a sum that her uncle had considered enough for her personal use, but it would not run to the cost of repairing Florence House.

'If only we had not lost money at last week's card party,' she muttered, staring unseeing at the bleak winter landscape.

However, it was not her nature to be despondent and she put her mind to ways of raising the capital she needed. Her fingers crept up to the string of pearls about her neck. She had inherited her aunt's jewel box. It was overflowing with necklaces, brooches and rings, most of them quite unsuitable for a single lady. Susannah did not want to sell any of them. They were part of her inheritance and she owed it to her uncle's memory to keep them if she possibly could. But Florence House was important to her, and she had to do *something*, and urgently. By the time she reached Bath she had come up with a plan, and when she spotted Gerald Barnabus on the pavement she pulled the check-string and stopped the carriage.

'Gerald, good day to you! I wonder if I might have a word...'

March had arrived. The first flowers of spring were in evidence and Jasper was conscious of the fact that he had planned to be back at Markham by now. He was receiving regular reports from his steward, which assured him all was well, but he wanted to be back before Lady Day. The yearly rents were due then and he liked to discuss future agreements with his tenants. Honesty compelled him to admit that there was no real reason for him to stay in Bath, so what was keeping him here? He might argue that it was the mystery surrounding Susannah Prentess, but an uncomfortable honesty forced him to admit that it was the woman herself who fascinated him. It would not do. It would be best if he forgot all about Miss Prentess. When Tuesday dawned he found himself looking forward to going to Royal Crescent that evening. It would be the last time, he promised himself. He would bid goodbye to Mrs Wilby and her enchanting niece and return to Markham.

Jasper went out for his usual early walk, but this time turned his steps towards Sydney Gardens, determined that he would not even look to see if Miss Prentess's carriage left the city that morning.

He returned to York House for breakfast and spent the next few hours at the desk replying to his steward and writing various letters. The afternoon was well advanced by the time he applied his seal to the last letter, and when Jasper glanced at the clock he was surprised to find it was so late. It had become something of a habit for Gerald to call in York House each afternoon, if they had not met earlier in the day, to discuss plans for the evening. Jasper shrugged. He was not his cousin's keeper. Gerald was of age, after all, and had gone on very well in Bath before his arrival. Jasper finished his letters and called for Peters to bring his hat and cane: he would call upon Gerald at his lodgings in Westgate Buildings and invite him to dinner.

In the event Jasper never reached Gerald's abode, nor did he issue the invitation. He had stopped in Milsom Street. It was in his mind to buy a little gift to send down to his godson at Rooks Tower, but his attention was caught by a reflection in the toyshop window. The shop was on the shady side of the street, so the image from the far side of the road was particularly clear. Gerald had emerged from the jewellers and paused to pull on his gloves. Jasper turned and was about to hail his cousin when he noticed the veiled figure of a lady being ushered out of the shop with much bowing by a black-coated assistant. It was obvious to Jasper that Gerald was waiting for the lady. He held out his arm to her, but before setting off she put up her veil to display the lovely countenance of Susannah Prentess.

Jasper froze. Susannah slipped her hand through Gerald's arm and they set off down the street. There was such a warm smile on her face that Jasper felt winded. He stepped back, almost reeling from the sudden bolt of jealousy that shot through him.

The low sun was shining upon them and they did not notice him watching from the shadows. Had Gerald proposed again, had he been accepted? No. He could not believe it. He *would* not believe it until he had spoken to his cousin. With an effort he forced his unwilling feet to carry him onwards. His brain seethed with conjecture, but he refused to admit his worst fears. He wandered about the town, visiting the Pump Room and the circulating library, but nothing could satisfy his restless spirit. He called at the White Hart but discovered that Charles Camerton had gone out. No matter, Charles was joining him for dinner, so he would see him then. However, as he turned his steps once more towards his hotel he saw Gerald walking down High Street towards him. He was somewhat reassured by the way Gerald hailed him cheerfully, but after they had exchanged greetings, Jasper could not resist telling him that he had seen him earlier.

'You were outside the jewellers with Miss Prentess. Would you like to tell me what that was about?'

'Actually, I am not at liberty to say at the moment.' Gerald's boyish face flushed. 'I promised Susannah.'

'I see.' Jasper's jaw clenched at the familiar use of her name and there was a hollow ache in his stomach.

'It is nothing terrible,' Gerald hurried on, watching him anxiously.

Jasper forced a smile to his lips.

'If that is the case then why can you not tell me?'

Gerald looked uncomfortable.

'It is just that I know Mama would not approve. She might quiz you, and if you do not know, then you cannot tell her anything, can you?'

'Gerald—'

His cousin cut him short.

'Will you be at the Crescent this evening? I will ask Susannah. If she is willing, I will tell you then. I promise. For now you must excuse me, I am on an errand.'

'Come and dine with me tonight,' said Jasper. 'Charles Camerton will be there, we can go on to the Crescent together.'

Gerald shook his head.

'I am sorry, Jasper, I should like to join you, but I do not think I will be back in time.'

'Why, where are you going?'

'I told you, an errand,' was all the answer Gerald would give before he dashed off, leaving Jasper prey to such a fierce anger that for several minutes he remained rooted to the spot. An engagement. It had to be. It was the only thing that could account for Gerald's odd speech, and the happiness he had seen in both their faces earlier. Clutching his cane, Jasper strode angrily back to York House. She had tricked him. Why should he be surprised? She had told him her actions were no concern of his, but Gerald *was* his concern. Damnation, he was head of the family. How dare she make Gerald act in this underhand manner!

* * *

By the time Charles Camerton arrived for dinner Jasper's rage was contained. Outwardly he was smiling, urbane, but it still burned, a steady, simmering fury inside him. Years of training came to his aid, allowing him to converse with seeming normality during the meal, but he tasted nothing of the dishes set before him and allowed his glass to be refilled more than normal.

Only when the covers were removed and the servants had withdrawn did he allow himself to think back over his day.

'I looked for you at the White Hart today, Charles, and you were not in the Pump Room. Did you go out of town?'

'Yes. It was such a fine day I took Mrs Logan for a drive.'

'Really?'

Charles shrugged. 'Just being friendly, you know.'

'I hope you are not developing a *tendre* there, Charles. I shall require you to be on winning form again at the Crescent tonight.'

Charles refilled his brandy glass.

'I am more than happy to accompany you there, Markham, but I am not sure your plan is necessary. I have been watching your cousin. He does not seem in any danger of making a cake of himself over La Prentess. At least, no more than any of the other young bucks who are fashionably in love with her.'

'I wish I could agree with you.' Jasper pushed back his chair. 'I plan to leave Bath soon, but before I do I want to make sure Gerald is in no danger.'

'Very well then.' Charles rose and followed him to the door. 'Let us to the Crescent, by all means.'

Jasper escorted him out of the hotel. During the meal

he had convinced himself that there was only one way to protect Gerald from that scheming woman: he would have to seduce her.

Susannah gazed about her with satisfaction. The drawing room looked very welcoming, the curtains were pulled against the darkness and the cheerful fire kept the icy weather at bay so effectively that she did not need to wear a shawl over the flowing creation Odesse had fashioned for her. The apricot silk was embroidered at the neck and sleeves with a pattern of vine leaves, the detail cleverly picked out in silver thread to catch the candlelight. She heard the distant rumble of voices. The first guests were arriving. Almost upon the thought Mrs Wilby hurried in.

'Is everything ready, my love? Tables set, new packs of cards… I have told Gatley to have plenty of mulled wine available for our guests as it is such a cold night.' She looked about her. 'Where is Mrs Logan?'

'She sent me word she might be a little late. She went out driving this afternoon.'

'Oh, with whom?'

'She did not say.' It was true, but Susannah suspected she had been in the company of Mr Camerton. She had seen them talking together after the Sunday service at the Abbey, and although Kate would tell her nothing, her smile had been very self-satisfied. She wondered if the widow had formed an attachment, then quickly dismissed the idea. Kate might smile and flirt with the men she encountered but Susannah knew it was a charade. Kate had often voiced her opinion of the male sex. They were at best deceivers, selfish brutes who cared for nothing but their own pleasure. It was much more likely that she was, to use Kate's own phrase, keeping

Mr Camerton sweet in the hopes of winning his money from him this evening.

'Well, I hope she will not be too long,' muttered Mrs Wilby. 'We need her to run one of the tables.'

There was no time for more. General and Mrs Sanstead were announced and after that there was a steady stream of arrivals. Susannah organised four guests at a whist table, found a partner to play picquet with Major Crommelly, explaining to him that she was unable to do so as she had to help her aunt entertain all the guests. Later, she gave in to the pleas of a group of young gentlemen to sit down with them to play a noisy game of *vingt-et-un*. She laughed and joked and flirted gently with them all, making sure that not one of them lost more than fifty pounds. Of course she could not dictate to her guests when they played amongst themselves, but it was her strict rule, and she insisted that her aunt and Kate Logan kept to it, despite many of the younger men bragging how much they could lose in one sitting at other houses.

She was pleased when Kate arrived and she could leave the table and tour the room, making sure that every one of her guests was occupied. No one would guess from her smiles and serene countenance that her mind was elsewhere, that she was watching the clock, and wondering what time Gerald Barnabus might arrive.

There was the bustle of another arrival and Susannah looked up hopefully. It was with mixed feelings that she saw Lord Markham and Mr Camerton walk in. Aunt Maude was already near the door to welcome them so Susannah made no attempt to approach. She watched Mr Camerton seek out Mrs Logan and join her table, while the viscount was persuaded to sit down with his hostess for a game of loo. Susannah could relax a little, at least until the game broke up and she saw the viscount crossing the room towards her.

The tug of attraction was as strong as ever. He moved between the tables with lithe grace, his tall, athletic form clad in the uniform black evening coat and black knee-breeches. She was forcibly reminded of a hunting panther.

And she was the prey.

Shaking off such nonsensical notions Susannah greeted him coolly, which he did not seem to notice. Her hand went automatically into his grasp without her even realising it. As he bowed she gazed at his dark head, trying to calm the fierce tattoo that was beating within her breast as his lips skimmed her fingers. It was as much as she could do to stand still. She must talk to Kate about what these sensations might mean—some instinct told her that Aunt Wilby would not give her an honest answer.

'Miss Prentess.' He straightened, subjecting her to that glinting smile. There was something else in his eyes, a dangerous recklessness that did nothing to calm her pulse. She withdrew her fingers, resisting the urge to cradle them in her other hand. She must act naturally, to treat him as she would any other guest.

'Are you tired of Lanterloo, my lord?'

'For the moment. I came to see if you would play picquet with me.'

She managed a soft laugh.

'You know I will not, my lord.'

'Then for the moment I shall be an observer.'

'As you wish.' He made no attempt to move out of

her way. 'How long do you intend to remain in Bath, my lord?'

'That depends.'

'Upon what?'

As soon as the words were uttered she knew she had fallen into his trap. He turned his dark eyes upon her again. She had no doubt that those handsome features and charming smile had undone many a young lady. Flirting with the other young gentlemen of Bath had always seemed an innocent, harmless pastime, but with Lord Markham no remark was ever innocent or harmless. Once again she found breathing difficult, she knew the colour was fluctuating in her cheeks. She wanted to move closer to that lean, muscular body and it was almost a physical effort to keep her distance.

'Mr Barnabus!'

The butler's sonorous announcement could not have been better timed.

She blinked, as if woken from a trance, and with a hurried 'excuse me!' she stepped past him and moved swiftly across the room.

'Mr Barnabus.' She held out her hands to him. 'You are very welcome.' She leaned a little closer, saying quietly, 'Well? Have you been to Florence House?'

He squeezed her hands.

'Yes. You may be easy. I have seen Tyler and given him the money. He will begin the new work next week.'

Susannah gave a little sigh of relief, her smile growing.

'Thank you, I can never tell you how grateful I am to you.' She tucked her hand into his arm and led him further into the room.

'I see my cousin is here,' he remarked. 'Would it—?' He stopped, looking about to make sure he could not be overheard. 'I do not like to keep things from him. May I tell him where I have been, why I am so late?'

'Oh good heavens, no!' she gasped, horrified.

'But Jasper is a great gun. I am sure he would understand—'

'And I am sure he would not.' She laid her hand on his sleeve, saying urgently, 'Please, Gerald, on no account would I have the viscount know anything about this.' When he looked uncertain she added, 'You promised. When I explained to you about Florence House, you gave me your word that you would not tell a soul.'

'Oh very well, Susannah, if you insist.'

'I do.' She squeezed his arm. 'Thank you, Gerald. Now what can I do to reward you? Shall we play at macao together?'

Jasper watched the little scene from across the room. There was no doubting her pleasure in seeing his cousin, and the boy was as besotted as ever. He had noticed when he had kissed her hand that she wore no rings—why should they keep their betrothal a secret? They were both of age and Gerald's nature was so open, so honest, that he would abhor any subterfuge. His eyes narrowed. It must come from the lady, then. She had secrets, and in his book that made her an unsuitable match for his young cousin.

He looked around for Charles Camerton and saw him sitting at a small table with Mrs Logan. From the pile of coins at his elbow Jasper guessed that he was winning. That was very good. Now he, too, must continue with his plan.

'How goes it, Aunt?'

Susannah took advantage of a break in the play to

speak to Mrs Wilby. The lady shook her head, making the lilac ostrich feathers on her turban tremble.

'Badly,' she muttered as she collected up the used cards. 'Lord Markham has taken two hundred off me already.'

'And Kate tells me she has just lost fifty pounds to his friend.' Susannah frowned.

'I have never known luck like it,' continued Aunt Maude. 'I admit I am loath to have the viscount play at my table again.'

'Then what do you propose I do with him?' Susannah felt the smile tugging at her mouth, despite the gravity of the situation.

'I do not know, my love, but I pray you will come up with something. He has made me so nervous that I cannot think clearly, and that, you know, is fatal to our success.'

Susannah was well aware of it. One needed a clear head if one was to succeed at card games. She hoped he would play at whist with Major Crommelly and the Sansteads, at least then any losses would not be hers, but the viscount seemed determined to play against Aunt Maude. Susannah watched as he won another game of loo and pocketed his winnings. A few pounds—a hundred at most. A paltry sum to Lord Markham, but Susannah was well aware that the losses this evening were mounting up. Thus, when the viscount asked if he might take her down to supper she agreed, reasoning that anything she could do to keep him away from her aunt would give that lady some welcome relief. However, as soon as he pulled her hand on to his arm she began to have doubts about the wisdom of being alone with him.

'Perhaps we should ask Mrs Logan and Mr Camerton if they would like to join us…'

'I have already ascertained that they would not.' Something of her disappointment must have shown in her face for he smiled. 'I vow, ma'am, I begin to think you are afraid of being alone with me.'

'Nonsense. Why should that be?'

'My reputation, perhaps?'

'I know nothing of your reputation, Lord Markham. Is it so very bad?'

'Perfectly dreadful,' he replied cheerfully. 'At least it is in London. I am relieved that no one here knows of it.'

She stopped as a sudden worry assailed her.

'And just what is your reputation *for*, my lord—gambling?'

'No. Breaking hearts.' Again his smiling eyes teased her. He covered her hand with his own and held it on his sleeve. 'Do you wish to run away from me now?'

Susannah's chin went up.

'I do not run away from anything, my lord.'

It was still early and the supper room was empty save for the servants. The viscount guided her to a table at the far end of the room.

Where we will not be overheard.

She stifled the thought. This was her house, her staff were in attendance. No harm could come to her here. The viscount insisted she sit down and went off to fill a plate for her. Susannah looked at the table, playing with the napkins and the cutlery. She would not watch him: she was all too aware of the graceful power of his movements. She would be better gathering her wits. The viscount had an uncanny knack of disconcerting her, she must be on her guard.

Susannah kept her eyes lowered until he returned and placed before her a plate filled with little delicacies.

'I congratulate you, Lord Markham. I gave you leave to choose for me, and I believe there is nothing here that I do not like.'

He slipped into the seat opposite and picked up his napkin.

'I took the opportunity to ask your estimable butler for his advice.'

She chuckled at that.

'I give you credit for your honesty, at least, sir.'

She applied herself to her food, gradually relaxing. Lord Markham was the perfect companion, asking nothing impertinent, amusing her with little anecdotes. As her nerves settled so her appetite improved and when her plate was empty she looked at the single syllabub glass on the table.

'Is that for you or for me?'

'For you.' He picked up the spoon. 'But I hoped you might let me share the enjoyment.'

She sat back, scandalised.

'No, that is an outrageous idea.'

He glanced around.

'Why? The room is empty at present. Even the servants are not attending.' He scooped out a small spoonful of the syllabub and held it out to her.

Susannah stared at it. She must not. She dare not. Yet she sat forwards, her eyes on that tempting spoonful.

'Go on,' he murmured, his voice low and inviting. 'While no one is watching. Tell me how it tastes.'

He held the spoon closer and automatically her lips parted. She took the sweet, succulent mouthful, felt the flavours burst upon her tongue. Nothing had ever tasted so delicious. Heavens, was this how Eve felt when she had tried the forbidden fruit?

Jasper watched, entranced. He saw the flicker of her eyelid, the movement of her throat as she swallowed. She ran her tongue across her lips and he felt the desire slam through him. By God, no wonder Gerald was besotted. He tore his eyes away and sat back. He was meant to be seducing *her*, not the other way around.

'Well, Miss Prentess, did you enjoy that?'

She would not meet his eyes. That was perhaps as well. He was not at all sure he could sound so cool if she was looking at him.

'Yes…no.'

'Another spoonful, perhaps?' He dug the spoon into the syllabub again but she lifted her hand.

'No! There are too many people now. We will be seen.'

'But you would like to do it again?'

Her blush gave him the answer but she said hurriedly, 'Of course not. You are quite outrageous, my lord. We will forget that happened, if you please.'

Her voice was perfectly steady but he noted that her hand shook a little as she picked up her napkin and touched her lips. Good. She was off balance, which had been his object. That he, too, was shaken by the moment was unfortunate, but it would not happen again.

'As you wish. But there is something else I want from you, something that is not at all outrageous.'

'What is that?'

'To play picquet with you.'

'Out of the question. You have already won more than enough from my aunt.'

'I am giving you the chance to win it all back.'

'No.' She rose and shook out her skirts. 'I must return to the drawing room.'

'As you wish.' He held out his arm. The fingers that she laid upon his sleeve trembled a little. He fought down the impulse to put up his free hand and cover them, to protect her. That was not his purpose at all. As they left the room he asked his question again.

'And shall we now play picquet?'

'I have told you, no, my lord.'

He threw her a teasing glance.

'After such a meal do I not deserve some reward?'

The look she gave him was indignant.

'After such a meal you deserve I should not speak to you again!'

Charles Camerton and Mrs Logan were descending the stairs and they waited to let them pass.

'We were just coming down to join you,' Charles addressed them cheerfully. 'Mrs Logan hopes the luck will change after a break.'

Jasper noted the rueful look the widow gave to Susannah as they passed.

'It seems your aunt and your friend are not doing so well this evening,' he commented as they went up the stairs.

'We shall come about.'

'You could recoup everything with a single game of picquet.'

'Or lose even more.'

'Not necessarily.' He had her attention. 'We need not play for money.' He glanced up and down the staircase. They were alone. 'I will wager my diamond pin against...' He paused.

'Yes?'

'Dinner,' he said at last. 'You will join me for dinner at York House on Thursday night.'

Chapter Seven

*M*adness.

Susannah wanted to shake her head, to tell him she would not countenance such a wager, but her eyes were fixed upon the diamond. It winked at her. It was worth a king's ransom. It would more than pay for the repairs to Florence House. She could recover the jewels she had sold today and there might even be sufficient to cover the running costs of the house until she came into her inheritance. She was silent as they made their way to the top of the stairs and when they reached the landing she allowed him to draw her to one side.

'Well, madam, will you accept?'

She ran her tongue over her lips.

'Dinner, you say?'

'Yes.'

'Alone?'

'Of course.'

It was not to be thought of. To have dinner with him, unescorted, would ruin her reputation.

Only if it was discovered.

As if reading her thoughts he continued, 'You need have no fear. The hotel is very quiet at present and you may come veiled. My man will serve us and he is very…discreet.'

'It seems you have thought of everything, my lord.'

'I like to think so.'

'If I win you will give me the diamond.'

'I will.'

'And if I lose, I will have dinner with you at your hotel. Nothing more.'

'Nothing more.'

'We will play the best of three games,' she declared.

'If that will suit you.' The viscount bowed.

'Perfectly.' Having made her decision, she led the way into the drawing room and headed for the empty table in the corner, collecting several new packs of playing cards on her way.

Susannah unwrapped the first pack, thankful that she had taken only a small glass of wine with her supper. She drew the low card and shuffled, holding out the cards for the viscount to cut. She could do this. It was merely a case of steady nerves and keeping a mental note of all the discards. She had done it hundreds of times before. As dealer she knew she must be on the defensive in the first game, but she had a strong hand and after making her discards she was slightly ahead on points when play started. Her optimism was dented when the viscount won the final trick.

'You were unlucky.' He reached for a new pack. 'But you showed some skill. You may do better this time.'

'I shall indeed.'

She studied her hand and chose her discards carefully. By the time play started she felt sure she had the stronger hand. Winning the first trick boosted her confidence and she played with conviction, narrowly winning the second game. The third, however, started badly and ended worse. The viscount won every trick.

'Capotted,' she declared, carefully putting down her cards. She sank her teeth into her bottom lip. She must admit defeat gracefully. 'Congratulations, my lord. You have won.'

'You play very well, Miss Prentess. I think you deserve one last chance.' He drew the diamond pin from his neck cloth and placed it on the table between them. 'What say you we play one more game, winner takes all?'

She laughed. It sounded a trifle reckless, even to her own ears.

'What do I have to lose?'

She reached out to take the pin between her thumb and finger. The viscount's hand closed over hers. A sudden flicker of candlelight made his eyes gleam with a devilish glow.

'There is one minor alteration to the terms of our wager.' His voice was smooth, as cold and deadly as steel. 'If I win this game you come to the hotel for dinner and you stay. All night.'

With a gasp she drew back. Unmoved, he continued.

'You have my word I will not seduce you. I will not even touch you without your permission. But you will stay in my rooms *until morning*.'

'What is the point of your assurances?' she challenged him. 'I shall be ruined whether you touch me or no.'

'Only if word of it gets out. And I shall tell no one.'

She sat up very straight, staring at him.

'Why are you doing this? Why force me to dine with you and stay in your rooms if you do not want to…to seduce me?'

His smile sent a shiver running down her back.

'Oh I want to seduce you, madam, but I have never yet forced any woman to accept my advances. So what do you say to the wager, Miss Susannah Prentess? A diamond worth thousands against a night with me?'

Susannah stared down at the glittering gem. She had beaten him once, and only lost the third game by ill luck. She had his measure now. Surely it was worth the risk. She realised that she was more of a gambler than she had ever known.

Slowly and deliberately she unwrapped a new pack.

'My trick, I believe, Miss Prentess. And my game.'

Susannah put down her cards. It had not even been close. The viscount had started with the strongest hand, and although she had recovered a couple of tricks the outcome had never been in doubt. She swallowed, suddenly feeling very numb. When she managed to speak, her voice seemed to belong to some other creature, someone calm and not at all shaken by the thought of what she had agreed.

'What time do you want me to join you on Thursday?'

'Shall we say seven o'clock? My man will meet you at the entrance, you will not need to announce yourself at the desk.'

She raised her chin.

'What if I do not come? What if I refuse to honour the wager?'

His eyes rested upon her. There was no hint of blue in them now. They were slate grey, dark and implacable.

'You will come. It is not in your nature to go back on your word.'

The little flicker of defiance died.

'You are right.' She put her hands on the table to steady herself as she rose to her feet. 'If you will excuse me, I have neglected my other guests long enough.'

'Of course.' He stood, his bow the perfect mix of deference and respect. 'Until Thursday, Miss Prentess.'

When she had gone Jasper resumed his seat. He took up the diamond pin and carefully secured it amongst the folds of his neckcloth. He had never before pursued a woman who was so reluctant to succumb to his advances. For an instant his conscience pricked him. He could be ruining an innocent woman.

No. He was *saving* his innocent cousin. Susannah Prentess must never marry Gerald. How that came about was up to her—if she refused to give him up, then Jasper would make sure Gerald knew about her visit to York House. His cousin might be naïve, but he would not countenance marriage to a woman who had been unfaithful to him.

'Your visitor, my lord.'

Peters ushered the veiled figure into the small parlour that doubled as a dining room and went out again, shutting the door behind him.

'Welcome, ma'am.'

Jasper went towards her. She stood unmoving, and at last he reached out and lifted the veil from her face. She allowed him to remove her cloak and bonnet. He noted the pleated muslin around her shoulders, ending in a fashionable neck ruff. Chosen deliberately, he suspected, to hide her charms. Her gown was a deep sea-green silk, with a matching silk cord tied in a bow beneath her breasts. The ends of the cord hung down almost to the hem and were decorated with silk tassels that bobbed and shimmered whenever she moved, drawing the eye towards the matching shoes and the occasional glimpse of a dainty ankle. Her hair was caught up in a knot on her head, from which a few golden curls dangled enticingly over her ears and glinted in the candlelight. She had never looked more beautiful, or more frightened.

He took her hand.

'You are ice-cold,' he remarked, drawing her down on to a sofa before the fire.

'I took a chair. I did not want any of my people to know my destination.'

'What of Mrs Wilby?'

'My aunt has gone to the Fancy Ball at the Upper Rooms with Mrs Logan. I told them I was…unwell.'

Again he was obliged to crush a prickle of conscience. He was doing this for Gerald. There need be no adverse consequences of this evening, as long as the lady agreed to his terms.

'There is no need for anyone to know you are here, except my man, Peters, and I can vouch for his discretion.' He smiled, hoping to dispel some of the anxiety in her face. 'I have sent him off for the night. There will be no one to disturb us.' He pointed to the table on the far side of the room. 'You see your dinner; everything is there so we may serve ourselves, when you are ready.'

'I am ready now. Let us get on.' She tugged off her gloves. 'I have urgent business that takes me out of Bath early tomorrow morning.'

She stalked to the table. Her whole demeanour indicated that she wanted to get this over with as quickly as possible. She was not intent upon flattering him, Jasper thought ruefully, as he poured wine into two glasses.

'Miss Prentess, we have a long evening ahead of us. It would pass much easier if we observe the basic civilities.' He handed her a glass. 'Will you cry quits with me, at least until we have finished our meal?'

There was a stormy look in her eyes, but after a brief hesitation she gave a little nod.

'By all means, my lord.'

'Good.' He held out her chair, his eyes drawn to the smooth curve of her neck between the frilled edge of the ruff and her upswept hair. He resisted the temptation to bend and plant a gentle kiss there—she was not to be won by such a liberty.

Susannah remained upright on her chair, her nerves at full stretch. She did not understand the man. The air was thick with tension, every word, every gesture, seemed loaded with meaning. When she had taken her seat all she could think of was his hands on the chair behind her, just inches from her shoulders. It made her skin tingle. He had not touched her, and when he took his own seat he looked cool and at his ease. From the soup to the syllabub he served her with skill and courtesy, carving for her the most delicate slices from the roast duck, helping her to a portion of the sole in red wine, a sliver of the potato pudding. There was never a hint that she was anything more than an honoured guest, but all the time she was aware of him sitting across the table from her. She kept her feet tucked beneath her chair lest they should accidentally brush his.

She watched his hands as he served her, remembering how he had held out the syllabub when he had taken her down to supper at Royal Crescent, his long fingers holding the spoon to her lips, the wonderfully decadent sweetness of the soft mixture on her tongue. Of course she would not allow him such outrageous freedom again, but there was no denying that the syllabub set before her this evening was dull and lifeless in comparison.

Her lips were dry, but she would not run her tongue across them. That would show weakness and might rouse in him the desire she suspected was just below the surface. Yet he insisted he did not wish to seduce her, that he would do nothing without her permission. She sipped thoughtfully at her wine. Was this tension, the awareness, only within her? A surreptitious glance across the table showed that he was watching her, a faint smile on his handsome face.

And he *was* handsome. Sinfully so. She thought back to when they had danced together, remembering the covetous looks of the other ladies. How they would envy her, here alone with him. It must be the dream, the fantasy, of so many females. Yet Susannah knew it should remain as nothing more than a fantasy—the reality of what could lead from such an encounter as this was too horrendous, too devastating to consider. She must be on her guard against the feelings he aroused in her. How many times had she heard a poor, misguided girl say, 'I could not help myself'?

'If you have eaten your fill, ma'am, shall we retire from the table? It would be more comfortable to sit before the fire.'

The viscount's words dragged her back from her reverie. He came around the table and held out his hand to her. Not by the flicker of an eyelid would she admit to the flash of awareness that shot through her when she placed her hand in his. She refused to lean upon him, even though her knees threatened to give way beneath her and her whole body was tingling and alive in a way that she had never known before. Her breasts were hard, pushing against the thin silk of her bodice and there was an ache of desire low down in her belly. She felt as if she was caught in some giant web. It wrapped around her, easing her closer towards her escort. When they reached the sofa it took all her effort to push against that invisible web and place herself at the very end, as far from that disturbing presence as it was possible to be.

The viscount did not appear to notice. Susannah held her breath, ready to leap up should he seat himself too close, or press himself up against her, but instead he stood a little to one side, looking down at her.

It was unbearable. If he had pounced, leered or directed lewd innuendo towards her she would have known how to react, but there was nothing lover-like or menacing in his behaviour. They might have been the best of friends, enjoying a meal together. Save that they were not friends. They were strangers, and they were totally alone in his suite of rooms in the most expensive hotel in Bath. Taking her courage in her hands, Susannah forced herself to look up and ask him a direct question.

'Why are you doing this?'

He hesitated a heart's beat before replying.

'I want to make sure you do not marry my cousin.'

She blinked at him. Was that all? Relief brought the first real smile of the evening to her face.

'Then you have gone to a great deal of trouble for nothing, my lord. I have already told you I do not mean to marry him, and I am pretty sure Gerald has told you the same.'

'I saw you,' he said. 'Coming out of the jewellers on Milsom Street.'

She raised her brows.

'And that convinced you we are to be married? You are very quick to jump to conclusions.'

'Then tell me what you were doing there.'

'I will not.'

'Then tell me where you go almost every morning, when you drive out of Bath in your carriage—and pray do not try to fob me off, I have seen you.'

'Very well, I will say nothing then.'

'You are an extremely obstinate woman, Miss Prentess.'

'And you are a fool,' she retorted. 'I told you at the outset I had no designs upon your cousin. Gerald has come to terms with that, so why cannot you?'

'You make use of him unmercifully.'

'He is happy to be of assistance to me.'

'You sent him off on an errand—'

'I did.'

'Where did he go?'

'That is none of your business.' She waved her hand. 'I doubt you would approve, if you knew.'

'But it might have stopped me from going to these extraordinary measures to prevent your liaison.'

His retort merely made her shake her head at him, smiling.

'You have led yourself a merry dance, have you not, my lord?'

He sat down beside her.

'It seems I have been well and truly bamboozled.'

He looked at her and his lips twitched. The corners of his mouth turned up. Susannah stifled a giggle, he tried not to chuckle, but the next moment both of them were laughing so hard they could not sit upright, but leaned against each other, helpless with mirth. He put his arm around her to support them and, still giggling, she turned towards him.

The laughter died away, but Susannah found she was still smiling, still looking into those dark, dark eyes that held nothing now but warmth and good humour. Without thinking she put up her hand to cup his cheek.

'How foolish you were to doubt me,' she whispered.

He turned his head to press a kiss into the palm of her hand and as he did so his arms slid around her. It seemed the most natural thing in the world to look up a little more, to invite his kiss and when his lips met hers it was as if the whole world relaxed with a sigh. She leaned into him, her lips parting under the soft pressure of his mouth. His tongue dipped into her, drawing on the ache that reached right through her body, down to her groin.

She wound her arms around him and kissed him back, tangling her tongue with his, pressing herself closer. Every inch of her skin was alive to the feel of his hands through the thin layers of her gown. When he stopped kissing her and slid one hand beneath her knees, lifting her effortlessly into his arms, she did not protest, but pressed her face against his neck, breathing in that faint, familiar scent she had come to associate with him and planting gentle kisses on the pulse beating beneath his skin.

He carried her through to the bedroom. A fire burned in the hearth, and candles flickered in the wall sconces, giving the room a warm, welcoming glow. He did not pause but made straight for the bed where he laid her on the covers. Her arms were still around his neck and she drew him to her, impatient to feel his mouth on hers again. He obliged, covering her mouth as he stretched out beside her, measuring her length with his body, arousing in her feelings she could not control.

She was almost swooning, transported to another world by the sensations he was creating in her. He had removed her ruff and was now kissing her throat, his hands unfastening the drawstring on her bodice so that he could caress her breasts. They were taut and hard, pressing against his questing fingers and when he began to circle one tender nub with his thumb she groaned aloud, her head going back as the pleasure of it surged through her whole body.

Susannah reached out for him. She did not know when he had cast off his jacket and waistcoat, but there was only the thin linen shirt between her hands and his flesh. She could feel the hard outline of his back, the contours of his shoulders, his spine. It was all so new, so exhilarating. She gasped as his mouth replaced the thumb at her breast and her body responded, softening, the very bones liquefying. His hand smoothed over her silken skirts, pushing them aside to stroke her thigh. She was drowning in the pleasure of him, opening, turning towards his questing fingers, inviting him to go further, to explore her fully.

Susannah moved sensuously against the covers. She had not known it could be so wondrous, this attraction between a man and a woman. That she could feel so alive, so at one with another person. Was it always like this? Was this how it had been for...

Memories and cold fear returned.

'No.' She was seized by panic and tried to push him off. 'No, please. Please, don't do this.'

Immediately he stopped and drew away. Instead of relief she felt merely chilled and bereft.

'Susannah? What is it, my dear, what is wrong?'

She rolled away from him and scrabbled to sit up, hugging herself.

'I never meant— I should never— I am so ashamed.' She buried her face in her hands as hot tears burned her cheeks. Trembling, she waited for him to curse her roughly for her wanton behaviour, to swear, maybe even to lash out at her.

After a deathly silence broken only by her muffled sobs she felt his hand on her shoulder. A light touch. Soothing, not threatening.

'I beg your pardon, Susannah. This is all my fault. I never intended… Oh, hell and damnation, what a coil!'

His gentleness made her cry even harder. He shifted until he was sitting beside her and gently pulled her against him.

'I promised you I would do nothing without your consent, my dear. If I misunderstood—'

She shook her head, unable to speak, unable to tell him how much she had wanted, *relished* every touch, every caress.

'I must go—'

He held her tighter.

'No, not yet. It is not yet midnight, there are too many people abroad. Someone might recognise you.'

'Then what shall I do?'

'You must stay here until dawn and I will find you a chair.'

'I cannot stay here, with you.'

'To leave my chambers now would be to risk being seen. You would be ruined.' He exhaled, a long, drawn-out sigh. 'I think I have misjudged you. We must talk.'

'No, not yet.' She held her head in her hands. 'I feel so tired.'

He pulled her unresisting on to the bed.

'Then lie here and sleep.' He added quickly, 'You will be perfectly safe. I promise I shall not molest you again. The bed is wide enough for us both to lie on it without touching.'

Susannah turned away from him and curled herself into a ball. Molest her? He had not molested her. He had awoken her to the delights of her own body. He had seduced her and she had succumbed most willingly. Oh heavens, she was no different from those poor unfortunate girls at Florence House. They too had been seduced by fine words and soft caresses, before they had been abandoned. How could she have been so weak? No wonder young ladies required a chaperon to be with them constantly. She had not known how it could feel, had not realised how wayward her own body could be. She thought of the man lying beside her. There was no doubt he was kind and gentle, but it made him no less a seducer.

She felt the bed move as he slid off it, heard him pad across the room. A moment later there was the soft click as the key turned in the lock. Her worst fears were realised. She was his prisoner. Hot tears pressed against her eyes. It was clear now that his gentle assurances were worthless. He had not kissed her because he wanted to, because he was attracted to her. It was a cold plan devised to protect his cousin. The tears spilled over, burning her cheeks. What a fool she was.

Jasper came back to the bed and lay down again, keeping very still. He listened to the quiet snuffling beside him. Sympathy put his desire to flight. And he *had* desired her, so much so that he had forgotten his planned seduction, forgotten all about Gerald Barnabus. When he had taken Susannah in his arms he had thought only of possessing her fully, wholly, for himself. Her distress made him realise that somehow he had got it badly wrong. Whatever secrets she had they did not involve marriage to his cousin, he would stake his life on that now.

When she was calmer he would talk to her, assure her that if there was the faintest hint of scandal resulting from this evening then he would do the honourable thing and marry her. But that would come later. For now she needed to sleep, as did he. At least, having locked the door, there was no danger that they would be discovered in this compromising situation by some over-zealous chambermaid coming in early to light the fire.

He dozed, his dreams filled with images of Susannah. He was even aware of the faint trace of flowery perfume he had noticed on her skin when they had kissed. In his dreams she was standing beside him and he reached for her. He sighed when she caught his hands and held them. The fog of sleep lifted and he realised that Susannah really *was* standing beside the bed, but she wasn't holding his hands, she was binding them together.

'What the—?'

'Please do not struggle, my lord, that will only make the bonds tighter.'

He blinked away the final remnants of his dream. She had used the silk cord from her gown to bind his hands together and had tied the cord around the bedpost. He tried to sit up, but his arms were yanked awkwardly towards the post and he collapsed back again.

'What the hell do you think you are doing?'

'I am leaving, and I am making sure you cannot prevent me.' She watched him tug hard against his bonds.

'It is silk, you know, and incredibly strong. I doubt you will break it.'

'There is no need for this. I told you I would not stop you.'

'You also told me you would not touch me,' she retorted.

The candles were guttering in their sockets but there was still sufficient light to see that she looked incredibly desirable with her flushed cheeks and those golden curls in disarray.

'Susannah—'

'Miss Prentess to you.'

'You cannot leave.'

'Oh, yes, I can.' She picked up the key. 'You should have hidden this, my lord, if you really wanted to keep me your prisoner.'

'Prisoner be damned! I locked the door to protect your honour.'

'Hah!'

He was not surprised as her scathing response, but he tried again.

'Please, Susannah. Think. It is not light yet. It is not safe for you to go out alone.'

'That is not your concern.'

As she walked away to the other room he pulled again at the silk rope, feeling it tighten on his wrists. There was no chance of freeing himself quickly. Frantically he searched his mind for any argument to stop her from leaving.

'But you promised, the wager—'

She returned with her cloak about her shoulders and her bonnet in one hand.

'I have dined with you, and it wants only an hour until dawn, so I have stayed with you until morning.

I think you will agree I have fulfilled my part of the wager.' She put on her bonnet and tied the strings. 'I will bid you *adieu*.'

'Good God, woman, you cannot leave me tied up—'

'I can, and I will. Do not worry, your valet will be back in an hour or so. Of course, you might try calling for help, but this could be a little embarrassing to explain, don't you think?'

'Damn it all, Susannah—'

She drew herself up to her full height, and despite the tumbled curls that escaped from her bonnet she was as haughty as any aristocrat.

'You have said quite enough, my lord. Our acquaintance is at an end. You are no longer welcome in my house and I shall not acknowledge you, should we meet in public.'

With that she swept out of the room.

Chapter Eight

Jasper stared at the closed door. One of the candles guttered and went out, increasing the gloom. With a growl of frustration he strained against the silk rope. He was not worried for himself, as Susannah had said, Peters would be back soon, but he did not like to think of her out in the darkened streets alone.

However, there was little he could do about it at present, so he tried to make himself comfortable. The fire had died away to a sullen glow and the air was growing chill, so he wriggled himself under the bedclothes. It took some time but at last he managed to cover himself sufficiently and he settled down to wait for morning.

Susannah kept her veil pulled over her face as she ran through the deserted streets. The ground was covered with a fine dusting of snow and the cold seeped through her thin slippers, numbing her toes. She had always disliked the way the silk tassels knocked against her when she moved, but now she was painfully aware of their lack. It had been her plan to use the cord tonight, if it should become necessary, and it had worked exceedingly well. She felt a twinge of guilt when she thought of leaving the viscount a prisoner. He would never forgive her for that.

A scuffle made her start and look around nervously, but although she saw shadowy figures in the alleyways and heard the occasional bark of a dog as she hurried on, no one approached her and she reached the Crescent without being accosted. She ran down the area steps and used her key to enter through the servants' door, which she had instructed Dorcas to leave unbolted. A single lamp burned in the small servants' hall, and Susannah saw her maid dozing by the dying embers of the fire. She stirred as Susannah secured the door.

'Ooh, mistress, thank the Lord you are back safe.'

'Thank heaven indeed,' murmured Susannah, sinking into a chair.

'My dear ma'am, you are shaking like a leaf.'

'Y-yes. I d-didn't realise how frightened I was.'

Dorcas was wide awake now, and approached her mistress anxiously. 'Heaven help us! If that rascally viscount has harmed you—'

'No, no, it was not Lord Markham,' said Susannah. 'It was coming back alone through the dark streets. And he is not rascally,' she added with something of her old spirit. 'He was merely trying to protect his cousin.'

'Well, 'twasn't right for him to go bullying you to dine alone with him. What Mrs Wilby would say if she knew...'

'It was very wrong of me, I know that.' Now that the danger was over, Susannah felt a great desire to weep and had to fight back the tears. 'It is done, and no one is any the worse.' She glanced out of the window, where the darkness was giving way to the first grey light of dawn. She hoped very much that Peters would return soon and free Lord Markham. Resolutely she turned her thoughts away from the viscount. 'Come along, Dorcas. I must sleep. My carriage is ordered for eight o'clock.'

'Never tell me you are going to Florence House in the morning.'

'You know I must. I have arranged to call for Mrs Logan. We want to see how they go on with the new housekeeper.' She crept up to her room, thankful that the early hour prevented Dorcas from voicing her opinions as they made their way through the silent house.

When Peters entered the viscount's sitting room at York House Jasper greeted him with an angry bellow. Peters rushed to the bedroom and stopped abruptly in the doorway.

'Well don't stand there gawping,' roared Jasper. 'Untie me!'

'Yes, m'lord, at once, but, what, who—?'

'I should think that was obvious,' growled Jasper, curbing his impatience as Peters struggled with the knots in the silken rope. 'Thank God the maid did not find me like this.'

'Knowing the nature of your engagement last night, I informed the staff that you were not to be disturbed,' replied Peters calmly.

'The devil you did. What time is it?'

'Nearing seven, m'lord.'

'Good. Then we are not too late.' At last he was free and Jasper sat up, rubbing his wrists. 'I want you to send a message to the stables. Have Morton come here. Now.'

'My lord?'

'I want him to go to Royal Crescent as soon as maybe.'

'Sir, if I may be so bold, if the lady is reluctant...' Under his master's frowning gaze the valet shifted uncomfortably from one foot to the other, finally saying in a rush, 'It's not like you, sir, to pursue a woman if she ain't willing.'

Jasper shook his head.

'Willing be damned. That has nothing to do with it. Miss Prentess said she was going out this morning. I want to know where she is bound. I'll find out what her secret is if I have to tear Bath apart!'

By nine o'clock the viscount was washed and dressed in his green riding coat and buckskins. His heavy caped driving coat was thrown over a chair and his hat and gloves rested on the table in readiness. He strode impatiently up and down the sitting room, stopping occasionally to look out of the window, where large feathery flakes of snow could be seen floating down. At last he heard a hasty footstep approaching. Morton entered upon the knock.

'Well?' Jasper barked out the word.

'I saw the carriage setting off, my lord, and followed it, as you ordered. It went as far as a house just this side of Priston. On the Wells Road.'

'And you can find it again?' demanded Jasper, shrugging himself into his driving coat.

'Aye, my lord. The curricle is at the door now, but the weather's turning bad. The snow is beginning to settle.'

'Then the sooner we get started the better.'

The horses were fresh and Jasper had to concentrate to keep them in check as they trotted through the quiet streets. It was early yet, and the snow was keeping all but the very hardy indoors. Once they had crossed the bridge and were settled upon the Wells Road he gave them their heads and they rattled along at a cracking pace. It was snowing heavily now, coating the ground and hedges and making it difficult to see far ahead. Beside him, Morton hunched down into his coat and muttered occasionally about the folly of travelling in such weather. Jasper was beginning to agree with him and was contemplating abandoning his journey when the snow eased and the dense cloud lifted a little.

'There, we shall go on easily now.'

'Aye, my lord, 'til the weather sets in again,' retorted Morton with all the familiarity of an old and trusted retainer. 'I mislike the look of that sky. If you was to ask me we should turn back now.'

Jasper looked up. The grey, sullen clouds matched his mood exactly.

'Well I am not asking you,' he snapped 'You applied goose-fat to the horses' feet, didn't you, to prevent the snow from balling? So we should be good for a few hours yet. We shall turn back once I have discovered Miss Prentess's secret and not before.'

The journey had done much to cool Jasper's temper but nothing to quell his determination to find out what could persuade Susannah to drive out on such a morning. This had nothing to do with Gerald, it was purely for his own satisfaction. His wrists were still sore from that silk rope, but he was not a vindictive man, he bore her no grudge for that... Well, not much of a grudge. The woman intrigued him. She had rejected him, and he was not used to that. On the contrary most women were only too willing to accept his advances.

When he and his twin had entered society as young men they had the advantages of being wealthy and handsome. The ladies had literally fallen at their feet and they had learned to take such adulation as their due. They had flirted outrageously and become known as the dark and notorious Coale twins. Now, Jasper had the added advantage of a title. He had never had to fight for a woman in his life. He had only to cast his discerning eye upon a female and in most cases she would fall eagerly into his arms. If a lady showed any reluctance then he shrugged and moved on. No rancour, no regret.

He wondered if he had become too complacent, arrogant, even, where women were concerned. He had never had to work for their good opinion, merely taken it for granted. He had always assumed that when he eventually fell in love the lady would feel the same and it had come as something of a shock three years ago when he had proposed to Zelah Pentewan and been refused. However, she was head over heels in love with his twin and he could understand that, only berating himself for not discovering the state of the lady's affections before offering her his hand.

Zelah had taught him a salutary lesson and Jasper had been content to leave his heart behind when he returned to town to continue his bachelor lifestyle. The women in London were as eager as ever for his attentions, but somehow the attraction of such a carefree life had palled. Perhaps it was seeing his twin so happily married, but for the past three years Jasper had felt a curious restlessness. He had hidden it well, continued to flirt with all the prettiest ladies, was the most obliging guest at any party, but knowing his heart to be safe at Rooks Tower with his sister-in-law he had never felt the least inclination to offer marriage to any one of the beautiful débutantes paraded before him, much to the chagrin of their hopeful parents. Not one of them had made any impression upon him, had stirred him to make the least effort. Yet here he was, risking his precious team on snow-covered roads to pursue a woman who had made it abundantly clear that she did not want his attentions.

But this was nothing to do with the fact that she was a woman, and a very beautiful one at that. She had got the better of him, and that rankled. Lord, what an arrogant fool he had become!

'Beggin' yer pardon, m'lord, I don't see there's much to laugh at,' grumbled Morton, sinking his chin deeper into his muffler.

'I am laughing at myself,' Jasper told him, still grinning.

'You'll be laughing yerself into the parson's mousetrap if you ain't very careful.'

'What?' Jasper's head whipped round and he stared at his groom. 'I have no interest in the woman in that way. Marriage to such a virago? Good God, I can think of nothing worse.'

'Seems to me you are putting yerself out a great deal over her.'

'Fustian! It's just that there is something smoky about Miss Prentess, and I am determined to find out what it is.'

Jasper gave his attention to his driving. Perhaps he *was* being foolish. He could have paid someone to find out everything about the woman and saved himself the trouble.

'Turning's up here, sir,' said the groom. 'On the right.'

And if this outing did not solve the mystery that is what he would do, he decided as he turned into a narrow lane,

The snow lay inches deep and unbroken through the lane. Jasper proceeded cautiously. There could be deep ruts beneath the snow, waiting to catch the unwary. The track was descending into a wooded valley and the groom pointed out their destination on the far side. Jasper slowed and peered through the trees at the collection of buildings.

'It looks like a gentleman's house, my lord. What will they say to us turning up uninvited?'

'I shall use the weather as my excuse.' Jasper gave a little flick of the whip to move the team on.

Ten minutes later they drew up in front of the house. No one came out to greet them and apart from the smoke spiralling up from a couple of the chimneys there was no sign of life. Jasper jumped down and went to the door. The weathered oak panels shook as he forcefully applied the knocker. A biting wind had sprung up and when a flustered housemaid opened the door he immediately stepped into the hall.

'Good day,' he said pleasantly. 'Pray tell your master or mistress that—'

He got no further. Standing in a doorway at the far end of the hall, and holding a baby in her arms, was Susannah.

Chapter Nine

'Miss Prentess. Good day to you.'

Jasper made his bow, his brain reeling. Whatever he had expected, it was not this. He had seen Susannah's horrified look when he had appeared, but she recovered quickly.

'Lord Markham.' She hesitated and glanced down at the sleeping baby. 'Will you not come in, sir?'

He could see behind her a comfortable parlour with a cheerful fire.

'I would be delighted, madam, but first I must look after the horses, I do not like to leave them standing in this weather.'

He let the words hang and watched her expression carefully. She would like to send him to the rightabout but she knew he would not go quietly. Her gaze shifted to the housemaid still hovering by the door.

'Bessie, direct my lord's groom to the stables, if you please.'

'Thank you.' Jasper followed her into the parlour and shut the door.

As soon as they were alone she turned on him.

'What are you doing here?'

'I followed you.' He stripped off his gloves, surprised to find his hands were shaking slightly. 'I am curious to know what you are about.' There was an odd lightness in his chest, but he dare not ask the question that was now uppermost in his mind. He must be patient. Now he was here she would tell him everything. She must.

She was looking uncertain and his surprise and anger gave way to concern. He said gently, 'Will you not sit down?

She did so, gently settling the baby more comfortably in her arms before fixing her eyes upon him once more.

'My lord, why do you persist in this? I can assure you this has nothing to do with you, or your cousin. Is that not enough for you?'

'No. I want to know what is this place, and why you are here. I will not leave until I have answers.'

With a sigh she sank back in the chair.

'Very well. You are in Florence House, sir. A home for…distressed gentlewomen.'

'And the child in your arms?'

'The son of one of our…guests. He is only a few weeks old. His mother is very tired and the babe was crying so I brought him downstairs to see if I could settle him.'

Jasper realised he had been holding his breath until that moment.

'But why have you kept this so secret?'

Her lip curled.

'You were in Royal Crescent when the Magdalen Hospital was discussed with Amelia Bulstrode and Mrs Farthing. I am sure you overhead the whole. It is considered quite…improper for an unmarried lady to have any interest in such matters. That I have strong views about it is considered shocking enough. If they knew the extent of my involvement—'

'And what *is* the extent of it, Miss Prentess?'

She put up her chin and looked at him defiantly.

'This is my house, one of the properties my uncle left me in his will. When I came to Bath last year I met up again with Mrs Logan. During one of our conversations it emerged that a young lady she knew was with child. She had eloped, left her home and her friends to run off with a man who had sworn to marry her, but later he abandoned her. She could not go back to her family, and fortunately Kate—Mrs Logan—came upon her and took her in. When she told me of it, I too was keen to help the poor girl, and others like her, so we decided to open up this house to give them refuge.

'At first we had no idea other than to take them in and give them somewhere safe to stay until the baby was born, but it soon became clear that more was needed. These are gently bred girls, they are not educated to be anything other than a gentleman's wife. They need more skills than that before we can turn them out into the world again. We teach them housekeeping—some are good with a needle and can earn their living as a seamstress, others have a talent for lacemaking.' She raised her eyes to his. 'We give these young ladies hope, my lord, and the opportunity to be independent.'

'And their families, their parents?'

'Most of these girls have been abandoned by their kin—some are in danger of being packed off to an asylum, as if…as if their predicament is some kind of mental affliction. When they come to us they are assured of anonymity. They come here and we treat them as guests, not inmates to be punished. At present only those involved in Florence House know of its existence, and I need that to continue for now, until I have control of my inheritance and can set up a trust fund to support it.'

'But if that is the case, how do those young ladies in need know where to find you?'

'We find *them*,' said Susannah. 'After that first unfortunate case, Mrs Logan heard of two more. And household servants gossip a great deal. A maid will know her mistress's situation almost as soon as the lady herself. My own maid is always ready to listen to the gossip, and if a young lady's family is not prepared to support her, then she offers an alternative. We have already helped about a dozen young women.'

'I did not know Bath had so many.'

'Word spreads, my lord. Some of them come from surrounding villages.'

'All very laudable,' he remarked. 'And how successful are you at finding employment for your, ah, guests?'

'Very. That first young lady had a remarkable eye for fashion. Kate and I purchased a house in Henrietta Street. She is now able to pay her rent and is quickly becoming established as a modiste.'

'Ah, would that be Madame Odesse?'

She nodded, smiling a little. 'The very same. I wear her gowns and the fashionable of Bath flock to copy me, but of course that will only continue as long as I maintain my place in Bath society. Odesse employs several of our young ladies as milliners and seamstresses, and she purchases lace from a little group we have established in another little house in Bath. They all earn enough to make a modest living.'

He looked about him.

'But a house like this does not come cheap.'

'No, indeed. And it is in need of repair. We have made a start, but much more is required. Once I have control of my uncle's fortune I will be able to do more, but for now...'

There was a knock at the door and Morton looked in.

'Beggin' yer pardon, m'lord, but it's started to snow again, and the wind is picking up. We had best be going.'

'Yes, very well.' Jasper looked at Susannah. 'Shall I order your carriage to be prepared?'

'I cannot leave.'

Jasper looked at the window. For the first time he noticed the howling wind rattling the frame and the soft white flakes swirling around outside.

'You must, I think, or risk being stuck here, possibly for days.'

She shook her head.

'There is no one here to look after the girls. Mrs Gifford, the housekeeper, was obliged to go away on Tuesday to nurse her sick sister. We engaged a temporary housekeeper, but I am afraid we were sadly deceived in her. When I arrived this morning I learned that she had packed her bags and left yesterday, as soon as the weather began to turn.'

'But *you* cannot stay—surely that was not your intention when you came here today?'

'No, I planned to visit with Mrs Logan.' She frowned a little. 'Only when I called for her I was told she was not at home. These young ladies—girls—are my responsibility, my lord. There are only three of them in the house. The eldest is but nineteen. I cannot abandon them.'

'What of the other servants?'

'There is Bessie, the scullery maid who opened the door to you.'

'That is all, no manservant?'

'Only old Daniel, who lives next to the stables and

does a little of the outside work. We decided that the girls would feel more at ease if there were no other menservants in the house.' She glanced at the window. 'You had best be gone, my lord. I would not have you snowbound on my account.'

Susannah shifted in her seat, no longer facing him. She had enough to think about without the viscount being here to distract her. The defection of Mrs Jennings was a blow and she had arrived at Florence House to find the household all on end. Jane had opened the door to her, looking desperately tired. She explained that Lizzie and Violet were too frightened to sleep in their own rooms, so they had spent the night huddled together in one big bed, with Lizzie's baby in its cot beside them. Susannah had helped Bessie to prepare a simple breakfast for them all before sending the girls back upstairs to rest and bringing the baby downstairs to make sure Lizzie's sleep was not disturbed. She had been walking up and down the little parlour, trying to decide what to do next, when she heard the imperious knocking on the front door and looked out to find Lord Markham standing in the hall, his broad shoulders made even wider by the many-caped driving coat so that he appeared to fill the small space.

For one dizzy, heart-stopping moment she thought he had come to rescue her, before common sense reasserted itself. She did not need rescuing, and Lord Markham was more her nemesis than a knight in shining armour. The sooner he left the better, then she could concentrate on the problem of what to do here.

'If you are staying, then so, too, am I.'

'Nay, my lord!'

'You cannot do that!'

Susannah's voice and the groom's protests were immediate but had no apparent effect upon the viscount.

'Morton, go back to the stables and make sure the horses are bedded down for the night. I take it there is space for my groom to sleep somewhere?'

He addressed this last question to Susannah, who answered distractedly, 'Yes…yes, there is plenty of sleeping space above the stables—my coachman will show him where to find straw to make a comfortable bed—and Daniel will arrange to feed him, too, but…my lord, I cannot, *cannot* put you up here.'

He dismissed his groom before turning back to her.

'You have no choice.' He looked faintly amused at her consternation. 'Pray do not look so alarmed. I am not expecting you to wait upon me.'

'But, last night—'

'We will forget that, for now.'

His smile grew, and with it her embarrassment. The baby stirred in her arms and she got up, murmuring that she must take him back to his mother. The viscount opened the door for her and with a mutter of thanks she fled from the room. The young ladies were gathered in the upstairs sitting room, but Bessie had informed them of the viscount's arrival and they looked anxiously to Susannah for an explanation.

'Who is he, Miss Prentess?' asked Lizzie as Susannah gently handed over the baby. 'Has he come to fetch you away?'

'He s-spoke to me at the ball once.' Violet Anstruther's voice quavered. 'Perhaps Papa sent him to fetch me…'

'You may all be easy, the viscount has not come to take anyone away. He is an acquaintance of mine and a perfect gentleman.' Should she have crossed her fingers against the lie? Despite all that had happened between them it felt like the truth. 'He is stranded here in the snow, as are we all now.' She hoped she sounded suitably reassuring. 'You are at liberty to come downstairs and join us, if you wish.'

This suggestion was quickly rejected, the girls declaring that they would prefer to remain above stairs.

'Very well, I believe there is a little soup left, so I will ask Bessie to heat it through and bring it up for you. I will ask her to bring more coal upstairs, too, so that you may keep the fire built up in here. Then we must think what we can do for dinner tonight.' She looked at the three girls. Lizzie was confined to her bed and had her baby to nurse. Jane was leaning back in her chair, her hands rubbing over her extended stomach. Only Violet Anstruther looked fit enough to help with the cooking, but when Susannah suggested it, she immediately shook her head and admitted that she did not know how to do anything more than boil a small kettle to make tea. She looked so frightened at the prospect of venturing into the kitchen that Susannah did not press her.

'I will help,' offered Jane, 'when my back has stopped aching.'

'No, you must stay here,' said Susannah quickly. 'Bessie and I will manage.'

'At least the larder is full,' observed Jane. 'I made sure Mrs Jennings sent Daniel for the supplies yesterday before she left the house.'

'I cannot forgive the woman for leaving you all in such a way,' declared Susannah. 'As soon as I can get back to Bath I will make arrangements for another housekeeper to come in to look after you until Mrs Gifford returns.'

She went downstairs to find that the viscount had

built up the fire in the parlour. A patch of melting snow near the hearth caught her eye.

'Did you send Bessie out to find my footman? I meant to do it before I went upstairs, and charge him with bringing in coal for the fire.'

'No, I brought it in myself.' He laughed at her shocked countenance. 'As Gerald told you, Miss Prentess, I am not at all high in the instep.' He pointed to a tray on the side table. 'I also found the coffee pot, so I have made some. I thought we might sit by the fire and take a cup together.'

'Why, thank you, sir. But I should really be looking out what we can eat for dinner...'

'There will be time for that presently. Sit down and talk to me.'

She allowed herself to be escorted to a chair and handed a steaming cup. She had to admit that after the trials of the morning it was pleasant just to sit, even if she was determined it could not be for long.

'I have been thinking about the cost of running this house,' he began. 'I take it Mrs Wilby's card parties help to pay for it.'

'Yes.'

'And you encourage the gentlemen of your acquaintance to attend, upon your aunt's invitation, of course.'

She shot him a defiant look.

'And why not? It is the *gentlemen* who have made this place necessary.'

Jasper sat back, surprised.

'Is that what you really think?'

'Of course. They court the young ladies, flatter and cajole them into allowing them to...' She paused to put down her cup, using the moment to gather her thoughts before continuing. 'These are young, innocent girls who have fallen for a seducer's lies, heedless of the consequences.' A dull flush coloured her cheeks as she remembered her own weakness. 'It is too easily done, I fear.'

'So you invite the men to your drawing room and fleece them.'

'I do not *cheat*, sir. It is merely that we—Aunt Maude, Mrs Logan and I—we are all better at cards than most of our guests. And we never take more than fifty guineas at any one sitting.'

He ran a hand through his hair.

'Susannah, it does not matter if it is fifty guineas or five thousand, you are still taking money off these people.'

'It is not illegal.'

'No, but it is not *right*. You are in effect running a gaming house.'

She crossed her arms, as if in defence.

'It is for a good cause.'

'Then tell your guests what you are about. Let them choose whether they want to support you.'

She gave a bitter laugh.

'Support a house for fallen women? You have seen the reaction when one mentions such a subject. They would not give so much as a sou.'

'You should set up a committee, get some of the Bath tabbies on your side.'

'No. I prefer to do it my way.'

Jasper sat forwards, frowning.

'But why? Why do you want to punish the young men so? Not all of them are wild and reckless, you know. Gerald Barnabus, for example.' He saw the flash of consternation in her eyes, before the lashes swept down to veil them and a new suspicion hit him. 'Does Gerald know about this place?'

There was a brief hesitation before she replied.

'Yes. I let something slip and was obliged to tell him. He has been very helpful.'

'And that is why you took two hundred guineas from him last year.'

'Yes. We needed extra funds urgently, to set up the house for Odesse.'

He kept his eyes on her face.

'Why was he escorting you to the jewellers the other day? You may as well tell me. If you do not I shall find out from Gerald when I get back to Bath.'

She was twisting her hands together in her lap and he remained silent, waiting for her to speak.

'I needed money to pay the builder. I asked Gerald to come with me to the jewellers, to sell some of my aunt's jewels.'

'Your inheritance.'

She hung her head.

'I thought the money could be better spent here.'

'And just what did you sell?'

'An emerald set, necklace, ear-drops, aigrette—totally unsuited to me.'

'While you are single, yes.' Jasper imagined how well the stones would look against her creamy skin, accentuating the green flecks in her eyes, and nestled amongst those glowing curls. 'Once you are married—'

'I shall never marry.'

The words were uttered with such force, such conviction, that Jasper's brows snapped together.

'That is a bold statement.'

'It is true, nevertheless.' She rose, shaking out her

skirts. 'I have seen how men treat women. It shall never happen to me. Now if you will excuse me—'

'No, I will not.' He jumped up and caught her arm. 'You are very harsh upon our sex.'

'And with some reason, my lord. Witness your own behaviour last night!'

'No,' he said slowly. 'I think it goes beyond that.'

She looked alarmed and tried to free her arm.

'Can you wonder if I am harsh, when the girls here tell me such tales? Now let me go, sir.'

'Not until you tell me.' He pulled her round to face him. 'I saw it in your eyes last night. You were terrified.'

Her eyes flashed.

'You flatter yourself!'

'Not of me, but something has occurred. Something in your past.' She stopped struggling and turned her head away, her lip trembling. He said gently, 'Will you not tell me? Susannah—'

He was interrupted by a hasty knock on the door and he released her arm just as Bessie rushed in. She did not appear to notice them stepping apart, too caught up in her own news which she uttered in a scared, breathless voice.

'I beg your pardon, Miss Prentess, but—Miss Jane sent me. She says…she says the baby is coming!'

Susannah did not exclaim or cry out. She stood for a moment, hands pressed to her cheeks as she dragged her thoughts to what the maid was saying.

'We must send for the midwife.' She went to the window. 'At least we must try.'

Bessie peered over her shoulder.

'But the snow is very thick, ma'am, and 'tis drifting.'

'My footman, Lucas, should go. He is young and strong.'

'It would be safer if there were two,' said Jasper. 'Morton shall go with him. Give me the midwife's direction and I will go out to the stables and tell them.'

Susannah did not hesitate. Instructions were given and even before the viscount had left the house she ran upstairs. Jane was leaning against the wall, clutching at her stomach.

'Mrs Gifford told me these pains would come,' she gasped. 'Slowly at first, but then more frequently.'

'And how do they seem to you?' asked Susannah.

Jane gave her a strained smile. 'They are coming very quickly. I hope we can wait for the midwife.'

'Oh my heavens, what shall we do?'

Susannah turned at the anguished cry to find Violet Anstruther standing in the doorway. Quickly she ushered the girl out of the room, telling her to look after Lizzie and her baby, then she turned her attention back to Jane, who was pacing up and down, her face very pale.

She calculated that the midwife could not be here for at least another hour and she busied herself with preparing the room, bringing in a crib and blankets and clothes for the new baby, then she helped Jane out of her gown. All the time she kept up a cheerful dialogue which was punctuated by Jane's gasps each time the contractions took hold.

The heavy cloud had brought an early dusk and Susannah had given orders for the lamps to be lit. It was with relief that she heard the thud of the outer door and the low rumble of voices in the hall. She ran down the stairs. The chill of the air as she descended confirmed that the front door had been opened, but there were only three figures in the hall: the viscount, his groom and Lucas, her footman.

The two servants were covered in snow.

'I beg your pardon, miss, but we didn't make it.' Lucas blew on his hands and his teeth chattered when he spoke. 'The snow is breast high across the road and we couldn't get through. And we daren't risk crossing the fields for the snow is falling so thick 'tis impossible to see more than an arm's length in front of you and we wouldn't have known which direction we should go.'

Susannah tried hard not to let her disappointment show.

'Very well, thank you for your efforts. If you go into the kitchen Bessie will find you something hot to drink.'

'If you don't mind, miss, we'll head back to the stables,' put in Morton. 'The old man said he would keep a good fire and have a kettle of something ready when we got back.'

'Yes, yes, you had best go then, and get yourselves warm.' The viscount waved them away and turned to look at Susannah. 'This is bad news,' he murmured, drawing her into the warmth of the parlour. 'What will you do now?'

'I must go back upstairs, I fear Jane is very near her time.'

'Is there anything I can do?' His readiness to help was comforting, but she shook her head.

'Not unless you are a man-midwife.'

'I regret I cannot help you there, my only experience of such things is when my favourite pointer whelped at Markham.'

Despite her anxiety she smiled at that.

'Then you know less than I do. I was here last year when one of the girls was in labour. She was very frightened and the midwife asked me to sit with her, to calm her.'

'So you are not totally inexperienced.'

Susannah clasped her hands together.

'On that occasion the midwife had very little to do. The baby came into the world quite easily. If Jane's birth is like that then there is nothing to worry about, but if not—'

She broke off, the horrors of what might happen crowding in on her. The viscount took her hands; the steady strength of his fingers around hers was oddly calming.

'We have no choice but to try our best.' A faint cry from above made him lift his head. He squeezed her hands. 'Do you feel up to this?'

She met his eyes.

'As you have said, there is no option. I must do what I can.'

'Then go back upstairs. If you need me you only have to call.'

The hours ticked by. Susannah sat with Jane while the contractions continued. She had heard that sometimes these pains could die away, and the baby might not come for days. For a while she hoped that perhaps this would be the case and they would be able to send again for the midwife in the morning, but as the evening wore on Jane grew more restless and the pains more frequent. Susannah fetched a bowl of warm water to bathe Jane's face and hands, and later Bessie came up with a tray, saying the viscount had ordered her to bring up tea and bread and butter for them both.

Susannah did not touch the food but she sipped gratefully at the tea, while Jane refused everything.

She shifted uncomfortably on the bed, becoming more and more restless until eventually she was gasping and straining. Susannah knew the crisis must be very near now and she held Jane's hand tightly, praying that nothing would go wrong.

The birth, when it came, was mercifully brief. Jane was crying out with the pain while Susannah stood by her, feeling helpless as she could do nothing but wipe her brow and murmur inadequate words of comfort. Jane's anguish was growing by the moment and Susannah was on the point of calling for help when she saw with a mix of terror and delight that the baby was coming. Tentatively she reached out to cradle the head while she continued to encourage Jane. She watched, entranced, as the little body gradually emerged and she found herself crying with relief. The tiny form looked perfect and its angry cries were oddly reassuring. With infinite care she wiped the baby and wrapped it in a soft cloth before lifting it into its mother's arms.

'Look, Jane,' she whispered, her voice hushed with awe and wonder. 'You have a little girl.'

Chapter Ten

While Jane reclined against a bank of pillows and sleepily watched her baby taking its first, tentative feed, Susannah summoned Bessie to help clear up, then she went to tell Violet and Lizzie that all was well. The hour was advanced by the time she made her way downstairs once more and there was no sign of the viscount in the parlour. She followed the rumble of voices through to the kitchen, where she stopped in the doorway, staring in amazement.

A black range had been installed in the huge fireplace and the viscount was standing before it, stirring the contents of a saucepan. He had removed his jacket, rolled back his voluminous shirt sleeves and tied an apron over his pristine white waistcoat. He glanced round.

'Ah, you are come down at last. Do come in and shut the door. Bessie told me the news. How are your patients?'

Susannah smiled at the term.

'They are not *my* patients. I did very little, and we still need the midwife or a doctor to visit them as soon as the weather improves. But for now mother and baby are both well and resting.' She looked towards the scullery, where Bessie was cleaning dishes. 'You have had dinner, then. I am glad.'

'There was a leg of mutton in the meat safe, so I have made collops for everyone.' He reached for a frying pan and settled it over the fire. 'Bessie and the ladies above stairs have already dined, but I was waiting for you to come down so that I could cook yours fresh for you.'

'Oh, but there is no need, I am so tired, a little soup will do…'

'Nonsense, you need to eat.' He came across and took her arm, guiding her to the cook's armchair at the head of the table. 'Sit down there and do not move, save to drink the glass of wine I have poured for you.'

She gave a shaky laugh. 'I do not think I *could* move if I wanted to, I am quite worn out.'

Outside the wind was buffeting the house and hurling icy pellets against the windows, but the kitchen was warm and comfortable, and Susannah was content to sit back and relax. She watched, entranced, as the viscount moved around the kitchen with all the assurance of an accomplished chef. Bessie, too, was completely at home, pottering between the kitchen and the scullery, responding to his instructions as if it was the most natural thing in the world to be directed by a peer of the realm.

'I did not realise how hungry I had become,' murmured Susannah as the viscount slid a plate in front of her.

'No, you have been far too busy.' He brought his own plate to the table, along with his glass and the decanter of wine. Before he sat down he went to the scullery.

'If you have finished those dishes you may go to bed, Bessie. The rest can wait until the morning.'

'Very good, m'lud. Goodnight, ma'am.' The scullery maid bobbed an awkward curtsy and hurried away. Susannah stared after her, shaking her head.

'I am amazed. You have fed everyone, with only Bessie to help you?'

'I have indeed. Her understanding is not great, but knowing everyone else was occupied upstairs, she was only too willing to help where she could. She showed me where to find everything, including Mrs Gifford's secret store of wine and cider, something I understand she did *not* share with Mrs Jennings! I hope you don't mind, but I used almost a whole bottle of claret to make the sauce for the collops.'

'Violet told me Bessie had brought them dinner, but she did not say… that is, I thought she had served them up a little bread and ham.'

'Oh, I think we did better than that.' Meeting her wondering gaze, he laughed. 'I had an eccentric uncle. When we were younger, my twin and I used to stay with him at his hunting lodge in Leicester, where we would fend for ourselves. We would hunt and fish and cook whatever we could find. My uncle was firmly of the opinion that a man should never be wholly dependent upon his servants, neither his valet nor his cook.'

'Then I am greatly indebted to your eccentric uncle,' she replied, savouring the delightful combination of flavours on her plate.

He grinned as he refilled their glasses. 'You were otherwise engaged and it soon became clear to me that if I did not do something we would be obliged to call in old Daniel to feed everyone.'

'You did very well. I am impressed by your abilities, my lord.'

'As I am with yours. Not many ladies of my acquaintance could have taken on the role of midwife.'

'And I am convinced no other gentleman of my acquaintance could have taken on the role of cook,' she replied, smiling.

He lifted his glass.

'Perhaps we should congratulate ourselves, then.'

She raised her own, meeting his eyes with a shy smile. All the old enmities were forgotten, for now.

The meal was delicious and she could not help comparing it with the elaborate dinner he had given her the previous evening. Then he had been aiming to impress and she had been far too anxious to enjoy it but now, this simple meal served in such lowly surroundings was by far the best thing she had ever tasted.

Better a dinner of herbs...

The old proverb came to mind but she banished it quickly lest it spoil the comfortable atmosphere they were sharing.

By the time they had finished their meal the kitchen fire was dying and the cold was beginning to creep back into the high-ceilinged room. Susannah pushed her plate away and gave a little shiver.

'Let us move to the parlour,' suggested Jasper, putting on his coat. 'I left the fire banked up in there. Unless, that is, you would like to retire to your room?'

It was at that point Susannah realised that in all the confusion she had made no provision for herself, or the viscount. With so much of the house uninhabitable due to the leaking roof and the unsafe chimney stack, it would not be easy to find two free bedchambers. She decided she would think about that later. For now the lure of a warm fire was much more seductive.

* * *

After the cavernous kitchen the parlour was snug and welcoming. The viscount used a taper to light a single branched candlestick while Susannah went to the window.

'The snow is still falling,' she said. 'I do not think I can ask Lucas to make another attempt to reach Priston until the morning.'

The viscount was bending over the fire, stirring the coals into a blaze.

'I agree. As soon as it is light we can send them out again.'

'We? I should have thought you would be anxious to return to Bath, my lord.'

'Not until I know all is well here.'

'That is not necessary…'

She trailed off as he regarded her, one dark brow raised.

'You cannot be nurse, housekeeper *and* cook, Miss Prentess, and from what I have seen of the other inhabitants of this property they are all incapable of helping you, for one reason or another.'

'It grieves me, but I have to agree with you.' She sank down on to a chair, trying not to sound too disheartened. 'Both Lizzie and Jane have young babies to look after, and Violet is quite unused to nursing or domestic work of any kind.'

'And your scullery maid, willing as she is, can only work under instruction.' The viscount pulled the spindle-legged sofa closer to the fire and sat down. 'Tomorrow we will send Morton and your footman to Priston with instructions to fetch the midwife and try if they can to find a good woman who is prepared to live here and run the house until your own housekeeper returns.'

He held up his hand as she opened her mouth to speak. 'Please do not argue. If that fails, as soon as the road is clear, Morton shall drive into Bath and find a suitable female through the registry office.'

'You seem to have thought of everything, my lord.'

'I know very well that you will not leave here until you know your guests are provided for.'

'True.'

'Then if we have settled that point, perhaps it is time we retired.'

'Ah. That might be a slight problem.' Susannah stared at her hands clasped in her lap. 'I did not think to have Bessie prepare rooms for us. I imagine Mrs Gifford's room will be usable, but the other three bedrooms in this part of the house are already occupied by the young ladies. If I had thought of it earlier I would have had a truckle bed made up in Violet's room for myself—'

'Out of the question. I shall sleep here on the sofa.'

She sighed with relief.

'That is very good of you. I will go and find you some blankets.'

'Not necessary,' he said. 'The fire and my driving coat will suffice to keep me warm.'

With a chuckle she rose and went to the door.

'Oh, no, I must show some respect for your position, Lord Markham.'

The corners of his mouth lifted.

'Why change now, Miss Prentess? So far in our acquaintance you have shown no regard for my position at all!'

With a laugh gurgling in her throat she whisked herself out of the room, returning a few minutes later with blankets and a pillow.

'Brrr, it is cold once you step outside this room,' she said, putting the bedding down on a chair. 'I looked in on the others while I was upstairs; everyone is sleeping peacefully, even the new mother and baby.' Jasper was kneeling by the hearth, stirring the contents of a large pewter jug. 'Cooking again, my lord?'

'Mulled cider,' he said. 'Watch.'

He pulled the poker out of the fire and carefully lowered the red-hot tip into the jug where it sizzled and hissed, sending a spicy aroma into the air. Susannah breathed it in, appreciating the scent of apples and spices. He filled two rummers with the fragrant, steaming liquid and held one out to her.

'Perhaps you would join me?'

Susannah knew she should retire, but she had peeped into Mrs Gifford's bedchamber. It was cold and unwelcoming, with no cheerful fire burning. She was loath to return to it, so she accepted the glass and sat down beside him on the sofa. They were enveloped in the warm glow from the fire and Susannah found the dancing flames strangely soothing

'Why are you doing this?' she asked him suddenly.

'I told you, my eccentric uncle…'

'No, I mean, why did you stay here today, why are you showing such kindness to me? After last night…'

He waved one hand, the heavy gold signet ring glinting as it caught the firelight.

'Last night I thought you were leading Gerald astray. I did not know he was a party to all this. Silly cawker, why did he not tell me?'

'Pray do not blame Gerald, I made him swear to tell no one.'

He said quietly, 'That was almost your undoing.'

She felt the colour stealing into her cheeks, and it had

little to do with the cider. She thought it best to keep silent and after a moment he continued.

'This place must be very important to you, to risk coming out on such a day.'

'It is.'

'More than just charitable goodwill, I think. I noticed the new sign as we came in. Have you changed the house name? Was that your idea, or Mrs Logan's?'

The cider was dispelling the chill inside, just as the fire was warming her skin. She felt very mellow, and comfortable enough for confidences.

'Mine.'

'Will you not tell me?' His voice was gentle. 'Who was Florence?'

'She was my sister.'

Jasper caught his breath. At last she was prepared to tell him the truth.

'Was?'

He waited while she sipped at her drink. She was staring into the fire, a faraway look in her eyes.

'She died five years ago.'

'I am very sorry.' Instinctively he reached out and covered her hand. She did not draw it away. 'Will you tell me about it?'

She sat up a little straighter but she kept her eyes on the fire, as if reading her words in the flames.

'When my father died in Gibraltar we—my mother, sister and I—went to live with his sister in London. My aunt was a strict Evangelical and when my mother died of the fever a year later we were left to her care. Our family was not rich, but respectable enough, and very soon after my mother's death my sister Florence was courted by a young man who promised to marry her.

'He was very dashing and handsome, a very fashionable beau and Florence believed his promises enough to...' He felt the little hand tremble in his. 'He disappeared, leaving her pregnant. When my aunt learned that Florence was with child she threw her out of the house. I was forbidden ever to see her again. I smuggled money and food to Florence, who managed to find lodgings nearby. My aunt discovered what was happening and she stopped my pin-money and kept me locked in my room. I think she must also have spoken to the landlady, too, because Florence left her lodgings and I heard nothing more of her.

'After six months my aunt thought it would be safe for me to go out alone again, and at the market one day a woman approached and told me Florence had died in childbirth a few weeks earlier. This woman was a milliner, earning appallingly little and living in the same house as Florence, close to Drury Lane. She said her landlady had a kind heart and had taken my sister in when she found her on the street. Florence would not say how she had got there, or what she had gone through, but she was very near her time so they gave her a bed and did what they could, although there was no money to pay for a midwife.

'I went to the house where Florence died, I had to see it for myself. It was very squalid, but the landlady was a kindly soul, and it was a comfort to know Florence had not been quite alone at the end. The landlady told me there were hundreds of women like my sister, gently bred girls who were pursued and courted by fashionable men who took their virtue and then abandoned them. It is the way of the world. Neither she nor the milliner would take any money for their trouble, but they said Florence had begged them to get a message to me, to let me know what had become of her.' Her mouth twisted and she added bitterly, 'By that kindness they showed more mercy to my sister than her family had ever done.'

She pulled her hand free and wiped a tear from her cheek.

'The letter from my Uncle Middlemass came soon after. If only he had come back to England a year earlier! As it is I left my aunt's house very willingly. It was too late to help Florence, but I vowed then that I would do something to atone for her death. That is why I set up Florence House, and using the money from those arrogant rich men goes some way towards making them pay for their cruelty.'

'Cruelty is a very strong word.'

She lifted her head.

'Not strong enough, I think.'

'But not all young men are cruel, Susannah. Some may be wild, yes, and thoughtless—this young man who courted Florence, you say he disappeared. Surely it is possible that he did not know of your sister's condition, or mayhap circumstance prevented him from coming back to her.'

'Believe me, my lord,' she said slowly, 'I know that man was an out-and-out scoundrel.'

In the dim light he saw a strange look flicker across her face—revulsion, horror, anger. Jasper's brows drew together. What was it she was not telling him? Before he could frame another question she gave a tiny shake of her head.

'This is a drear conversation when we should be celebrating having come safely through a most trying day. Is there any more of the mulled cider?'

She held out her glass

'I do not think I should give you any more. You will accuse me of trying to befuddle you with drink.'

She laughed. 'No, that was last night, when you were trying to seduce me. Today you have been a true friend, my lord.'

A friend. He smiled ruefully. No woman had ever called him friend before.

'If we are friends then surely you should not be calling me my lord.'

She turned her head to give him an appraising glance from those clear hazel eyes. They twinkled now with mischief.

'What should it be, then—viscount? Or perhaps Markham?'

His smile grew.

'Try Jasper.'

'Jasper.' He liked the sound of it on her lips, the slight hesitation in her voice as she tried it out. She nodded, apparently satisfied. 'And you must call me Susannah.'

'Thank you.'

She leaned back on the sofa and sipped at her drink, comfortable in his company, not worrying when her shoulder brushed his.

'No, you have been most gentlemanly—' A giggle escaped her. 'Perhaps that is the wrong word—I have never known a gentleman prepare a meal before. And it was delicious. The baby is safely delivered and peacefully sleeping with her mother, the other girls are resting. Did I tell you the meal was delicious, sir? All is right with the world.'

'A good day's work, Miss Prentess.'

'Yes indeed.' She smiled, and as he watched her eyelids began to close. Deftly he reached across and took the rummer from her fingers as she dropped into a deep sleep.

Susannah opened her eyes. She was lying on the sofa, her head cradled on a pillow, and she was tucked around with blankets. She shifted her head and saw the viscount stretched out in the chair opposite, his feet resting on a footstool and his many-caped driving coat thrown over him. He stirred in his chair.

'Good morning, Miss Prentess.'

She sat up and immediately put one hand to her head as it began to pound in the most unpleasant manner.

'I did not sleep in Mrs Gifford's bed, then.'

'I did not like to disturb you.'

'I brought this bedding downstairs for you…'

'There was plenty for two.' He rose, throwing off the coat and the blanket beneath it. His hair was a little tousled and stubble shadowed his cheeks, but she thought he looked remarkably well after spending the night in an armchair. 'I shall see if Bessie has built up the fire in the kitchen. I think we should have some coffee.'

Susannah said nothing as he went out. She remembered sitting here last night, talking to him. She remembered drinking the cider but then…nothing. She looked down. She was still fully dressed, neither she nor anyone else had made any attempt to disrobe her. Her hand crept to her neck. She had been alone, asleep and in the company of a strange man—a nobleman, moreover, with a reputation for breaking hearts—and he had made no attempt upon her honour. In fact, he had given her his own pillow and wrapped her in the blankets she had brought down for his comfort.

She stood up and was relieved to find her head did not feel any worse for the effort. Walking to the window, she drew back the curtains to let in the morning light. It was still early and the sun had not yet risen but its effects could be seen in the clear blue sky with its scattering of blush-pink clouds. A movement caught her eye and she saw Jasper step out on to the drive.

When had she begun to think of him as Jasper? A memory surfaced. She recalled declaring that they were friends now. With a groan she put her head in her hands. Had she been drunk last night? What else had she said to him? She raised her head to watch him striding towards the stables. He was hatless, his thick black hair gleaming and he moved with an easy grace that made her pulse stir. Quickly she turned away from the window. It was madness to think of a man in that way. It was frightening.

She bundled up the bedding and carried it upstairs, taking the time to wash her face and hands and re-pin her hair before returning to the parlour, where she busied herself relighting the fire. She wanted the coffee Jasper had promised and he did not disappoint her. He entered with a tray balanced on one hand and looking so assured that she laughed.

'You add the accomplishments of a waiter to your many skills, my lord.'

'Obviously a misspent youth.' He put the tray down on the small dining table and held out a chair for her. 'I'm afraid there are no fresh-baked muffins but there is some toast, if you would care for it.'

She joined him at the table and helped herself to a piece of toast while Jasper poured coffee for them both.

'I suggested Morton and your menservants should take the shovels and try to force a path to drive the carriage to the village. I think you would like the midwife to come here as soon as possible?'

'Yes, thank you. I did check on Jane. She and the baby are well but I shall be happier once the midwife has seen them.'

'Of course. I have given instruction that if the midwife is not available then they must bring the doctor.'

She murmured her thanks, once more shaken by his kindness.

Susannah was relieved to feel a little better once she had broken her fast and the rest of the morning passed quickly. She coaxed Violet Anstruther down to the kitchen and showed her how to prepare breakfast for the others, then she busied herself with household duties until the noise and bustle at the front door heralded the arrival of the midwife. She was accompanied by a cheerful-looking woman who introduced herself as Mrs Ibbotson and said she had come about the position of housekeeper.

'I am a widow, you see, Miss Prentess,' she explained, when Susannah took her aside to interview her. 'All my children have flown the nest, so there is nothing I would enjoy more than to be looking after the young ladies until Mrs Gifford returns. The viscount's man told me what is expected and a few extra shillings is always welcome. I took the liberty of bringing a bag with me in the hope that you would agree to me starting immediately, which I am free to do.'

With a recommendation from the midwife and Bessie's statement that she had known Mrs Ibbotson for many years and knew her to keep an excellent house, Susannah felt it safe to think of returning to Bath.

'The men say the main road is passable,' Jasper informed her. 'I will follow you in my curricle, to make sure you come to no harm.'

'Pho, I have my coachman and footman to look after me, I shall be safe enough,' she declared, but she was pleased to know he would be there, all the same.

Suddenly it was time to go. Susannah said goodbye to the girls, forbade any of them to come outside to see her off and found herself being handed into her waiting carriage by the viscount.

'I will take another route once we reach Bath,' he announced. 'There may be talk.'

'I suspect the weather is providing the Bath residents with plenty to discuss for the moment.'

'Nevertheless, we should avoid giving them fuel for gossip.' He stood back as the servant put up the steps and closed the door. 'It may be best if we do not meet for a few days, just to be on the safe side. You may rely upon me to say nothing of Florence House, or of our being here together.'

'Thank you.' It was too soon, there was more she wanted to say, but she had to content herself with a small wave. Jasper raised his hand in salute and was lost to sight as the carriage pulled away.

Chapter Eleven

Susannah found her aunt and Mrs Logan waiting for her in Royal Crescent when she returned. Kate's immediate greeting included an apology for not accompanying her to Florence House.

'I admit I was concerned when you were not at home,' remarked Susannah.

'I had business I was obliged to attend to.'

'At eight in the morning?'

She was surprised to see her friend looking a little ill at ease, but she had no time to reflect upon it for her aunt was already fussing over her.

'With Edwards driving you, and Lucas in attendance I was not overly worried,' declared Aunt Maude, hugging her. 'And when the snow set in I guessed you would be obliged to put up at the house overnight.'

'Knowing how few habitable rooms there are in Florence House perhaps it was a good thing I was not with you,' remarked Kate. 'I said to Charles—'

'Charles?' Susannah turned to her. 'You were with Charles Camerton? Was that the reason you could not come with me.'

She had never seen Kate blush before. Could it mean

that her friend was truly attracted to the gentleman? Susannah tried to be happy for Kate, but she had to acknowledge a slight disappointment, a vague feeling that somehow her friend had let her down.

Susannah kept them occupied for the next hour discussing the snow and the situation at Florence House. She did not mention the viscount's presence in the house, salving her conscience with the thought that do to so would give rise to unnecessary speculation. At length she escaped to her room to dress for dinner, only to suffer an uncomfortable half-hour as Dorcas bemoaned the loss of the tasselled cord from her mistress's green-silk gown. She was scandalised by Susannah's airy admission that she had never liked the cord and had thrown it away. Her declaration that she was going to send the gown back to Odesse to be fitted with a ribbon tie instead met with even more condemnation.

'Never did I think you would be guilty of such extravagance, Miss Prentess,' declared her maid, shaking her head. 'Why, as high and mighty as a viscountess you are getting.'

'No, I am not,' declared Susannah, blushing hotly. 'Why on earth should you say such a thing?'

Dorcas turned to stare at her.

'It's just a saying, miss, as well you knows. And I'm sure if you want a gown altering then 'tis no business of mine.'

Susannah quickly begged pardon and sat meekly while her maid dressed her hair, fervently hoping that she would be able to get through the rest of the evening without blushing again over the events of the past few days.

* * *

By Sunday the snow was melting, leaving the ground waterlogged and the sky grey and overcast. Susannah wondered if Jasper had left Bath, now that he knew she had no intention of marrying Gerald. She realised she would be very sorry if she did not see him again. Then she remembered his final words to her—*it may be best if we do not meet for a few days.* Her hopes rose. Surely that could only mean he was remaining in Bath? With this in mind she took particular care over her choice of walking dress for the Sunday morning service in the Abbey. A watery sun broke through the clouds as she descended from the carriage, prompting her aunt to hope that they had seen the last of the winter weather.

The walk to the Abbey doors was a short one, but Susannah was aware of the frowning looks that were cast her way as she accompanied her aunt. A *frisson* of nerves tingled down her spine. Did they know about her meetings with Lord Markham? To dine with him in York House had been a risk, but that was compounded by being stranded with him at Florence House the following night. Head high, she tucked her hand in Aunt Maude's arm and accompanied her into the Abbey. A quick look around convinced Susannah that the viscount was not present. She was disappointed, but considering the looks she had received, she thought perhaps it was for the best.

The service seemed interminably long and Susannah was impatient to be outside again where she could confront those who were casting such disapproving stares in her direction. Better to know the worst immediately. At last they were making their way out through the doors and into the spring sunshine. Aunt Maude had been blissfully unaware of the frosty looks and now

sailed up to Mr and Mrs Farthing, who were conversing with Amelia Bulstrode.

'Oh, Mrs Wilby, I did not see you there.' Mrs Bulstrode stopped, flustered, her eyes flickering to Susannah and away again. 'Heavens, I did not expect—that
is, with all the talk, I thought you might prefer not to
come here today.'

'Talk?' Aunt Maude glanced at Susannah, a crease
furrowing her brow. 'Perhaps I have missed something.
I have not been outside the house since Thursday.'

'Then you will not know that everyone is talking
about the new establishment you have seen fit to cre-
ate,' Mrs Farthing's strident tones cut in. She turned to
Susannah, her rather protuberant eyes snapping angrily.
'I suppose you think yourself superior, Miss Prentess,
to be setting up your own house for fallen women. Our
establishment in Walcot Street is not good enough for
you. I wonder what your uncle would think if he knew
you had put one of his houses to such use.'

So it was Florence House that had started such a
fluttering in the dovecotes. Relief allowed Susannah
to respond mildly to the accusations.

'I beg your pardon, ma'am, but you said yourself
the Walcot Street home cannot cope with the number
of applicants. My own small attempt to help distressed
gentlewomen...'

'Gentlewomen!' Mrs Farthing snorted. 'Trollops,
they are. Wanton hussies, flaunting themselves before
the young men. Is it any wonder that they find themselves in difficulties? Rather than trying to set up your
own establishment, you should contribute to ours. I do
not know why you want to pander to these females,
setting them up in their own house out of town with a
cook and a housekeeper and treating them as guests.

Guests! They should be made to work, to understand the error of their ways. And if she were *my* niece, Mrs Wilby—' she turned her attack towards Aunt Maude '—I would strongly counsel her to leave these matters to those who understand them.'

'I'm afraid she is right,' added Mr Farthing, smiling at Susannah in a very patronising way. 'You young ladies like your worthy causes, I know, but my dear wife has the right of it. You should not be associating with these creatures, lest you become tainted.'

Susannah's temper reared at that, but Aunt Maude nipped her arm. Somehow she managed to hold her peace while Mrs Wilby smiled and nodded and said all that was necessary before leading her away.

'Tainted!' Susannah almost ground her teeth in annoyance. 'Why, Aunt, if anyone is to talk of arrogance—'

'I know, my dear, but few people are as liberal as you.' Aunt Maude patted her arm as she guided her firmly towards the waiting carriage. 'It is the reason we told no one about your little scheme, is it not? How on earth did word get out?'

Susannah wondered this, too, and she considered the matter during the short drive back to Royal Crescent.

'I do not believe it could have come from the servants, I pay them very well for their discretion.'

'Mrs Farthing did seem to be particularly well informed,' mused Aunt Maude as the carriage pulled up at their door. 'I suppose the truth was bound to come out at some point.'

'But not yet,' muttered Susannah. 'Not now.'

She followed Aunt Maude into the house, where they divested themselves of their coats before repairing to the drawing room.

'It could be very damaging if the connection between Odesse and Florence House is known,' said Aunt
Maude. 'She is not yet well established, and the knowledge might affect her business. If that happened we
would have to find another market for the lace, too. But
who could have let it slip? Apart from the servants only
you, me and Kate Logan know the truth.'

Susannah walked to the window and stared out. Suddenly the spring sun did not seem quite so bright.

'There is another,' she said slowly. 'Lord Markham
knows the truth.'

'What?'

Susannah turned from the window. She could not bring
herself to meet her aunt's astonished gaze.

'He followed me on Friday morning. I was obliged
to explain to him. Everything.'

'Oh heavens!' Aunt Maude fell back in her chair,
one hand pressed to her breast. 'Why did you not say
earlier, my dear? I suppose you thought it not worth a
mention. And when I recall how bad the weather was
on Friday, I suppose we must think ourselves lucky that
he was not snowed up with you.'

'Well, actually, ma'am…'

It took all Susannah's reassurance and the judicious
use of her aunt's silver vinaigrette bottle to bring Mrs
Wilby back to a semblance of normality. She would
not rest until she had heard the whole story. She was
shocked, scandalised, not least when Susannah told her
that the viscount had cooked dinner for them all.

'Well he is a very odd sort of man,' she declared,
fanning herself rapidly. 'To remain in the house while
you were all at sixes and sevens with the birth. And you

say he did not insist upon taking the best bedchamber? Very odd indeed.'

'He was content to sleep in the parlour and leave Mrs Gifford's room for me.' Susannah was relieved when her aunt accepted the inference. She feared that not even the vinaigrette would help if she had to confess to spending the night in the same room as the viscount.

'Oh good heavens, what a tangle,' declared Mrs Wilby. 'It is bad enough that everyone knows you are involved in Florence House. If they should discover that you spent the night there, alone, with Lord Markham—'

'I was hardly alone, Aunt,' objected Susannah. 'There was the scullery maid, three other ladies and two babies in the house, too.'

'As if that makes it any better! I suppose it is too much to hope that the viscount has left Bath. He was not at the Abbey.'

'Neither was Mr Barnabus.'

'That is true.' Mrs Wilby sighed. 'Perhaps we should attend the ball in the Upper Rooms tomorrow night, after all, to make a show of indifference.'

Susannah shook her head.

'We agreed we would go to the Fancy Ball on Thursday this week. We mentioned it to several of our acquaintances. I do not see that we should change our plans because of a little talk.'

'Then we must wait until Tuesday to see what effect this has upon our card party.'

Susannah was inclined to be optimistic.

'It is a matter of little importance to anyone but ourselves. I hope we will find our rooms as busy as ever.'

But when Tuesday arrived several of their usual guests sent their apologies and there was a depressing number of empty tables in the room. Susannah was relieved to see Gerald Barnabus arrive and several other young gentleman came in shortly after, but Susannah heard them telling her aunt that Mr Warwick would not be joining them.

'He said he had a prior engagement, but we think otherwise,' declared Mr Edmonds, grinning at his friends. 'Your links with a certain house in the country appear to have upset him badly.'

'Aye, guilty conscience, most likely,' added William Farthing with a grating laugh that reminded Susannah very much of his mother.

Mrs Wilby raised her brows. The young man coloured and immediately begged pardon before moving off quickly with his friends to find amusement at one of the card tables. Susannah turned away, pretending to be busy until they had passed. Their amusement was almost worse than the disapproval of the older members of Bath society. She hoped her aunt's obvious displeasure at their laughter would prevent the matter being raised again, but when several of them joined Susannah at the loo table, she discovered that they were more than ready to tease her about Florence House. She tried to keep her temper, but their constant gibes made her call a halt.

'I pray you will say no more, gentlemen. This is a cause that should be supported by every Christian, not ridiculed. You at least should realise that, Mr Farthing, since your own mother is so closely involved with Walcot Street.' She handed the cards to the gentleman on her right and rose from the table. 'Pray continue the game for me, Mr Edmonds, I have had enough for tonight.'

She walked away, trying to calm herself. She should have known what to expect.

'Miss Prentess.' She turned to find Gerald beside her. He gave her a rueful smile. 'So Florence House is no longer a secret.'

'And the subject of much merriment,' she said bitterly. 'The jokes and winks, the innuendo—'

'They are young and thoughtless,' he said pacifically. 'It is unusual for an unmarried lady to be involved in such a charity. You know yourself most young ladies would deny all knowledge of such matters.'

'I would very much like to know how the secret got out,' she said. 'I don't suppose it was you…'

'Good Gad, Susannah, you know I would not say anything! I did not even tell Jasper about it.'

'No, of course not.' She smiled, and after a few moments he went off to join in a game of whist.

Susannah moved to a corner table, ostensibly to trim a flickering candle, but this was only an excuse to have a few moments to herself.

'You are very pensive.' Mrs Logan approached her.

'Kate,' Susannah kissed her cheek. 'I did not see you arrive. How are you?'

'Well, thank you.' Kate searched her face. 'But you are looking pale, Susannah. What is wrong?'

'Oh, nothing.' She tried to dismiss it with a smile. 'I am merely wondering how everyone knows about Florence House. I have spoken to the servants, and I am convinced not one of them has said anything about it. Gerald, too, swears he has not said a word.' She bit her lip. That left only Jasper.

You may rely upon me to say nothing of Florence House.

In her mind's eye she saw his image again, standing at the carriage door, solid, secure…and unreliable. He had let her down, and it hurt all the more because she had been so sure she could trust him. Giving herself a mental shake, she dragged up a smile.

'Well, it cannot be helped. We must do what we can to continue. Will you play *vingt-et-un* tonight, Kate? The winnings from the table are badly needed. I have paid Mr Tyler for the moment, but there will be more bills.'

'Of course, although only until Char—I mean, Mr Camerton arrives.'

'Oh, will he be coming then? Is be bringing the viscount?'

'I can only vouch for Mr Camerton,' replied Kate, a heightened colour in her cheeks. 'I do not think he has seen Lord Markham at all this week.'

'My biggest problem with Mr Camerton is that he wins far too often.' Susannah said it lightly, but she was half in earnest. She had noticed that when Charles Camerton was at the table, Kate's attention was not given fully to the game, and she could ill afford more losses.

The following morning Susannah's worst fears were confirmed. Their rooms had been only half-full, and when Mrs Wilby totted up the figures she reported sadly that they had made only thirty pounds.

'Hardly enough to pay for the supper.' Aunt Maude put down her pen. 'And nothing from Kate. She was playing picquet with Mr Camerton for most of the evening. One can only guess what her losses must be. I cannot understand why she continues to play against him.'

'Can you not, Aunt?' Susannah rubbed her arms. 'I think she is in love with him.'

'Kate? I do not believe it. She has completely forsworn men.'

'That is what I thought, too. I thought she felt as I do.'

'But if she is in love…'

'I know,' said Susannah in a hollow voice. 'Everything has changed. And it is all Lord Markham's fault, damn him!'

'Susannah!'

She coloured and quickly begged pardon. 'But it was the viscount who brought Charles Camerton to our rooms, and he betrayed me—us.'

'I am inclined to be philosophical,' her aunt responded. 'Florence House could not remain a secret for ever, and I cannot be sorry if Kate has found a man to love her.'

'Her first husband was a brute,' declared Susannah. 'In Gibraltar his viciousness was the talk of the regiment. I only hope she will not be hurt again.'

'My love, not all men are undeserving scoundrels,' said Aunt Maude gently. 'I was happily married to a good, kind man for fifteen years. Why, even Lord Markham may have his good points. At least he does not appear to have told anyone about Odesse.'

'He should not have told anyone *anything*,' retorted Susannah. 'He promised me—' She broke off, determined not to give in to the dull aching misery inside her. 'Enough of this. We shall come about, so let us not be too despondent. The sun is shining, Odesse has just delivered my new walking dress, so I shall take a stroll in Sydney Gardens. Will you come with me?'

No more was said about the card party and Aunt Maude was content to accept Susannah's assurances that all would be well. A visit to Odesse confirmed that her business was still doing well. In fact she reported that the number of customers was increasing, but despite that, Susannah felt the leaden weight inside. It was not that the secret of Florence House was out, but the fact that she had trusted Jasper, and he had let her down.

* * *

As they made their way to the Upper Rooms for Thursday's ball Aunt Maude wondered aloud how many of their acquaintance knew about her patronage of Florence House, and how many would show their disapproval. Susannah made a brave response, but she was secretly relieved to find that they were not completely ignored when they entered the ballroom.

A short distance from the door a group of young bucks stood talking. Susannah knew them all, but as they approached one of them looked up. For a moment he glared at her, then turned and strode off.

'Dear me, it appears we have indeed offended Mr Warwick,' murmured Aunt Wilby.

She spoke quietly, but a young gentleman making his bow to Susannah overheard and grinned.

'Take no notice of Warwick, Miss Prentess, he's been like a bear with a sore head recently. Probably worrying over some female.' He laughed heartily, then he leaned closer, saying confidentially, 'We've told him, ma'am, that if it's *that* sort of trouble...' he tapped his nose '...then the gal might be glad of your little, ah, charity.' With a knowing grin he linked arms with his companions and walked away.

'I suppose we shall have to accustom ourselves to such talk,' remarked Mrs Wilby in a tone of long-suffering. 'It will die away soon enough, once there is some other juicy gossip to replace it.'

Susannah knew this to be true, but it angered her to think all her careful preparations for Florence House might be jeopardised because the secret had been revealed too soon, and by a man who assured her she could trust him.

She had convinced herself that she never wanted

to see Lord Markham again, that she could shrug her shoulders and put him from her mind, but when she saw him conversing with Gerald Barnabus all the pent-up anger of the past few days came flooding back.

As if aware of her eyes upon him, the viscount looked up. He touched Gerald's arm and the two men approached. Susannah watched in growing anger and amazement as Jasper made his bow to her aunt. He was completely at his ease. She glared at him, but it had no effect. When he addressed her she quickly turned away from him, causing her filmy muslin skirts to flounce around her. How dare he think he could betray her and get away with it!

'Miss Prentess, are you not well?'

'Perfectly, thank you.' She wanted to ignore him but he took her elbow and in the confusion of the crowded room he adroitly moved her away from her aunt.

'Are you cross with me for staying away for so long?' he said quietly. 'I beg your pardon, but I had business to attend to, and thought, in the circumstances—'

'In the circumstances, my lord,' she interrupted him savagely, 'it would be better if you stayed away for good,'

'What is this? What have I done to offend you?'

'As if you did not know!'

His brows snapped together.

'No, I do not know. When we parted on Saturday—'

'On Saturday you promised not to mention Florence House to anyone.'

'And I have not done so.'

'Why, then, is everyone talking of it? Why have I been subjected to cold stares and even been snubbed by my erstwhile acquaintances?'

'Susannah, I give you my word—'

'Don't you dare use my name,' she shot back at him. 'How dare you even *speak* to me!'

She went to move away but his fingers tightened on her arm.

'I do not know who has given away your secret, but it was not me.'

She shook off his hand.

'Everyone else who knows about Florence House has been party to the secret for months and not a hint of it has leaked out. But only days after I tell you, it is common knowledge.'

'However that may be, it is not my doing, and not my groom's either. He knows better than to talk out of turn.'

'I do not believe you.' Her lip curled. 'Pray leave me, Lord Markham. I have no wish for your company this evening.'

Susannah turned away and this time he made no attempt to prevent her. She made her way back through the crowd to her aunt's side, prepared to explain the angry flush on her cheek, but Aunt Maude merely gave her a distracted smile.

'Mr Barnabus has gone, Susannah, but he said to remind you that you promised to dance with him later. Oh dear, I have received the cut direct from at least two ladies, and Mrs Sanstead says I should persuade you to distance yourself from Florence House if you are not to be ostracised by Bath society.'

'Really? How dare these small-minded matrons think they can dictate to me!'

'Now, Susannah, pray be careful,' Aunt Maude begged her. 'Do not let your temper carry you away. We need the good offices of these ladies. How else are we to fund Florence House for the rest of this year?'

'I neither know nor care,' Susanna ground out furiously.

'Perhaps we should close the house, until we have more funds.'

Aunt Maude's tentative suggestion brought Susannah's outraged eyes upon her, but after a moment her fury died down.

'No, I will not do that, unless there is no other way.' She looked around. 'I expected to see Kate here.'

Mrs Wilby tutted.

'Oh, my dear, it completely slipped my mind. She sent a note to say she was going out of town for a few days.'

'That is a pity, I would have liked her support tonight. Never mind.' Susannah put on a brave smile. 'We shall stand our ground, Aunt. One or two may turn away from us, but our true friends will stand by us, and I hope once the gossip has died down we shall recover.' She smiled mischievously. 'Besides, I cannot leave yet. Odesse assured me this latest gown she has created for me will look its best when I am dancing.'

There was no lack of partners for Susannah, but the numbers soliciting her to dance were sadly diminished, and the high-nosed stares she received from a group of matrons standing with Mrs Farthing suggested that many of them were shocked to learn of her involvement with Florence House. Keeping her head high, Susannah smiled and laughed with her dance partners, but by the time she rejoined her aunt after a series of lively country dances her cheeks ached with the effort.

'Heavens, I never thought dancing could be such a chore,' she muttered, following Aunt Maude to a space where they might not be overheard, but when asked if she wanted to go home, she quickly disclaimed, 'I beg

your pardon, Aunt, I should not be complaining. There
are still many here who do not care a fig for my association with Florence House.'

'Yes, my love, but they are not the high sticklers
who can make a difference to our long-term plans. If
the cream of Bath society should turn against you, then
your patronage of Odesse could count against her—'
Aunt Maude broke off and gazed past Susannah, a wary
look in her eye.

'Miss Prentess, would you do me the honour of
standing up with me for the next dance?'

Jasper's cool voice brought the angry flush back to
Susannah's cheeks. Had he not understood what she
had said to him? Without turning, she said coldly, 'No,
my lord, I will not.'

Aunt Maude gasped in horror, but Susannah merely
hunched one white shoulder. Instead of moving off, the
viscount stepped closer. She was aware of his presence, the heat of his body at her back. She could feel
his breath on her cheek as he spoke quietly in her ear.

'Think carefully about this, madam. Your credit in
Bath is sadly diminished. Can you afford *not* to dance
with me?'

She bit her lip. He was right. It did not take Aunt
Maude's beseeching stare to tell her so. Slowly she
turned around. He smiled and held out his arm, but the
steely glint in his eye told her he was not in the mood
to be refused. Reluctantly she placed her fingers on
his sleeve.

'That is better. Let us see what we can do to repair
the damage.'

'I am doing this under sufferance,' she muttered as
he led her on to the floor. 'I have not forgiven you.'

'Since I am not at fault there is nothing to forgive,'

he retorted. They took their places facing one another, more duellists than dancers. He bowed to her as the music started, and as they passed in the dance he continued, 'Do you know, you are the most stubborn female I have ever met.'

'It must be a novel experience for you, my lord, to find a woman who will not toady and flatter you.' She bit the words off quickly as they circled about the other dancers. Angry as she was, Susannah did not wish anyone else to hear their argument. When Jasper took her hand again he carried on the conversation.

'Not at all—' they separated, circled, returned '—there are many such, but few who would be as ungrateful as you.'

Susannah's eyes flashed, but she was obliged to hold back her retort until they were once again holding hands.

'Oh, so I should be obliged to you, should I, because you deign to stand up with me?'

'No, you tiresome wench, because I am trying my utmost to prevent you from becoming a pariah. My attendance upon you may persuade those ladies whose support you need to think better of you.' His lips curved upwards as he watched her struggle. He reached out and took her hand as the last notes of the music died away. 'You know I am right,' he murmured as he bowed over her fingers. 'I can make you or break you tonight.' He straightened and bestowed on her his most charming smile. 'Well, Miss Prentess, what is it to be? Shall we stay for the cotillion?'

The fact that he was right did nothing for Susannah's temper. In any other circumstances she would have swept off and left him standing alone on the dance floor, but she was well aware that such an action would only increase the disapprobation already surrounding her. She cared nothing for her own standing in Bath, but at present Florence House could not survive without the extra revenue she could provide. In the future she hoped there would be sufficient money from Odesse and the lace-makers to help maintain the house, but this was a critical time. She needed the viscount's support.

With enormous effort she forced herself to smile at him, saying through her clenched teeth, 'With the greatest of pleasure, Lord Markham.'

'Well, that passed off exceeding well,' declared Mrs Wilby as she waited for Susannah to extricate herself from her chair in the hallway of Royal Crescent. 'Lord Markham's timely intervention had a profound effect on everyone. Even before you had finished the cotillion Lady Horsham and Mrs Bray-Tillotson came up to speak to me, and I have received no more than a nod from either of them before.' She took Susannah's arm and led her into the morning room on the ground floor, where candles burned and the fire had been built up for their return. 'And then to join Mr Barnabus in escorting us to supper. Why, even Mrs Farthing and her cronies could not quite snub us after that!'

'No' Susannah moved towards the fire to warm her hands. 'His lordship was most accommodating.'

'Indeed he was. I think he must regret letting slip our secret.'

'He maintains he said nothing.'

'Well then, it was even more considerate of him to give us so much of his time tonight.'

It was clear to Susannah that her aunt had been very anxious about their reception at the ball and her relief now took the form of continuous chatter. Susannah let it wash over her for a few minutes before making her excuses and fleeing to her bedroom.

She was obliged to be grateful for the viscount's attentions but she would have preferred a simple apology. In that he was no different from most men, so arrogant that he would not admit he had been at fault, that he had made known her connection with Florence House. His refusal to do so had quite spoiled her evening. Jasper was a good dancer and in other circumstances she would have revelled in standing up with him for the cotillion, holding his hands, laughing up into his face, but his perfidy hung between them like a cloud. She had kept her smile in place, concentrating on the intricacies of the dance and determined not to allow her anger to be visible to the constantly changing partners, but it had been difficult.

The viscount had been most attentive at supper, too. Outwardly Susannah had been serene and smiling, but he had not been deceived, and once Dorcas had undressed her, brushed out her hair and departed, Susannah slipped between the sheets and relived her brief, final meeting with the viscount.

They had been waiting for their cloaks when Jasper came up to take his leave. He had taken advantage of the noisy, bustling chatter to speak to her alone.

'You will not cry friends with me?'

'I am, of course, grateful for what you have done tonight, my lord…'

'Well that is something, I suppose.' He took her hand. 'I have much ground to make up, but I will come about, Susannah, believe me.'

But, of course, she could not believe him. She could not trust him ever again.

* * *

When Jasper awoke the following morning his first conscious thought was of Susannah Prentess. How she had ripped up at him when she thought he had broken his word to her. She had looked quite magnificent, those hazel eyes flashing with emerald-green sparks of anger. It would take time and patience to convince her he had not been to blame but it would be worth it. For the present he hoped he had deflected some of the disapproval away from her—surely the attentions of a viscount would count for something with the Bath harpies.

He jumped out of bed and rang the bell. He was eager to see Susannah again—it surprised him a little to realise how much he wanted to see her—but he must allow her a day or two. At present she was too angry to listen to reasoned argument. There was plenty to do. He had letters to write to his man of business, and he and Gerald had discussed plans for a riding party with Charles Camerton and a few of the other gentlemen of their acquaintance, so perhaps he should talk to Gerald about that. Still, he might take a walk this morning, and if he should happen to bump into Miss Prentess, well....

He made his way to the Pump Room, stopping off on his way to call at the White Hart, where he was told that Mr Camerton was gone away.

'We are expecting him back in a day or so, though, m'lord,' said the servant, pocketing the coin Jasper pressed into his hand. 'He's left his bags here.'

With an inward shrug Jasper left the inn. His plans to form a riding party must wait, then. He crossed the road to the Pump Room, but a quick tour of the crowded room informed him that Susannah and her aunt were not present. However, having ventured into the busy meeting place, he could not leave before speaking to a number of his acquaintances and listening to the latest gossip. He was pleased that this no longer centred on Susannah—she had been supplanted by the news that the Dowager Countess of Gisburne was in Bath.

Jasper received the information with interest, and set off for Laura Place, where he was shown into the countess's drawing room by her stately butler.

He found himself in the presence of an elderly lady dressed in black satin. She was sitting in a large, carved armchair, her back ramrod straight, and the bright eyes that watched him cross the room were remarkably piercing.

'Markham...' she held out her hand '...I did not expect to find you here, but it is a pleasant surprise. You will take wine with me? Good.' She paused while he bowed over her fingers and did not object when he then leaned forwards to kiss her cheek. 'You can tell me how your family go on. I saw your sister in town, looking radiant, as ever. And how is Dominic, my godson? I wanted to get to Rooks Tower for the christening, but the weather...' She waved one beringed hand. 'I would have risked it, but Gisburne and my doctor were adamant.'

'And quite right, too, ma'am,' Jasper agreed, pulling up a chair and sitting down. 'Dominic would never forgive you for knocking yourself up with such a journey. He is inordinately happy, you know.'

'Having met his wife I can believe it,' replied the dowager. 'Zelah Coale is a very sensible gel, and a reliable correspondent, too.'

'Yes, she has won all our hearts.'

Even as he uttered the words, Jasper realised with

a slight jolt of surprise that Zelah had not been in his thoughts for some weeks now.

'And how are you, my boy—still leading the young ladies a merry dance?'

'Rather the reverse, ma'am,' he replied, thinking of Susannah. 'But tell me, what brings you to Bath?'

'The winter left me a trifle fagged and my doctor thought it would do me good to take the waters.'

'As long as it is nothing serious.'

'Not a whit, although I don't doubt Gisburne and his wife would like it to be. They must wish me at Jericho.'

Jasper grinned, too well acquainted with the dowager's easy-natured son to believe any such thing.

'You know he would dispute that, and your many charities would miss you, too.' He paused, gazing down at the large signet ring on his finger. 'And talking of your charities, I think you may be able to help me.'

'Go on.'

Jasper took advantage of the servant's entrance to consider his words. Once the glasses had been filled and they were alone again he began.

'A friend…' He hesitated, knowing that in her present mood Susannah would object strongly to the term. 'An acquaintance has set up a home for young ladies of gentle birth who have been abandoned by their families for, ah…'

'For being pregnant,' she finished for him. 'There is no need to be mealy-mouthed with me, Markham.'

He smiled.

'I beg your pardon. Let me explain…'

When he had finished telling her about Florence House, the lace-makers and Odesse, Lady Gisburne nodded slowly.

'Exemplary.' She put down her empty wineglass. 'What is it you want from me?'

'Ostensibly all this was set up by Mrs Wilby. Now it is known that her unmarried niece is closely involved with Florence House and the Bath tabbies are sharpening their claws. Some have already cut the acquaintance. If they learn of the connection with the modiste it could destroy the small income that keeps the house going.' He refilled the glasses and held one out to the Dowager. 'The niece is an heiress and I believe she intends to fund the scheme, once she comes into her inheritance, but that will not be for a year or two yet. I would like to help them.'

She looked at him over the rim of her glass.

'Repenting past sins, Markham?'

'Certainly not,' he replied, in no way offended. 'Seducing innocents has never been my style, and despite my reputation I have always been alive to the consequences of my actions. I am tolerably certain there are no bastards of mine in the world. No, it is purely altruistic.' He found he could not meet that searching gaze and studied the contents of his wineglass instead. 'Any offer of assistance from me would be rejected, but you could tell Mrs Wilby there is an anonymous benefactor who wishes to invest in some worthy cause.'

The dowager sipped at her wine, a slight crease furrowing her brow. Jasper waited patiently, knowing better than to disturb the old lady. At last she looked up, a glimmer of a smile on her sharp features.

'Very well, I will do it. If only to confound the Bath tabbies!'

Chapter Twelve

When Saturday dawned wet and windy, Susannah and Mrs Wilby decided to remain indoors. They settled quietly to their sewing, although Susannah's work remained untouched on her lap for most of the time. Her thoughts kept going back to the viscount and his refusal to admit he had spoken to anyone about Florence House. She had seen too many of the young men in Bath bluster and boast. One could not rely on any of them, but it surprised her how much it hurt her to know the viscount was one of their number. She had thought him different from the rest. She had hoped—quickly she stifled her half-formed thoughts. She would think no more about it. When Mrs Wilby addressed some remark to her she replied briefly and bent her head over her tambour frame once more. She had thought herself quite content with her lot, but recently she had to admit that the future as an unmarried lady seemed rather a lonely one.

Susannah was surprised out of this melancholy train of thought by Gatley coming in to announce a visitor.

'The Dowager Countess of Gisburne?' Aunt Maude dropped her sewing in amazement. 'But we do not know—I saw her name in Mr King's visitors' book, but—oh, show her up, Gatley, show her up! Good heavens, what on earth has brought a dowager countess to our door?'

'I have no idea, Aunt, but we shall soon know.' Susannah quickly put away the sewing things while her aunt patted her cap and straightened her gown.

The Dowager was a thin, formidable-looking figure, her severe black gown relieved by a vast quantity of white lace. Her dark, bird-like eyes rested for a moment on Susannah as she entered the room, before she turned her attention to Aunt Maude.

'Mrs Wilby, we have not been introduced, but I hope you will forgive the intrusion when you know my business.'

Murmuring, Aunt Maude rose from her curtsy and begged the dowager to be seated.

She moved to a sofa and sat down, saying in her forthright manner, 'I believe you are responsible for an establishment near here. Florence House.'

Susannah looked up.

'Goodness me, ma'am, however did you hear of that?'

Those sharp eyes flickered over her again, and Susannah saw the gleam of amusement in their depths.

'The rumour mill in Bath is quite inexhaustible, Miss Prentess. You may know, Mrs Wilby, that I am very interested in such causes. I would like to help you.'

Aunt Maude threw an anguished glance towards Susannah, who replied cautiously, 'That is very gracious of you, ma'am, but I am not sure…'

'Oh come, ladies, I have not been in Bath long but one visit to the Pump Room was sufficient for me to know that your little scheme has set up the backs of the

Walcot Street committee. Will you deny that your present funding is inadequate?'

'No, we will not deny that,' replied Susannah.

'Good.' The dowager put down her cane. 'Then let us discuss it!'

When at last Lady Gisburne had been shown out, Mrs Wilby fell back in her chair.

'Heavens, my head is fairly spinning.'

'I admit she is a very forceful personality,' agreed Susannah, smiling slightly, 'but her patronage—and her money!—will be most welcome.'

'But can we believe her when she says she will leave the control of Florence House in our hands?'

'Oh, I think so, but that is something we can go over once the papers are drawn up.' Susanna stood by the window, watching the dowager being helped into her carriage. 'I liked her plain speaking. She is very knowledgeable about how we should proceed. With Lady Gisburne as patroness I think the future of Florence House is assured.'

'And Odesse,' added Mrs Wilby. 'My lady agreed we should not make her connection with Florence House public knowledge, but she was keen to see her work.'

Susannah chuckled.

'From the prodigious amount of lace on the dowager's gown, her patronage alone should bring plenty of work for the modiste and the lace-makers.' She turned back to her aunt. 'It is a great relief to me,' she admitted. 'I do not mind if Bath society shuns me, but the thought of not being able to support the house, or the girls—' She broke off, shaking her head to dispel the tears that threatened.

'Well,' declared Mrs Wilby, taking up her sewing

again. 'I believe with the Dowager Countess of Gisburne as an acquaintance, Bath society will not dare to shun us!'

And so it proved. On Sunday the Dowager had attended the morning service at the Abbey and once she had acknowledged Susannah and her aunt, others followed suit, even Mrs Bulstrode and Mrs Farthing, although it was clearly an effort. A visit to Henrietta Street on Monday was also encouraging.

'I have had no one ask me about Florence House,' said Odesse, going to fetch a large box from a shelf. 'And this morning, I received a visit from a most superior personage: a dowager countess, no less. She has ordered a new morning gown and hinted that she might place even more business with me, if I can turn it round quickly. Thank goodness I stayed up last night to finish this for you, Miss Prentess, otherwise heaven knows when I would have time to do it.'

She opened the box and pulled out a new evening gown of apricot silk.

'Oh it is beautiful,' exclaimed Susannah.

'I hoped you would like it.' Odesse held up the gown for Susannah's inspection. 'The flounced skirt is hemmed with lace, like the neck and the puff sleeves, and I have found a pair of long gloves that match the colour exactly.'

'Quite exquisite,' declared Mrs Wilby. 'You must wear it at the ball, my love.' She beamed at the modiste. 'It is quite the finest gown you have made yet, Odesse.'

'Thank you, ma'am. And the walking dress with the lilac-sarcenet petticoat that you ordered for yourself is ready now, if you wish to take it, Mrs Wilby, but I'm

afraid I have not had time to finish the green pelisse,
I am very sorry.'

'Oh, never mind about that.' Mrs Wilby happily
waved aside her apology. 'I do not need the new pelisse yet and would much rather you satisfied your other
customers.'

'Lady Gisburne has lost no time in seeking out
Odesse,' remarked Susannah, when the ladies were once
more in their carriage, surrounded by their purchases.
'I have every confidence that she will be well satisfied
with her services.' She put her hand on the box beside
her and chuckled. 'Perhaps now I can stop buying so
many new gowns!'

That same evening, Susannah smoothed the long
gloves over her arms and stood back to look at herself
in the glass. There was no doubt that the apricot silk
was most becoming. Dorcas had dressed her hair à la
Madonna, with a centre parting and the curls falling
from a topknot so that they would bounce and shim-
mer about her head when she danced at the ball tonight.

She wondered if Jasper would like it, but resolutely
stifled the thought. He was still not forgiven, so it was
of no odds to her at all whether he liked it or not. With
something like a toss of those guinea-gold curls she
picked up her shawl and hurried downstairs to join Aunt
Maude.

Their reception at the Upper Rooms was noticeably
warmer than it had been the previous week. There were
smiles and bows from most of the matrons as they entered, and more than one lady promised Mrs Wilby an
invitation to drink tea with her the following week.

Aunt Maude caught Susannah's eyes, a glow of triumph in her own, and Susannah was forced to bite back a smile. A sudden commotion at the door was followed by a reverent hush. Susannah and her aunt stood back as the Dowager Countess of Gisburne was announced. The old lady progressed regally and Susannah noticed that although she carried a stick she rarely leaned on it as she made her way through the crowd with a nod here, a word there. When she reached Susannah she stopped.

'Miss Prentess.'

Susannah rose from her curtsy to find the dowager was regarding her through her quizzing glass.

'Hmm. Elegantly turned out, as always. I think you are in a fair way to becoming the best-dressed lady in Bath, my dear.' She had not raised her voice, but her words carried effortlessly around the room.

'Thank you, ma'am.'

Susannah inclined her head to acknowledge the compliment but she was almost startled into a laugh when the old lady winked at her before continuing her regal progress towards the ballroom.

Gerald Barnabus had begged her to keep the first dance for him and he came to find her when the orchestra began tuning up. He too cast an appraising eye over her.

'I have never seen you looking lovelier,' he declared, pressing a fervent kiss upon her gloved fingers.

Susannah laughed.

'I am immune to your compliments, Gerald, you give me too many of them.'

'That is because I am violently in love with you,' he replied gallantly.

'I fear you have just fallen into the habit of saying so,' she retorted, shaking her head at him.

'How can you say so? I have been your most loyal suitor.' A faint frown marred his boyish countenance when he spotted a group of gentlemen at the far side of the room and he added quietly, 'At least I am not one of those fairweather suitors, who abandon you at the first hint of adversity. Most of that crowd over there have not been to one of your card parties since it was known that you are the patroness of Florence House.'

'We are grateful for your constant support, and Lord Markham's,' she added conscientiously. 'Is, um, is the viscount coming tonight, by the bye?'

'Oh, yes, we dined together. He is here somewhere,' said Gerald carelessly. 'He agrees with me, your support for Florence House is to be applauded.'

'Thank you, I am glad to know that. However, we have another patroness now, although she does not wish to be named yet. It means the house's future is much more secure. Our card parties are less important now. We may even discontinue them.'

'I should be glad of it,' he replied earnestly. 'While I understand the necessity I have always thought—' He broke off, flushing. 'But never mind that. The first set is forming. Shall we join them?'

Susannah stood up for the first two dances with Gerald, and after that there was no lack of partners. The music lifted her spirits. She no longer needed to worry about Florence House, she could relax and enjoy herself. As she was waiting for another dance to begin she saw Jasper at the side of the room. He looked very handsome in his dark coat, his black hair gleaming in the candlelight. Perhaps she was being unfair to him. Mayhap he had not intended to tell anyone about Florence House. Surely she could forgive such a slip?

* * *

By the end of the dance she had made up her mind she would speak to him. She gracefully excused herself and moved off the dance floor. The crowd was so thick it was impossible to see very far and Jasper's dark head was not visible in any direction. On one of the higher tiers of benches she could see her aunt, part of a large crowd gathered around Lady Gisburne. Susannah had no desire to join that throng and she decided she would sit out on the lower benches until the dancing stopped and tea was served, then she would join her aunt in the tea room. Perhaps she would find Jasper there. She began to make her way through the crowd. Ahead of her she could see Mrs Bulstrode and Mrs Farthing at the centre of a little group of ladies. Susannah had no wish to push past them and endure their insincere greetings so she stepped to one side, where she was shielded from their view by two large gentlemen deep in conversation. However, she was close enough to hear Mrs Farthing's sneering tones.

'I see Miss Prentess is wearing yet another new gown. I wonder she can afford so many, with her little "interest" to keep up.'

Her cronies laughed. Susannah's lip curled slightly and she was about to move away when she heard Mrs Bulstrode give an angry titter.

'My dear, she can afford anything she wants now she has Markham in her pocket. I wager we will be calling her "Viscountess" before the end of the summer.'

Susannah froze. She folded her arms across her breast, hugging herself. Markham in her pocket? Nothing was further from the truth and yet…perhaps that is how it looked, to those who had been watching them at the last ball. Jasper had been very attentive. The blood that had earlier drained from her body now returned in an angry rush. How dare they! How dare they couple her name with anyone, least of all the viscount?

She remembered their last meeting. His insouciance, his confident assertion that he would *come about*. Perhaps Jasper himself had started these rumours, perhaps he was misguided enough to think that the hint of such a liaison would protect her from the disapproval of Bath society.

Fustian, she told herself savagely. *Only a nodcock would believe it would do anything other than make me look foolish!*

She looked about her. She must find Jasper and have it out with him. Now.

Another perambulation of the ballroom convinced her that the viscount was not present and she made her way to the Octagon. That, too, was crowded, but still no sign of him. Her last hope was the tea room. That was the least crowded of all, for the dancing was still going on and the waiters had not yet completed setting out the refreshments. One or two couples stood about the room and Susannah was about to give up and return to the ballroom when a movement on the balcony at the far end of the room caught her eye. Someone was on the upper level, and even in the shadows she recognised the familiar form of Lord Markham.

Susannah hurried up the stairs to the landing. The light from the three grand chandeliers did not reach this far and the soaring pillars threw further bands of shadow across the narrow gallery.

'Lord Markham. I have been looking for you.'

He turned at her voice and she saw the flash of white teeth as he smiled at her.

'Really? I came up here to escape the crowds. I am honoured that you have sought me out.'

'You should not be. I have come to pick a crow with you!' She began to pace up and down, too angry to keep still. 'Do you know that everyone is saying we are betrothed?'

'Are they?'

'Yes, they are,' she said furiously. 'Perhaps you can tell me how that rumour came about?'

'Your spending the whole evening with me at the Fancy Ball, perhaps?'

'That was to protect Florence House. You should have scotched this rumour.'

He spread his hands.

'I beg your pardon, but I was not aware of it.'

'Well you are aware of it now, and I demand you put a stop to it.'

He caught her hand as she went to pass him.

'Pray do not put yourself into a passion over such a little matter, Miss Prentess.'

'It is not a little matter,' she flashed at him, tearing her hand free. 'It is—it is a slur on my good name!'

His black brows went up.

'That you should be considered a fit wife for a viscount? I see no slur there.'

'This is all your fault,' she railed at him, too furious for reason. 'First you betray a confidence and then—'

With a growl of exasperation he caught her arms and turned her towards him, giving her a little shake.

'How many more times do I have to tell you I did *not* give away your secret? And no more have I set it about that we are to be married. Thunder an' turf, what would I want to do such a thing for?' His hands slid up to her shoulders, she could feel their heat through the thin silk of the tiny puff sleeves.

'I don't know—to make mischief, perhaps!'

His thumbs moved gently over her collar bones, caressing the bare skin. It was strangely arresting. Her mind might still be angry with him, but her limbs were locked, she was unable to move away.

'I am not in the habit of making mischief of that sort.'

His low voice resonated through her body. A tingle ran down the length of her spine. Gently he pulled her back against the wall, where the shadows were deepest. She should protest, push him away, run back to the safety of the crowded ballroom.

She did none of these things. His hands continued to hold her shoulders. He was standing so close now that she could smell the spicy tang of cologne on his skin. Her breasts seemed to swell and pull her forwards, responding to the attraction of his lean, muscular body.

He put the fingers of one hand beneath her chin and forced her to look up at him. His face was in shadow, but she could sense his eyes on her face, feel them burning into her very soul, laying it bare. It was as much as she could do not to whimper in fear.

'S-stop this,' she stammered. 'Let me go.'

In response he lowered his head and touched her lips with his own. She found herself reaching up, standing on tiptoe to prolong the contact.

'You may leave whenever you wish.'

The words whispered over her skin, their meaning lost. She closed her eyes, shivering with delight as his kisses strayed to her neck. Her head went back and she clutched at his jacket, a wave of dizziness washing over her. He planted kisses on her throat and along the length of her jaw before returning his attention to her mouth and then she was drowning in his kiss, opening her lips, inviting him to plunder her mouth, her own tongue tentatively flickering to meet his.

He gave a groan as his arms tightened around her. She was crushed against his body—it was every bit as hard and demanding as she remembered. She wanted to tear at his clothes but instead drove her hands into his hair, revelling in the silky strength of those black locks between her fingers. Her body was on fire, her thighs aching for his touch and when he raised his head she clung to him, trembling. Only his encircling arms prevented her from collapsing in a heap at his feet.

'Tell me you did not plan this,' he murmured into her hair.

'Plan what?'

He laughed softly.

'You bewitch me.'

Susannah took a few deep breaths and fought to regain control of her unruly body. Not just her body, her mind, too. Jasper spoke of being bewitched. Surely something of that kind had happened to her? This was not normal, rational behaviour.

Steeling herself, she pushed him away. She felt a little unsteady, but her legs did not crumple beneath her.

'Pray to not think I came up here to, to...'

'No, I acquit you of that. As you must acquit me of spreading rumours about our impending marriage. But you know, perhaps it is not such an impossible idea.'

'I beg your pardon?'

'Perhaps we *should* marry,' he said.

'P-pray do not tease me, my lord.'

'No, I am in earnest. After forcing you to dine alone with me, then our being together at Florence House, it occurs to me that I should offer you the protection of my name.' His wicked smile flashed. 'Especially if we have this effect upon each other.'

Another tremor ran through her, but this time of fear.

'No. Never.' She crossed her arms, thoroughly alarmed. 'Th-this is not natural. It is to be avoided. It leads to, to debauchery and decadence.'

He smiled. 'I am becoming more enamoured of the idea every minute.'

He reached out for her but she whisked herself away from him, putting her hands on the iron railings behind her for support.

'I c-cannot marry you.' Panic welled up inside her. 'You—I—you frighten me.'

'No, you have frightened yourself,' he said gently. 'These feeling are natural. When we are married you will see—'

'No! I have made a vow to myself never to marry.'

'Because of what happened to your sister? It is time to let that go, Susannah. It is time to live your own life.'

She gazed up at him. His words were gentle, but there was something in his eyes, a warm glow that promised much and threatened her self-control. It terrified her. A sudden burst of laughter echoed around them. Jasper looked down into the tea room.

'The dancing has ended. Everyone is coming in here now. You had best go and find your aunt.'

She took a step away from him.

'I c-can't marry you, my lord. I c-can't...'

'Yes, you can.'

He reached out and touched her cheek with his fingers. The skin burned, sending white-hot shards of pleasure pulsing through her. Did he not understand this should not be happening to her? She could not allow any man such control over her.

'I have to leave Bath for a few days,' he said. 'There are papers I have to sign at Markham, but I will be back on Wednesday evening. I will call on Thursday and we will discuss it further. You need not fear, everything shall be done properly. I shall ask your aunt for permission to pay my addresses.'

She shivered. It must not happen. She could not live in such a way, turning into a wanton, unrestrained wretch every time he came near her. She knew only too well the pain and heartache she would suffer if she allowed it to continue. Ladies were to be respected, worshipped—the way Gerald respected and worshipped her. Those baser instincts that Jasper unleashed in her must be controlled at all costs. Biting her lip, she began to back away, yet when he put out his hand she gave him hers, trying to ignore the little arrows of desire that darted along her arm as his thumb grazed the soft skin of her wrist.

'Go now, then. Until Thursday.'

He let her go and she stood irresolute. She wanted to throw herself back into his arms, to surrender to that overwhelming passion he called up so easily within her, but that would mean disaster. He was the flame, she the moth. He would destroy her. Summoning up every reserve of energy she could find, she nodded to him and forced herself to turn and walk away.

Susannah did not go in search of her aunt, instead she wandered around the ballroom, which was deserted now save for little chattering groups that had no wish for refreshment. How had it happened? How had this man come into her world and turned it upside down? She did not need this, did not want it. She wanted only to go back to the safe certainties of the life she had known, where she was in control, in charge of her own happiness. She sank down on a chair, unseeing eyes staring at the empty dance floor. He did not want to marry her but he felt obliged to, because he had compromised her reputation. Despite that he would come to the Crescent, as he had promised. He would talk to Aunt Maude, he would propose. He would take her hand, look into her eyes and she would be powerless to refuse him.

'I can't let that happen,' she whispered. 'I c-cannot let myself be subjugated by him. No man shall ever be my master.'

She wrapped her arms about herself and began to rock backwards and forwards. There must be a way to prevent it.

'Miss Prentess, are you unwell?'

General Sanstead was bending over her, his kindly face creased with concern. She forced herself to get up, to smile at him.

'I am perfectly well, thank you General. I, um, I need to find someone...'

She walked off, her limbs feeling strangely stiff and difficult to control. She must go home immediately. She would leave Bath, go away where no one could find her. People were beginning to return to the ballroom now, and one of the first to come through the door was Gerald Barnabus. He saw her immediately.

'Good heavens, Susannah, you are as white as a sheet. Are you unwell?'

'Yes—no—I must get away from here.' She clutched at his outstretched hand, trying to remain calm and not burst into tears.

'Yes, of course, my dear. We will find Mrs Wilby. But is there anything I can do?'

'Oh, Gerald, I have made such a mess of everything. I am afraid—'

'Afraid of what?'

She could not bring herself to tell him about Jasper. She said distractedly, 'Of being alone.'

His grip on her hand tightened.

'Well that is easily resolved,' he said cheerfully. 'Have I not asked you to marry me countless times? You only have to say the word and you need never be alone again. I will protect you from everything.'

She stared up into his smiling face. Good, kind Gerald, who had been a friend to her and had never asked more than to be allowed to kiss her hand. He would protect her.

'Oh, yes, Gerald,' she said quickly. 'I will marry you. And as soon as possible.'

Chapter Thirteen

Gerald stared at her for a long, long moment before a grin of delight broke over his face. 'Truly? Why, Susannah, you have made me the happiest of men.'

He pressed a kiss upon her fingers and she waited for the reaction, for her skin to tingle and burn, for that ache deep in her body. It did not come. She was safe.

'We must tell my aunt,' she said.

'By all means, let us go and find her.'

Mrs Wilby was sitting beside Lady Gisburne on the first row of benches. Susannah was inclined to hold back, but Gerald was eager to impart the good news, so she stood silently beside him as he made his announcement.

Mrs Wilby looked a little startled at first, but then she smiled and held out her hand for him to kiss. Lady Gisburne's congratulations were more restrained, and she gave Susannah a quizzical look.

'I did not know you were considering matrimony, Miss Prentess.'

'I have been pestering her to marry me for months now,' said Gerald happily. He turned his smile towards

Susannah. 'And at last my persistence has been rewarded.'

'And when will the engagement be announced?' the dowager enquired. 'Or is it to be a private affair?'

'Of course it will be made public,' replied Susannah, frowning a little. 'Everything shall be done properly.'

The words reminded her of the encounter with Jasper and she had to force her wandering mind to concentrate upon the dowager's next words.

'And will this affect our plans for the charity?'

'Not at all, except…' Susannah hesitated as she thought of a way to delay her next meeting with the viscount. 'Perhaps we could put off our visit to Florence House until Thursday morning?'

'Very well, my dear, Thursday it shall be.'

'Thank you, ma'am.' The sudden scrape of the fiddles caught Susannah's attention. She wanted very much to go home, but to leave so suddenly after the announcement would cause comment, Instead she turned to Gerald.

'The dancing will be starting again very soon. Shall we join them?'

'Why not?' He grinned. 'And now we are betrothed I need not give you up for the rest of the evening!'

Jasper stood back, watching the dancers. He could not keep his eyes from Susannah, who skipped and twirled about the room, her bouncing curls gleaming in the candlelight. She was going down the dance with Gerald, and although she was smiling Jasper thought her enjoyment a trifle forced. He considered seeking her out for the next dance but decided against it. Their earlier meeting had flustered her. He grinned to himself. It had thrown him, too, to discover just how much he wanted her. His inner smile grew and he shook his head a little, thinking of the mull he had made of his proposal. For once his charming address had deserted him, so it was no wonder he had startled her. But she was no fool. She would know he was in earnest, so he would leave her to become accustomed to the idea of being Lady Markham.

A movement nearby caught his attention. Lady Gisburne was making her way towards the door.

'Going so soon, ma'am?'

'I am. These late hours no longer agree with me.' She paused, her eyes following his gaze to the centre of the room.

'Are you hoping to dance with Miss Prentess? You will be disappointed, I think.'

'No, let Barnabus enjoy himself. I shall be calling upon Miss Prentess on Thursday.'

'Will you now?' She paused. 'And does the lady know of it?'

He smiled.

'She does indeed.' He dragged his eyes away from the dancers and fixed them upon the old lady's face. 'Why do you ask?'

She did not reply and for an instant Jasper wanted to take her into his confidence, to tell her he intended to make Susannah Prentess his wife. But no. She was Dominic's godmother, not his. His family must be informed first, and he would tell them just as soon as he had made his formal proposal to Susannah.

The dowager waved her hand as she finally replied, 'Oh, no reason. But if you are not going to dance again, Markham, then you can make yourself useful and escort me back to Laura Place.'

He laughed at that.

'Of course, ma'am. With the greatest of pleasure.'

Jasper had never been so impatient to be done with his estate business, but at length it was concluded and he could return to Bath. On Thursday morning he rose early and dressed with particular care, honouring the occasion with a morning coat of midnight blue, a white-embroidered waistcoat and buff coloured pantaloons tucked into shining Hessians. He arrived at Royal Crescent shortly before ten o'clock. He was shown into the morning room, where he found Mrs Wilby engaged with her tambour frame. She quickly put it down when he entered, and rose to greet him.

'Lord Markham, this is a pleasant surprise.'

He bowed over her hand.

'Did Miss Prentess not tell you I would be calling?'

'No, my lord, she did not.' She waved him to a seat. 'She has gone out.'

'Oh? And when do you expect her to return?'

'Not for some time, my lord. She is gone to Florence House with Lady Gisburne.' She noticed his frown and added quickly, 'They arranged it some days ago, I believe.'

'Then she did not tell you I intended to call?'

She fluttered her hands.

'No, but with all the excitement of the past few days I expect it slipped her mind.'

'Excitement, ma'am?'

She looked at him in surprise.

'Did you not know? She is engaged to Mr Barnabus.'

It took all Jasper's self-command to get him through the rest of the interview and back out into the street. While his mouth uttered the congratulations expected of him, his mind was seething with conjecture, none of which made any sense.

So she had accepted Gerald's proposal. But why now, when she had consistently turned him down in the past? And to do so within days of their explosive encounter on Monday evening? The two events must be linked. She had said she could not marry him—was that because she had already accepted Gerald? He paused, rubbing his chin. If that was so, why did she not tell him as much?

By the time he reached York House he was no nearer an answer and he strode on to Westgate Buildings, where he was informed Mr Barnabus had not yet left his room. He took the stairs two at a time and his knock upon the door was answered almost immediately.

'Jasper, come in.' Gerald was in his shirtsleeves, his cravat hanging loose about his neck. He stood aside to let Jasper enter. 'I thought you were at Markham.'

'I returned last night. I understand I should congratulate you.' Jasper watched him carefully. There was nothing but genuine pleasure in the young man's smile.

'Ah, you have heard then. She has accepted me at last.'

Jasper forced his own lips into a smile and said casually, 'You have been very busy while I have been away.'

'It was all agreed at the Upper Rooms on Monday. I was coming out of the tea room when we met and, well...' He paused while he deftly knotted his neckcloth, then grinned at Jasper. 'Suddenly we had agreed it all.'

'Extraordinary,' murmured Jasper.

'Isn't it?' said Gerald. 'I can't tell you how happy I am.' He glanced down at his watch. 'I cannot stay longer, I am afraid. I am off to Hotwells to see my mother.

I want to tell her myself and give her time to become accustomed to the idea before I take Susannah to meet her. Then we can decide upon when and where we are to be married.'

Jasper had been holding on to some faint idea that this was all a hoax, but now that hope died. Susannah would not deliberately serve Gerald such a trick. But something was wrong, he was certain of it, and if he was to prevent her making the biggest mistake of her life then he had to call a halt to this engagement, before it was too late.

He went back to his hotel and sent a note to Royal Crescent, formally begging for an interview with Miss Prentess as soon as she returned. Shortly before dinner he had his reply. He read the words aloud. 'Miss Prentess regrets she is not at home to callers.'

With a savage curse he screwed up the paper and hurled it into the fireplace.

Susannah and Lady Gisburne's visit to Florence House took the best part of the day, but Susannah was well satisfied with the result. Mrs Gifford was now back as housekeeper, and after accepting their condolences upon the death of her sister she sat down with them to discuss the running of the house. Lady Gisburne approved of all that had been achieved and promised to provide funds to enable more extensive repairs on the house to begin immediately. Before leaving, Susannah took some time to speak to the young ladies still in residence. There were only two, Lizzie and her baby having moved to Henrietta Street. Violet Anstruther was inclined to be tearful and required a great deal of comforting from Mrs Gifford, but Jane and her baby were doing well and Susannah was touched when Jane asked permission to call her daughter Susan.

'You were wise to start on a small scale,' Lady Gisburne commented as the carriage trundled back to Bath. 'Now word of Florence House is out I expect applications to increase rapidly.'

'Yes, sadly I believe that is true. There are any number of young women requiring our support. The rent from Odesse and the lace-makers helps, but it will not cover everything. Your help is very welcome in keeping the house running.'

'The papers are being drawn up even now, and I have sent out invitations for the little party on Saturday, to formally announce my patronage of Florence House.' The dowager gave a thin smile. 'There are times when a title is very useful, Miss Prentess. I have had very few refusals.'

'I am glad to hear it, My aunt and I are very much looking forward to coming to Laura Place for the event, I only wish Gerald could be back in time, but he writes to say Mrs Barnabus needs him for a few more days yet.'

With an alarming want of tact he had also written that his mother had been thrown into strong hysterics by the news of their betrothal, but she did not intend to share this news with anyone.

'Once you are married you may not be able to play such an active role,' remarked the dowager. 'You will have a family of your own to consider.'

Susannah looked away, uncomfortable with such thoughts. She had become engaged to Barnabus because he had seemed safe, he was inclined to worship her reverently, but she was well aware that once they were married he would expect her to allow him more than a chaste kiss on the cheek.

'My aunt has always been the main player in this, Lady Gisburne.'

'Tush, everyone knows now that you are the force behind Florence House.' The dowager smiled. 'It does not matter too much. Mrs Gifford is perfectly capable of handling the day-to-day running of the charity, and we will merely be patronesses, something that you can do even if you were to live many miles from here.'

Susannah frowned.

'Why should you say that? Mr Barnabus is very happy to make his home in Bath.'

From her corner of the carriage the dowager gave her an enigmatic smile.

'Sometimes one's plans can change,' she said.

The news that Lord Markham had called was no surprise to Susannah, although she told Aunt Maude she had quite forgotten about it. The viscount's subsequent note gave her a momentary panic, but her response was soon sent back to him and she hoped that would be the end of it.

'Indeed, I am quite fatigued with all the recent excitement,' she remarked as she sat down to dinner with her aunt. 'I think, while Gerald is away from Bath, I should like to have Gatley deny all visitors.'

Aunt Maude was immediately concerned.

'My love, this is quite unlike you, you usually have an abundance of energy. Are you sure you are not sickening for something?'

'No, no, of course not. I have been trotting a little too hard, as Gerald would say. I shall come about again very soon, you will see.'

'I sincerely hope so.' Aunt Maude picked up her knife and fork. 'Very well, we shall cancel all our engagements for a few days, and do nothing more strenuous than stroll to the Pump Room, where I am sure a glass of the waters will soon restore your spirits.'

The Pump Room was always popular, but any hope Susannah had that she might lose herself in the jostling crowd soon disappeared when she saw Jasper making his purposeful way towards her.

His greeting was abrupt, and when he suggested they might take a turn about the room together she politely declined. She remained resolutely beside her aunt, conversing with friends, then she took a cup of the waters, sipping at it reluctantly and doing her best not to screw up her face at the sulphurous taste, but all the time she was aware of the viscount's dark presence, waiting for his chance for a private word with her. It could not last, however. Lord Markham was far too distinguished a visitor to be allowed to stand idle. He was soon accosted by those claiming an acquaintance and he was obliged to move away. Eventually he left the Pump Room and the tension in her spine eased. She could relax again, and when she saw Kate Logan she hurried across the room to greet her.

'My dear, where have you been for such an age?' Susannah took Kate's hands and pulled her forwards to kiss her cheek. 'To go off for such a time, and never a word to me to say where you had gone.'

'I know, and I apologise,' said Kate. 'We arrived back too late last night to call upon you.'

'Never mind that, you are here now.' Susannah took her arm. 'Let us walk about the room and you can tell me where you have been.'

'I believe you have news, too, Susannah—'

'Yes, but you must go first,' she interrupted her. 'I insist.'

'Very well.' They walked on for a few steps and Susannah watched her friend biting her lip. She looked unusually pensive. 'I have been to Radstock.'

'Radstock!' Susannah laughed. 'What on earth can have taken you there?'

'Mr Camerton's mother lives there. Mr—that is—Charles and I are to be married.'

Susannah halted.

'But I thought—' She stared at her friend. 'I don't understand. I thought you had vowed never to marry again. After the last time…'

'I know, I thought I would never meet anyone who would make me change my mind on that, but I have.'

'No.' Susannah turned to her, taking her hands and giving them a little shake. 'Kate, you are funning. You must be. Your last husband was a monster, you told me he— That no man was worth the risk…'

Kate blushed and shook her head.

'I was wrong,' she said simply. 'When I met Charles I knew I was wrong.' She looked up suddenly. 'But you are a fine one to be admonishing me for my change of heart! I hear you are engaged, now, to Gerald Barnabus.'

'Yes, yes, but that is different,' argued Susannah. 'I will not be diverted, Kate. How can you be engaged to Mr Camerton? You have known him for only a few short weeks.'

'I know, but I love him, Susannah.' The smile and the soft look that transfigured the widow's face made Susannah's heart sink. 'He is a gambler, like me. We fell in love at the card table, then he came to call and took me riding, and we went walking in Sydney Gardens, and…' Kate looked up, her eyes shining. 'He has turned my whole world upside down, Susannah. He sends my spirits soaring heavenwards just by holding my hand. His smile lights up my day. And he feels the same way about me. I can hardly believe my good fortune. He loves me, he really does. So we are to be married, just as soon as the banns have been called.'

A cold, dark cloud wrapped itself around Susannah's heart as she listened to her friend. She thought of Gerald Barnabus, her own fiancé. She imagined him holding her hand, smiling at her and she felt nothing. Nothing at all.

Mrs Wilby was as good as her word and cancelled all their engagements for the whole week, with the exception of Lady Gisburne's party at Laura Place. Susannah was adamant that they must attend, but she was uncharacteristically nervous as she allowed Dorcas to dress her in her cream satin with the green ribbon ties.

'Stop fidgeting, miss, do,' Dorcas admonished her as she nestled tiny cream rosebuds amongst the golden curls piled up on her head. 'I've never known you in such a fret before a party.'

'Tonight's soirée means Florence House is no longer a secret, Dorcas,' Susannah told her. 'I am very anxious that it should be a success.'

But to herself she acknowledged that this was not the reason for her unease. Since her engagement to Gerald she had avoided Jasper's company, but tonight there could be no escape. She would have to face him.

'Well this is most satisfactory,' murmured Aunt Maude, looking around the crowded reception rooms in Laura Place, 'I believe all of Bath is here tonight.'

Susannah could only nod in agreement. Lady Gisburne had specifically noted on her invitations that the evening was to acknowledge her patronage of Florence House, a home for distressed gentlewomen, but only one or two people had stayed away. Everyone else was keen to congratulate the dowager upon her support of such a cause. Even Mrs Bulstrode was present, as well as Mr and Mrs Farthing, a generous donation from Lady Gisburne to the Walcot Street Penitentiary helping them to bury their resentment.

'A very different reaction to the one I received,' murmured Susannah.

'Unmarried ladies are expected to be more circumspect,' came her aunt's comfortable response. 'When you are Mrs Barnabus no one will think anything of you supporting such a cause. What a pity Gerald could not be here tonight.'

Susannah thought so, too, especially when Jasper appeared. Her heart began to hammer uncomfortably when she saw him walk in, his gleaming black hair brushed back from that handsome face. He bowed over the dowager's hand, and as he straightened his dark eyes raked the room. It was as if some second sense brought his gaze straight to her.

She squared her shoulders. It would be better to get this first meeting over, then they could be easy. Her confidence began to wane as he made his way towards her. He stopped to speak to others on his way, his easy manners and charming smile much in evidence, but when at last he stood before her there was a fierce, uncompromising look in his eye that made her want to run away. Instead she forced her knees to bend a little. She kept her hands firmly clasped about her fan.

'Lord Markham.'

'Miss Prentess.'

Aunt Maude was addressing the viscount, nervousness making her garrulous, but Susannah did not hear her and she suspected Jasper too was not attending. He was holding her eyes.

'I believe you have been indisposed, ma'am.'

'I, er, I have been resting, but I could not miss this evening.'

'I guessed as much, which is why I came.' He lowered his voice. 'You cannot avoid me for ever, you know.'

A sudden constriction in her throat made it difficult for Susannah to swallow. She kept her eyes on her fan, studying the intricate pattern on the sticks.

'I have no idea what…' Her voice tailed away when she looked up and met his hard eyes again.

Someone had claimed Mrs Wilby's attention. For the moment no one was attending to them and Jasper made the most of the opportunity.

'We will talk, alone.'

'No, I cannot. I—'

'You can and will.' He leaned closer. 'There is a small sitting room downstairs. The door to the left of the hall table. I will meet you there at midnight.'

'No.' She cast about wildly for an excuse. 'That is…'

In the press of the crowd no one saw him grip her arm.

'Midnight,' he said again. 'Be there, madam. You owe me that much.'

Jasper moved away and Susannah was free to circulate, to talk, but even while she conversed and smiled her mind was racing. He was angry with her and she could not blame him. She tried to tell herself he could not touch her now, she was engaged to Gerald, but somehow that thought did not reassure her as it should. She took a glass of wine to steady her nerves and tried to interest herself in the proceedings. She knew most of the people present, even the various single gentlemen who attended her card parties had turned out in force. At one point she found herself face to face with Mr Warwick. He looked confused for a moment, she thought he might speak to her, but after acknowledging her with a tiny nod of his head he hurried away. She wondered why. If it was true that he was the father of Violet Anstruther's child then he should be grateful to her. Florence House would take on the responsibility that he had shirked. Hunching one white shoulder, she turned away. Her eyes strayed to the clock on the mantelpiece. Eleven o'clock. Another hour and she would have to join Jasper in that downstairs room. Alone.

You do not have to go, a little voice in her head whispered seductively. *Think of the scandal. You are promised to another man. You should not go.*

But she would go, if only because she knew that Jasper would come after her if she did not. The minutes ticked by with agonising slowness. Lady Gisburne carried her away to introduce her to Lady this, and Lord that, but she could concentrate on nothing, only the hands of the clock steadily moving towards twelve.

The noise from the reception rooms died away behind her as Susannah slipped down the stairs. The hall was deserted save for a porter dozing in his chair by the front door. She could see the hall table, flanked by two identical doors. Pausing only to collect herself, she moved to the one on the left.

Susannah closed the door quietly behind her and

looked around. At first she thought the room was empty. A small fire and the single-branched candlestick provided only enough light to show her the empty satin-covered sofa and armchairs. Then a shadow moved by the window and she saw Jasper.

'I cannot stay long, my lord. I shall be missed.'

'Tell me why you are marrying Barnabus.'

She moved towards the fire, holding her hands out to the glow, more for distraction than any need of warmth.

'Is it not obvious?'

'Not to me.'

She ran her tongue across her lips. They were dry, a sign of her nervousness.

'He...he has courted me for months.'

'But you knew I was going to offer for you. Why did you not tell me then?'

'I did not think you were serious.'

'After what happened on the balcony of the tea room?' He gave a savage laugh. 'How passionate does a man have to be, madam, before you consider him *serious*?'

She did not move, keeping her attention on the hearth. She heard his hasty stride behind her.

'How passionate was Barnabus, when you accepted him?'

Her head came up at that.

'Gerald is a gentleman—'

'You mean he has not touched you.'

She fluttered her fan.

'He does not need to. We—'

'You have promised yourself to a man for whom you feel nothing.'

'That is not true!'

'Is it not?' He grasped her shoulders and turned her

to face him. 'Does the blood pulse through your veins when he touches you? Does Barnabus drive you to the brink of madness with desire?'

She shrugged him off.

'I do not want that.' Her cheeks were burning and she fanned herself rapidly.

'Did you accept him to escape from me?' When she did not reply he continued, 'So that's it. You are afraid of what is between us—'

'There is nothing between us!'

He took the fan from her and threw it down on the chair. Before she could protest he pulled her into his arms and kissed her savagely. Immediately her body sprang to life. The blood not only pulsed, it positively sang in her veins. She knew she must not give in. She put her hands on his chest, resisting the impulse to cling to his coat.

'Tell me you feel nothing for me.' His breath was hot on her neck as he covered her skin with kisses, each one burning even further through the defences she had erected. 'Tell me you do not want to lie here with me now and let me make love to you.'

With a superhuman effort she pushed herself away from him.

'That is desire, my lord, but it is not *love*.'

He towered over her, his face in shadow and his shoulders rising and falling with each ragged breath.

'If it is love to know I cannot live without you, that every day we are apart is a day in hell then, yes, Susannah, I love you.'

Lies, said the voice in her head. *He is a seducer. He will say anything to bend you to his will.*

She backed away, the pain of the separation tearing at her skin.

'Well, *I* do not love *you.*'

The words fell like lead weights into the silence between them.

'Do you love Gerald?'

She hesitated.

'We have mutual affection and respect. Love will follow.'

'Are you sure, Susannah?' He was closing in again, and once more desire and panic warred within her. 'Are you sure it won't be boredom that will follow? Dull complacency?'

She gave a sob.

'You do not understand. I am *safe* with Gerald. I can live my life in comfort, I will not be forever wondering if he is faithful to me, I will not risk…' she turned away, squeezing her eyes shut, trying to hold back the tears as she forced out the final words '…breaking my heart.'

Silence. Susannah could hear only the ticking of the clock. Surreptitiously she wiped away a rogue tear.

'Ah.' He uttered the word like a sigh. 'I would offer you my hand, my heart, my *life*, Susannah, but there is an element of risk in all things. This passion we feel for one another may burn out, though I do not believe it. You would have to trust me on that, but you have never trusted any man, have you?'

'Men in the grip of passion are unreliable,' she muttered. 'Even my own father, though he swore he loved my mother and came crawling back, begging for forgiveness on more than one occasion.'

'I cannot argue against that,' he said quietly. 'I know some men are feckless creatures, but not all of us. However, if you would rather have Barnabus—

'He loves me!'

'Then let us hope that is enough for both of you,

and that I have been mistaken in my own feelings.' He walked to the door. 'Goodbye, Susannah. I will not trouble you again.'

He went out, the door closing behind him. The emptiness and silence pressed in on her. Susannah felt then that she had lost something in her life. As though some prop, something necessary to her comfort, had been taken away.

Chapter Fourteen

Jasper did not go back upstairs. He was in no mood for company so he let himself out of the house and walked back to his hotel. He was promised to escort the dowager to the Abbey in the morning, but after that he would quit Bath. He had spent far too long here already and there was work on his estates that needed his attention. That should help to keep his mind from dwelling on Susannah Prentess. He should be glad to be leaving her behind. He had found her a patroness for Florence House, he had even endured an uncomfortable night in a chair there, to say nothing of slaving away in the kitchen to feed everyone, and for what? She was not even grateful. He shook his head and swung his cane at a clump of weeds pushing up at the roadside. He did not want her gratitude, he wanted to protect her, to make her comfortable—to make her happy. And if that meant he had to disappear from her life then so be it.

Susannah and her aunt did not attend the Abbey service the following morning. Jasper sat beside Lady Gisburne during the long sermon, impatiently waiting for the service to end so that he could get back to his rooms, where Peters was packing up everything in readiness for an early start in the morning. It was not until he was helping Lady Gisburne back into her carriage that Jasper told her he was leaving, hoping to fend off any questions by adding that he had business at Markham.

'No doubt it can wait a few more days.'

'I regret it cannot. My stay in Bath has been far longer than intended.'

'Because of Susannah Prentess.'

Her shrewd gaze was on his face but he kept his countenance impassive as he took his seat beside her.

'She was a distraction, I admit.'

'Hmm. I wondered how you would take it when you learned that she was to marry. What happened last night?'

He raised his brows.

'Last night, ma'am?'

The slight note of hauteur in his tone had no effect on the dowager.

'It was obvious to me that the two of you have been playing cat and mouse. Then you both disappeared last night. What did she say to you?'

He decided not to deny it. The old lady was too astute to be fobbed off.

'She intends to marry Barnabus.' He added bitterly, 'She feels safe with him. Safe! What she means is she thinks she can keep him under her thumb, poor devil!'

'Yes, I thought as much.'

He shifted his eyes to her face.

'You knew she was engaged to Barnabus, didn't you? You knew it that night, at the ball, before I went off to Markham. For pity's sake, why did you not tell me?'

'Would it have made any difference?'

'Yes! I might have reasoned with her—'

'As you did last night? When Susannah came back upstairs she looked positively distraught.'

A dull flush crept into his cheek.

'She inflames me,' he admitted. 'I find myself attracted to her like no other, and she feels the same, though she will not admit it. That is why I am going home in the morning. There is nothing here for me now.'

'Much as it pains me to contradict you, Markham,' replied the dowager untruthfully, 'you are not leaving Bath tomorrow. Dominic and his family are on their way, and he will expect you to be here to meet him.'

'I don't believe it!'

Ignoring his exclamation, the dowager continued impassively, 'I had an express from my godson this morning, telling me they will be arriving tomorrow.'

Jasper found a similar note waiting for him when he returned to York House. Peters received the change of plan with unimpaired calm, merely enquiring if he should instruct the hotel to prepare rooms in readiness for their arrival.

'No need. The dowager has invited them to stay with her at Laura Place.' He crumpled the note in his fist. 'It means we will not be returning to Markham tomorrow after all. I must at least stay to welcome them.'

'So tell me all about your engagement to Mr Barnabus.'

Susannah was strolling through Sydney Gardens with Kate, and was half-expecting the question. She had managed to avoid the subject since Kate's return to Bath, but had known that at some point she would have to explain.

'Oh well, he has been very persistent, you know, and he is such a sweet boy.'

'I thought you had turned your face against marriage.'

'No more than you, Kate,' she countered. 'I have heard you say many times that nothing would persuade you to take another husband.'

'I know.' Kate looked down, and Susannah saw the tell-tale blush mantle her cheeks. She could not remember Kate ever being out of countenance before Charles Camerton appeared, but recently she had changed, become much…softer, somehow. Now she gave a self-conscious laugh. 'I thought myself too old, too embittered to risk marrying again, but meeting Charles has changed my mind.' She glanced up. 'I am afraid he rather swept me off my feet, so much so that I confided in him about Florence House.'

'You did?'

'Yes, and I am very sorry for it. It is entirely my fault that your secret is known. You know how it is when you meet someone and you just want to talk and talk for ever? I am afraid I was not very discreet, and since I did not impress upon Charles that it *was* a secret he spoke of it in the Pump Room and—well, it went on from there. I suspected as much when we were so thin of company at your card party, and when I asked Charles he said he had mentioned it to Mrs Bulstrode, although thankfully he said nothing about the connection with Odesse. I know I should have told you immediately, but I did not want you to be cross with Charles. I hoped it might soon be forgotten. I beg your pardon, Susannah. Can you ever forgive me?'

So Jasper had not betrayed her. A dozen disjointed thoughts raced through her brain. If she had not been so quick to condemn him they might still be friends—more than friends. No. He roused in her such uncontrollable passions that friendship was not possible. She was engaged to Gerald now. Safe, dependable Gerald. That was what she wanted. She summoned up a smile.

'Of course I can forgive you, Kate. In fact, it has all turned out very well. If it had remained a secret then Lady Gisburne would not have learned of it and wanted to become our patroness. What I find it harder to understand is your sudden decision to marry.'

Kate's mouth twisted into a rueful smile.

'I was very strident, was I not, in my condemnation of all men? It comes from my years married to one who...'

Susannah squeezed her arm.

'You do not need to tell me, Kate. I knew you then, I saw what you went through, even though I was very young and everyone did their best to keep these things from the children. Infidelity was rife in Gibraltar. Even my own father was not above taking advantage of the camp followers.'

'How do you know that?' asked Kate quickly. 'I do not believe he would tell you such a thing, nor your mother.'

'I heard them arguing one night.' Susannah blushed at the memory. 'He said if Mama would not let him into her bed then he had to relieve his—his *passions* elsewhere.'

'Oh my dear, I am so sorry.' Kate squeezed her arm. 'Your mother had become very religious, had she not?'

'Yes, like her sister, although not quite such a zealot.' Susannah shivered. 'But that does not excuse his behaviour.'

'Do not be too hard on your father, my dear. He was a good man, in his way. Certainly not vicious, like Logan.'

'That is why I was so shocked when you told me about you and Charles Camerton.'

Kate sighed.

'I did not mean to fall in love with him, but I could not help it.' She laughed suddenly. 'I have broken all the rules I set for myself, have I not? I have listened to my heart, and not my head. But you must have done the same, my dear. Why else would you have decided to marry— Susannah, why do you look like that?'

Susannah shook her head, suddenly tears were crowding her eyes.

'Oh, Kate,' she whispered. 'I think I have made a terrible mistake.'

'Dom.' Jasper touched his brother's shoulder. 'I was told I would find you in the Pump Room, but I didn't believe it.'

Dominic turned, grinning. It was like looking into a mirror, thought Jasper. He still felt it, despite the livid scar that stretched across his twin's cheek.

'My godmother must drink the waters and my wife wants to gossip.' Dominic gripped his hand. 'How are you, Brother?'

'Well enough, thank you. I received your note yesterday, but I thought you would need the evening to recover.'

'Aye, after a whole day on the road the children were fractious and Zelah and I too tired to be good company.'

'I am pleased I did not take up your invitation to join you for dinner then! What brings you to Bath?'

Dominic's hard eyes flickered towards Lady Gisburne.

'Summoned. She told us *you* have been here for some time.'

'I came here after visiting Gloriana. She was afraid Gerald had fallen into the clutches of some harpy.'

'And had he?'

'Not at all.' Jasper spotted a speck of dust on his sleeve and flicked it away. 'The lady is an heiress. Considerably richer than Gerald, I believe.'

A soft voice called his name. Zelah was beside him, holding out her hands.

'Welcome to Bath, Sister.' He kissed her cheek. 'What brings you here? Your glowing looks tell me it is not for your health.'

'No, of course not.' She tucked her arm in his. 'Take me for a promenade about the room, Jasper.'

He glanced at Dominic, who nodded his approval.

'Aye, off you go, but don't keep her too long. I won't spend all day here.'

'Surly as ever,' commented Jasper as he led his sister-in-law away.

She laughed. 'No, no, he is much better now. When I met him he would not have dreamed of attending an assembly such as this. Now he is completely at his ease, and is not even conscious of his scars.'

'That is down to you, Zelah. We are all grateful for that.'

'Nonsense.' She blushed. 'He would have come about, in time. But this not why I wanted you to myself. Tell me about this lady who has stolen your heart.'

He stopped, exclaiming explosively, 'Who the devil—!'

'Lady Gisburne told us all about it last night.'

'Then she has been a great deal too busy!'

'Dom says he has never known you to take so much trouble over a woman.'

'Hell and damnation, I won't have my affairs discussed in this way,' he muttered in a furious undertone.

Zelah was not noticeably abashed, and merely made him walk on.

'So is it true? I do hope so, Jasper, because I never liked the idea of your pining over me. Tell me all about her.'

That drew a reluctant smile from him.

'You have grown very forward since you married my brother. But there is nothing to tell you, since she is going to marry Gerald Barnabus.'

'He is some sort of cousin of yours, is he not? And does she love him?'

'She will drive him to distraction.'

'That does not answer my question.'

'Does it matter?' he said impatiently. 'They are to be married. Barnabus has gone off to see his mother to arrange everything. There is nothing to be done.' Zelah's questioning gaze goaded him to add, 'Yes, I had some hopes there, but nothing serious.'

'Everyone tells me she is a great beauty.'

'Matchless.'

'But you have known many beauties, Jasper. What makes this one so different?'

He considered the question.

'Her spirit,' he said at last. 'She saw an injustice and has fought to do something about it, even at the expense of her own good name. She is very courageous…' he remembered the alarm in Susannah's hazel eyes when he had reached out for her '…at least, in some things.'

'Then I hope I shall meet this paragon, very soon.'

Jasper looked up.

'You shall do so now. Gerald is here, and he has Miss Prentess on his arm.'

Introductions were performed and Jasper sensed an air of unhappiness about Susannah. There was nothing in her manner to suggest she was melancholy, she smiled and conversed with her usual ease, save that she would not look at him. Perhaps it was his imagination, perhaps he merely wished to believe she was regretting her choice.

He was too distracted to take note of the conversation and suddenly realised that Zelah had left his side and was walking away with Susannah, declaring with a smile that they were off to talk of fashion and furbelows.

'We shall not see them again for some time,' he remarked, turning to Gerald. 'When did you get back from Hotwells?'

'Yesterday.'

'And how is Gloriana? How did she take your news?'

Gerald's eyes were fixed on the ladies as they walked away and he did not answer immediately.

'Very much as I expected. She was overset at first, but she saw I was not to be moved, and after a night's reflection she came round. I am to take Susannah to meet her next week.'

'That is good news then.' Jasper hoped his reply was sufficiently cheerful, but his companion did not respond. 'You do not seem particularly elated by your success.'

'Hmm? Oh, I am tired, I suppose.'

Jasper gave a crack of laughter.

'Tired, after a journey of just over a dozen miles? My dear boy, you should go and drink a cup of that foul-tasting water immediately.'

Gerald's smile was perfunctory.

'No need for that, it is just...' He sighed. 'I don't know if I can explain it to you. You will say that a fellow cannot be euphoric for ever, but…oh, you know how it is, Jasper. You want something so badly for a long time, then when you eventually achieve it, it is a trifle—' He broke off and gave a self-conscious laugh. 'This is all nonsense, of course. Susannah is everything I ever dreamed she would be.' He looked past Jasper. 'By Jove, is that your twin over there? I didn't know Dominic was here, too, that is famous, I must speak to him immediately.'

He dashed off, leaving Jasper to follow more slowly in his wake.

Susannah was never quite sure how Mrs Coale had managed to carry her off. One minute she was holding Gerald's arm and trying to steel herself to meet Jasper, who was watching her approach with a dark, unfathomable look in his hard eyes, the next she was promenading around the Pump Room with the slight, dark-haired lady that was Jasper's sister-in-law, telling her all about Florence House. At first she was a little wary, but Zelah's gentle manner and genuine interest soon had its effect and she found herself answering her questions quite freely.

'The dowager countess is most impressed with your efforts there,' remarked Zelah. 'That is no small compliment, believe me.'

'I am only too thankful that she thought the cause worthy of her attention.'

'Lady Gisburne loathes being bored and she was most thankful that Jasper brought your project to her attention.'

Susannah blinked.

'I did not know it was the viscount who told her

about Florence House. I thought she had merely heard the gossip.'

'Oh, no, she told me Jasper argued the case very strongly. And I believe there is a good modiste here that I must visit,' added Zelah, with a twinkling look. 'I intend to order at least one gown from Odesse while I am in Bath.'

The conversation turned towards fashion and in no time at all they had completed another full promenade of the room.

'Oh dear, I can see my husband is looking out for me.' Zelah chuckled as they came within sight of Lady Gisburne's party. 'Come along, let us join them.'

'Oh, but there is no need for me to come with you,' declared Susannah, hanging back. She could see Jasper standing beside his equally tall brother and was reluctant to go any closer.

'Nonsense, I must make you known to Dominic, and I can see Mr Barnabus is with them, too, so where else would you want to go?'

Unable to withstand the pressure of that small, determined hand on her sleeve Susannah accompanied Zelah to join the little group and said all that was proper when she was introduced to Dominic Coale. She resolutely kept her eyes averted from Jasper, but it was impossible not to think of him when she looked at his twin.

Even with the livid scar dissecting his cheek, she thought Dominic Coale as heart-stoppingly handsome as his brother. They shared the same thick, glossy black hair, the same regular features, the lean cheek and finely carved jawline, and if she fancied Jasper's smile a shade warmer and the glint in his blue-grey eyes a trifle more wicked, that was surely her imagination. While Dominic spoke to her she did her best to ignore Jasper, standing so close and silent, almost within touching distance. She could feel his presence, like a tangible force drawing her closer. She told herself that since Gerald was distantly related to the brothers she would have to grow accustomed to meeting Jasper. And she would do so. She had told Kate as much when they were strolling in the gardens yesterday.

Her tears had taken her by surprise and she had found herself admitting to Kate that she did not love Gerald.

'But he loves *me*,' she had said, wiping her eyes with the handkerchief Kate supplied. 'I cannot cry off, it would break his heart.'

'Better that he should be disappointed now than he should discover it later.'

'He shall *not* be disappointed,' Susannah declared. 'I will be a good wife to him. I *will*.'

'You are in love with someone else.' Kate's shrewd eyes did not miss the tell-tale flush that immediately coloured Susannah's cheek. 'Is it Markham? Are you in love with the viscount?'

'No.' Susannah knew her hasty denial was too vehement. She added quickly, 'And if I were it would make no odds. He cares nothing for me.'

'Oh, my poor girl, you have lost your heart to a rake!' Kate's sympathy had almost overset Susannah again. 'I can see how one might easily fall in love with such a man, but it will not do. He is too much a flirt, universally charming to any pretty woman, but you could never be happy for long with such a man. He is far too insubstantial for you.'

Susannah thought back to the night she had spent with Jasper at Florence House. There had been nothing insubstantial about him there when he took charge of the cooking, his orders to Bessie echoing around the cavernous kitchen. Nor had there been anything rakish in his manner when they were sitting together later, in the parlour. Not that it made any difference now.

She raised her head and said again, 'I shall make Gerald a good wife, I promise you.'

'...my love, shall we go? We arranged to meet your aunt at the circulating library.'

Gerald touched her elbow. Susannah turned to look at him, yesterday's words still ringing in her head.

'Yes, of course.' She waited until they were out in the sunshine before she spoke again and when she did it was with studied coolness. 'I thought Lord Markham and Mr Coale were only distant relations of yours, Gerald. Do you...do you expect to see much of them, when we are married?'

'Oh, I shouldn't think so,' he replied carelessly. 'Dominic rarely leaves Exmoor and Jasper divides his time between Markham and London. By Jove, I never thought!' He stopped, clapping his hand to his head. 'Should we look around for a country house, Susannah? It had not occurred to me that you might want to live elsewhere.'

'No, I would rather stay in Bath,' she said quickly. 'I have the house in Royal Crescent, after all. My aunt has already told me she intends to find a little place for herself once we are wed.'

'That will suit me very well, although perhaps we will make the occasional jaunt to town.'

'Of course, whatever will make you happy, Gerald.'

'Good heavens, marrying you will make me the happiest of men, my dear.' He kissed her hand. 'Now, here we are at Duffields—shall we go in and find your aunt?'

Chapter Fifteen

Jasper was glad to get up after a restless night and he was putting the finishing touches to his cravat when Peters announced that Mr Barnabus wished to see him.

'So early?' He took out his watch. 'You had best send him up.'

Jasper did not turn round when Gerald came in, but one glance in the mirror showed him that the young man was looking unusually serious.

'What is it, my young friend?' Jasper fastened his diamond pin into the snowy folds before turning away from the mirror. 'Are you in dun territory, perhaps? Do you need money?'

'Good heavens, no.' Gerald looked suitably shocked. 'My fortune ain't nearly as large as yours, Jasper, but it is sufficient for my needs. No, I need some advice.'

Jasper took another look at Gerald and knew a craven desire to fob him off.

'I am engaged to ride out with Dominic this morning,' he said, picking up his coat. 'Walk with me and tell me what is troubling you.'

They were out on the street before Gerald began.

'I think I have been a little rash in asking Miss Prentess to be my wife.'

'Oh?'

'I wonder if it is a mistake, for both of us. After all, as Mama pointed out to me, Susannah is a couple of years older than I.'

'That is no reason to cry off,' objected Jasper. 'You have chosen a lady who is both beautiful and rich. An ideal choice, most people would think.'

Gerald looked even more tortured.

'I know and she is. I have even convinced my mother that Susannah is the perfect partner for me.'

'Then what is the problem?'

'I thought I was in love with her, but recently, I am not so sure. She is the kindest, most generous of women, but there is not that grand passion that I expected to feel with the woman I intend to make my wife.' He looked up, his blue eyes troubled. 'I am afraid I am making a mistake, Jasper. I am very much afraid we shall both be rendered unhappy. What shall I do?'

Jasper regarded him steadily. This was his moment. One word from him and Gerald would break off his engagement. Susannah would be free again. The temptation was extreme, but Jasper knew he could not do it. At last he said abruptly, 'I am not the person to advise you on this, Gerald. You must make up your own mind. At the very least you should talk to Miss Prentess about it.'

With that he turned on his heel and walked away.

Susannah was gazing out of the drawing-room window. The snow had mostly disappeared from the Crescent, but there was still a covering of snow on Crescent

Fields. Kate stood at her shoulder. They had been going over the same subject for more than an hour.

'If you are unsure then you must talk to Gerald,' said Kate firmly.

'I cannot do that. It would wreck his dreams.'

'So you would marry him without love.'

Susannah turned away from the window.

'You are forgetting he loves me,' she said with a sad little smile. 'That must count for something.'

'But if you are in love with Markham—'

Susannah stopped her.

'Even if I were not to marry Gerald there is no hope for me there.' She thought of Jasper's frowning looks, the hard silence he maintained when she had seen him in the Pump Room. 'Lord Markham no longer cares for me. So I will marry Gerald, and at least one of us will be happy.'

'Your happiness is important, too!' Kate gave her a little shake. 'Promise me you will at least talk to Gerald. You are rich. You have no need to marry to secure your future comfort.'

Susannah gave a dispirited shrug. 'Loneliness is not comfortable.'

'It can be a great deal better than marriage to the wrong man,' returned Kate. She glanced out of the window. 'Barnabus is approaching now, another minute and he will be here.' She swept up her bonnet. 'I will leave you to talk to him alone. But remember, Susannah, treat him honestly now, or face a lifetime of regret.'

The news that the rich Miss Prentess and Mr Gerald Barnabus were *not* to be married spread even faster than the rumours of their engagement. Gossip-mongers like Mrs Farthing and Mrs Bulstrode might disapprove of Miss Prentess's fickleness, but mothers with daughters to dispose of were very happy that a genial young gentleman of independent means was once more on the marriage market.

Jasper was dining at Laura Place when the dowager countess announced the news as they commenced upon their soup.

'This is not Pump Room gossip,' she declared, looking around the dining table. 'I saw Miss Prentess myself today, to discuss Florence House. She told me she and Mr Barnabus had agreed they should not suit.'

Her sharp eyes flickered over Jasper, who maintained his outward calm.

'Will you call upon her?' Zelah was sitting beside him and she took advantage of the dowager's conversation with Dominic to ask her question.

'No. I have no reason to do so.'

She laid down her spoon.

'Jasper, I declare you are even more stubborn than your brother! As soon as I saw you and Miss Prentess together I knew you were in love.'

'You are right in so many cases, my dear Sister-in-law, but not in this.'

'Am I not? I think—'

'No.' He gave her a warning glance. 'Pray do not meddle in what you do not understand!'

He was thankful that no more was said and engaged to join them the following day for a party of pleasure, to drive out to Lansdown.

However, when he called the next morning he was met with the news that the children were too fractious to go out, and Lady Gisburne had bethought herself of urgent business to discuss with Dominic.

'Which leaves me at a loose end,' explained Zelah, buttoning her spencer. 'I thought you might like to escort me to Sydney Gardens.'

Jasper's eyes narrowed.

'I mislike that look in your eye, madam,' he said. 'What are you planning?'

Zelah opened her eyes at him.

'Why, nothing, Brother dear, 'tis merely that I want to see the canal. I am told it is perfectly charming with its overhanging trees and pretty iron bridges.' She took his arm. 'Come along, it is such a lovely morning and a walk in the fresh air will do us both good.'

Jasper's suspicions were not fully allayed, but he accompanied his sister-in-law to the gardens. The fine weather had brought out many visitors and their progress up the sweeping gravelled walk was slowed by the need to stop and speak to their numerous acquaintances, but at last Zelah guided her escort off the main path towards a much quieter part of the gardens.

'I believe there is a grotto down here where Sheridan courted Elizabeth Linley. He wrote verses about it, you know.'

'I thought you wanted to see the canal,' objected Jasper.

'I do, of course, but let us look for the grotto first.'

Jasper's earlier suspicions began to stir again. They were roused fully when he saw Susannah coming towards them. She was accompanied by Charles Camerton and Mrs Logan, and a swift glance at Zelah's countenance convinced him their meeting was not unplanned.

Mrs Logan waved to them. 'Mrs Coale, Lord Markham, what a surprise.'

Susannah's look of shock seemed real enough.

'I did not know you were acquainted with Mrs Coale, Kate.'

'We met at the Pump Room yesterday.' Kate quickly passed on to introducing Mr Camerton, and Jasper took the opportunity to observe Susannah.

She was a little pale but otherwise composed. She looked as if she would prefer to be anywhere but in his vicinity. His inner demon took a perverse satisfaction in it. If this was a ruse to throw them together then it was not going to work. However, he had reckoned without his resourceful sister-in-law. After a few moments' conversation she clapped her hands in delight.

'Well, is this not my great good fortune? Mr Camerton is taking the ladies to see the grotto, too, and he has been regaling them with all sorts of stories about Mr Sheridan's time in Bath. It is clearly the most salacious gossip, and I am desperate to hear it!'

'Can events that happened forty years ago be considered gossip?' Jasper enquired.

Charles Camerton had the grace to look a little guilty. 'The ladies seem to like it.'

'Well, since you do not wish to listen you may give your arm to Miss Prentess for a little while,' said Zelah. 'She will not want to hear the stories again. There, now we can all be comfortable. Shall we walk on?'

The party thus rearranged they began to move, Jasper and Susannah following the others. Jasper sought for something to say to break the awkward silence.

'I fear we are the victims of two extremely managing female minds. I acquit Charles of being anything more than a pawn in their hands.'

'I beg your pardon.'

Her despondent manner wrenched at his heart.

'Come now, this is not like you,' he said in a rallying tone. 'You are more like to rip up at me.'

She gave a little shake of her head, keeping her face averted.

'I have treated you very badly. Kate told me it was Mr Camerton, and not you, who divulged the secret of Florence House.'

'To good effect, since you now have a patroness.'

She looked round at that.

'I am aware that I have you to thank for that, too.'

He raised his hand and touched her pale cheek.

'You have had a very horrid time of it recently, I think. Were you sorry to terminate your engagement?'

'No. I was more concerned for Gerald, but when he told me the true state of his feelings I knew we must call it off.'

Jasper hesitated before saying slowly, 'Perhaps you are afraid of marriage.'

'Perhaps I am, a little.'

'Because of what happened to your sister.'

'Not just that.'

Her fingers trembled against the crook of his arm and he brought his hand up to cover them.

'Will you not tell me?'

'I have tried for so long to blot it out,' she whispered. 'I have told no one.'

Jasper looked up. They had fallen some way behind the others.

'There is no one to hear us, only the trees.' He pressed her fingers. 'Have we not shared enough for you to know you can trust me with your confidences?'

'Every experience I have had has shown me that men are not to be trusted.'

'You trusted Gerald enough to become betrothed.'

'Gerald was never a town beau.'

'Yet still you cannot bring yourself to marry him.'

'I began to think, to realise. At some stage he would want to— I would have to...' She shuddered. 'I could not bear the thought of it.'

'Tell me, Susannah.'

They walked on in silence. Jasper kept his hand over hers where it rested on his sleeve. He wanted to pull her into his arms, to kiss away her sadness, but she was tense, like a filly on the edge of bolting. She began to speak.

'My Uncle Middlemass took me to London when I was eighteen. You know his money came from trade, so there was no formal presentation at court, but he had many acquaintances in town, so our society was not limited. On one evening at a party I recognised the young man who had courted Florence. He did not recognise me—even when we were introduced he did not remember the name. I was incensed. I followed him and his friends to the card room. I told him what had happened to Florence—' She broke off. A gentle wind was sighing through the trees and making the spring flowers dance around them, but she did not notice any of it, her eyes fixed upon some unseen point in the distance.

'He laughed. He said if she had been foolish enough to give herself to him then she deserved her fate. They were all laughing, all those fashionable young men with their windswept hair and elegant neckties, laughing at the fate of my poor sister. Then he grabbed me and began to...to kiss me. He said he'd wager I was as wanton as my sister. If it had not been for the timely entrance of a servant I do not think he would have stopped. And the others were standing by, watching.' She shivered. 'I managed to make my escape but I will never forget. He was laughing as I fled down the stairs. He saw women as nothing but playthings for his pleasure.'

'And then?' demanded Jasper, his temper rising. 'Surely Middlemass took action against this man?'

'No, I never told him of it. My uncle had a weak heart. I was afraid if he knew, it would make him ill.'

Susannah looked back over the years. It was all such a long time ago. She had never spoken of it, not even to Kate, but somehow, telling Jasper was a relief. Now perhaps he would understand her panic. Suddenly, walking with him here in Sydney Gardens with the spring sunshine warm on their backs, the past did not seem quite so horrific. She stole a glance at Jasper. He was scowling as he digested all she had told him. He, a man of fashion with a reputation as a breaker of hearts, was part of that set that she despised, but somehow he did not quite fit. Perhaps she was wrong. Perhaps not all men were the same.

He turned his head suddenly, his blue-grey eyes locking with hers and she was aware of that familiar breathlessness, but the panic she had felt before did not engulf her. Instead she was relieved that he was beside her. She was comfortable in his company. Thinking back, she realised it had been the same when they had been together at Florence House. Perhaps...

'I am honoured by your confidences, Miss Prentess, but I think we should catch up with the others. Mrs Logan will be anxious about you.'

How formal he was, how polite. He lengthened his stride and she was obliged to quicken her own step to keep up with him.

'I am quite capable of looking after myself, my lord.'

She uttered the words almost as a challenge, hoping he would contradict her. When he did not, she tried again. 'I think you were correct, sir, when you surmised that Mrs Logan and your sister-in-law engineered this meeting to throw us together.'

'Yes, but you need have no fear, madam. I have no intention of importuning you.'

'Oh.'

Susannah's spirits swooped even further. He threw her a quick smile.

'I am well aware of your low opinion of me, madam. My actions in the past have only reinforced that, but I do not intend to repeat them.'

Susannah swallowed her disappointment. They had caught up with the others so there was no time to reply. Jasper offered his arm to Zelah as they approached the secluded grotto and did not address Susannah again until the two parties split up. Then he took her hand and saluted it before walking off with his sister-in-law on his arm.

'Well?' Kate waited only until the viscount was out of earshot before turning to Susannah, an eager question in her eyes. Susannah merely returned her look and Kate almost stamped her foot. 'What did he say to you?'

Susannah gave an exaggerated shiver.

'The wind is growing a little chill. Perhaps, Mr Camerton, you would escort us back to town now?'

'Susannah!'

Mr Camerton chuckled as he offered both ladies an arm.

'You had best tell her, Miss Prentess. She can be extraordinarily tenacious.'

'There is nothing to tell.'

'You mean he did not make you an offer?'

Susannah shook her head.

'No. He behaved like a perfect gentleman.'

Zelah was less complimentary about her brother-in-law.

'You are a complete nodcock,' she told him bluntly as they strolled back through the gardens. 'We gave you every opportunity to put things right with Susannah Prentess—'

'There is nothing to put right,' he argued. 'And I am shocked that you and the lady's so-called friends should design to place her into such a position, alone with a man and unchaperoned.'

'The lady was clearly not averse to your company,' she observed. 'You had your heads together for most of the time you were together.'

'She confided in me. I understand perfectly now why she does not wish to marry.'

'Why not, when she is clearly in love with you?'

'Do you think so?'

Zelah laughed.

'Of course. Why, her eyes followed you from the moment we met. Dear heavens, Jasper, you have never doubted your attraction before!'

It was true, but it had never mattered so much to him before. The knowledge that he was in love with Susannah Prentess had shaken him badly. Until he had actually uttered the words at Lady Gisburne's party he had not realised it.

And for once in his life he was not sure how to proceed.

'She has been hurt,' he said at last. 'Frightened very badly. I must go gently, give her time to recover. Besides…' another objection reared its head '…I am not convinced she and Gerald are not in love.'

However, a chance meeting with that young man later that day put all doubts to flight. They met in Stall Street and Gerald explained that he was off to the theatre with friends that evening.

'You are not regretting your new-found freedom then?' said Jasper, smiling.

Gerald grinned.

'Not at all, I am supremely happy about it. And the added bonus is that I don't have to go to the Upper Rooms tonight.' He took Jasper's arm and began to walk with him. 'You know I had my doubts about the betrothal, and I went to Royal Crescent to discuss it with Susannah, as you suggested, but I had hardly begun when she interrupted me to say that she had changed her mind, that we would always be friends but that she could never love me. I cannot tell you how relieved I was. In fact, we laughed over it, once we had agreed to part. She is such a darling girl, but I can see clearly now that we would never suit. The hardest part will be telling my mother. After working so hard to convince her that Susannah was the only woman for me I now have to tell her it was all a hum!' They had reached Stall Street and prepared to part. 'I am going to see her tomorrow,' said Gerald, moving away. 'Wish me luck!'

Smiling at the memory, Jasper made his way back to York House. It would appear Miss Prentess was indeed free. If Zelah was correct and Susannah did feel something for him, then why wait to put it to the touch again? He thought back to what she had told him in Sydney Gardens, the confidences she had shared. What if she was not warning him off but merely trying to explain to him her previous actions? The thought raised his spirits. He must talk to her.

Jasper took out his watch. It was nearly dinnertime, he would write to her, making his intentions perfectly clear and telling her he would call tomorrow morning. He would send the message tonight, so that it would be waiting for her when she returned from the Assembly Rooms. That would give her time to make up her mind. If she did not wish to see him a short note by return would spare her the pain of a meeting, although it would be sufficient to end his hopes. But that would be her choice. Perhaps all was not yet lost.

Susannah had no inclination for dancing, but they had promised to attend the Fancy Ball and she must keep her word. The Upper Rooms were as full as ever, and there was no shortage of partners, but she did not enjoy herself. By the time the interval came to take tea she had given up all hope of seeing Jasper, which made the evening even more dull and she was relieved when eleven o'clock struck and she could go home.

Susannah and Aunt Maude took chairs to Royal Crescent, but being a fine night they alighted on the pavement and shook out their skirts before ascending the scrubbed steps to the front door. They had barely entered the house when a body hurled itself off the street and into the hall, causing panic. Mrs Wilby shrieked as Gatley laid hands on the intruder. In the ensuing struggle they fell against the hall table, sending the silver tray clattering to the floor. Above the mayhem Susannah heard the man call out to her.

'Miss Prentess, a minute of your time, I beg you!'

She peered through the gloom.

'Mr Warwick? What in heaven's name is the meaning of this?'

'I must speak to you.'

The young man gazed at her. His hair was dishevelled and there was a wild look in his eyes, but when the butler tried to hustle him out of the door she put out her hand to stop him.

'Wait, Gatley. Let him speak.'

'I called earlier, but you were out.'

'Aye, that he did, miss,' averred the butler, panting slightly. 'About eight o'clock.'

'Goodness, and you have been waiting outside ever since?'

'Yes.' He raked his hand through his hair. 'I have been walking up and down, waiting for you to return. You are my last hope.'

Mrs Wilby tutted loudly. 'I hardly think this is the time—'

'Hush, Aunt.'

Susannah regarded her visitor with some concern. With his crumpled neckcloth and haggard eyes he looked more like a ragged schoolboy than the fashionable gentleman she had welcomed into her drawing room on countless occasions.

'Come along into the morning room, Mr Warwick. We will talk there.' She observed the shocked faces around her. 'You must come, too, Aunt, and Gatley shall remain in the hall, where we may call him if necessary.'

She handed her cloak to the goggling footman and ushered her unexpected guest into the morning room. He allowed himself to be pushed down gently into a chair and once Susannah had made sure that the door was closed and Aunt Maude was comfortably seated, she took a seat opposite Mr Warwick and asked him the reason for his visit.

Immediately he jumped up and began to stride about the room, wringing his hands together. She waited patiently. At last he stopped and turned to her.

'Miss Prentess. I want to see Miss Anstruther!'

Aunt Maude gave a little gasp, but Susannah said merely, 'Go on.'

'I have treated her abominably.' He began to pace the room. 'I cannot eat, cannot sleep—I cannot forget her. She has been on my conscience ever since I knew—' He broke off and returned to his chair, burying his face in his hands.

'I have been to Shropshire, to visit her parents, but they told me they have no idea where she is.' He pushed his fist against his mouth. 'They abandoned her. She might be dying in a gutter for all they know! How could they be so cruel?'

'And what of your own actions, sir?' Susannah demanded, her voice icy. 'Do you hold yourself blameless in all this?'

'No, no, not at all! When she told me, I w-was frightened, I refused to acknowledge that the child was mine. I thought Mr Anstruther would call me out, that I should be disgraced.'

'As you deserved to be,' put in Aunt Maude, with uncharacteristic severity.

He turned to look at her.

'I know, ma'am. I am well aware of that. It took me a long time to come to my senses, to realise that I had to present myself to her parents, to own up to my actions and ask for Violet's hand in marriage. But then, when I arrived at the house and was told she was not there—'

'So why do you come to me, Mr Warwick?'

'I have scoured the city, I called at Walcot Street, but they denied all knowledge of Miss Anstruther. Your charity is my last hope. I have no idea where the house may be, but I remember hearing that it is a refuge for young ladies such as Violet. So I came here, hoping, praying, that she might be one of the lucky ones.' His wild, frightened eyes fixed themselves upon Susannah. 'Tell me if she is there, Miss Prentess.'

Susannah watched him. There was no doubt of his distress.

'And if she should be under my care,' she said slowly, 'what do you intend by her?'

'To throw myself at her feet, to beg her forgiveness and to make amends. I want to marry her, Miss Prentess, if she will have me. If not, I want to support her and my child. I must make some reparation for what I have done.'

Mrs Wilby sat forwards, saying gently, 'That is all very well, Mr Warwick, but we would need to ascertain the young lady's wishes in this case.'

'But that is not the end of it.' Mr Warwick was on his feet again. 'William Farthing told me that his mother had written to Mrs Anstruther, suggesting Violet might be at Florence House. He said his mother had received a reply this morning. Mr Anstruther is even now on his way to Bath, intent upon taking his daughter back to Shropshire with him. You do not know him, Miss Prentess. He is a cruel man, he will incarcerate her and force her to give up the child, if it is allowed to live. And Violet is under age—he is still her legal guardian.'

'Well goodness gracious me!'

Susannah paid little heed to her aunt's exclamation. She was thinking quickly.

'Very well, Mr Warwick. Can you have a travelling

carriage here first thing tomorrow morning? I will take you to Florence House to see Violet. If she is agreeable, then my maid shall accompany you both to Gretna Green. However, the decision must be Violet's. If she does not want to go with you then I will find somewhere to hide her.'

Mrs Wilby gave a little shriek.

'But, Susannah, if her father should bring the law down upon us…'

Susannah shrugged. 'We will deal with that problem if and when it arises.' She rose. 'I suggest you go home now, Mr Warwick, and get some sleep.'

He came up and clasped her hand, kissing it fervently.

'Thank you, ma'am, thank you. I shall be here at eight, without fail!'

Chapter Sixteen

The sun streaming through the curtains roused Jasper. He looked at his watch. It was very early, but he knew he would not sleep again. Today he was going to ask Susannah Prentess to marry him. There had been no reply from Royal Crescent, and he was sure that if Susannah was going to refuse him she would have replied immediately. He got up, calling for Peters to bring hot water. He would shave now and get dressed. Not in the clothes he planned to wear for his visit to Royal Crescent, but the plain dark riding coat and buckskins that he could walk out in, to pass the hours until he could see Susannah. He strode out of the town and up on to Beechen Cliff. The wind was warm, a promise of the summer to come. Jasper smiled to himself. A good omen, perhaps? A sign that the gods were smiling upon him. He heard the distant chiming of a bell on the breeze as he headed back towards York House. As long as there was no note waiting for him, he would call on Susannah at ten o'clock. There was plenty of time for a leisurely breakfast and to change into his morning coat and knee breeches before setting off for the most momentous meeting of his life.

'Peters, Peters! Where the devil are you?' He strode through the rooms, frowning. Then he heard the scurry of footsteps behind him.

'My lord, thank heaven you are back!' Peters ran in, one hand on his chest which was heaving alarmingly as he gasped out his explanation. 'I was out collecting your best shirt from the laundrywoman. Knew you would want to wear it this morning. I was about to cross Gay Street when a travelling carriage comes down the road. Naturally I stepped back out of the way, but happened to look up as it went past me, and I saw who was in it.'

'Well, what of it?'

Jasper looked at him impatiently, he had more important things on his mind. Should he wear his white quilted waistcoat or the oyster satin with the pearl buttons?

'It was Miss Prentess, my lord. Large as life.'

Jasper forgot about waistcoats.

'*What?* Are you quite sure?'

'Yes, my lord. The carriage was forced to slow to wait for a bullock cart to get out of the way and I had plenty of time to look.' Peters paused to regain his breath.

'And is there a note for me from Royal Crescent?'

'No, my lord. I left word at the desk that any messages were to be brought upstairs immediately.' The valet added in a colourless voice, 'She was travelling with young Mr Warwick, my lord.'

His words hit Jasper like cold water. She was running away from him. She knew he intended to make her an offer and she was too afraid to tell him to his face that she could not marry him. So that was it. Over.

Peters was still talking.

'It was a smart turn-out, my lord, four horses, no expense spared, I'd say, and a couple of trunks strapped to the roof. I've got a lad following the carriage to see which way they are heading and to report back. And I sent word to the stable for Morton to bring your curricle round.'

Jasper turned on him with and growl.

'Dammit, Peters, I have never yet chased after any woman!'

The valet gave him a long stare.

'This isn't any woman, my lord. It is Miss Prentess.'

Aye, and she didn't want to face him. First she had used Gerald Barnabus to protect her. Now Warwick. Devil take it, why should he care?

Only Warwick was not Gerald. Warwick was not a diffident young man who would treat Susannah gently if she refused his advances. Jasper did not know the man well, but if the rumours were anything to go by he was a hot-headed young buck who had already ruined one lady's reputation.

He picked up his hat and gloves.

'By God you are right. I must go after her!'

Susannah paced up and down the parlour at Florence House, anxiously pulling her gloves through her hands. Mrs Gifford was sitting by the window quietly mending a pillowcase.

'Perhaps I should not leave them alone.'

Mrs Gifford looked up, her kindly old eyes twinkling.

'My dear, Violet was quite happy to afford the young man a private interview.'

'I know, but perhaps he is coercing her.'

'They are only in the next room. She has but to raise her voice and we would hear it.' The housekeeper picked up her scissors and snipped the thread. 'Be patient,' she said, putting away her needle and folding up the pillowcase. 'You were sufficiently convinced of Mr Warwick's sincerity to bring him here. Now let him make his case to the lady.'

Susannah stopped pacing.

'I may be wrong,' she said. 'Until very recently I would not put my trust in any man—' She broke off as the adjoining door opened and the young couple came in. One look at Violet's happy face told her that everything was well.

'Miss Anstruther has consented to become my wife,' declared Mr Warwick, following Violet into the parlour. He caught her hand and smiled down at her. 'We want to be married immediately, so that no disgrace shall be attached to my child.'

The proud note in his voice as he uttered the last two words was unmistakable. Mrs Gifford caught Susannah's eye and smiled.

'That is settled then.' The housekeeper got up from her chair and came forwards to envelope Violet in a motherly embrace. 'I wish you very well, my dear.'

'You understand what you must do?' Susannah asked Violet.

The girl nodded. 'We fly to Scotland immediately, I understand that.'

'But Miss Prentess is sending her own maid to act as your chaperon and look after you until we can be married,' Mr Warwick told her. He addressed Susannah. 'I will not risk a meeting with Anstruther until Violet is my wife, but once I have her safe then I shall write to him. I hope he will recognise the connection.'

'And if he will not?' asked Susannah gently.

'Then I shall take Violet to my own family. I have

already written to apprise them of the situation.' The young man met her gaze steadily. 'I have told them what a fool I was not to accept my responsibilities immediately.'

'Oh, no, no,' cried Violet. 'You were shocked, frightened, I quite understand.'

His arm went about her.

'Ah, sweetheart, you are an angel to be so forgiving, but I must bear some blame...'

'Yes, yes, you can discuss all this in the carriage,' Susannah interrupted them. 'If you are going to make any headway at all today then you need to be setting off as soon as may be. We know your father is on his way to Bath, Violet. It would be better if he did not find you here.'

'No indeed.' Violet's eyes darkened with fear. 'I will go and collect my things, and I must say goodbye to Jane and Lizzie, and the babies.'

She hurried away, returning a few minutes later with her meagre belongings packed in a single portmanteau and her travelling cloak around her shoulders. Mrs Gifford provided a basket of food and a flask of wine to refresh them on their journey and Susannah accompanied them to the door, where the carriage was waiting.

'I cannot tell you how very grateful I am to you, Miss Prentess.' Violet hugged her. 'Without your kindness I do not know what would have become of me.'

'You need not think of that now. You have no doubts about marrying Mr Warwick?'

'Oh, no, none at all.' Violet's eyes positively shone at the prospect. 'But how will you manage without your maid? Who knows how long we will be gone?'

'I shall miss her, of course, but she is by far the best person to look after you on your long journey,' replied

Susannah, sending a laughing glance towards her servant as she helped Violet into the carriage. 'You have sufficient money with you, Dorcas? I do not want you to leave Miss Anstruther until she has hired a suitable maid.'

'Don't you worry, miss, I'll make sure she takes on someone that knows how to look after her. 'Tis you I am more concerned about, miss,' said the maid gruffly. 'Without me to dress you.'

'I shall fetch Mary upstairs to help me,' replied Susannah. 'You said yourself she has ambitions to be a lady's maid. Now go along, and look after your new charge.'

A flurry of goodbyes, a few last minute words of advice and the carriage was shut up.

'Ah, they are such children,' declared Mrs Gifford, wiping her eyes with the corner of her apron. 'I pray they will be happy.'

'So, too, do I,' muttered Susannah fervently.

She stepped back and raised her hand in a final salute as the coachman gathered up the reins. He was about to pull away when the clatter of hooves announced another vehicle approaching.

'Oh, good heavens, who can this be?' exclaimed Mrs Gifford. 'Never say Mr Anstruther is here already!'

'No indeed.' Susannah's voice faltered as she recognised the curricle sweeping through the gateway. 'It is Lord Markham.'

He had seen her. He checked his horses and turned on to the carriage circle. Susannah looked at the coachman.

'He is not obstructing the gates, you can go. Quickly.' She turned to the housekeeper. 'You too should go inside, Mrs Gifford. I will join you presently.'

She stepped on to the drive in front of the approaching curricle. If the viscount had any thoughts of pursuing the carriage then she would at least delay him.

'Lord Markham,' she hailed him cheerfully. 'What brings you here?'

He brought the horses to a plunging halt, just feet away from her.

'I might ask you the same question.' He waited until his groom had run to the horses' heads and jumped down. 'And *who* was driving away in that carriage?'

She knew of no connection between the viscount and Mr Warwick or Violet Anstruther, but she could not be sure. She kept her smile in place.

'There is a cold wind, my lord, and I have left my cloak in the parlour. Shall we continue this discussion indoors?' She heard his firm step on the gravel as he followed her to the house. The parlour was empty and the viscount closed the door upon them with a snap.

'Now will you tell me what the devil is going on?'

Jasper sounded angry and she turned to him, frowning slightly.

'I do not understand you.'

'You were seen leaving Bath this morning. In the company of Mr Warwick.'

'What of it?'

'You could have told me you would not be at home.'

Her frown deepened.

'Why should I do that? This is no business of yours.'

He looked as if he would argue, then thought better of it.

'So why has he left you here? Where has he gone?'

She regarded him in silence for a few moments. She did not understand him. Yesterday he had been so friendly, so understanding that she had wanted to confide in him, to have no secrets between them. But that had been a mistake. He had clearly been shocked and appalled at what she had told him, for he had left her abruptly, with no word of comfort, nothing to say he wanted to continue the acquaintance. Now here he was, frowning at her, demanding to know what she was about. Did he think because he had stayed at Florence House, helped her during the birth of Jane's baby, that he was entitled to an explanation? She tried to put aside her own hurt feelings and think logically.

'You had better sit down, my lord, and I will try to explain.'

'Thank you, I prefer to stand.'

'Very well.' She sank down into the armchair beside the fire. 'There was talk in Bath—you may have heard it—that Mr Warwick was the father of Violet Anstruther's baby.'

'What of it?'

'It is true. Mr Warwick initially denied all involvement in the case, but when Violet disappeared he had a change of heart. He has been searching for her for some time, I believe. He came to me last night to ask if she was here. He wanted to make reparation, to marry her. He appeared to be in earnest so I brought him to see her.'

'In a travelling carriage.'

'He has taken her to the border.'

'So you were not running away with him.'

'Of course not!'

'But it was very convenient for you, to go out of Bath so early this morning, Miss Prentess.'

She blinked at the scathing note in his voice. She had cried herself to sleep last night over the loss of his friendship, but that was over. He could not touch her heart, hurt her, ever again.

'It was necessary,' she said coldly. 'Mr Warwick believes Mr Anstruther is even now on his way here to wrest his daughter away from us. May I ask why you are so interested in this case, my lord? What is it to you?'

'I have no interest at all in Warwick and Miss Anstruther.' He was pacing up and down, his black brows drawn together. 'But it is not the first time you have left Bath to avoid meeting me.'

'I do not know what you are talking about.'

He stopped pacing and stared at her.

'Did you not receive my note?'

'Note, sir? What note? What did it say?'

She fancied a dull flush tinged his cheek, but he turned away and she could not be sure.

'Nothing. It is not important. Tell me, Miss Prentess. How do you intend to get back to Bath?'

'Do you know, my lord, until this moment I had not considered. I have no idea.'

He came to stand before her, calm and assured.

'Then I can offer you a solution, madam. My curricle is outside. I will convey you to Royal Crescent.'

Susannah might tell herself she felt nothing for him, but when Jasper was standing over her, the capes of his driving coat making his shoulders look so impossibly broad, it was difficult to ignore his powerful presence. Her heart was thudding painfully in her chest but she tried to think sensibly. It was a perfectly logical solution. A dignified, graceful acceptance was all that was required, but her nerves had been at full stretch the whole morning and she could not control the torrent of words that poured forth.

'Thank you. Unless perhaps I should remain here in

case Mr Anstruther should appear. What do you think? I do not consider it at all likely that he will arrive today, and I have every confidence that Mrs Gifford will be able to convince him that his daughter was never here— we keep a record of all our residents of course, but she enters false names for them, you see.'

Susannah listened to herself, horrified, knowing she had only stopped because she had run out of breath.

'I believe you can leave Mrs Gifford to deal with Mr Anstruther, if he should arrive,' replied Jasper. 'You should come back to Bath with me, now.'

'Very well.' She rose and went to the table to collect her bonnet and gloves. 'I must say that your arrival is very convenient. I would have had to ask old Daniel to take me home in the gig.'

His lips twitched.

'I fear that a common gig would never do for you, Miss Prentess.'

He picked up her cloak and put it around her shoulders. The touch of his hands, fleeting though it was, instantly brought a reaction. Her body tensed, every nerve on end, anticipating the next contact. Dear heaven, she must get over this! She quickly stepped away from him.

'I shall take my leave of Mrs Gifford and our guests, and join you outside.'

Jasper stood on the drive and breathed deeply, taking the cold, clear air into his lungs. She had not seen his message. She did not know he had intended to make her an offer. The mixture of frustration and rage that had consumed him during his headlong dash to Florence House was still simmering within him. She was the most infuriating woman he had ever met. He could not pin her down, she was constantly surprising him.

Perhaps he should not propose to her. He never knew

where he stood with Susannah from one moment to the next. And the emotions she aroused in him—would he ever be in control if he allowed her into his life? He turned in time to see her coming out of the house, tying the ribbons of her bonnet beneath her chin as she walked towards him. The bonnet was not the frivolous, over-decorated confection preferred by most fashionable ladies, but its stylish simplicity was very becoming. The pale satin lining of the wide brim gave her countenance an added glow, and the jaunty angle of the bow drew attention to the dainty chin and those cherry lips, just waiting to be kissed.

No! After what she had told him yesterday he dare not indulge in such fantasies. No wonder she was so afraid of his embraces. He schooled his features into what he hoped was a polite smile and waited to help her into the curricle. The hesitation she showed before allowing those slender fingers in their kid glove to touch his hand was confirmation that she was still wary of him.

He set the team in motion, waiting for Morton to scramble up behind him before settling them into the swift, comfortable pace that would carry them all the way to Bath. She made an innocuous comment about the weather. He responded with a monosyllable. Jasper kept himself rigidly upright, trying not to react when the jolting of the curricle threw her against him. The silence between them seemed to grow more awkward as the miles passed. Finally he cleared his throat.

'I shall be leaving Bath tomorrow.'

'I am surprised you have stayed so long, my lord.'

Her cold response disappointed him. Not even a polite word of regret. He retorted bitterly, 'It was not my original intention.'

'I hope you do not blame me for that.'

'Who else should I blame? It was my cousin's interest in you that brought me here in the first place.'

She stared at him.

'I told you at the outset I had no intention of marrying Gerald.'

'And then you became engaged to him.'

She turned away again, but not before he had seen the shock in her eyes. He might as well have struck her. Remorse flayed him, but it only added to his frustration.

'You know that was an error.' She added, with something of her old spirit, 'But it is not one I intend to repeat.'

'I am glad to hear it. I pity any man who falls into your clutches.'

He regretted the words immediately, but they had reached the old bridge leading into Bath and the sudden appearance of a barouche made his team shy. He was obliged to give his attention to preventing a collision before he could reply.

'I beg your pardon, Susannah. I—'

'Do not *speak* to me,' she commanded him in arctic tones. 'I will not spend another moment in your company. You will set me down immediately, if you please.'

'The devil I will. You cannot walk alone through this part of the town.'

'I can do whatever I want!'

'Do not be so foolish. No lady should walk near the docks, and beyond that are the poorest stews of Bath. Heaven knows what would become of you if I set you down here.'

'If you will not stop I will jump down.'

'Oh, no, you won't.' He reached out and grabbed

her wrist. 'You are in my care and I shall deliver you to your house.'

'Your *care*, my lord, has almost resulted in my ruin on at least two occasions.'

Jasper glanced behind. Morton was sitting in the rumble seat, wooden-faced. He would stake his life on Morton's discretion, but she must be very angry with him, to speak so in front of a servant.

Susannah tried to shake off his iron grip.

'Let go of me!'

His hold on her wrist did not weaken. The heat from his fingers burned through her sleeve.

'Only if you promise that you will not try to jump down. Quickly,' he growled. 'I cannot control this team with one hand and if you will not give me your word then I shall instruct Morton to hold you in your seat.' He showed his teeth. 'Only think how that would look.'

'You wouldn't dare!'

'Morton—'

'Very well!' Hastily and with a burning look of reproach she made her promise. How could she have ever thought him a gentleman!

'Good.' He released her and she cradled her wrist in her other hand, convinced she would see a bruise there if she were to peel back her sleeve. 'Now you will sit still until we reach Royal Crescent. If you move so much as a finger then Morton will lay hands on you, is that understood?'

She sat upright, staring rigidly before her as they picked up speed. The sense of injustice was fanned by the ensuing silence.

'You are a monster,' she told him. When that elicited no reply she added, 'A brutish beast. You should be locked up.'

Still he did not reply. She tried again.

'I have never known why everyone thinks you so charming. You are a fraud, Lord Markham. You are nothing but a rake. A—a libertine. A wolf in sheep's clothing. A seducer of innocent females.'

His frown grew blacker with every word she threw at him, but he said nothing until he had guided the curricle into the Crescent and pulled up at her front door.

'We will continue this conversation inside.'

'If you think I am going to allow you into my house after this—!'

With a total want of decorum she scrambled out of the curricle and ran up the steps. Unfortunately Gatley had not been prepared for their approach and she was obliged to hammer upon the knocker. Behind her she heard Morton addressing his master.

'I'll take 'em back to the stables, shall I, m'lord? You're in a fair way to ruining their mouths, the way you've been jerking at the ribbons.'

Glancing back, she saw that Jasper had jumped down and was even now on the pavement. The door opened and she ran inside, but before she could order Gatley to deny him, Jasper had followed her into the hall.

'I am afraid Mrs Wilby is not at home,' offered the butler. 'She left a message to say she is visiting Lady Gisburne today and after dinner they are going on to a concert at the Lower Rooms.'

Ignoring him, Susannah confronted Jasper.

'Get out of my house. Immediately!'

'Not until we have had this out. You have hurled every insult at me and I think you owe me the opportunity to reply!'

'There is a note for you, madam,' Gatley went on. 'The maid found it beneath the hall table when she was cleaning this morning. I have put it on the mantelshelf in the morning room.'

She paid no heed to him but continued to glare at Jasper. It was like confronting a wild animal. If she took her eyes off him he would pounce.

'Well?' His own eyes narrowed, anger darkening them to slate-grey.

'I have nothing to say to you,' she threw at him.

'But I have plenty to say to you.' With a growl he caught her wrist and dragged her towards the nearest doorway.

Gatley dithered beside them.

'Madam—'

The viscount turned upon him, saying imperiously, 'We are not to be disturbed!'

He dragged Susannah into the morning room, closed the door and turned the key in the lock.

Chapter Seventeen

'No, do not shut the door on us, Gatley,' Mrs Logan called out to the butler as she trod up the steps to the house. 'Mrs Coale and I have come to see if Miss Prentess has returned yet.'

He held the door wide to admit them and as Zelah followed Kate into the hall she cast another glance at the butler. He was definitely looking a little flustered.

'Miss Prentess has come in, madam. She is in the morning room. With Lord Markham.' He stood before them and if he had not been a most stately personage, Zelah would have sworn he was hopping from one foot to the other. He continued, as if the words were wrenched from him, *'They have locked the door.'*

Kate's eyes widened and the look she cast at Zelah was positively triumphant.

'Well, this is a most interesting development,' she murmured.

Gatley cleared his throat. 'I was wondering if I should call Lucas…'

'No, no, if you will be advised by me you will leave well alone,' said Zelah.

'I agree,' said Kate. 'We will come back another time, will we not, Mrs Coale?'

Zelah was having difficulty concealing her smile.

'We will indeed,' she managed. They stepped out of the door and she paused as a final thought occurred to her. 'And, Gatley, I suggest you fetch up a bottle or two of your finest claret. For a celebration.'

A rare gleam entered in the butler's eye and a smile broke over his usually austere features.

'I will indeed, madam!'

Susannah tore herself free, saying furiously, 'You cannot give my staff orders!'

He stripped off his gloves and threw them on a side table.

'You could have told him to throw me out.'

'I should not need to. It should be perfectly clear to him that you are unwelcome in this house.'

The angry light faded and he grinned.

'I doubt if your butler has ever been called upon to eject a peer before.'

She bit her lip, fighting back an answering smile. He was standing in front of the door so she could not escape, but she was not prepared to forgive him so easily.

'Very well, my lord, say what you have to and be gone.' Rather than look at him she removed her bonnet and cloak and set them carefully over a chair.

'When I heard you had left town with Warwick I thought you were running away from me again.'

'I never run away,' she told him haughtily, then spoiled the effect by adding, 'but it would be understandable if I should do so, after the way you have treated me. You tried to seduce me. You used me shamelessly.'

'I did,' he agreed. 'And you gave me my own again for that, did you not, madam? Leaving me tied to the bedpost.'

She grew hot at the memory. Her cheeks burned.

'I am not proud of my actions that night.'

'You should be.' He paused. 'You are a woman to be reckoned with, Miss Prentess.'

Embarrassed by his praise she turned away.

'Nonsense. I did what was necessary to protect myself.' As she was doing now, closing her mind to the attraction she felt for him. After all, he would soon be gone and she would be alone again. She had a vision of the bleak, cold years stretching ahead of her and felt the sudden sting of tears.

Susannah rubbed her eyes. She felt incredibly despondent. If Jasper did not leave soon she knew she would begin to cry. She summoned up every ounce of energy to say angrily, 'If that is all, perhaps you will go now, and leave me in peace.'

'No, it is not all,' he retorted. 'You have thrown a great many accusations at my head, madam. I demand the right to defend myself.' He walked to the window and stood looking out, his hands clasped behind his back. 'You accused me of being a rake. I am not, madam. I admit I have indulged in many a flirtation, but the women have never been unwilling.'

'Hah!' She curled her lip. 'Would they have been quite so willing if you had not had a title, and a fortune?'

'I would like to think there is more to me than that, but you are right, Miss Prentess, I cannot be sure.' He added quietly, 'Since meeting you, madam, I am not sure of anything.'

She had to steel herself not to crumble at this sudden diffidence. To distract herself she went to the mantelpiece and picked up the note that was resting against the clock. She said, as her fingers broke the seal, 'Your doubts will fade once you are gone from Bath.'

'Oh, you may be sure I shall do my best to forget this,' he retorted.

She paid no heed to his words, her attention given to the paper in her hands.

'This is the note you sent me yesterday?'

He gave a quick look over his shoulder. 'Yes, I—'

'Oh, heavens.' One hand crept to her cheek, she could *feel* the colour draining from her face. 'You were g-going to, to—'

'Yes,' he interrupted her. 'I was going to offer for you.'

'B-but why?' She felt almost dizzy.

'I have already told you, I love you.'

She lifted her hand.

'No, no, that was an error. You don't even *like* me.'

He laughed harshly.

'You are quite right. You are the most maddening, exasperating woman I have ever encountered, but it has not stopped me falling in love with you.'

She could only stare at his back, groping for words that would not come. After an uncomfortable silence he continued.

'Oh, pray, don't be alarmed, madam. I may love you to distraction but after what has passed this morning I will not put you to the trouble of refusing me. You have made your sentiments perfectly clear.'

She shook her head.

'No. You do not understand. I—I cannot allow you to be near me…'

'I *do* understand,' he said gently. 'You honoured me

with your confidences and they made me realise how repugnant my advances must have been to you.'

He still had his back to her, his gaze fixed on the view over Crescent Fields. Her heart was beating so hard it was difficult to speak, even to *think*, but she knew she had to try, and she must get it right, or she would never see him again.

'N-not repugnant,' she whispered, moving closer. 'I cannot allow you to touch me because of what happens to me when you do.' She reached out and put her hand on his shoulder. 'I want you so much it terrifies me.' He turned at that and with his eyes upon her it was twice as hard to go on, but continue she must. 'I have never felt such an overwhelming desire for anyone, for anything in my life before. When you kiss me I am in danger of forgetting everything, my fear of men, of losing control, of falling in love…' her voice faded until it was little more than a breath '…of you breaking my heart.'

He raked his fingers through his gleaming black hair, saying unsteadily, 'Oh my dear, I swear I will never do that. But you have to trust me.'

'I do, Jasper, I do trust you.' She put her hand up and touched his cheek. 'Do you see what this means, Jasper, do you know what I am asking? I *want* you to seduce me.'

Still he did not move. Placing her hands on his shoulders, she reached up and touched her lips against his. Immediately his arms came round her and with a sigh she leaned against him, twining her arms about his neck. Their kiss was long and languorous and incredibly gentle, but when at last he broke away she rested her head on his shoulder, aware that not one of her bones felt strong enough to support her.

'Oh dear.' She clung to him, murmuring the words into his neckcloth. 'I do not think I can stand.'

With a laugh he swept her up and carried her across to the sofa, where he sat down with her on his lap and began kissing her again. She responded eagerly, her lips parting to allow his tongue to roam wherever it would. She drove her fingers through his hair, revelling in the silky feel of it. Every nerve was alive and aching for his touch. She wanted to feel his skin against hers and she began to tug at his cravat. He stopped kissing her and put his hand up over her fingers.

'Susannah, I cannot do this.'

Cold fear clutched at her heart.

'Have I offended you, have I been too forward? I know some men do not like that in a woman...'

He gathered her into his arms and held her close, his cheek resting against her curls.

'No, sweetheart, that is not it, but I do not want to do anything you might later regret.'

'No...' she ran her tongue over her lips '...I won't regret this. It is what I want. Truly.'

'Then I won't seduce you.' His smile was warm. 'But I will make love to you, if you will let me?'

The burning look in his eyes sent a shiver of anticipation through her.

'Oh yes, yes, please.'

With a look that promised everything he slid her from his lap on to the sofa and knelt on the floor beside her.

'First we must dispose of some of these garments.'

He divested himself of his driving coat and jacket then slowly, and with infinite gentleness, he removed her walking dress, pausing occasionally to kiss the newly exposed skin.

Susannah lay back against the satin cushions, her eyes closed, revelling in the touch of his hands as they roamed over her body. He pressed kisses on her breasts where they rose up from the confining corset, his tongue flicking over the soft flesh and causing her to moan softly. When he stopped she opened her eyes and saw that he had transferred his attention to her feet. Gently he untied her ribbon garters and rolled down each stocking, caressing her calves as he did so. He kissed her ankles and toes, nibbling at their rosy tips while his hands slid up to her thighs. Her body tightened as his fingers moved upwards and immediately he stopped.

'Tell me if you don't want this,' he murmured.

In response she reached out for him, pulling him down on the sofa with her, capturing his mouth and kissing him with a ferocity that left them both gasping. Susannah kissed him again while his gently roving fingers caressed her inner thighs until she was arching against his hand. She heard him groan and even as she was swooning with the new and delightful sensations he was rousing in her, he covered her with his body. Her hips rose up to welcome him. She gave a little cry but when he hesitated she gripped him even tighter.

'No, no, don't stop,' she murmured, her mouth against his cheek. 'I want this, I *want* this.'

She sought his mouth again and they kissed, their bodies moving as one, faster, harder. She clung to him, her fingers tracing the hard muscles of his shoulders while she matched his movements, delighting in their union. It was too much. She threw back her head, dragging air into her lungs while her limbs bucked and twisted, beyond her control. She felt rather than heard Jasper's muffled cry and held on as he tensed above her, and she gave herself up to the delicious sensation of flying and drowning at the same time.

As their bodies relaxed together he held her closer.

'Oh, my dearest love. I hope I didn't frighten you.'

Her heart swelled with the words. She reached up and stroked his hair.

'Now I know what they mean by taking one's pleasure,' she said, smiling. She grew still and he raised his head.

'What is it?'

'Did you mean what you said?' she asked him shyly. 'About loving me to distraction?'

'Of course. Have I not just proved it is so?' After another kiss he helped her to sit up. 'I am afraid we will not be able to marry immediately. It will have to be a big ceremony, at Markham, with all the family and tenants as witnesses. I hope you do not object—' He broke off. 'What is it? What have I said?'

She looked away.

'It is what you have *not* said. You have not yet asked me to marry you, my lord.'

With a growl he pulled her back into his arms.

'On the contrary, I suggested it some time ago, but you refused me. However, I am taking what has just happened as a sign that you have changed your mind. Well, strumpet?'

She lowered her eyes, saying provocatively, 'I suppose I *must* marry you now, even without a formal proposal.'

Her teasing provoked just the reaction she had hoped for. She was swept up into another passionate embrace and within minutes Jasper had once more carried her to such ecstatic heights that afterwards she could only lay docile and compliant in his arms, agreeing with all his plans for the future.

'We must buy you a ring,' he decided. 'We will do that tomorrow. And while we are in Milsom Street we will retrieve the emeralds you sold.'

'If they still have them. The manager said it was a very fine set.'

His grin was pure wickedness.

'It is and they do still have it. I purchased it and asked them to put it aside for me. I had meant to give it to Lady Gisburne to return to you, once I had left Bath.'

She shook her head, distressed.

'Oh, how can you be so good, when I have treated you so abominably?'

He gave a soft laugh and kissed her again.

'You have made up for all that now.'

'No, this has pleased me, too.' She cast another shy look at him. 'I did not realise being in love could be—'

His arms tightened.

'Is that true?' he demanded. 'You love me?'

'To distraction,' she said, smiling. 'I would have told you sooner if I had realised how wonderful it would be to have you make love to me.' She cast a glance at her stays and chemise. 'And we have not yet removed all our clothes.'

'Your morning room is not the place for that.' He dropped a kiss on her forehead. 'But believe me, my darling, when I finally undress you, I shall make love to you even more thoroughly.'

Three months later Jasper was as good as his word, when he carried his new bride to the marriage bed at Markham. The costly linen nightgowns were soon thrown off and they lay together, exploring and enjoying each other until their mutual passions could no longer be denied and they gave themselves up to the consummation that carried them to new and exhilarating heights.

Later, in the first flush of dawn, Jasper knelt beside Susannah, gazing at her perfect, creamy body. She lay on the silken sheets, her hair spread across the pillow like a golden cloud.

'My viscountess,' he murmured. 'When will I ever grow tired of looking at you?'

'Never, I hope.' She opened her sleepy eyes and reached for him. 'My darling husband, seduce me again.'

* * * * *

MILLS & BOON®

The Regency Collection – Part 1

Let these roguish rakes sweep you off to the
Regency period in part 1 of our collection!

Order yours at **www.millsandboon.co.uk/regency1**

MILLS & BOON®

The Regency Collection – Part 2

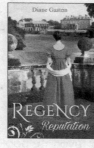

Join the London ton for a Regency
season in part 2 of our collection!

Order yours at **www.millsandboon.co.uk/regency2**

MILLS & BOON®

Why shop at millsandboon.co.uk?

Each year, thousands of romance readers find their perfect read at millsandboon.co.uk. That's because we're passionate about bringing you the very best romantic fiction. Here are some of the advantages of shopping at www.millsandboon.co.uk:

* **Get new books first**—you'll be able to buy your favourite books one month before they hit the shops

* **Get exclusive discounts**—you'll also be able to buy our specially created monthly collections, with up to 50% off the RRP

* **Find your favourite authors**—latest news, interviews and new releases for all your favourite authors and series on our website, plus ideas for what to try next

* **Join in**—once you've bought your favourite books, don't forget to register with us to rate, review and join in the discussions

Visit **www.millsandboon.co.uk**
for all this and more today!

MILLS_WEB